if
you only
knew

KRISTAN HIGGINS

if you only knew

HQN™

ISBN-13: 978-0-373-78929-0

If You Only Knew

Recycling programs
for this product may
not exist in your area.

This edition published by arrangement with Harlequin Books S.A.

For questions and comments about the quality of this book,
please contact us at CustomerService@Harlequin.com.

® and TM are trademarks of Harlequin Enterprises Limited or its
corporate affiliates. Trademarks indicated with ® are registered in the
United States Patent and Trademark Office, the Canadian Intellectual
Property Office and in other countries.

www.HQNBooks.com

Printed in U.S.A.

To Shaunee, Jennifer, Karen and Huntley,
with heartfelt thanks for the laughs,
the wine and especially the love.

Jenny

TODAY IS ONE of those days when I realize that staying friends with my ex-husband was a huge mistake.

I'm at the baby shower for Ana-Sofia, Owen's wife and my replacement. Indeed, I'm sitting next to her, a place of honor in this circle of beaming well-wishers, and I'm probably beaming just as hard as everyone else. Harder, even, my "gosh, isn't it wonderful, she's so radiant" smile that I give at work quite often, especially as my brides get bitchier or their mothers get more critical or their maids of honor get more jealous. But this smile, the baby-shower smile…this is superhuman, really.

I know that coming today is incredibly pathetic, don't worry. It's just that I didn't want to seem bitter by not showing up—though I'm pretty sure I *am* bitter, at least a little. After all, I'm the one who always wanted kids. Every time I brought it up, though, Owen said he wasn't sure the time was right, and he loved our life the way it was.

Yeah. So. That turned out not to be quite true, but we did stay friends. Coming today, though…pathetic.

However, I woke up this morning utterly starving, and I knew the food would be amazing at the shower. Ana-Sofia *inspires* people. Plus, I'm moving out of the city, so for the past three weeks, I've been trying to eat or give away every morsel of food in my apartment. Let's also mention that I couldn't figure out an excuse that people would buy. Better to be an oddity here than Poor Jenny at home, scrounging through a box of Wheat Thins of indeterminate age.

Ana-Sofia opens my gift, which is wrapped in Christmas paper, despite it being April. Liza, my host, glowers; the red-and-green cocoa-swilling Santas are an affront to the party vibe, which Liza noted on the invitations.

In an effort to create a beautiful and harmonious environment for Ana-Sofia, please adhere to the apricot-and-sage color scheme in your clothing and gift-wrapping choices.

Only in Manhattan, folks. I'm wearing a purple dress as a middle finger to Liza, who used to be my friend but now posts daily on Facebook that she's LOL-ing with her BFF, Ana-Sofia.

"Oh! This is so lovely! Thank you, Jenny! Everyone, look at this! It's beautiful!" Ana-Sofia holds up my gift, and there are gasps and murmurs and exclamations and a few glares that I have brought the best present. I cock an eyebrow at the haters. *Suck it up, bitches.* My gift was actually dashed off last night, as I kind of forgot to buy a present, but they don't have to know that.

It's a white satin baby blanket with leaves and trees and birds stitched into it. Hey. It only took me two hours. Nothing was hand-stitched. It wasn't that big a deal. I sew for a living. A wedding-dress designer. The irony is not lost on me.

"Couldn't you have just bought a stuffed animal like

a normal person?" murmurs the person on my left. Andreas—born Andrew—my assistant, and the only man here. Gay, of course—do straight men work in designer bridal wear? Also, he hates and fears children, which makes him the perfect date for me under the circumstances. I needed an ally.

Have I mentioned that the shower is being held in the apartment I once shared with Owen? Where, so far as I could tell, he and I were extremely happy? Yes. Liza is hosting, but the power went out in her apartment, thanks to the ham-fisted construction crew installing her new glass countertops—granite being so very last decade—and so we're here instead. Liza is sweaty and loud, rightfully worried about being judged on her prowess as hostess. This is the Upper East Side, after all. We're all about judgment here.

The gifts—including mine—border on the ridiculous. The shower invitation—engraved from Crane's—asked, at the behest of the parents, for donations to the clean-well-water charity Ana-Sofia founded—Gushing.org, the name of which brings to mind a particularly bad menstrual period, but which raises funds for wells in Africa. Yeah. Therefore, everyone donated fat checks *and* tried to outdo each other with gifts. There's a Calder mobile. A 1918 edition of Mother Goose stories. A mohair Steiff teddy bear that costs about as much as the rent on my soon-to-be former apartment in the Village.

My gaze drifts across the now-tastefully furnished apartment. When I lived here, it was cozier and boho—fat, comfortable furniture; dozens of pictures of my three nieces; the occasional wall hanging from Target, that bastion of color and joy for the middle class. Now the decor is incredibly tasteful, with African masks on the wall to remind us what Ana-Sofia does, and original paintings from around the globe. The walls are painted those boring neutral colors with sexy names—October Fog, Birmingham Cream, Icicle.

There's their wedding photo. They eloped, so thank God I didn't have to go to that—or, heaven forbid, make her gown, which I would've done if asked, because I'm still pretty pitiful where Owen is concerned and can't figure out how to divorce him out of my heart. Though the photo was taken by the justice of the peace in Maine, it's perfect. Both bride and groom are laughing, slightly turned away from the camera, Ana's hair blowing in the sea breeze. The *New York Times* featured the photo in the Sunday Vows section.

They really are the perfect couple. Once, it was Owen and me, and while I didn't expect perfection, I thought we were pretty great. We never fought. My mom felt that since Owen is half-Japanese, he was a better bet than "those simpletons" I dated—all of whom I hoped to marry at one point or another, starting with Nico Stephanopolous in eighth grade. "The Japanese don't believe in divorce," Mom said the first time I introduced her. "Right, Owen?"

He agreed, and I can still see his omnipresent, sweet smile, the Dr. Perfect Smile, as I called it. It's his resting expression. Very reassuring to his patients, I'm sure. Owen is a plastic surgeon, the kind who fixes cleft palates and birthmarks and changes the lives of his patients. Ana-Sofia, who is from Peru and speaks five languages, met Owen eleven weeks after our divorce when he was doing his annual stint with Doctors Without Borders in the Sudan and she was digging wells.

And I make wedding dresses, as I believe I've already said. Listen, it's not as shallow as it sounds. I make women look the way they dreamed they would on one of the happiest days of their lives. I make them cry at their own reflections. I give them the dress they've spent years thinking about, the dress they'll be wearing when they pledge their hearts, the dress they'll pass on to their own daughters someday, the dress that signifies all their hopes and dreams for a happy, sparkling future.

But compared with what Owen and his second wife do, yeah, it's incredibly shallow.

In theory, I should hate them both. No, he didn't cheat with her. He's far too decent for that.

He loves her, though. Ostensibly, I could hate him for loving her and not me. Make no mistake. I was heartbroken. But I can't hate Owen, or Ana-Sofia. They're too damn nice, which is incredibly inconsiderate of them.

And being Owen's friend is better than being without Owen entirely.

The quilt has made the rounds of admiration and is passed back to Ana. She strokes it tenderly, then looks at me with tears in her eyes. "I don't have the words to tell you how much this means."

Oh, shut up, I want to say. *I forgot to buy you a gift and dashed this off last night with some leftover Duchess satin. It's no big deal.*

"Hey, no worries," I say. I'm often glib and stupid around Ana-Sofia. Andreas hands me another cream puff. I may have to give him a raise.

"I'm so excited about your new shop," Ana continues. "Owen and I were talking about how talented you are just last night."

Andreas gives me a significant look and rolls his eyes. He has no problem hating Ana-Sofia *and* Owen, which I appreciate. I smile and take another sip of my mimosa, which is made with blood oranges and really good champagne.

If I'm ever pregnant, though the chances of that are plummeting by the hour, I imagine I'll have the unenviable "I sat on an air hose" look that my sister had when she was percolating the triplets. There was no glow. There was acne. Stretch marks that made her look as if she'd been mauled by a Bengal tiger. She gnashed on Tums and burped constantly, but in true Rachel fashion, my sister never complained.

Ana-Sofia *glows*. Her perfect olive skin is without a blemish or, indeed, a visible pore. Her boobs look fantastic, and though she is eight and a half months pregnant, her baby bump is modest and perfectly round. She has no cankles. Life is so unfair.

"We just found out that our daughter's classmate is her half brother," says the taller woman in Lesbian Couple #1. One of them just became a partner in Owen's practice, but I don't remember her name. "Imagine if we hadn't known that! She could've ended up dating her half brother! Marrying him! The fertility clinic gave out *fourteen* samples of that donor's sperm. We're filing a lawsuit."

"It's better than adopting," says another woman. "My sister? She and her husband had to give back their son the fourth time he set fire to the living room."

"That's not so bad. My cousin adopted, and then the birth mother came out of rehab and the judge gave her custody of the baby. After two years, mind you."

On the other side of the circle, there seems to be a heated debate over whose labor and delivery was most grueling. "I almost died," one woman says proudly. "I looked at my husband and told him I loved him, and the next thing I knew, the crash cart was there…"

"I was in labor for three *days*," another states. "I was like a wild animal, clawing at the sheets."

"Emergency cesarean eight weeks early, no anesthesia," someone else says proudly. "My daughter weighed two pounds. NICU, fifty-seven days."

And we have a winner! The other mothers shoot her resentful looks. Talk turns to food allergies, vaccines, family beds and the sad dearth of gifted and talented programs for preschoolers.

"This is fun," I murmur to Ana-Sofia.

"Oh, yes," she says. Irony is not one of her skills. "I'm so glad you are here, Jenny. Thank you for giving up your afternoon! You must be very busy with the move."

"You're moving?" one of her extremely beautiful and well-educated friends asks. "Where?"

"Cambry-on-Hudson," I answer. "I grew up there. My sister and her family are—"

"Oh, my God, you're leaving Manhattan? Will you have to get a car? Are there any restaurants there? I couldn't live without Zenyasa Yoga."

"You still go to Zenyasa?" someone says. "I've moved on. It's Bikram Hot for me. I saw Neil Patrick Harris there last week."

"I don't do yoga anymore," a blonde woman says, studying a raspberry. "I joined a trampoline studio over on Amsterdam. Sarah Jessica Parker told me about it."

"What about brunch?" someone asks me, her brow wrinkling in concern. "What will you do for brunch if you leave the city?"

"I think brunch is illegal outside Manhattan," I answer gravely. No one laughs. They may think I'm telling the truth.

Now, granted, I love Manhattan. To paraphrase the song, if you make it here, the rest of the world is a cakewalk. And I *have* made it here. I've worked for the best—even Vera Wang, as a matter of fact. My work is sold at Kleinfeld Bridal and has supported me for fifteen years. I was named one of the Designers of the Year when I was at Parsons. I've been to not one, but two parties at Tim Gunn's place. He greeted me by name—and yes, he's as nice as he seems.

But while I love the city, its roar, its buildings and smells, its subways and skyline, in my heart of hearts, I want a yard. I want to see my nieces more often. I want the happily-ever-after that my sister nailed, that's unfolding for my ex-husband and his too-nice wife.

I hope I'm running to something, not away. The truth is work has felt a little flat lately.

Cambry-on-Hudson is a lovely little city about an hour north of Manhattan. It has several excellent restaurants—some even serve brunch, shockingly. The downtown has a movie theater, flowering trees, a park and a Williams-Sonoma. It's hardly a third-world country, no matter what these women think. And the latest shop is Bliss. Custom-made wedding gowns. My baby, in lieu of the human kind.

My phone beeps softly with a text. It's from Andreas, who has put in his earbuds in order to drown out the stories of blocked milk ducts and bleeding nipples.

Check out the nose on the great-aunt. I hope the baby inherits that.

I smile at him gratefully.

"Did you hear about the obstetrician who fathered fifty-nine babies?" someone asks.

"That was an episode on *Law & Order*."

"Ripped from the headlines," someone else murmurs. "Someone in my building was one of his patients."

"Oh. Oh, dear," Ana-Sofia says.

I turn to her. She looks a bit startled. "It's probably not true," I tell her.

"No… I think… It appears my water has broken."

There is a silence, followed by a collective roar.

I'll spare you the details. Suffice it to say that, despite there being a dozen women who've given birth all jockeying for position, my hand is the one Ana-Sofia clutches. "Oh, Jenny, it's happening," she says. "I feel something." Her beautiful brown eyes are wide and terrified, and then I'm easing her onto the floor and crouched between her still-slim thighs—really, it's like she's showing off. I slide off her thong—she's maintained her bikini wax, FYI—and, holy Mother of God, I can see the head.

I fumble in my purse for the travel-size Purell (if you ride the subways on a daily basis, you carry Purell) and slather some on my hands. "Get some towels and quiet down!" I bark at the other shower guests. I'm kind of good in emergencies. Liza hands me a stack of towels— very soft and about to be ruined by whatever comes out of a woman during childbirth.

"Let me help," Liza whines. Indeed, this would make a great Facebook post. Just delivered my BFF's baby, LOL!—with Ana-Sofia Marquez-Takahashi.

"I need to push," Ana pants, and she does, once, twice, a third time, and a face appears—a baby! There's a baby coming into my hands! One more push, and I'm holding it, slimy and covered in white gunk and a little blood and incredibly beautiful.

Dark hair, huge eyes. A miracle.

I ease her out all the way and put her on Ana's chest. "It's a girl," I say, covering the baby with a towel.

It seems like just a few seconds later that FDNY clomps in, and I entertain a quick and deeply satisfying fantasy—*The head firefighter is filled with admiration for my cleverness, checks me out and asks me to dinner in the cutest Brooklyn accent the world has ever heard. His biceps flex hypnotically, and at the end of the date, yes, he does pick me up to demonstrate just how easy it would be for him to save my life, and a few years later, we have three strong sons, twin daughters on the way. And a Dalmatian.*

But no, their attention is quite taken with Ana-Sofia—as it should be, I guess, though it would be nice if just one of them checked me out. Someone cuts the cord, and Ana is weeping beautifully over her daughter, and Liza holds her phone to Ana's ear so my ex-husband can sob his love and admiration for his wife, who just set the land-speed record for labor and delivery.

From down the hall, I can hear Andreas dry-heaving in the tastefully decorated powder room over the murmurs of admiration from the shower guests and the brawny firefighters as they tell Ana how amazing she is, how beautiful her daughter is.

Seems as if I'm leaving the city in the very nick of time.

Rachel

---❖---

THE LAST TIME my husband and I had sex, I fell asleep.

Not after. During.

Just for a second. Adam didn't even notice; I think he just thought I was having my mind blown and it was all part of the grand finale.

But I did. I fell asleep. And it felt *so* good. The sex felt good, too…but the sleep! That gentle floating sensation, the skittering thoughts, the warm, comforting smell of my husband, the rocking rhythm, and just for a second there, I was…away.

This has been bothering me. I told Jenny about it, and she laughed till she cried. And I did, too, but I was thinking about how I'd vowed never to be that woman. The kind who's too tired for sex. The kind who regards making love as just another chore in an endless blur of days.

"Cut yourself some slack," Jenny had said, patting my hand. "You're an amazing wife. But tell Adam you need a nap, for the love of God! Or have him give you a massage instead next time."

Except I don't want to be one of those wives who'd rather have a back rub instead of sex, though if Adam did give me a back rub, I'd probably cry with gratitude. Fourteen hours a day of lifting kids, buckling car seats, picking up toys, sitting on the floor, lugging diaper bags because Charlotte is still holding out with potty training… Of course my back hurts.

But it's a small price to pay. Our girls are so lovely, so wonderful and precious and miraculous that I can't even believe they're mine.

"Mama!"

My middle daughter, lifted out of me one minute after Grace and one minute before Rose, snaps me out of my reverie. Charlotte's chubby little torso is smeared with paint—nontoxic, made from organic vegetable dye… Once you learn there are products like that out there, it's impossible to ignore them, and the Perfect Mommy faction here in Cambry-on-Hudson, New York, makes sure you know exactly what kind of paint *their* toddlers are using.

We've been finger-painting, and I always strip Charlotte and Rose down for that, Charlotte in her Sesame Street diaper, Rose in her tiny flowered underpants. Rose has moved from her poster board to the kitchen floor, but that's okay. I'll wash the floor later. Grace, on the other hand, is fully clothed, because even at three and a half, she's very tidy. Her little brow is wrinkled as she carefully draws on her paper. My serious baby. Not for the first time, I worry that she's on the Asperger's spectrum; she's too neat, too fastidious. Then again, she has cut my cleanup by one-third.

"What is it, Charlotte?" I ask, stroking her blond curls.

"I poop, Mama. My bum hot." She shoves a hand in her diaper, then withdraws it to show me. "Sticky."

Where's that chapter in the parenting books, huh? "That's fine, honey. Let's get you cleaned up."

I glance around the kitchen; all the drawers and cabinets have safety locks on them, and the girls and I are fenced in with baby gates. "Rose, Grace, I'm taking Lottie to the bathroom, okay? Stay here."

"No! I coming, too, Mama!" Rose demands. Both Rose and Charlotte are behind Grace in the speech department, which the pediatrician assured me was normal with multiples. Still. I worry a little.

"Grace, are you okay on your own?" I ask.

"Yes, Mama. I'm making circles."

"They're beautiful, honey."

I scoop Rose up, hold Charlotte so she can't touch anything with her poopy hand, and walk down the hall to the powder room. Dang it. Somehow, Charlotte just managed to wipe her hand on my leg, so I'll have to change again. Well, that's life with three kids. Laundry every day. Besides, I was going to change anyway before Adam came home.

In the triplet group the girls and I occasionally go to, there are moms who look fifteen years older than they are. Who have inches of gray roots showing, who wear their husbands' clothes and smell like stale milk and spit-up, who are weepy and exhausted. They terrify me, because some days, I feel as if I'm one inch away from that myself. I never want my girls to think they're exhausting me; they're the loves of my life. I'm the mother who actually misses them the four hours they're at preschool three days a week. Being a stay-at-home mommy was all I ever wanted.

"Time to wash hands, Lottie," I say now, setting Rose down and turning on the water. "Rose, do you have to go?"

"No," she says. "No fanks, Mama, I fine." She smiles,

and my heart floods with love. I'll have to write that down on one of my note cards so I can tell Adam about that. *No fanks, I fine.* I try to store up those little moments to tell him, since he has such long hours. Also, my memory isn't what it used to be.

I wash Lottie's hands, then take off her diaper and clean her up.

"I poop more," she says.

"Okay," I say, putting her on the potty. Rose and I wait. Charlotte grunts, her face going red. "No poop!" she announces grandly, and the three of us laugh.

I love being a mother so much, it's a wonder my heart fits in my chest anymore. Adam and I *made* these perfect girls, and I can't quite get over that. For most of my life, I've fought shyness. I'm still shy, even around Adam sometimes. You know how it is… If I have a stomach issue, I use the guest bathroom. I still have to give myself a pep talk before we go to a party.

And while I still blush and feel awkward when I'm out in public sometimes, I have *this*, the knowledge that my girls adore me, that I know exactly who I am and what I'm doing as a mother. The memory of my days as a graphic designer at Celery Stalk, a company that made computer games for kids, are shadowy now, but I remember the effort it took, talking to everyone, trying not to worry so much. How it took an hour for my shoulders to drop after I got home.

This…this is what I'm made for.

We wash hands again, all three of us. The soap dispenser is new, and the girls are still fascinated by its wonders. I put a clean diaper on Charlotte, and we're good to go.

Just as we leave the bathroom, Rose squats and pees on the floor, soaking through her panties.

"Oopsy," I say.

"I sorry, Mama."

The usual stash of paper towels isn't under the sink. Dang. "No, that's okay, honey. Don't worry a bit." I glance down the hall. "Grace? How are you, sweetheart?"

"Fine."

I can tell by her voice she's not fine.

"What are you doing, honey?" I walk down the hall to the kitchen, holding Rose by the hand. She's dripping, which means I'll have to wash the hall floor, too.

"Nothing," Grace says. Then there's the sound of something spilling.

Cheerios. All over the kitchen floor. Those things have impressive sliding power. "Don't dump the cereal, sweetheart. That's our food."

"I want more circles," Grace says, emptying the box. "I want to color all circles."

Charlotte is already stomping on the Cheerios, grinding them into fine powder, which makes Grace scream in fury. Rose hesitates, then joins in the stomping. "Settle down, girls," I say, scooping up Grace.

"My circles! My circles!" she wails, arching her back so that I nearly drop her.

Nap time. Such blessed words. I am eternally grateful that my daughters are such good sleepers.

Twenty minutes later, Rose is in clean clothes but weeping because I won't let her drink the Windex I used to wipe up her pee. Grace is angry and stony-faced and has told her sisters she hates them, which made me flinch; I don't think Jenny and I *ever* said that to each other, and I have no idea where the girls learned the word *hate*, especially in reference to other humans.

Charlotte is making the strained poop face again.

"Mama, more pooping," she confirms.

"Great," I say. "Not a problem."

It's 1:34 p.m. Bedtime is six hours away.

But no, it's not that bad. It's just…well, it's tiring, having three kids at once. People like to tell me how blessed I am, and trust me, I know that. Four years of trying to have a baby, three on hormones, four in vitro attempts…four years of hope and yearning… Adam and I went through a lot to have this family.

Which doesn't mean it's not tiring some days.

"I not sleeping," Charlotte tells me. "I hate sleeping. I hate! I hate!" Grace's anger seems to have infected her.

"Sleeping is a happy time," I say, kissing her head. She rubs her eyes and glares at me, but she'll be the first one asleep. Grace will be the last, and she'll need a good twenty minutes of snuggling when she wakes up, flushed and confused. Rose already has her little butt in the air, thumb in her mouth. She gives me a drooly smile and closes her eyes.

Their room is my favorite place in our gorgeous house, yellow and green with mobiles that I made, an overcrowded bookcase and three hammocks filled with stuffed animals. Unlike a lot of the houses I've seen, this room isn't a showplace, an adult's idea of how a child's room should be, with four tasteful stuffed animals and books arranged by height. No. This room is real *and* beautiful, sunny and light and airy. These books are read. "Sleep tight, my babies," I say, closing the door.

Charlotte kicks the wall a few times, but that's tradition. I now have an hour and a half of what Adam calls "your time."

Me Time is spent vacuuming and washing the kitchen floor, cleaning the bathroom, putting the lids back on the paint pots, washing the brushes, chipping dried paint off the table, hanging up Grace's picture on the fridge. I then wash out the sink and check the menu I made on the weekend. Being organized is kind of a must when you have to grocery shop with three little ones. Tonight's dinner is salmon with couscous and roasted almonds and a broccoli salad. I stick a bottle of sauvignon blanc in the fridge, take the broccoli and red cabbage out of the fridge, then pause, glancing at the computer.

It'll just take a second.

I Google "five star hotels, new york city" and scroll through the list. The Surrey—nah, too fussy. The Peninsula—just looked at that one last week. Anything Trump—no, thanks, too overdone.

Ah ha. The Tribeca Grand. I click and look at their suites, then call up. "Hi, I'm interested in booking a suite for a weekend in September," I tell the woman, who has a gorgeous accent. Swiss, I decide, not that I'd know. "No, just for one person…Business with some entertaining thrown in…Well, I'm looking at that one right now, but I'm not sure that'll be big enough. Is the penthouse suite free the weekend of the twenty-first?… It is? Great. And the rooftop terrace…that's for penthouse guests only, correct?"

The dishwasher kicks on as the woman tells me about the cost, the amenities, the restaurant, and I imagine lying on a chaise longue on the terrace, looking at the city, or sliding into that giant bed, the thrill of those polished cotton sheets. I'd get a martini at the bar; a specialty martini, not something on the menu, but something I'd ask the bartender to make just for me.

Then I glance at the clock, realize I only have forty minutes of Me Time left, thank the Swiss woman and switch the laundry.

WHEN ADAM COMES home just before seven o'clock, I'm clean—thanks to taking a shower while the girls played on the bathroom floor with my makeup brushes—and dressed in clean clothes. The house is picked up, I managed to put some flowers in a vase—after scooping a tulip head out of Rose's mouth and calling the poison hotline to ascertain that she'd be okay. Dinner is in the oven, the wine is in an ice bucket, the table is set, the girls are fed and bathed and sweet and in their little jammies, jumping up and down with excitement at the sight of their father coming through the door.

"Princesses!" he exclaims, kneeling down to hug them. He smiles up at me.

God, I love him.

He's still *so* good-looking. Better-looking, one of those boyish faces that's improved with age since we met ten years ago. His black hair is starting to gray, and smile lines fan out from his eyes. He's the same weight he was when we got married. So am I, though I've had to fight for it, and some of my parts aren't exactly where they used to be. But Adam is nearly unchanged.

"Sorry I'm late," he says, standing up to kiss me.

"That's fine," I tell him. "We can eat after they go to bed." We try to eat all together every night, but sometimes life interferes. And honestly, how nice this will be! Almost a date. Hopefully, Grace won't keep getting out of bed, because if she does, Rose will, too.

"Daddy! Daddy! Daddy!" Charlotte chants.

"Rose, put that down, honey," he says as she tries to carry his briefcase. "Rach, I'll put them to bed, how's that?"

"That would be great," I say. "They'll love that."

A lot of people in this area work in Manhattan. Two of my friends have apartments in the city, and one's husband lives there during the week. A lot of folks don't get home from work until eight or nine. But Adam has always worked here, in Cambry-on-Hudson, ever since he graduated from Georgetown, and it's just one more thing I'm grateful for. He spends more time with the girls than most of my friends' husbands, the type of dad who has tea parties with our daughters, pushes them too high on their swings and has promised a puppy for their fourth birthday.

In Cambry-on-Hudson, being a stay-at-home mom is common, and the lovely neighborhoods are full of slim, highlighted mothers in Volvo Cross Countrys and Mercedes SUVs, moms who get together for coffee at Blessed Bean and go shopping together for a dress to wear to the latest fund-raiser.

I do some of those things, too—Mommy and Me swim class at the country club that I'm still a little embarrassed about joining. Adam said we needed the membership to schmooze for his job as a corporate attorney. But I still feel shy. And incredibly lucky, too.

Adam takes off his suit jacket and drapes it over the railing. "Story time!" he announces, then scoops all three girls into his arms and carries them upstairs. Grace's dark cloud has lifted, Charlotte is shrieking with delight and Rose has snuggled her head against his shoulder and waves to me.

I pick up Adam's jacket automatically and put it in the dry-cleaning bag in the hall closet, then go into the kitchen and pour myself a glass of wine. Fifteen more minutes for the salmon. From upstairs, I can hear Adam singing "Baby Beluga" to the girls.

This little window of quiet is a gift. I look around the kitchen, which I love. I love our whole house, a big 1930s house that has no particular style, but is gracious and warm and interesting. Jenny teases me about being a throwback, and it's true, I love all the homey stuff—baking and gardening and decorating. Our childhood home was nearly perfect until Daddy died, and Mom and Dad were so happy, so solid, so together...that was what I wanted, ever since I can remember.

From the hall closet, I hear a phone chime. I guess Adam's phone is in his suit pocket. Can't have him lose that, because, like most people these days, it's practically an appendage. I retrieve the phone and glance at the screen.

The text is from Private Caller. There's an attachment. No message.

"Baby Beluga" is still being sung upstairs.

The phone chimes again, startling me. Private Caller again, but this time, a message.

Do you like this?

I click on the attachment. It's a slightly blurry picture, but of what, I'm not sure. A...a tree, maybe, though it doesn't look so healthy. It looks diseased, moist and soft. There's a knothole that looks damp and sick. Whatever it is, I can't imagine why someone would be sending it to Adam. He doesn't know anything about trees.

A vein in my neck throbs. The vampire vein. Maybe it's an artery. I don't know.

Baby Beluga, Baby Beluga...

This was clearly sent to Adam by mistake. That's it, because otherwise, Adam would have this person in his contacts list. His phone is always completely up-to-date. In fact, he lost it last week, and he went a little crazy looking for it. All those contacts, he said. All those saved texts and apps and calendar notes and everything that I don't use on my phone. I just use it to call or text him or Jenny, or in case the nursery school needs to get in touch with me.

I think it's a tree. I'm almost positive.

But Adam doesn't know anything about trees. This was probably meant for the...the...the tree warden or something.

Baby Beluga... Baby Beluga...

I forward the picture to my phone.

Then I delete it from his.

That throbbing vein makes me feel sick. I put the phone back in his jacket pocket, put the jacket back in the bag, and then I go back into the kitchen and take a big sip of wine, then another.

The girls' door closes upstairs. Adam is always faster at tucking in than I am.

His feet thud down the stairs. "Babe," he says. "Have you seen my phone?"

"No," I lie. "But I did just put your jacket in the dry-cleaning bag. Maybe it's in your pocket?"

"Right." He goes to the closet, retrieves the phone, checks it. Then he looks at me with a smile. "What's for dinner? It smells fantastic in here."

"Salmon."

"My favorite."

"I know." And then I smile, though I have no idea how my face actually looks, and pour him some wine.

I remember what I wanted to tell him. *No fanks, Mama, I fine.*

I don't tell him. I keep that to myself.

When we go to bed a couple of hours later, Adam checks his phone, kisses my temple and is asleep within seconds.

Usually, we make love on Friday nights, since the next day is Saturday and Adam doesn't have to get up early. He tells me I can sleep in, too; the girls are big enough to play in their room for an hour or so, and he's even offered to get up with them. But he never hears them, so I wake up anyway, and then wake him up, and then I can't ever get back to sleep once I hear the girls moving and talking.

But this Friday night, nothing. A kiss on the temple. No expectant smile, no nuzzling, no "you look beautiful" or "you smell fantastic," his traditional opening volley when it comes to sex.

Maybe he noticed that I fell asleep last time after all. Maybe he's being thoughtful.

Or maybe it's something else.

Jenny

THE DRIVE FROM Manhattan to Cambry-on-Hudson is one I could make in my sleep. COH is my hometown, a place my sister never left except to go to college, a place I visit at least twice a month.

But it's different, coming here to live. On many fronts, it's perfect, because I never did want to stay in Manhattan forever. COH is a pretty town on the banks of the Hudson, saved from true depression by its proximity to the city and some really smart planning on the part of the town council. Years ago, they preserved the riverfront, which is now home to restored brick buildings filled with dress boutiques and home goods shops, a bakery and café, an art gallery and a few restaurants and salons.

And Bliss.

There, in the center of the block, is my new business, the shop name announced in sleek steel letters over the door. Rachel designed the logo, a simple branch of cherry blossoms, and three days ago, we tackled the window display—pink silk cherry blossoms tied to dangling white ribbons. The interior of the shop is the palest pink, the floors a dark cherry, newly sanded and polished.

In the window, being admired by three young women,

is a strapless *peau de soie* dress with lace overlay, a pattern of tiny rosebuds woven into the Chantilly.

Cambry-on-Hudson also is home to three country clubs, an equestrian club and a yacht club—it's on the very border of Westchester County, you see. With all those wedding venues and deep pockets in town, Bliss should do just fine. And maybe I'll get the old tingle back, now that I'm not surrounded by memories of Owen.

I'll miss the city, but I admit that I feel a little relieved to get out of there, too. It's a hard place to live—the constant noise, the endless blur of humanity, the exhaust and pavement and strangely sweet steam rising from the subway grates. It takes a toll, all the walking in heels, navigating through crowds, grabbing on to subway poles and stair railings that have been touched by thousands of people. And last I checked, I was allowed to go back to visit, though my friends and colleagues made it feel a bit like I was walking the green mile to my execution. Such is the nature of New Yorkers.

So, yes. This is a good move, a year in the making, and I can't wait to get settled. Life will be quieter here. Easier. I'm not just moving because Owen and I got a divorce. Honest.

I head up the hill from the riverfront, where there is block after block of gentrified old row houses. Some streets are a little careworn and rough, and the other side of Broadway gets seedy fast, as we are not quite as Westchester County as the rest of Westchester County. The Riverview section of the city, where my sister lives, is quite posh, with big sprawling houses and glimpses of the Hudson.

But Magnolia Avenue, where I'm renting, is lovely

without being snooty. Real people live here, people who have to work for a living.

As I pull up to Number 11, my phone rings.

I sense my hard-won optimism is about to get a smackdown. The Angel of Death, also known as my mother, Lenore Tate, long-suffering widow and professional pessimist.

Best to take the call; otherwise, she'll call the police to check on me.

"Hi, Mom," I say, making sure I sound chipper.

"I'm just checking in. Honey, I'm so sad for you. Horrible that you have to move," she says in her trademark tone—mournful with a dash of smug.

"I don't have to, Mom. I chose to."

"You sound so depressed. Well, who can blame you?"

My eye twitches. "I'm not depressed. I'm really happy. I'll be closer to you, and Rachel, and—"

"Yes, but these aren't exactly ideal circumstances, are they? It should've been *you* and Owen, not him and Ana-Sofia. Though she is quite beautiful. The baby, too. Did I tell you they had me over last week?"

"Yes. You've mentioned it nine times now."

"Oh, you're counting. Poor thing. I can only imagine how hard it was, delivering the baby who should've been yours…"

"Okay, I'm hanging up now." She's not exactly wrong, and she knows it. Such is her evil power.

"I'm coming over to help you unpack. Do you have pepper spray? The neighborhood is seedy."

When I went to college, Mom moved across the state border to a posh little town in Connecticut and began viewing COH as akin to the slums of Calcutta. It's irritating, but at least she doesn't live too close by.

"Mom, the neighborhood is gorgeous," I tell her, using my "calm the bride" voice.

"Well, it's not what it was when your father was alive. If he hadn't died, it still might be a nice place to live."

This is one of those illogical and unarguable statements so common from Mother Dear. Westchester County is hardly a hotbed of crime and urban decay. Even if COH was hit by urban blight—which it hasn't been—it's not as if Dad, who was a dentist, would've single-handedly stepped in and saved the day.

"You should've moved to Connecticut, Jenny. Hedgefield would've been perfect for your little dress shop. I still don't understand why you didn't want to come here."

Because you live there. "I have to go, Mom. Don't come over. I'll have you up over dinner later this week, okay?"

"I can't eat dairy anymore. It gives me terrible diarrhea. Ana-Sofia made empanadas that were delicious. Maybe you could call her for the recipe, since you're not the best cook."

Cleansing breath, cleansing breath. "Anything else?"

"Well, don't make duck. I'm morally opposed to duck. Do you *know* what they do to ducks at a duck farm? The cruelty! It's barbaric. But I do love veal. Can you make veal? Or is that too hard for you?"

"I'll make something delicious, Mom." I won't. I'll buy something delicious.

"See you in a few hours, then."

"No, no. Please don't come. I won't even be here. I have a bride coming in." A lie, but it's de rigueur when dodging a maternal visit.

"Fine. Maybe I'll call Ana-Sofia. She asked for some advice on getting the baby to burp, so…"

"Okay, bye." I stab the end button hard. My twitch has grown into a throb.

I'd like to say that Mom means well, but that wouldn't really be true. When things are good, she looks not for the silver lining, but for the mercury toxicity. When things are bad, her eyes light up, she stands straighter and her life is filled with purpose. She views my move to COH as both my inevitable failure at marriage—she always hinted Owen was too good for me—and also a gauntlet I've thrown at her feet. If I do better after my divorce—personally and professionally—it might imply that she should, too.

Well, no point in crying over spilled milk. Spilled wine, yes. But I have a long day of unpacking in front of me, and I want to get started. Unfortunately, the moving truck is nowhere in sight. Luis said he knew the street, but they're late just the same, even if they left just a second after I did.

Hopefully, this will be the last time I move—which is exactly what I said when I moved in with Owen. He was the fourth boyfriend I lived with, but I thought he had staying power. But seriously, this could be the last time, because my new place is flippin' beautiful. The real estate lady said it's possible that it'll go up for sale next year; it was an impulse buy on the part of the owner, and my lease is only for one year—a hint, she said, that the owner might want to sell it.

So I *could* live here forever, and why not? It's elegant and cozy at the same time, a four-story brick town house painted dark gray with black trim and a cherry-red front door. Iron window box holders curl up in front of all the windows, and I immediately picture planting trailing ivy and pink and purple flowers in a few weeks. The trees along the street are dressed in green fuzz, and the magnolia across the street is in full, cream-and-pink glory.

My apartment consists of the middle two floors of the building—living room, dining room, tiny galley kitchen and powder room on the first level, then three small bedrooms and a full-size bath up the wide wooden staircase. The Victorian claw-foot tub was impossible to resist. There's a tiny backyard with a slate patio, which I get to use, and a tiny front yard that belongs to the super, who has the first floor—the pied-à-terre, the Realtor called it, which made it sound very fabulous and European. The fourth floor is being used by the owner for storage. With the three dormered windows up there, the light would be fantastic. If I owned the place, I could use the entire floor as a home studio. Or a nursery for my attractive and cheerful babies.

A man comes down the street, walking a beautiful golden retriever.

He looks my way, and our eyes meet. He lives right next door in that gorgeous brownstone, and he's single, go figure, a chef who's just signed a contract to let his name be used on a line of high-end French cookware. His sister is engaged, and guess who's making her dress? Jenny Tate, that's who! What a small world! The Christmas wedding is at St. Patrick's Cathedral, and I wear a wine-red velvet dress to the reception and he's in a tux, and as we dance together, he slides an engagement ring onto my finger and drops to one knee, and his sister— in her gorgeous satin modified A-line dress with green velvet trailing sash—is all for this. In fact, she's in on the proposal and is already crying happy tears. We get married and buy a charming old farmhouse with views of the Hudson so our twin sons and little daughter can run and play while we harvest vegetables from our organic garden and we'll breed Jeter, our faithful Goldie, and the kids will all be valedictorians and go to Yale.

The man fails to make eye contact. Instead, he's yelling something into a phone about "your bitch of a sister," so I regretfully cross him off my list of potential second husbands.

Owen never yelled. One of his many qualities. I never, ever heard him raise his lovely, reassuring voice.

I wait till the guy is safely past—just in case he's a serial killer, as my mother would no doubt assert—and get out of the car, swing my cheerful polka-dot purse onto my shoulder and check myself out in the window. Eesh. Andreas and I killed the last two bottles of Owen's wine last night while watching *Thor*s 1 and 2 for the eye candy. Part of my divorce was that I got half of Owen's small but wonderful wine collection, and I didn't object.

An image from our marriage flashes like lightning—Owen and me, on a picnic in Nova Scotia a few summers ago, holding hands. He picked a daisy and tickled my ear with it, and the sun reflected off his shock of black hair so brightly it almost hurt my eyes. His hair was—is—adorable, standing up in a way that defied gravity, perpetual bedhead that made him instantly appealing and almost childlike. No wonder his patients love him instantly.

The bewilderment is the worst part. That's what they don't tell you in divorce articles. They talk about anger and loneliness and growing apart and starting over and being kind to yourself, but they don't tell you about the untold hours in the black hole of *why*. Why? What changed? When? Why was I the one you chose to *marry*, but all of a sudden, I'm not enough anymore?

But I'm not about to start off this phase of my life bewildered. *Fuck you, Owen*, I think, and it's oddly cheering.

The super is supposed to meet me here and give me my keys. I tighten my ponytail, summon a smile and go through the iron gate to the super's door. This courtyard could be adorable with some plants and a little café table, but right now, it only holds a ratty lawn chair that's seen better days... It's the aluminum-frame kind, the seat woven from scratchy nylon fiber. The image of a fat, unshaven man wearing an ill-fitting bowling shirt, scratching his stomach with one hand and nursing a Genesee with another, a mangy dog by his side, leaps to mind with unfortunate clarity.

But no. No negativity! In ten minutes, I'll be unpacking in my beautiful new place. I can put the kettle on, even though I don't like tea, but the image of tea is very cozy on this cool, damp day. Red wine is even cozier.

Maybe I'll invite the super to have a drink with me. Or not, if he looks like the guy I just envisioned. Did the Realtor say if it was a man or a woman? I can't remember. Better yet, a neighbor will come over—not the angry golden retriever man, but a different neighbor. An older man, maybe, someone who has a good bottle of wine in one hand. *I saw the moving truck*, he'll say, *and wanted to welcome you to the street. I teach Italian literature at Barnard. Are you free for dinner? I happen to be cooking a roast.* Then again, what kind of single man cooks a roast? Scratch that. I'll come up with something better.

I knock cheerfully on the super's door—*shave-and-a-haircut, two-bits!*

There's no answer. I knock again, less cheerfully and

more loudly. Still nothing. Pressing my ear to the door, all I hear is quiet. One more knock.

Nothing.

I go back to my car and call the Realtor, getting her voice mail. "Hi! It's Jenny Tate. Um, the super doesn't seem to be here, and the moving truck will be here any sec, so…maybe you could call him? Thanks so much! Bye!"

On cue, the phone rings, but it's not the Realtor.

It's Owen.

"Hi," I say.

"Hey, Jenny." His voice is low and holds that intimate timbre that makes the parents of his patients name their next baby Owen, boy or girl. It also works well with women. Between that and his omnipresent faint smile, it always seems as if he's about to tell you a secret, and you're the only one he *can* tell, because you're just that special. We women get a little feeble-minded around Owen Takahashi, MD. He could say, "Hey, I've been thinking about strangling a few kittens. You in?" and you'd find yourself answering, "You *bet* I'm in! When can we get started?"

"You made it okay?" he asks now.

"Yeah! Just fine," I say, eyeing my house. "I can't wait for you and Ana-Sofia to see it. And the baby! How is she? I love her name! Natalia! It's so gorgeous!"

We've been divorced for fifteen and a half months. Soon, I hope, my need to be überchipper will fade.

"She's beautiful. Jenny, I can never thank you enough."

"No!" I sing, rolling my eyes at myself. If Andreas were here, he'd give me a nice brisk slap. "It was an honor." Make that a punch.

"So listen, Jenny. We'd like to use *Genevieve* as a middle name. After you."

Oh, God. "Uh, well, that's not my name," I say. For some reason, Mom just wanted Jenny. Not even Jennifer.

"Yes, I remember," he says in that "I've got a secret" voice, evoking late Sunday mornings in bed. "But still."

You know what, Owen? Don't. Okay? I don't want your baby to be named after me. Come on!

"That's very…nice. Thank you."

There's a silence. A drop of rain slaps the windshield, but just one, lonely and useless.

"You'll always be special to me," Owen says softly.

I clench my teeth. What he means is *I'm sorry I stopped loving you and found all that meaning with Ana-Sofia and discovered that I was dying to be a father—once I had the right wife, that is—and am living the dream right now, thanks to your clever hands and my perfect wife's amazing uterus that just pushed the baby out in a matter of minutes. No hard feelings, right?*

"Well," I say in the same idiotic, chipper voice. "You're special to me, too! Obviously! I married you, right? But I mean, you and Ana are *both* special to me. And so is Natalia! Right? How often do you get to deliver a baby, after all? It was fun."

He laughs as if I'm the most delightful person in all the world (which he once told me I was, come to think of it). "I miss you already. We'll see you for dinner next week, right?"

"You bet." Because, yes, I'm going to their place for dinner next Friday. How civilized! How urbane! We're so New York! You couldn't pull this shit off in Idaho, let me tell you. Probably because people are more honest out there. "Give Ana-Sofia and the baby my love."

Before I can say anything else that's stupid or spineless or inane or all of the above, I click off, grab the steering wheel and shake it. "Do you have to be such a dickless wonder?" I ask out loud. "Do you, Jenny? Huh? How about a little dignity, hmm? Is that so much to ask?"

My phone dings with a text.

Mom:

I bought you a rape whistle. There was a gangland slaying on your street last week.

"No, there wasn't, Mom!" I yell, strangling the steering wheel with even more gusto. "There was no gangland slaying!"

"Hey. You okay, Charlie Sheen?" comes a voice, and I jump against my door, grappling instinctively for the handle to escape my would-be rapist or gangland murderer. A man is leaning down, peering at me through the passenger window.

"Uh...can I help you?" I squeak.

"You were screaming. You seem to be the one who needs help." He looks pained, as if I'm the nineteenth crazy person he's dealt with today.

"I— It was... I was talking to myself. I work alone for the most part. Occupational hazard. Anyway. Sorry." I try to remember that I'm a fabulous and creative person with an impressive work history in a very competitive field. Nevertheless, I feel like an ass. "Hi."

"Hi."

His hair is flippin' beautiful, chestnut-brown and curling. His eyes are blue. Blue-gray, really. Or maybe green-blue. Yes, he's looking at me like I'm insane, but those are some very nice eyes.

"Keep it down next time," he says. "There are children around."

I feel my cheeks start a slow burn, which is generally what happens when I'm confronted with an attractive man under the age of ninety-five. I clear my throat and get out of the car, the cool, damp air making me wish I'd worn a sweater.

"I'm Jenny," I say. "I'm moving in, but the super's not around, and he has my keys." *See? All perfectly normal, pal.*

"You're moving in?"

"Yes. This house. Number 11. Do you live around here?"

"I do." He doesn't elaborate. Probably doesn't want to point out his house to the crazy woman.

"Well, do you happen to know the super?"

He's tall. And thin. Suddenly, I want to feed him. Also, that's some *seriously* gorgeous hair, even better than at first glance. Married. Hair like that wouldn't remain single. He's wearing an unbuttoned flannel shirt over a T-shirt, and while he looks like he just rolled out of bed, it kind of…works.

He brings me a bottle of wine and flowers to welcome me to the neighborhood. He's a boatbuilder, and he invites me for a sail on the Hudson next weekend, and the stars wink and blaze overhead, and he's never felt this way before; he always believed the universe would give him a sign, and what's that, a comet? If that's not a sign, then he doesn't know—

"You eye-fucking me?" he asks.

"What? No! I'm just… I'm not, okay? I just need my key, but the stupid super isn't here."

"The stupid super is right in front of you."

I close my eyes, sigh and then smile. "Hi. I'm Jenny. The new tenant."

"Leo. Keep your eyes to yourself, for the record."

"Can I please have my keys?"

"Sure." He tosses them over the car roof, and I catch them. "So why the screeching?" he asks.

"I wouldn't call it screeching, really," I say.

"Oh, it was screeching. Let me guess. Man trouble?"

"Wrong."

"Ex-husband?"

"No. I mean, yes, I have one, but no, he's not the trouble."

"Did he remarry yet?"

"Would you like to help me carry some stuff in?" I ask, forcing a smile.

"So yes, in other words. Is she younger? A trophy wife?"

I grit my teeth. "I have to unpack. And no. She's fourteen months older than I am, thank you." I yank a canvas bag from the backseat. I'm not the most organized person in the world—my sister holds that title—and I forgot to pack my underwear drawer in my suitcase, so it's in with my drill and hammer and a pint of half-and-half. Leo the Super looks in but refrains from commenting.

"Feel free to help," I say, grabbing a Boston fern with my free hand.

"I'm afraid you'll read into it. I already feel a little dirty."

"Great." The guy seems to be a dick, his hair notwithstanding.

I lug my bags up the eight stairs to my front door, then fumble for the keys, nearly dropping my fern.

"Hey, Leo!" calls a feminine voice, and we both look

down the street. A woman about my age—younger, let's be honest—is dragging a small child with one hand, holding a pie in the other. "Happy weekend, you!"

"Same to you," he calls. "Hi, Simon."

"Your son?" I ask.

His eyes flicker back to mine. "My student. I teach piano."

"Oh. Nice. I love piano music." I mean, I guess I do. I've never thought about it much. I like Coldplay, and Chris Martin plays piano, so that counts, right?

"Classical piano?" His voice implies that an unstable woman such as myself has never heard classical piano. He's almost right; aside from what I hear at weddings, I tend to veer toward things written in this century.

"As a matter of fact, yes," I lie. "I love classical piano. Beethoven and, uh...those other guys."

He cocks an eyebrow. "Name two pieces."

"Um...'Piano Man' by Billy Joel."

"Oh, God."

"And 'Tiny Dancer' by Elton John."

He grins suddenly, and his face, which is already too nice of a face, transforms into gorgeous.

"Simon's been practicing so much this week!" says the mom, and speaking of eye-fucking, she's not very subtle. I gather Leo the Super is single. A quick glance to his left hand shows no ring.

So he's single. Hello! I feel a prickle of interest. After all, I do want to get married and have kids...

"God," he mutters. "I'm a person, okay? Not a piece of meat." He opens the gate of his courtyard and holds it for the mom, ruffling Simon's hair.

The mother thrusts the pie—and practically her boobs—into his hands. "Strawberry rhubarb," she an-

nounces. "I thought you could use some feeding." A
husky, fuck-me laugh ensues. Her kid, who's about six,
rubs his nose on his arm, then wipes the arm on his
mother's very short skirt. I hope she's cold.

"This is very nice of you, Suzanne," Leo says. "Come
on, Simon, let's hear you play, buddy." He puts his hand
on the kid's shoulder and steers him in through the gate.
I only realize I'm still watching when Suzanne gives
me a pointed look, then follows Leo into his apartment.

By 4:30 P.M., my furniture is in place, hauled in by the
brawny movers who arrived five minutes after I un-
locked my front door. Rachel was supposed to come by
this afternoon, and I texted her a little while ago but she
hasn't answered. She's not one of those people glued to
her phone. Probably got lost in baking or stenciling or
something. Adam was going to take the girls to the children's museum so she could help me, but maybe something came up.

Still, it's not like her to blow me off. Not at all.

I start unpacking one of the boxes labeled Kitchen.
Cooking has never really been a great love of my life.
Eating, sure. But Owen was the better chef. Once we
divorced and I moved to the Village, my tiny apartment
was two doors down from an Italian restaurant. Problem
solved. But maybe I'll cook more now. It could happen.

My kitchen windows overlook the little courtyard.
All day, Leo's had a steady stream of students, rang-
ing in age from four or five to middle-aged. All the
adult students seem to be women, and there is not one
father in sight. Many women carry foil-wrapped good-
ies. The sound of easy piano pieces floats up to me, as
well as some popular songs; I recognize "Clocks" by

Coldplay—see? I wasn't that far off—as well as a few Disney songs. I also recognize a lot of flirting going on between Leo and the females.

Owen never flirted. He was—is—earnest and kind, which smothered any flirting ability he had.

I take out a weirdly shaped whisk and wonder what it's for. I'm going to miss Phil's Wok and Porto Bello, that's for sure. I had six restaurants on speed dial in the Village. But Cambry has a few cute places and, of course, Rachel will feed me whenever I want. She *lives* to feed people. I love eating with her and Adam and the girls, in that big sunny kitchen where Rach always seems to have cut flowers in a vase on the table, where the girls say grace before they start eating.

The biggest plus to moving back here—I'll get to see them whenever I want. Every day, even.

The thought brings a warm rise of happiness. My sister is and always has been my best friend, and I adore her husband, who's handsome and charming and just dull enough. And my nieces are the lights of my life. Nothing feels better than their little arms around my legs when I come through their door, or their tiny, soft hands in mine, or their heavy heads on my shoulder when they've fallen asleep on my lap. When they were first born, I spent two precious weeks living with Rachel and Adam, changing the tiny diapers, swapping girls with Rachel depending on which one was hungry, changing the laundry and folding the little preemie outfits.

Even if I never get to be a mommy, at least I'm a beloved aunt.

I unpack a pretty wooden bowl I got in Australia when I was doing an internship down under. The red-and-orange polka-dot chicken I bought at Target; not exactly an irreplaceable artifact, but so cheerful and happy. Another pair of misplaced panties. A picture of Rachel and me, which I place in the living room in the built-in bookcase.

I really love this place. I can make curtains for the big windows, lace panels that would look perfect and still let in light. A big old Oriental carpet for in front of the gas fireplace. My red velvet couch and leather club chair look as if they were made for this living room. I think I'll buy a butler's table and get a few orchid plants. Rach will tell me how to keep them alive.

Some movement on the street catches my eye. Oh, hooray! Speaking of my sister, she's here, standing in front of her minivan. She looks a little…strange. Her hair is in a messy ponytail, as is mine, but for me, it's normal.

Also, she's wearing jeans and a T-shirt. As someone who wears a uniform to work—I own five black pencil skirts, five sleeveless black silk shirts, five long-sleeve black silk shirts and four pairs of black Jimmy Choo pointy-toe heels—the first thing I do every day when I get home is rip off my sleek clothes and get into pajamas or jeans. My days off—Sunday and Monday—are for sloth, I've always felt.

But Rachel is always turned out, as Mom says, usually in a dress and cute shoes. I don't know how she does it, to be honest, raising the girls, keeping that house so beautiful and still looking great.

I knock on the window and wave, but she doesn't hear me, so I head out onto my stoop. I should get some pansies or something for out here. A planter full of flowers would make it look so cheerful.

"Hey, Rachel!" I call.

She looks up, and I realize she's been talking to Leo,

who is now sitting on his lawn chair, drinking a beer. A multicolored lump of fur lies beside him. I presume it's a dog, as it is dog-sized. Seems like I wasn't too far off in my mental image of a super.

I go down the steps to give my sister a hug. "Hi! Thanks for coming!"

"Sorry I'm late."

I glance at Leo, who's petting the dog with one hand. His expression is...naughty. "You okay? Did he say something to you?" I ask my sister in a low voice.

"Who?"

"Him. Leo. The super."

"Oh, no. He's very nice."

"Well, come on in. The movers were great, and I'm just putting stuff in drawers. Want some tea?"

"Do you have any wine?"

"Shoot, no. I can run downtown and get some, though."

"I have wine," Leo says.

"It's okay," I tell him. "But thanks."

"That would be great," Rachel says.

"My pleasure." He unfolds himself from the chair. Six-three, I'd guess. "Loki, stay," he orders. The dog, who looks rather close to death, doesn't twitch.

My sister looks a little pale. "Are you okay, Rachel?" I ask.

She doesn't answer, just goes up the stairs into the little foyer. "This is great," she says unconvincingly. And the thing about Rachel is, she loves home decorating and all that stuff. It's her art form. She's Martha Stewart meets Maria Von Trapp; in fact, she found me this place, and when we came here with the Realtor a month ago, Rachel raced around like a kid at Christmas.

"Thanks," I say. "Rach, you seem weird, hon."

Then she takes out her phone and taps a button. "Do you know what this is? Is this a tree? With some kind of disease or blight or something?"

I look, then flinch. "No. It's… Where did you get this?" Because, shit.

"What is it?"

I swallow. "It's…um, it's a va— It's girl parts. A crotch shot." Hey. Owen and I watched a little porn from time to time, back in the day. The picture is blurry and super close-up, which is quite icky, so yeah, I guess I could see how Rachel, who is very innocent, could think it was a diseased tree. "Who sent this to you?"

But my sister doesn't answer, because now her face is the color of chalk, and her legs buckle, and Leo catches her just as he comes in the door.

Rachel

A DISTANT PART of me is so, so embarrassed that a total stranger has seen me faint. I've never fainted before. I mean, I've *wanted* to, a thousand times, usually when I'm at a party, trying to pretend that I'm having fun, and trying to eat when no one else is looking. I'm always worried about how I look when I'm eating. I think people who throw parties should offer private little carrels where guests can go and eat in private. So I generally don't eat at parties, then the wine goes right to my head, like now, and that makes me feel even more self-conscious, because I'm afraid people will say, "That Rachel got so drunk at our party last night!" so in the end, I neither eat nor drink. I just stand around, hoping to faint, because leaving the party, even by ambulance, would be preferable to trying to look like I'm having a good time.

But I suppose I really earned the faint today. And Jenny's friend is very kind. He has sad eyes. Sad for me, because I'm an idiot.

I guess I knew what the picture was. All morning long, I smothered the thought, watched as Adam read on his iPad and accepted gifts from the girls—a picture from Rose, drawn in nursery school, a tulip head from Charlotte, a rubber band from Grace. Charlotte was chattering, Grace sitting at his feet with a notepad and pen, pretending to write a book, all three girls content to bask in his half attention. Before, I never would've faulted him for that, those delayed responses and absentminded pats on the head. He works hard. He deserves time to relax.

But this morning, I wondered what he was looking at. Who might be messaging him. And, as ever, his phone was on the table next to him. That's nothing new. I wouldn't let myself read into it. It was a tree sent by mistake. I didn't look at the picture again.

Instead, I went to the computer and looked up that hotel again. The soothing colors, chocolate and cream and white. The lobby bar, with its palm trees and beautiful clock. Looked at that for a long time after he took the kids to the museum, and though I had to go to my sister's, all I did was sit there, looking at the penthouse suite, imagining how calm and confident I'd feel there, sipping that martini and looking out over the city.

"Rachel. Drink some more water, honey." My sister's dark eyes are worried. I obey. I'm sitting on Jenny's lovely, soft old couch, and my sister is teary-eyed and furious at the same time. Leo—that's his name, Leo Killian, a nice Irish name—is looking at me too sympathetically. Tears are leaking out of my eyes, but they're faraway tears, tears I'm not really even aware of, except Jenny keeps handing me tissues.

Adam loves me. I know he loves me.

To think I thought it was a tree. A knothole. *Some* kind of hole, yes, but really, I am *such* an idiot. Almost forty, and pathetically naive.

I hope he's not giving the girls macaroni and cheese for supper. Yes, it's organic, but I like to save it for when I've had a really hard day. If he uses it, he preempts me.

And you know what? *He* should never make macaroni and cheese from a box! *I'm* the one who gets to do that. I stay home with them all day, every day. I get to be lazy once in a while. He should make them chicken and broccoli and…and…

Oh, God, he's cheating.

My thoughts surge and roll like a riptide, crashing into each other from all directions, then shushing back before I can figure out the current. I just… I just don't know what to think or where to swim.

Leo hands me a glass of wine. "Thank you," I say.

Is my life over? Life as I knew it?

My heart starts thudding in hard, erratic beats. I *love* my life. *Our* life. Finally, we seemed to hit the sweet spot. Before, even though I liked my job and my coworkers and friends, I was waiting for my *real* life to begin. Marriage. Motherhood. Just as I was starting to worry that I'd never meet anyone, I met Adam. The courtship and marriage part was strangely easy. But then came four years trying to get pregnant. Hormone injections and trying desperately to keep our love life fun and spontaneous—and, please, there is *no* spontaneity when you're trying to get pregnant, but I did my best to trick Adam into believing I was just incredibly horny and creative. Then thirty-three weeks of sheer terror, because when you're pregnant with triplets, you're a time bomb, and all you pray for is to make it to twenty-seven weeks, then another week more, and another week more.

Those first few weeks, when Rose and Grace got to come home but Charlotte had to be in the hospital, and then with all three of them, at least one baby always awake, always hungry, always crying, always needing to be changed, the pain of my huge cesarean incision, my rock-hard, ever-leaking breasts... Even then, I loved it.

But this past year, with the girls all sleeping through the night, eating regular food, and the no-dairy restriction lifted from Grace, and nobody having a peanut allergy, and Rose seeming to have outgrown the asthmatic bronchitis... I've loved every day of so many months, been so grateful for every day.

Please don't let these days be over. I don't want things to change. Please, God, don't let Adam be cheating.

I guess I said that last thing out loud, because my sister squeezes my hand.

"Maybe..." I begin. My voice sounds as thin and weak as rice paper. "Maybe whoever sent it just hit the wrong number?"

"Sure," Jenny says, but she's stiff and tight next to me, so it's clear what she thinks. I look at Leo.

"Do *you* think it's a wrong number?" I ask him. He's a man. Maybe he'll know.

He hesitates, then runs a hand through his hair. "No."

"Why?"

"Because if you were going to send a picture like that, wouldn't you make sure it was going to the right person?"

Yes. Except I would never send a picture like that.

I gulp a mouthful of wine. My head is starting to pound.

My husband might be having an affair.

My husband is having an affair.

The words don't sink in.

"So you're a piano teacher?" I ask him.

"That's right."

The wine in my glass trembles, as if we're having an

earthquake. Oh, no, it's because my hands are shaking. "Some of my friends use you. Elle Birkman? Her son is Hunter. And um, um…Claudia Parvost. Her daughter is Sophia."

"Sure. Nice people."

Elle and Claudia aren't really my friends. We're in the same book club. We all belong to the COH Lawn Club. The girls and I take Mommy and Me swim classes there. Elle just had breast implants and now wears a string bikini that makes the teenage-boy lifeguard extremely uncomfortable.

Apparently, my brain will think about anything other than that…picture.

"My girls… We want them to take an instrument. I always thought piano would be the nicest."

He smiles. It's a sad smile, because he *knows*. "How old are they?"

"Three and a half."

"Twins?"

"Triplets." I smile, but my smile is broken and weak, wobbly as a newly hatched baby bird. "Are they too young?"

"Not necessarily. If they can sit still for half an hour, they're not too young." It's a kind answer, because he doesn't want to deny me anything right now, because I'm a pathetic, stupid wife, the wife is always the last to know, my wife doesn't understand me, my wife will never find out, I'm leaving my wife.

I chug the rest of the wine in my glass.

"Why don't I go?" Leo says.

"Yes. Thank you," Jenny says, standing up. She walks him to the door, and they murmur for a second, no doubt expressing their horror and sympathy for me.

Jenny comes back and sits next to me, her pretty face concerned. This was supposed to be *her* weekend. I was supposed to help *her*, and the girls were supposed to come to cheer her up, because it's really real now, her divorce from Owen, Owen's new family, and she loved him so much, and God, I hope he never cheated on her, she said he didn't but who can really know anything anymore? No one. That's who.

Suddenly I'm crying very hard, not just leaking tears but full-on, chest-ripping sobs that hurt, they're so vicious.

"Oh, honey," Jenny whispers, holding me close. "Oh, sweetie."

"Don't tell anyone. I have to figure out what to do first," I choke out between the awful, shuddering convulsions.

"No, I won't," she says. "And…Rachel, whatever you need, I'm here. If you and the girls want to stay here—"

"No!" I yelp, startled out of my tears. "No! It's way too early to think about anything like that. I don't even know if it's true. Please, Jenny."

"No, you're right. I'm sorry."

My phone chimes with a text. Adam:

We're home. How's Jenny's place? Should we come over?

A completely normal text. Normal husband talk. "Look at this," I say, wiping my eyes on my sleeve. "I mean, seriously, it was probably a mistake. Whoever sent that just dialed the wrong number."

"It… Sure. It could've been."

I stare at the phone, then hand it to my sister. "Could

you answer? Just say the place is a mess and I'll be home later?"

She types my response, then hands me back the phone.

Adam replies, Okay, babe. Love you.

See? He loves me. Of course he does.

When we were engaged, we talked about cheating. I brought it up, even though it was hard, even though my heart was sledgehammering through my chest wall. I mean, I'm not really the ultimatum type, but certain things have to be said. *I wouldn't be able to stay with you if you ever cheated*, I told him, and he said he'd never, ever do such a thing. He only loved me. He only wanted me.

He didn't feel the need to warn me that cheating would be a deal breaker for him, too. Obviously, I'd never cheat on him. It went without saying, even back then.

He loves our life as much as I do. He wouldn't risk it.

"I think this was all a mistake," I say with more conviction.

Because if it's not, everything is different now.

The doorbell rings. Jenny stands and looks out the window. "Shit. It's Mom. I'll get rid of her. Why don't you hide in the bathroom?"

I obey. My legs feel weak, and that wine is throbbing in my brain, thick and sluggish.

"Hey, Mom, I'm not feeling so good," I hear Jenny say. "I have a wicked headache. And I'm almost done, really."

"You must be so depressed," Mom says. "You look awful. Was it heartbreaking?"

"Um…not really. We've been divorced for more than a—"

"Of *course* it was. Oh, honey. I'm so sorry for you. Even though Rob's life was cut short, at least we never had to even *think* about divorce. We might not have had many years together, but we made them count. You don't even have that, you poor thing. Want me to rub your head?"

"I'm good."

Nothing makes our mother happier than discussing the troubles of those around her—even her daughters, and sometimes especially us—so long as she can come out the winner. Those four years that I tried so hard to get pregnant, all she could talk about was how easy it had been for her. When the girls were born by C-section, all of them just about four pounds—which was great, given that they were triplets—Mom delighted in telling me for the thousandth time about how both Jenny and I came into this world at twice that weight. *Both you girls were perfectly healthy*, she said, sounding slightly perplexed. *Well. I'm sure yours will grow.*

If she saw me now, she'd home in on me like a missile. And unlike Jenny, I can't hide anything.

My face in the mirror is nearly unrecognizable. I look terrified. I can't lose Adam. I can't. I love him so, *so* much. There has to be a mistake.

After my father died, I couldn't look in the mirror, because the heartbreak was written over my face so clearly.

I look the same now. Eyes too wide. Skin too white.

They're still talking; Mom doesn't want to leave, wants to talk about Owen's new baby and hear again how Jenny had to deliver her.

"Look, Mom, you're right," my sister says. "I'm incredibly depressed, I have a migraine—"

"I've never had a migraine. I never even get headaches."

"—and just want to be alone so I can wallow. Maybe we can have lunch this week. Come by the shop, okay? It's really cute."

"Yes, but it's hardly Manhattan, is it? I hope you won't go bankrupt. You should've moved to Hedgefield. You could live with me until you get on your feet, and we—"

"Okay, Mom, thanks! Bye." The door closes, and another minute passes. "It's safe," Jenny calls.

My college roommate was from Los Angeles, and she described being in an earthquake. If you can't trust the ground to stay still, she'd said, the entire world seems wrong.

I feel that way now.

"What can I do?" Jenny asks as I come out on my fearful legs.

"I don't know."

I have to believe that Adam was not the intended recipient of that hideous, disgusting picture. How do gynecologists do it all day, look between the legs of their patients and not just…just throw up?

My sister takes my hand. Even though she's younger, she's always been more certain.

I take a deep breath. I'm a mother. I'm not a weakling, and I have to be logical and smart. I have three children with this man. I can't just react. "I have to talk to him, I guess."

"Want me to babysit, and you guys can go somewhere? Or I can take the girls out. They can even stay over here tonight. I'd love that."

"I don't know. I just… I don't know."

My sister nods, then takes a slow breath. "I hate to ask this," she says, "but are there any other…red flags?"

Anything that would prove beyond a shadow of a doubt that he was cheating, she means.

"I don't think so. He's been tired lately. But people get tired. He's been working on this really complicated case, and… Well. He's been tired."

It's just that *tired* never meant *too tired* before.

She doesn't say anything. Is she pitying me? Disagreeing? Agreeing?

Adam's a corporate attorney. He knows things that save his clients millions of dollars each year. He's great at his job, was made partner at the firm, second in seniority only to Jared Brewster, who grew up down the street from us and used to sit on the bus with me. And since Jared's grandfather founded the firm, I'd say Adam is doing even better, maybe. He's important. He works a lot, it's true.

Maybe his lover is a client.

His *lover*. My stomach heaves at the word. I've always hated that word. It's too intimate, too romantic, too smarmy. I don't want my husband to have a lover. I've never even thought of myself as his lover. I was his girlfriend, then his fiancée, then his wife.

"There's a lot to lose here," I whisper.

"Yes." Jenny squeezes my hand, and I hate that I need a hand squeeze. I'm usually the giver of the hand squeezes…well, in the past year or so, anyway.

It's now past 7:30 p.m., so the girls are almost certainly in bed and sound asleep.

I guess I have to go home.

For the first time in my life, that thought fills me with dread.

I SLIP IN the house like a shadow and go right upstairs when I get home. Opening the door to the girls' bedroom, I feel a rush of love so strong that it momentarily crushes all the horrible worming thoughts that have twisted through my mind for the past twenty-four hours.

This room is pure. I know exactly who I am in this room.

My little girls are asleep; Charlotte is snoring slightly, Grace is sucking her thumb, Rose is sleeping upside down, her feet on the pillows. I kiss Grace first, then Charlotte, then turn Rosebud right-side-up and kiss her, too. I whisper "Mommy loves you" to each of them, breathing in their sweet and salty smell.

Here, in this room, I know everything that really matters. I was born to be a mommy. These girls are my life.

Some of the sticky fear slips away.

I go downstairs, through the living room and into the den, where Adam is talking on the phone. "I feel the same way," he murmurs, then catches sight of me and jumps.

Guilty.

"Hi," I say.

"Eric, my beautiful wife just came home," he says, smiling. Not guilty? "Can we talk on Monday? Great. Thanks. You bet." He clicks off the phone and stands up. "Hi, babe! I didn't hear you come in. Want a glass of wine? I made the girls mac and cheese, but I could make you an omelet or something."

Of course he made the mac and cheese.

And yet, these are not the words of a cheating husband.

"I'll have some wine," I say. We go into the kitchen, he pours me a glass of white, and I take a sip. The kitchen is sloppy; granted, I'm almost obsessive about neatness, but the pot from the girls' unnutritious dinner is sitting in the sink, the powdery cheese sauce hardening, and mail is strewn over the counter, which hasn't been wiped down.

Usually I'm just grateful that Adam doesn't view spending the afternoon with his children as a heroic feat, like some fathers do. But it would be nice if he just once cleaned up the way I do a thousand times a day.

"How's the new place?" he asks, grabbing a beer from the fridge. "Is Jenny happy with it?"

"It's great," I answer. My heart pumps too hard, and I picture a big ugly hand around it, squeezing ruthlessly, forcing the blood to gush through my veins. Arteries. Whatever. "It's really charming." What are we talking about? Oh, yes. My sister's place.

He waits for more. He likes my sister.

I wonder if he finds her attractive.

God, where did *that* come from?

"Adam, I need to talk to you about something."

"Sure, babe." He waits, his dark eyes expectant. I love his brown eyes. Mine are boring blue; Jenny got our father's dark, dark eyes, almost black. But Adam's are light brown, whiskey-colored and special.

"Um…how were the girls today?" I ask, suddenly dreading what I'm about to say next.

"They were great. Well, Rose was a maniac at the museum, and Grace's shoe came untied, and you know how she hates that, and I had to take all three of them into the ladies' room. Got a lot of dirty looks from some women, but really, what am I supposed to do? Take them into the men's room? No way." He grins. "My babies aren't going to see a man's junk for forty more years."

I smile. A tiny ray of relief seems to break through the clouds around my head, checking to see if it's okay to stay.

This is not how a cheating husband talks. It had to have been a wrong number.

"So what did you want to talk about?" he asks.

I fold my hands, which still seem to have a tremor. "Well, um, yesterday, something happened."

"What?"

Should I even show him? Maybe it would be better if I didn't. Maybe—

"Rachel? Hello? What, honey?"

I showed Jenny, and I asked Leo, and he's a stranger. I have to show my husband of the past nine years. He deserves to know.

I pull my phone from my bag and tap on the text so the disgusting picture fills the screen. Slide it across the counter to him.

Color rises from the collar of his polo shirt, up his neck, into his jaw and cheeks, a heavy, dark red.

Guilty.

Oh, God. Guilty.

Adam clears his throat, then slides the phone back to me. "What is that?"

"You know what it is, Adam." My voice trembles.

"Yeah, okay, I can guess. Who sent it to you? And why would they do that?"

"It was sent to you."

He blinks. Is his face getting redder? "What are you talking about?"

"When you were putting the girls to bed last night, someone texted this to you. I forwarded it to myself and deleted it off your phone."

"You deleted it? Why? Why didn't you say something? Why didn't you tell me last night?" He presses his lips together. "And why are you checking my phone all of a sudden? Why would you do that?"

"I was putting your jacket in the dry-cleaning bag, and I saw it."

"So you just... You... Why didn't you tell me someone's sending me porn?"

"Who sent it?"

"I don't know!" His voice slaps off the stainless-steel appliances. "How should I know? Did you call them back? Let me see that again." He grabs the phone back. "Private number." He looks up at me. "Could be anybody."

"Anybody sending a crotch shot, that is." I sound like Jenny.

He stares at me. "Do you think I'm *cheating* on you?" His eyes are hard.

I don't answer. All of a sudden, the tables are turned, and my face is the one that grows hot.

"Jesus, Rachel! Are you kidding me?"

"Keep your voice down," I say. "Don't wake the girls."

"I'm sorry! I'm a little upset! My wife thinks I'm cheating on her. I guess she thinks I'm a really shitty person!"

"Adam, there's a picture of...*that* on your phone. What am I supposed to think?"

"Maybe you could think 'Hey, this must be a mistake, because my husband isn't some douche-bag scum.'"

"I—I'm sorry, okay?" I take a breath, feel the burn of tears in my eyes. "It doesn't seem like the kind of thing that would be sent by mistake, that's all. I'd think you'd be really careful about getting the right number if you were sending *that* to someone." *Thank you, Leo.*

"You told Jenny about this, didn't you? I bet she had a fucking field day. She hates men these days."

"She does not. And no, she didn't have a field day. I showed her because…well, I wasn't sure what it was. I *hoped* it was a mistake. I did. But I needed to talk to you about it, and it's new territory, okay?"

He gives a short laugh. "Yeah. I guess so." He takes a breath and releases it slowly. "I love you, Rachel. I thought you loved me, too. I'd hope you'd at least give me the benefit of the doubt."

"Of course I love you, Adam. It's just very…weird and horrible, and I didn't know what to ask, or how to talk about this, or…or…"

"Do you believe me?"

His voice is cold and sharp, and suddenly, that terror rears up again.

I don't want things to change. I have cupcakes to make tomorrow, six dozen, because the girls are all in a different preschool class, and each class needs two dozen cupcakes. Also, I call my mother-in-law every Sunday morning to give her a grandchild report, and what would I say if Adam is cheating on me? And Jenny's just moved, and there are going to be long, happy dinners and lovely spring evenings on the back patio, and Adam… Adam cried when the girls were born. Really cried. He loves me, and he loves our daughters, and he loves our life.

"Rachel, do you believe me?" he asks again, more loudly.

"Yes. I do."

He closes his eyes and lets out a long breath. "Thank you." Then he comes around the counter behind me and slides his arms around me from behind. Kisses my neck. "Baby, I love you. The picture is disgusting, but come on. Don't be so dramatic next time. Not that there'll be a next time, please God."

"You're right." Two tears slide down my cheeks, and honestly, I don't know how to feel. Relieved? Sick? Happy?

I was wrong. It was a mistake.

We go upstairs. We make love. It's good. It's *us*. We know what the other likes, what to say and when, what moves to employ, where to touch for the best effect. It occurs to me that I'm glad our birth control is condoms, and then I push that thought out of my head.

We're okay. We're still us. Adam and me and the girls…everything is the same.

It's just that everything feels so different.

Jenny

❖━━●━━❖

THE NEXT DAY, I have to go to the city for a fitting from a bride who's so high-maintenance that asking her to come to Cambry-on-Hudson might well cause a brain aneurysm. The gown hangs in its blush-colored bag; I had a hundred of them ordered for Bliss, as well as special hangers that can hold up to twenty-five pounds, because some of these dresses are heavy. The bride, Kendall, is the kind who treats me like a servant, texting and complaining as I kneel at her side, pinning her last-minute changes and adjusting the seams since she's lost ten pounds in the past two weeks out of sheer rage. To call her bridezilla would be unkind to Japan's favorite monster.

But first, my sister.

Rachel texted me last night around ten, saying it was all a mistake, and she felt terrible for thinking Adam had cheated. I asked if I could call, but she said she was really tired.

I'm not sure I believe my brother-in-law, and I hate that I'm not sure.

When I first met Adam, Rachel was already overwhelmingly in love. Her first love, really, though she'd had a few boyfriends, always these rather nice, shy, geeky man-child types who wore *Doctor Who* T-shirts and spoke Klingon. But Adam was different, very sure of himself, and very charismatic. She glowed around him. They dated only a month or so before he proposed—asking for permission from Mom and me first, which won serious points with me and turned the event into an "I Miss Rob" occasion for Mom.

Adam cried when he saw Rachel in the church on their wedding day—it wasn't just the dress, which, trust me, was amazing, a modified A-line satin and French lace with a sweetheart neckline and delicate capped sleeves. He kept his sense of humor through the infertility years, and he brought Rachel flowers twice a week all through her pregnancy.

He's also a really good dad, though perhaps not as good as Rachel thinks he is... He's a little too aware of the fact that he does more than some of his peers, but he's content to let Rachel do the hard stuff, the getting-up-in-the-middle-of-the-night-when-someone-has-the-pukes stuff, the grocery-shopping-with-all-three-of-them-at-once stuff. But he's there, and he loves them, and he does contribute. And let's face it. Rachel loves being a stay-at-home mom.

I call Rachel just before I leave the house. "Oh, hey," she says. "Just a minute, okay? Charlotte, honey, I have to take this, okay? Can you please give that to Daddy? Thank you, sweetheart." There's a pause, and I hear a door close. "Hi," she says.

"How are things today?" I ask.

"Well, I showed him the picture," she whispers, "and he was really confused and then he got upset that I thought...you know. He has no idea who sent it. But he was really nice about it."

"Nice about what?"

"About me thinking that maybe he…strayed."

I press my lips together. "Hmm."

"So we're good. I think this is just a case of a mistaken phone number. I just feel really bad for what I thought."

"Rach, I don't think it's unreasonable to think your husband is having an affair when Private Number sends him a crotch shot," I say. "I hope he got that."

"No, no, he did," Rachel says. "We're past it. Actually, we're just leaving for church, so I have to run, okay? Listen, I'm so sorry about yesterday. I really wanted to help you get settled. I just freaked out."

"It's really okay. You deserved to freak out." I pause. "And I'm glad things aren't what they seem."

Except I smell a rat. Leo, a total stranger, smelled a rat. Yes, yes, there's a chance Adam is telling the truth.

But my gut is telling me he's not.

"He's a great husband," Rachel says. "And you know how the girls adore him."

"Yeah. I do. You go, hon. I have to run down to the city with a dress."

"Okay. Hey, tell your friend thanks for me. I'm so embarrassed."

"My friend?"

"Leo."

"Oh, right. Okay, have a good day. Talk to you later."

If Adam is cheating on my sister, I will rip off his testicles. Through his throat.

I pick up the dress and my purse and head outside. Leo is lying on his lounge chair, eyes closed, dog by his side, bottle of beer in his hand. "Hi," I say. "A little early for drinking, isn't it?"

"It sure is, Mom," he says, taking a swig without opening his eyes. The dog lifts his head and growls at me.

"My sister wanted me to say thanks."

"She's welcome."

"And thank you from me, too. You were very nice."

"No problem. I excel at catching women when they faint." He scratches behind Loki's ear, and the dog makes a guttural sound.

There's something arresting about Leo's face. Angular and a little thin, unshaven. Despite his easy words, there are two lines between his eyebrows. He looks up at me.

"No eye-fucking," he says.

"Because you're gay?" I suggest.

"Only where you're concerned, darling." He winks, and though I've just been rather brilliantly insulted, I can't help a smile. "Are you going to the prom?" he asks, gesturing with the beer bottle at the dress bag.

"No." Placing the dress carefully on the backseat, I secure the hanger onto the hook. "I'm a wedding dress designer."

"Seriously?"

"Seriously."

"That's a real job? I mean, they all kind of look alike, don't they?"

"Have a nice day," I say, waving. Well, my middle finger waves. Leo laughs, and there it is again, that warm pressure in my chest.

"I WANT YOU to take all the rosettes off," Kendall says.

We're in the living room of her parents' Upper West Side apartment, and I'm kneeling at her feet, my pincushion strapped to my wrist, taking the dress down from a size 00 to microscopic. It looks like her bones are about to slice through her skin.

"Your wedding is in six days, Kendall," I say. "It's a little late to change the design completely."

"Look, I hate them, okay? Just lop them off or something."

Being a custom wedding dress designer means one thing—the bride gets what the bride wants. We start the process, which takes a year on average, with the bride emailing me pictures of wedding dresses she loves. But there's a reason she's not getting one of those, and it's either that she's a hard size to fit, or she wants something completely unique.

Kendall wanted something unique. She sent me thirty-nine pictures of dresses she loved, from a minidress to a ball gown with twelve-foot train. I made her seventeen sketches, then, when she finally settled on one—the one festooned with beautiful, creamy rosettes—I ended up making twenty-two alterations to that sketch. Then, when she said she was deliriously happy with the design, I made the pattern. Cut the dress out of muslin and had her come in for a fitting. She wanted the dress changed again; not a problem, but from then on, it would cost her. A lot.

Alas, money was no object. Seven muslin dresses and thousands of dollars later, she signed a contract saying yes, I could proceed with the actual dress. A sleeveless sheath dress with a crisscrossing tulle bodice, a belt made from Swarovski crystals that tied in the back with a long, floating tulle sash and a skirt that made her appear as if she were rising from a giant pile of white silk roses, each of the 278 flowers made by the hand of yours truly. It's pretty. Of course it is.

All told, the dress will cost almost twenty grand.

"If I cut off the rosettes," I say patiently, "I'll have to make another skirt."

She doesn't bother looking up from her phone, which chimes with a text. "Oh, Christ, you gotta be kidding me! Mom? Mom!" the blushing bride roars. "Ma! Where the hell are you? Now *Linley* doesn't want to be in the wedding, either! Those bitches! How dare they bail on me!"

One wonders.

A half hour later, it's decided that yes, Kendall will get another skirt, made from tulle to match the bodice, and a full skirt with a sweep train that will trail out six feet behind her. I request payment in full plus aggravation pay—I call it an emergency alteration fee—and wait as her poor mother writes me out a check.

"You've been wonderful," the mom says. "Kendall, hasn't Jenny been wonderful?"

"What?" Kendall says, dragging her eyes off the phone. Her thumbs continue to tap out her message. "Who's Jenny? Oh. Yeah. Sure."

"She'll make a beautiful bride," I tell the mom.

"You're very kind," she says. "I'll refer you to all my friends."

"I really appreciate that."

Granted, I'm used to badly behaved brides. It can be a stressful time. But believe it or not, even women like Kendall can morph into a sweetheart on the big day. Not always, but sometimes. And happily, most of my brides are much nicer.

The lobby doorman holds the door for me. I stash the dress back in the car and stretch my lower back.

The sky has cleared, the cherry trees are in bloom and I decide to take a walk through Central Park. I love the happy noise of the throngs—kids laughing and yelling, the blur of languages I don't speak, a homeless man wishing everyone a blessed day, the thunk of bass music from an area where kids are doing backflips, entertaining the tourists.

The city has been my home since I was eighteen, and though I've only lived in COH a day, I feel as if I've been away for weeks.

Central Park is truly the crown jewel of the city, with its curving trails, the statues and flower beds awash in red tulips and yellow daffodils. People are out in droves—runners and parents and nannies and students. A lot of babies are being aired out today. I would pick that one, I think, eyeing a beautiful little boy with bushy black hair and enormous eyes. Or maybe that little girl in the purple windbreaker and red plaid skirt.

There's a man sitting on a bench, reading. An actual book, too, not a phone. I can't quite make out the title, but that doesn't matter. He's blond and wears glasses, and he has a scarf around his neck, but it's not dreadfully self-conscious. He seems to be about forty. No wedding ring. Nice face.

I consider talking to him. What to say, though? "Hi! Want to father some kids?" seems a little blunt. I glance around, hoping for inspiration.

Oh.

I seem to have wandered all the way across the park to the East Side. Two blocks from my old place. Owen's place, rather. *Paging Dr. Freud*...

I could visit them. You know…for self-torment purposes, in case my bride wasn't difficult enough. I could ask to smell Natalia's head. Maybe put her in my purse, which would easily fit a baby. I actually look to judge the baby-capacity of my bag. Yep. It could work. I'd make sure to move my sewing scissors first.

I turn around and face the scarf-wearing reader. "Hi. Beautiful day, isn't it?"

He doesn't look up. New Yorkers.

"What are you reading?" I ask more loudly.

He raises his eyes to me. "I'm sorry, were you talking to me?" he asks with a nice smile.

"I was just wondering what you were reading."

He holds the book up. "*Lord of the Rings.* My third or fourth time, actually. I'm sort of a geek about it."

My wedding dress looks like Arwen's when she finally sees Aragorn again. (Yes, yes, I'm referencing the movie, not the book. Sue me.) *My nieces are our tiny flower girls, and Rachel wears pale green as my matron of honor. Mom has a boyfriend and doesn't sob about Dad. For a wedding gift, I give him a first-printing edition of* LOTR, *and—*

And my fiancé's boyfriend sits down and kisses him. "Hi, darling, sorry I'm late. Brought you a cappuccino, though."

"Have a nice day," I say, but they're busy kissing.

It only takes me two minutes to get to Owen's place. I still have the code to the building, but I buzz 15A just the same. "It's Jenny," I say, cringing a little.

"Jenny! How wonderful!" comes Ana-Sofia's voice.

Five minutes later, I'm sitting in my former living room, holding my former husband's child, accepting a cup of coffee from his current wife, who's back in her regular clothes. It's been thirteen days, after all. Why go through all that mushy belly stuff when you're clearly on Darwin's list of favorite children?

"Do you remember Jenny?" Owen asks, smiling down at his daughter. "She helped you into this world."

"She's incredibly beautiful," I say honestly. Not a pore to be seen. Rosebud mouth, full, lovely cheeks. "She looks like—" *you*, I was about to say, but I clear my throat. "Like Ana-Sofia." I smile at my replacement.

"Thank God for small favors," Owen says, leaning over my shoulder to stroke his daughter's cheek with one finger.

She doesn't. She looks just like Owen, the same shock of black hair, the same sweet eyes, and I remember in a furnace-blast of embarrassment how I used to look at Owen when he was asleep and picture our children.

Funny how I didn't think this was going to be so hard.

There's a flash. Ana-Sofia has taken my picture. I imagine Ana-Sofia showing it to Natalia someday. *There's poor Aunt Jenny, just before she went crazy. We should visit her in the asylum this week.* "I'll send it to you, yes?" she asks.

"Sure," I say. Who wouldn't want a picture of her ex and his baby and her doleful self, after all? Maybe I'll blow it up and hang it over my couch. "So I just wanted to stop by. I had a fitting a couple blocks from here, but I should head home. Still have lots of unpacking to do."

"We can't wait to see the new place," Ana-Sofia says, taking the warm little baby from my arms. It's all I can do not to grab the baby back. "And we're so excited about the grand opening of Bliss!"

The thing is, she's sincere. I want so much to hate her—to hate them both—but they're just too fucking nice.

"I can't wait, either," I say in that oh-so-jolly voice I adopt around them. I wonder if there are any escort services in COH.

I should really get out of this friendship, I think as I walk back across the park to the garage where I parked. I know hanging around Owen and Ana-Sofia isn't doing me any favors.

It's just that when Owen broke my heart, he also begged me to stay friends with him, saying he couldn't picture life without me, that ever since we'd met, I'd been incredibly important to him, and even if we weren't working out (news to me), it would kill him if this was the end.

I'm still not sure if that was kind or incredibly self-ish of him. I've been going with kind.

I moved out of our apartment the day after Owen told me he didn't want to stay married, and it felt like I'd slept through the apocalypse. The air had seemed too heavy to breathe, and panic had flashed through me in razor-wire slices. *How can I do this? How can I do this? How can we be apart? How can he not want me anymore? What the fuck went on here? Where was I when it all went to hell?*

The only island on the horizon had been the idea that the following week, I'd be having lunch with him.

You may think I'm quite an ass for hanging around, hoping for a few kind words. I understand. I feel that way myself quite often. The thing is, there will be a *lot* of kind words. Let's not even bring up the great food those two always have on hand.

Owen still asks about my work. He loves my sister and nieces and mother. He thinks I'm pretty and funny and smart. He admires my creativity. We have a similar sense of humor. Conversation comes easily, and since the day I met him, and even through our quickie divorce and his marriage, I have yet to go three days without hearing from him. Even when he's been in a third-world country with Doctors Without Borders. Even now.

So. Being Owen's ex-wife is still better than any relationship I've ever had, except for one—when I was his actual wife.

It's not just his job—Dr. Perfect of the Great Hands and Compassionate Heart. It's not just his looks, which sure don't hurt. I always had a thing for Ken Watanabe, after all.

It's all those things and just how golden he is. How privileged I felt as the chosen one, Owen Takahashi's wife.

In most marriages, lust and love become tempered by normalcy. If you hear your husband farting in the bathroom seconds before he emerges and asks if you want to fool around, you generally *don't* want to fool around. You might, after a few minutes, but you have to forgive your husband for…well, for being human. For eating a bean burrito. After all, you ate the bean burrito, too.

You discover his irritating habits. He uses your shampoo and doesn't mention when it's gone. He leaves his workout clothes in a sweaty pile in the bathroom. When his parents visit, he runs out to the package store around the corner to buy his dad's favorite beer, even though you reminded him yesterday to pick it up, and that errand takes him ten times as long as it should, and you have to text him twice to say Where the hell are you? Your mother wants to know why I'm not pregnant yet! and he doesn't respond, claiming not to have received that text when he finally walks in the door.

Maybe he grunts at you when he comes in home from work, but he gets down on all fours and croons to the dog for ten minutes, using that special voice that sounds vaguely familiar because he used to use it for you.

Maybe he's just boring, and you sit across the table from him night after night as he drones on and on about the tuna sandwich he had at lunch, amazed that this man is the reason you didn't go into the Peace Corps.

Yeah. But it was never like that with Owen and me. I'm serious.

If he was sick, which hardly ever happened, he insisted on staying in the guest room—and using the guest bathroom. I'd make him soup and he'd accept it, but the man is a doctor, and the last thing he wanted to do was spread germs. A day or two later, he'd emerge, clean and showered, and he'd apologize for his downtime, and then make me dinner.

But if *I* was sick…oh, happy day! I *loved* being sick. And here's a secret. In the five years Owen and I were married, I was never once sick. Just don't tell him that.

I admit, I was feeling a little neglected one night. I'd made a really nice dinner, but he was late coming home from rebuilding children's faces, so I could hardly complain, could I? As the risotto coagulated on the stove, I waited. He texted that he'd be half an hour late. After half an hour, he texted again. So sorry. Closer to 8. At 8:30 p.m., he came through the door. I pretended not to mind, but I'd had this fabulous call—*Bride* magazine was featuring one of my dresses on the cover, and I'd been saving the news all day long, because I wanted to tell him in person.

So I poured the wine and Owen and I sat down—I'd set the table beautifully—and we ate the now-gelatinous and slimy risotto, which Owen proclaimed delicious. He was late, he explained, because he'd had to rebuild a child's nose in a particularly difficult surgery, and he'd wanted to stay until the little guy woke up from anesthesia, and then the little guy wanted to play Pokémon with Owen, and he just couldn't say no, and the parents were crying with amazement that their son was once again so beautiful and would no longer have to endure the stares and cruelty of the unkind, and the horrible fire that took the kid's nose could now be a memory and not a flashback every time the kid thought about, touched, saw or had someone look at his face.

The cover of *Bride* now seemed pretty unimportant.

"Is something wrong, darling?" Owen finally asked.

And because I couldn't say *I'm tired of you being so damn perfect, especially when I made risotto!* I said, "No, no." Pause. "I'm not feeling that great. I'm sorry, babe."

"Oh, no! *I'm* sorry! And here I've been going on so long! What's the matter, honey?"

I spewed out a few made-up symptoms—aches, some chills, a sore head—feeling perversely happy with my lie and my husband's subsequent guilt and attention. He tucked me into bed, found a movie I loved, then went to clean up the kitchen. "I'm running out for a few minutes," he called. "You need anything?"

"No," I said, immediately peeved once again. Stupid hospital.

But he returned fifteen minutes later with a pint of the notoriously hard-to-find Ben & Jerry's Peanut Brittle ice cream. My favorite. "I thought this might be the best medicine," he said with that sweet smile. Then he lay on the bed next to me as I ate straight from the carton.

Later, we held hands. There was no guest-room sleeping for me, no sir. Owen wanted to be close, in case I needed him. He stroked my hair as I fell asleep, told me he loved me.

And he did. But he never needed me. I didn't complete him. He felt we both deserved more.

All those other marriages—those imperfect marriages with their smelly bathrooms—had something ours didn't. That moment when you've had the worst day ever, and you come home, and you can't go one more step without a long, hard hug from your spouse. Only they have the arms that will do. Only they really understand.

I don't think Owen *ever* had a day when his life was in the shitter. When we met, he was already a star resident, on his way to greatness. And when *I* had a crappy day, when someone shot down my work, or when a buyer treated me like an assembly-line worker, when a bride had a tantrum because I had done exactly what she asked, I felt as if my complaints were petty and unimportant. After all, I still had my nose, didn't I?

I told myself that it was good, keeping things in perspective. In order to have interesting things to talk about with my husband, the heroic saver of faces, the smiter of deformities, the changer of lives, I'd listen to TED Talks on my computer while I worked. I'd read important novels. Listen to NPR in order to have interesting things to contribute to our dinner conversations.

But I never let myself have regular feelings when I was with Owen. I was almost afraid to bitch about Marie, the mean and less-talented designer who trashed me to our coworkers after Vera told me my work was "glorious." When a homeless man peed himself on the subway, and I only noticed because it leaked into my own seat, it was such a sad and horrifying occurrence that I wept as I gave him all the money in my wallet to the disapproving stares of my fellow riders. I cried all the way home and took a forty-five-minute shower. Threw that skirt in the trash and triple bagged it. It was one of my favorites.

But I didn't tell Owen. He'd just returned from Sri Lanka, fixing faces marred by war, after all. My brush with the homeless man…pah. It was nothing compared to what Owen had seen. So I kept that, and all the other little vagaries and irritations of life, to myself.

There's that saying—true love makes you a better person. I thought at the time that this was my evolution into a better person. What I didn't realize was that I wasn't better; I was just less me. I *wanted* to vent about Marie and her petty little pecks. I *wanted* to be consoled about sitting in someone else's urine.

But it was nothing compared to what Owen dealt with every day.

And so Owen and I had a very happy marriage, a seamless relationship of mutual affection, love, interesting conversations and enjoyable trips. When I felt the need to be human, I faked a mild virus, and Owen would attend to me as he might a patient, and I felt more special and loved than at any other time in our years together.

We were happy.

Except I saw it, that slow erosion of love. Of interest. Of that delight that Owen used to feel toward me, from the very first day we met, that incredibly flattering sense that Owen believed I was the most charming, adorable person he'd ever encountered. For a year, maybe two, I saw Owen's love flickering, like electricity during a thunderstorm. He was never cruel, never impatient. He was simply leaving me, a surgical centimeter at a time.

I don't think he was consciously aware of it, but I saw it, and I fought it, believe me. Tried to rock his world in bed, though sex had always been lovely and comfortable and intimate. After reading an article in *Cosmo*, I talked dirty to him one night as we were making love—dropped the f-bomb, as instructed. He pulled back and said, "What did you just say?" looking as stunned as if I'd just slit his throat.

I invited our friends over more frequently to show Owen that we were the couple to be, that we had this great life, of course we did, we were having a wine-tasting dinner! See? I tried to book a vacation, but Owen said he couldn't take the time. I booked a weekend in Maine instead, so we could walk on the stony beaches and take a boat ride to the Cranberry Islands, so we could get sloppy eating lobster and laugh and hold hands and sleep late. But Owen had an emergency surgery that day—a little girl shot in the face—and he had to stay the entire weekend at the hospital.

So, in all honesty, I wasn't all that surprised when he came home that fateful night and told me he wasn't living the life he felt he was meant for. That though he loved me, he couldn't help feeling a little...empty...lately. It wasn't my fault, of course. It was just a feeling that his destiny lay elsewhere.

I knew it was coming. It didn't make it any easier.

Is there anything more humiliating than begging someone to stay with you? To keep loving you? The answer is no. I begged anyway. For five solid hours, I begged and sobbed and shouted. He couldn't leave me.

He was everything to me. Please, everything should just go back to how it was when we were happy.

But he was resolute. "You're my best friend," he said, and there were tears in his eyes. "Jenny, I'm so, so sorry. I hate doing this, but I feel like I have to. The same way I knew I had to go to medical school, even though my dad wanted so much for me to be a lawyer. It's not you. It's just… I have to."

It's not you. The stupidest line in the history of lines. I moved out the next day. Of course it was me.

Three months later, Owen proved that fact by meeting Ana-Sofia. We were having our weekly lunch, and he hadn't said anything. I just knew. I could tell, because I recognized the look on his face; he used to look at me that way. "So you've met someone," I said.

He hesitated.

"Please be honest, Owen."

"Yes," he said. "I think I have."

A month later, he introduced me to Ana-Sofia, whose first words to me were, "Owen has sung your praises for so long! I've been dying to meet you." She hugged me. I hugged her back.

And that's how it's been. I want to get away from them. I want to be close to them. I love them. I hate them. I feel hateful that I have to love them, and I guiltily love that I hate them. I vow to be busy the next time they call.

My phone rings as I pull up onto Magnolia Avenue. "Hi, it's Ana-Sofia! Jenny, I'm so distracted, I completely forgot to ask you. I have tickets for the Alexander McQueen exhibit, and you were the first person I thought of! Would you like to go?"

That exhibit has been sold out for months. Of course she has tickets.

"Yeah, I'd love to," I say. "Thanks, Ana!"

"Wonderful! I'll email you details. Bye!"

I take a deep breath and get out of the car.

Leo is once again in the lounge chair. He seems sound asleep. I can tell he got up at some point, though, because he's wearing a dark gray suit, white shirt, a striped tie. His arms are folded tight across his chest, and there's a slight frown on his face. The wind, which has gotten nearly cold, ruffles his hair. Beside him is a bouquet of flowers.

He looks…sad. No, not sad. Lost, as if he forgot he was supposed to go to a party and just gave up, found this chair and hunkered down for the night. A well-dressed homeless man and his mangy dog.

I wonder if I should wake him.

Instead, I go inside, lugging Kendall's dress with me. A second later, I come out again with the red plaid blanket Andreas gave me for Christmas—cashmere…it pays to have friends with exquisite taste—and open the gate.

Loki growls. I ignore him; he's not terribly big, and he doesn't look as if he could spring to his master's defense without a trampoline. Indeed, his lip curls back, but the rest of him remains lying on his pillow bed.

Trying not to indulge in too much gooey tenderness—after all, I've known Leo for all of twenty-seven hours—I spread the blanket over him, then go back up the steps to my new home, put Pandora on Kelly Clarkson and start unpacking.

A FEW HOURS later, there's a knock on the door. It's Leo, holding my blanket in one hand, the bouquet of flowers in the other. "Is this yours?" he asks, lifting the blanket.

"Yes. You looked cold."

"I was fine."

"You're welcome." I give him a pointed look and take the blanket.

"Thank you."

We look at each other for a minute. "Come on in," I offer, and he does. "I was going to ask you to come up anyway. The living room light doesn't work." It's a gorgeous fixture, authentic Victorian, I think, ivory with a leaf pattern embossed into it.

"What the hell are you listening to?"

"This? This is Toby Keith." Leo stares at me like I'm an exhibit at the zoo. Right. He's a pianist or a musician or a snob. "Who are the flowers for?"

"Oh. Uh, my mother. She didn't like them."

"They're beautiful."

"She decided she didn't like orange."

"Ah." I wait for him to offer me the flowers. He doesn't. "How about fixing that light, Leo?"

He sits on the couch, puts the flowers down and takes a bottle of beer out of his suit pocket, pops the top off with the opener on his key chain and sits back, putting his feet on the coffee table. "Have you tried changing the lightbulb?"

"Make yourself at home. And yes. It's not the lightbulb."

"Sounds like the switch is broken. Maybe a problem with the wiring. Good thing there's a lot of natural light in here."

"Still, it would be even better if the super would fix my light. I believe you are the super, Leo?"

"I am. But I'm not that good at fixing stuff. I got this job because of my looks." He smiles.

"Well, then, since you're inept, would you call an electrician for me?" I ask.

"I'll make it my life's new mission. Can it wait till tomorrow, or are baby sea otters dying because your light won't go on?"

I sigh with exaggerated patience. "It can wait till tomorrow."

He takes another drink. It's an IPA, which I quite like.

"Bring me a beer next time," I say.

"Buy your own beer." He smiles as he says it, and damn, he's just too adorable. "How's your sister?"

Right. I sigh and sit down. "She's… I don't know." I grab a throw pillow and smoosh it against my stomach. Rachel had texted me a picture of the girls earlier, all of them on the slide at the park. No note. "She says she's good."

"But she's not good?" Leo says.

I pause. He *was* awfully nice last night. Caught Rachel, scooped her up in his arms and set her on this very couch. As I was saying, "Rachel? Rach? Rachel!" in a panicked voice, he got a damp dishcloth and put it on her forehead, then stuck around to see if she was okay. I guess he has a right to ask.

"It seems her husband has no idea who sent it," I say.

"Ah. It was all a mistake, then?"

"That's what we're going with."

He shrugs, a Gallic gesture that belies his very Irish name, a shrug that says, *Ah, poor kid, people are stupid, whatcha gonna do.* "She seems sweet."

"She is." I pause, not wholly comfortable with the topic. "So why the suit, Leo? Do you have a date? Those flowers aren't really for your mom, are they?"

"Yes, they were. I don't date. I'm strictly for recreational purposes."

I feel an eye-roll coming on. "Then were you giving a performance?"

"Nope."

"Shall I keep guessing, or does your dog need you and you really should be leaving?"

"I visit my mom every Sunday."

"You sure you're not gay?"

He laughs. "You're all right, Jane."

"Jenny."

"Whatever." He looks around my apartment. "So you like the apartment?"

"Sure. It's beautiful. Bigger than what I'm used to. And Cambry's my hometown, you know."

"No, I didn't."

"Did you grow up around here?"

He looks at me carefully, taking another drink from his beer bottle. "Iowa."

"A corn-fed Midwestern boy, huh?"

"That's me." He takes another pull of beer. "So what did you do today? You're a wedding planner?"

"We need to work on your listening skills," I say. "I'm a wedding dress designer. I just opened Bliss here in town." This fails to elicit any reaction. "I had a fitting in the city for a very irritating bride, and then I took a walk in Central Park, and then I went to see my, uh, friends."

He gives me an incredulous look. "Not the ex-husband and his lovely wife?"

"How did you— Yes." He cocks an eyebrow. "And their beautiful new baby," I add.

"Are you shitting me?"

"Not that it's your business, but we've stayed friends."

"No, you haven't."

"Yes, we have. Your dog growled at me, by the way. While I was covering you with your blankie."

"You put Mother Teresa to shame. Back to the ex... Why would you stay friends? Isn't that torture?"

"Are you married, Leo?"

"Do I look married?"

"Divorced? Separated? Are you a therapist? In other words, do you know anything about me or Owen or Ana-Sofia or marriage and divorce? Huh? Do you?"

"No on all fronts, and Ana-Sofia, sweet. That is a *smokin'* hot name. Is she beautiful?"

"Some people find her attractive."

He smiles. Just a little, but it works.

"Yeah, she's gorgeous," I admit. "As for why we stayed friends, maybe he was so devastated by our breakup that he couldn't stand the thought of not seeing me anymore. Maybe we still share a very special bond and despite marriage not working out, we want to stay in each other's lives. Maybe I really admire and respect his—"

"Stop, stop, I can't stand any more." Leo gets up and glances at the ceiling. "Call someone about that light. I just moved here myself and don't know anyone. Oh, and could you have him stop down at my place? My toaster doesn't work unless I plug it in the hallway."

I look at him for a second. "You blew a fuse. That's probably why my light won't go on."

"Ah. Fascinating."

"Where's the fuse box?"

"What's a fuse box?"

"Are you serious? How did you get this job?"

"I already told you. Good looks and charm."

"I can't wait to meet the charm part. Come on, I'll show you what a fuse box is, pretty boy. Take me to your cellar. Do you know where that is?"

We go out my front door, through the gate, where I earn another snarl from Loki. "That dog is really good-looking and charming," I say.

"He's old. Be respectful. The cellar's through here." He lets me into his apartment, into a tiny foyer, which opens into a large living room. There's an upright piano topped with piles of paper and music books. It's too dark to see anything else.

"This way," he says, pointing toward the small, sleek kitchen. He opens the cellar door, and we go down. It occurs to me that I'm going into a dark place with a stranger, and even as I think the thought, I know this guy is no threat to me at all.

"You're surprisingly quiet," Leo says, clicking on a light.

"I'm assessing the odds of you murdering me down here."

"And?"

"I hereby deem you harmless."

"How emasculating," he says. "What are you looking for again?"

"This, my son. Behold the fuse box," I say, pointing to the gray box on the wall. I flip open the panel and, sure enough, a switch is over to the right instead of the left. I push it back. "Modern technology. Show me your toaster."

His toaster is plugged into the same outlet as the cof-feepot, which is on the same circuit as the microwave. "Just move the toaster in over there and you should be fine," I tell him. "This is an old house. You might get an electrician in here to update the amperage."

"Did you learn all this in wedding school?"

He's tall. The kitchen light makes his hair gleam with copper, and the line of his jaw is sharp and strong.

"The eye-fucking, Jane. It has to stop." But he smiles as he says it.

"So you teach down here?" I ask, stepping back. Since he made himself at home upstairs, I do the same, flipping on a light and wandering through the living room. A gray couch and red chair complement the red-and-blue Oriental rug. There's a bookcase filled with tomes about the great composers. A bust of Beethoven glares at me next to a photo of a lake surrounded by pine trees.

The place is very, very neat and, aside from Beethoven, oddly devoid of personality, which isn't what I'd expect from Leo, not that I know him well, obviously. But still. I'd expect sloppy and welcoming, not sterile and...well, sterile. It looks like a model home, aside from the sheet music.

"So you just teach piano, or do you play anywhere?" I ask.

"I just teach. Sometimes I compose a score for something."

"Like a movie?"

He smiles. "No, nothing that complicated. Audio books, mostly."

"Neat. Did you go to school for music?"

"Yep. Juilliard."

"Really? Wow, Leo. Very impressive. Why don't you perform anywhere? You must be great."

"In the world of concert pianists, I'm probably a B minus."

"In the world of humans, I bet you're great."

"What do you know? You listen to country music." Another smile.

"How narrow-minded of you. Taylor Swift is a musical genius."

"Stevie Wonder is a musical genius, Jane. Taylor Swift is a woman still bemoaning what happened to her in high school."

"It's Jenny. My name is Jenny. So you *do* listen to Taylor Swift."

"I don't. But I don't live in a cave, either."

"No, this is a very nice place. Very tidy." I reach out to touch a key on the piano. "Can you play me something?"

"Sure," he says. He leans over the keys and taps out a few notes. "And that was 'Lightly Row.' Any more requests?"

"How about 'Paparazzi' by Lady Gaga?"

"Get out," he says, leaning against the piano. There's that smile again. He slides his hands into his pockets. "Thanks for fixing my toaster."

"I didn't touch your toaster."

"Well, you can touch my toaster anytime you want, Jenny Tate."

So. He *does* know my name. And he's flirting. And he's tall and lanky and his face is really fun to look at, all angular planes and wide smile and lovely crinkles around his eyes.

His smile drops.

"Don't get any ideas, missy," he says.

"Like what?" I ask.

"Like, 'Hey, my husband married someone else and has a new baby and I'm still single but there's an incredibly hot guy who lives downstairs, so why not?' I'm for recreation only."

"I'm not thinking those things, but bravo on your excellent self-esteem."

He goes to the foyer, opens the door and waits for me to follow, which I do. "You're thinking all those things. It's written all over your face."

"You know, Leo, in the day and a half we've known each other, I don't remember pinning you to the ground and forcing myself on you—"

"Yeah, I hope I'd remember that, too."

"—but I'm really not interested in you. Besides, you have all those moms and thirtysomethings who are dying to learn piano, as the kids are calling it these days. So go recreate with them, pal."

A smile tugs at his mouth. "You want to have dinner this week?"

I open my mouth, close it, then open it again. "On a date?"

He throws his hands in the air. "What did I just say? No, not on a date."

"For recreation?"

"For dinner."

"Why?"

"Because I have to eat, or I'll die," he says. "Never mind. It's a bad idea. The offer's been revoked. Bye, Jenny. See you around."

He smiles as he closes the door, gently, in my face.

It's only when I get back to my apartment that I realize he left the flowers on my coffee table.

Rachel

❖

MY MOOD OVER the next few days is shiny and hard and relentless. Nothing can get me down—not Charlotte putting a meatball in her diaper, not Rose's tantrum at the grocery store when I wouldn't let her swim with the lobsters, not Grace stonily telling me she loves Aunt Jenny more. I'm so, so relieved about Adam, and filled with energy. The house has never been cleaner. The girls and I weeded the flower beds—well, they played with shovels while I weeded. I baked and froze eight loaves of banana bread.

It's only at night that my stomach aches.

On Monday, I take the girls to nursery school for their four hours of doing exactly what we do at home—reading, singing, crafts, snacks—and then go over to Jenny's to help her unpack and organize and clean. She asks how I am; I tell her I'm great, and we leave it at that. I invite Mom to have lunch on Tuesday, and the girls are sweet and affectionate with her. I listen to her stories about Dad—I even encourage them, nodding and smiling as if I've never heard them before. When she leaves and the girls are still asleep, I bake so much that when the girls wake up, I put them in the minivan and drop off cupcakes for Jenny, another batch for her nice building super—though why a two-family house needs a super is a mystery—and three dozen for the homeless shelter.

On Wednesday, we have Mommy and Me swimming, and when we're in the pool, Clarice Vanderberger tells me I sure am in a good mood. I smile and say yes, what's not to be happy about, gorgeous weather we're having. Then I slosh over to Grace, who's a little too good of a swimmer and seems to be in love with Melissa, the swimming instructor, and resentful of the fact that Melissa is helping Rose.

"Can you believe Jared Brewster is actually going ahead and marrying that woman?" Elle Birkman asks me as her son laps pool water. God knows what kind of chemicals and germs and bodily fluids are in the pool, but she doesn't tell him to stop.

"Mama! Mama! Mama! Watch!" Rose orders as she dips her chin in the water as Melissa holds her. "Face in, Mama!"

"Honey, that's so good!" I say. "Oh, Charlotte, honey, don't drink the water. It's only for swimming."

"Hunter's drinking it!" Charlotte says. Grace tugs my hand.

"Hunter, honey, it's yucky."

Elle doesn't chime in. "I mean, men will be men, but he doesn't have to marry her," she says instead. "Has he talked to you about it? It's hard to believe he'll go through with it."

Jared is my oldest friend. Jenny and I have always been so close that it was hard for me to find another person I liked as much, but Jared was special. The Brewsters lived up the hill from us, so technically, we were neighbors, though his house was really posh; they even had a live-in housekeeper. He was that rarest of boys—

clean, for one, and nice, the type who'd ask you if you'd read a book or seen a TV show, then listen as you answered. Riding the school bus cemented our friendship; we sat together every day from kindergarten through eighth grade. He went to Phillips Exeter Academy for high school, but even then, we stayed in touch. Mom used to ask if we were dating—and pray that we were—but we weren't. It wasn't like that. But he's kind and nice and funny and comfortable as flannel pajamas. In addition to being my oldest friend, he's Adam's coworker at Brewster, Buckley and Bowman, or Triple B, as they call it.

So I'm not about to gossip behind his back.

"You guys talking about Jared?" Claudia calls from the other side of the pool, unfettered by loyalty.

"Yes," Elle says at the same time I say no. Grace yanks on my hand again, and Elle tows Hunter through the water to Claudia's side of the pool for a better gossip partner.

In the changing room as I wrestle my damp daughters back into their little dresses, Elle strips off her suit to make sure everyone—including the kids—is treated to a view of her new breasts. Claudia rolls her eyes, and I smile back. Personally, I thought the "before" pair was more attractive, but Elle insisted that Hunter had ruined her body.

The body looks pretty great to me.

She has a bikini wax.

So did the woman in the picture.

In fact, Elle's body is pretty damn perfect. No stretch marks... She had a C-section two weeks before her due date. The Hollywood, she called it. The scar is barely visible. Her ass is round and high, her stomach perfectly toned.

I'm suddenly cold.

Is it possible that Elle sent the picture?

"Mommy, wrong foot, wrong foot, wrong foot!" Rose yells cheerfully. She loves the echo in here. She's right, though. I switch feet and have better luck getting her little sneaker on.

Adam doesn't even like Elle. Says she's a climber. But maybe he does like her. I don't know why I'm thinking about it. That picture was sent by mistake.

My stomach doesn't feel so good.

"Okay, girls, sit tight. Mommy's going to get dressed, too."

"I'll keep an eye on them, Rachel," says Kathleen Rhodes. She has two sets of twins, ages seven and four—another in-vitro mom—and she's been really kind and helpful, loaning me books on getting your baby to sleep through the night, inviting us to playdates. Not many people want three kids in addition to their own. Kathleen doesn't mind a bit.

"Thanks," I say.

I pull the curtain behind me in the changing room and peel off my wet suit. It's a retro-style one-piece, red with white polka dots and wide shoulder straps. I liked it when I bought it, but now it seems matronly.

Well. I am a matron, after all.

I look at my reflection in the mirror. Unlike the mirrors in Nordstrom or Bergdorf, it's not a magical mirror, making me look taller and more slender than I really am.

For the most part, I love my body. I'm proud of what it did, percolating three babies at once, nursing them afterward. There's a little pooch of skin that no amount of crunches has been able to vanquish, but I'm the same size as I was in college. My breasts fared pretty well, too. Granted, they're not what they were when I was twenty, but they're hardly embarrassments. In fact, Kathleen once said she envied how I bounced back from pregnancy. Told me it took her four years. She still carries some extra weight, but she carries it well.

Adam has always been complimentary...though now that I think of it, maybe not as much lately.

My body is a mother's body. It's hopefully a MILF's body, but it's a mother's body, no doubt. My stretch marks, once a lurid red, have faded to tiny silvery marks, like a small school of fish. I can feel them more than I can really see them. On the rare occasions that I get to take a nice long bath, I find myself stroking them as I read.

I'm average. That's the word for it. This is an average body. It's not bad. For a nearly forty-year-old mother of triplets, it's really good.

But it's not Elle's body.

"Elle works out with a personal trainer five days a week," Kathleen tells me ten minutes later when I admit my insecurity. We're hunched over, buckling the kids in their car seats. Our cars, both minivans, are side by side. "Do you want to stick your kids in day care so you can go to the gym? Or drink kale shakes for breakfast?"

"No," I said. "I definitely don't."

"And you're fucking gorgeous, Rachel," she says. I've always been both shocked and impressed by her potty mouth. "Edward, if you bite me again, you won't have any dessert until Christmas." She turns back to me. "You okay, Rach?"

"Oh, sure," I say, sliding the door shut. "I just… I don't know. I guess I'm at the age where I'm getting…"

"Invisible?"

I hadn't thought of it that way, but there it is. Very few men look at a woman wrangling three toddlers. And I don't have time to look at them. "Yeah. Invisible."

"I know how you feel. The other day, this guy at the deli—you know, Gold's? The short guy with earrings?" I nod. "Well, he handed me my baloney and said, 'Here you go, beautiful,' and I was so fucking grateful! I mean, I used to get that all the time. All the time. And now, nothing. It takes longer and longer to pull off even *not bad. Beautiful* left on my thirty-fifth birthday. So I wanted to kiss this guy and buy him a car." She hands Edward a juice box, gives one to Niall and closes the door. "Enjoy it while you still have it. You want to get coffee?"

"Maybe next week," I tell her. "I think I'll drop by Adam's office for lunch."

I call our babysitter from the car. "Hi, Donna, it's Rachel Carver."

"Donna! Donna!" Charlotte shouts happily, and the other girls pick up the chant.

I smile. "I know this is last-minute, but I was wondering if you were free to babysit the girls today."

"I'd love to," she says instantly. "When do you want me to come by?"

"Twenty minutes?" I suggest.

Donna Ignaciato is every mother's dream—a retired widow who lives down the street, loves children and was deprived of her grandchildren when her son moved to Oregon last year. She's the kind of grandmother my mom is not—hands-on, affectionate, completely at home, the kind of babysitter who will take the laundry out of the dryer and fold it, and leave the girls cleaner and happier than when you left. I haven't used her much—just when Jenny hasn't been free, because she loves to spend time with the girls. My mom isn't the babysitting type. "All of them?" she said when I asked her to watch the kids this past winter. "At the same time?"

"No, Lenore," Adam said. "We want you to lock two of them in the cellar, and just rotate them out." I smiled, and Mom whipped out her ultimate guilt answer.

"If your father was alive, we could do it together, but…"

I let her off the hook, as I always do. It's sort of my job—the softer, more understanding sister. Besides, I'd worry constantly if Mom was in charge.

When Donna gets to the house, the girls swarm her, and I go upstairs and shower. Blow-dry my hair, put on makeup, dress carefully in a pink-and-black-checked dress and pink cardigan, the dangly silver earrings Adam gave me for Christmas, and the trifold, heart-shaped locket that has a picture of each of my girls. A bracelet. Black heels—but low, because it's daytime. Perfume, even.

Five days ago, I accused my husband of having an affair. And while it's understandable why I thought what I did—and though he's very generously let it go—damage has been done.

"You're pretty, Mama," Grace says when I come downstairs. She kisses my knee, and I stroke her silky hair.

"I should be back around three," I tell Donna, who's already cutting up apple slices for a snack. "Girls, listen to Donna, and have fun, okay? Give Mama kisses!"

I stop at the gourmet shop that's just around the corner from Jenny's shop. Maybe I'll drop by after my lunch, if I have time.

"Can I help you?" the girl asks, and I order Adam's favorite sandwich, a turkey-and-avocado-and-bacon panini. Broccoli salad. Two green teas. Three chocolate cookies. For myself, a green salad. That pooch of skin is all too clear in my mind.

Brewster, Buckley and Bowman, Attorneys at Law, is in a dignified old building overlooking the Hudson River. It's on the same block as my father's old office, which always gives me a pang; I loved visiting him at work, seeing him in his dentist whites.

I go into the venerable lobby of Triple B, which has been around for seventy years and employs more than forty lawyers. They handle everything from divorce to taxes to criminal defense. Adam's specialty is corporate law; boring to the outsider, but quite interesting once you understand what he does. Well. I have to think so. I'm married to the guy.

"Rachel!" the receptionist exclaims when I go into the office. "It's been too long. You here to see Adam?"

"I brought him lunch," I say, feeling the start of a blush. You'd think I wouldn't feel shy; I've been coming here for years.

"I'll just buzz him and let him know you're here," Lydia says. "In case he's with a *client*."

"Thank you very much," I say. I flash another smile, gripping the handles of the deli bag more tightly.

"You don't have to be so shy, you know," Lydia says. *Oh, okay. I'll stop, then. All I was waiting for was you to say that.* I know she means well. I smile—awkwardly—and let my eyes slide away.

"Hey!" A man comes into the foyer. "How are you, Rach?"

"Hi, Jared," I say, feeling a genuine smile start.

"Bringing the luckiest guy in the world some lunch?"

"I am indeed. How's Kimber?"

"She's great. Want to see a picture? We went to Provincetown last weekend. Had a blast."

"Sure." Got to love a guy who whips out his phone to show off pictures of his fiancée.

He shows me seven pictures of his beloved. I've met Kimber a few times, and she's quite a beauty, though I admit to being surprised the first time I saw her. Her hair is dyed a pinkish red that was never intended to be thought of as natural, she has a full-sleeve tattoo on one arm and wears brilliant peacock colors for eye shadow and liner. "You can just feel how happy she is in these pictures," I say.

Jared grins. "Thanks, Rach. Listen, I have to run. Got a lunch that's so boring, I might actually stab myself in the eye just to keep from falling asleep. Hey, let's have dinner, the four of us, okay?"

"That'd be great."

"Give the girls a kiss for me," he says.

"Adam will see you now," Lydia says.

"Lydia! Did you make her wait? Honestly. Rach, just go down to his office next time. You're his wife. You have rights." Jared gives me a mock-serious look, then leaves.

Dinner with him and Kimber would be nice, I think as I make my way down the hall to Adam's small but lovely office. It's so nice to see Jared smitten. In the past, he'd always dated country-club types, and I can't remember one relationship lasting even a year. With Kimber, he met her and it was the thunderbolt, as he said.

Same with Adam and me.

"Babe!" Adam says as I go in.

"Hi. I brought lunch," I say, going behind his desk to kiss him on the cheek.

"Oh. Wow, that's so nice of you. Um…well, uh, no, it's fine."

"Did you have plans?"

"No, no. I mean, yeah, I was going to grab something with another lawyer, but it's fine. Just let me send him a text." His thumbs fly, his phone cheeps and he stands up. "Close the door so we can have some privacy, okay? What did you bring me?"

"Turkey and avocado."

"'Atta girl." He smiles at me and gets up.

Adam's office has a little couch and chair, in addition to his desk, and we sit there as I unpack our lunch. He checks his phone, then slides it into his pocket.

Sometimes I feel like whipping that thing out a window. My cheeks hurt, which means I've been clenching my teeth.

"How are the girls?" he asks. "Are they with your sister?"

"No, with Donna," I say. "Jenny's working."

"Right. But does she have regular hours and stuff?"

He's never really understood how much work Jenny has had to do to get where she is, or how much time goes into making a wedding dress. He's a guy, after all.

"She does. Regular hours and then some." I take a bite of salad.

Then Adam's door opens, and in comes Emmanuelle

St. Pierre, one of Adam's coworkers. "So where were we?" she says.

Then she sees me and freezes for the briefest second.

"I'm sorry," she says. "Adam, I thought we were having lunch today. Did I have the wrong day?"

Just let me send him a text.

Him.

And so I know. I *know*.

Adam is cheating on me with *her*.

"Emmanuelle, you remember my wife, right? Rachel, you've met Emmanuelle, I think. The holiday party at the club?"

I've seen your vagina, I want to say.

"Um, mmm-hmm," I mumble, because my mouth is full of unchewed arugula.

You fucking slut, is my next thought, but then again, of course she's a fucking slut; she couldn't be a slut without fucking, could she?

"Emmanuelle and I are working on a case together," Adam says.

"Really," I say, swallowing the mouthful of roughage without chewing. *Really, Adam? Because you do corporate tax law, and she's a criminal defense attorney, and even your stupid little housewife knows that you would not work on a case together.*

"Adam, I didn't mean to interrupt your little…picnic," she says, and her eyes run over me, making me feel childish in my pink sweater, silly with my "trying to be artistic" earrings, like a failure in my little wifey-goes-out-to-lunch dress. She's wearing a sleeveless black turtleneck dress, Armani, maybe. Jenny would know in a heartbeat. Her glossy, dark red hair is pulled into an unforgiving twist. Tiny gold hoop earrings. A

wide, hammered gold ring on her right forefinger. No
other jewelry. Black ankle boots with thin, thin heels
that must be four inches high. Red soles. Those are…
What's that name? Christian Louboutin, right. Ridiculously expensive.

These details are razor-sharp, slicing through my
brain with barely any blood spilled.

I'm wearing a heart necklace. As if I'm in third grade
or something.

No. There are pictures of my children inside there.
I'm a *mother*. Emmanuelle is not a mother, no sir.

Not yet.

"I guess I'll talk to you later, Adam," Emmanuelle
says easily. "Nice to see you again, Rachel." Then she's
gone. The smell of her perfume lingers like radiation.

Adam exhales. "So. What else have you got planned
for today?" His face is studiously bland.

"You fucking liar," I say, and then I throw his iced
tea in his face and walk out of his office.

THE UPSIDE OF having three toddlers is they don't leave
you much time for thinking. I make the girls supper, read
them poems as they eat, then finish their macaroni and
cheese, because that stuff is delicious. I let them have
a longer bath than usual, and read them extra stories
and play Animal Kisses, in which they close their eyes
while I woof, meow or moo softly in their hair till they
guess which animal I am, or giggle so hard they can't.
For once, they're all smiling and sweet when I give out
their final hugs. No one gets out of bed, no one asks for
water, no one cries.

Clearly, I'm the world's most amazing mother.

I go downstairs, pour what has to be a ten-ounce glass of wine and sit on the couch and wait.

The look on his face, his wet, green-tea-drenched face, was almost funny.

Oily black anger twists and rises inside me. I try to dilute it with a few swallows of wine, but it stays.

I can't be too angry about this. Well, of course, I can be… I am. But I can't make decisions in anger. There are five of us to consider, not two.

Jenny has left two messages for me. Does she sense something? I haven't answered.

Adam has not contacted me. That terror I felt last weekend shudders back to life.

Does he want to leave me?

An image of my daughters in the future flashes in horrible clarity: all three resentful, whiny, confused at having to go spend a weekend with Daddy—and Emmanuelle. They'll become horrible teenagers, piercings and tattoos, and I'll find condoms in Rose's backpack, get a call from the school that Grace beat someone up, that Charlotte sold pot to her classmates. I'm already furious at Adam for doing this to our girls.

Furious, and terrified.

And then there'd be me. Divorced. Alone. I picture myself trying to date again—me, forty, with a cesarean scar and a pooch of skin made by another man's babies. Me, shy at best, socially terrified at worst, making conversation in the bar in the Holiday Inn while the Yankees are on, a sticky tabletop and a glass of cheap wine, uncomfortable vinyl seats.

Adam comes home at 8:07 p.m. Our girls have always been the early-to-bed types, so I'm sure he's lurked somewhere—the office, a bar, his whore's house—until he's sure they're asleep. He might be a cheating douche bag, but he doesn't want the girls to hear us fight.

He comes into the living room, looks at me, sighs and pours himself a scotch. "So I guess we have to talk," he says, and my eyes fill with traitorous tears, because I love his voice, and now I have to listen to him tell me that I'm right. This living room will never be the same again. It will always be the place where he told me he cheated.

He sits down across from me. I can see the stain from the green tea on his shirt.

"I'm sorry," he says.

"How long?" I ask.

"About three months."

Three months? Holy Jesus! It's late April now, so most of April, all of March, all of February.

He gave me the locket on Valentine's Day.

"Tell me everything," I say, and my voice is choked and brittle.

He sighs, as if I'm exhausting him, the asshole, and starts talking. He *didn't plan it*. It *just happened*. She came on to him. He *couldn't help himself.* He's a guy, and when a beautiful woman comes on to a guy, it's *hard to say no*. He loves me. He doesn't want a divorce. He's *sorry*.

And the thing is, I knew. I knew when I saw that picture. I knew when he took me upstairs for sex. I knew before Jenny told me.

Stupid, *stupid* me.

"Why didn't you end it?" I ask. My real question is *Why would you ever look somewhere else? What am I lacking that made you whip out your dick*—my God, my language is deteriorating by the second—*and stick it where it didn't belong?*

I can't look at him. I hate his face. If I look at him now, I might swing that empty wine bottle right at him.

"I did end it," he says, but there's too long of a pause.

"Don't lie to me, Adam," I say calmly. "You've already cheated on me. You lied to me when I showed you that picture, and you're lying now. Why haven't you ended it?" There. I manage to look at his face. My own feels as if a swarm of bees is under my skin buzzing and stinging, full of venom.

He shrugs again, not looking at me. "The sex is amazing."

The room spins.

"Look, you asked," Adam says, and yes, that's accusation in his voice. *You're the one who made me tell you!* "Rach, I love you. I do, you know that. And I love our life. But Emmanuelle… I don't know. She's very aggressive. I turned her down at first, I did!"

Does he want me to praise him? Give him a sticker? Write his name on the kitchen blackboard, like I do when one of the girls does something especially sweet or helpful?

"And then one day she came into my office to talk about a case, and she crossed her legs, and she wasn't wearing panties, and I couldn't help myself. It was—"

"Shut up, Adam. Shut the fuck up."

I'm quite sure today is the first day Adam has ever heard me use the *F* word. He stops talking.

"I told you if you ever cheated on me, I'd divorce you," I say calmly.

"I don't want a divorce. Think of the girls, Rachel."

"I *always* think of the girls," I hiss, the fury writhing in my stomach. "All I *do* is think of the girls. Were you thinking of the girls when you fucked another woman? Hmm? Is that what a great father does?"

"Look. I'm *sorry*. I really am, Rachel. I was weak. But I don't want to lose you."

How I would love to tell him to piss off right now. That there's no going back from this. That he can talk to my lawyer.

But just the thought of a divorce makes cold fear shoot through my legs. I don't want a divorce! No adored husband coming through the door every night, no father in the house for the girls, no "Baby Beluga" sung at bedtime. We'd have to separate our things, all our lovely things that have made our house so welcoming and happy. All the pictures of the girls; he'd obviously get to take some with him.

How could I live without things the way they are now?

My rage has been snuffed out by icy-cold terror.

"When you knew I saw the picture," I whisper, "did you tell her things had to end?"

"No," he admits. "I haven't yet."

The big question is waiting in the back of my throat like bile. "Do you love her?"

He hesitates. "I... No. Not like I love you. But yes, there are...feelings."

Oh, God.

My temples throb, and I have to force my teeth apart.

I get up to leave. I'll sleep in the guest room, take a long bath in the tub, maybe get another bottle of wine. Watch *Game of Thrones* and...and...

I stumble before I even make it out of the living room.

Adam's arms are around me. "Baby, I'm so sorry. I'm so, so sorry." His voice is rough with tears. "Please don't make any decisions now. I love you. I love our family. Let's not throw that away. I made a mistake. I'll fix this. We can get counseling, or go on vacation, whatever you want. But please don't leave me. I couldn't live without you."

I love him so much. I hate him so much. He picked me—out of all the women who would've loved to have been Adam Carver's wife, he wanted me. We made this beautiful family, this happy life—well, obviously not happy enough that he kept it in his pants, did he?

"I'm going to bed," I whisper. "I don't know what I want right now. Except to be alone."

"Sleep in," he says. "I'll get the girls to school tomorrow. I'll go in late."

I can't bear to look at his eyes anymore. Those beautiful caramel eyes that lied so well.

Feeling more tired than I've ever felt in my life, I climb the stairs, holding the railing with both hands. Past the picture of my parents on their wedding day. Past the photo of Jenny and me when we were little, dressed in frilly Easter dresses. Past the picture of Adam, smiling hugely, his eyes wet as he holds three little burritos with pink caps.

Past our wedding photo. Me, in that stunning, amazing dress Jenny made for me, looking more beautiful than I ever knew I could, smiling at Adam with such adoration and…and…gratitude that it makes me sick.

Without thinking, I take the photo off the wall and toss it down the stairs behind me, the sound of glass shattering on tile bright and clear.

"Rachel." His voice is hard and sharp.

I look down the stairs.

"Before you break anything else, just…just make sure

you know what you want. Think about our life together, and what life would be like apart." His voice softens. "Our marriage is worth fighting for. I screwed up, I admit that. But it would be smart to go slowly here."

I turn around again and go into the guest room and close the door.

It seems I've just been warned.

Jenny

———◆———

"OH, GOD," ANDREAS says. "Look at the hordes. This is awful." Though he threatens weekly to quit, I don't think he will, despite the reverse commute to the city. Who else would let him work on his novel during work hours?

"Hordes are good, Andreas," I say patiently, looking at the line that snakes down the block. "This is great. It's our grand opening. Smile. Be happy. And do not open that door until the stroke of twelve, okay?" It's Sunday, the sun is shining, and the streets of Cambry-on-Hudson are filled with people strolling around, having brunch— yes—shopping. Outside my shop is a huge tin bucket filled with early peonies, bought from the florist across the street. A chalkboard sign says "Bliss: Open House today from 12-5. Come in, look around and enjoy!"

My mother is the first person in line. This does make my shoulders droop a little. But no, no. While my mother will talk endlessly about her wedding to Dad, she at least does it in a highly romantic manner. It could be good for business. Still, it would've been nice if she hadn't worn sweats. She looks a teeny bit homeless. Sneakers, too. Her hair is messy. It's all part of the "I'm A Widow" package, lest there be any doubt that her life was ruined when Dad died.

As ever, a cold needle pricks my heart.

Well. I have too much to do to rehash the past.

Andreas pops the champagne at the little bar I've set up for today. Pink champagne and pale pink-frosted cupcakes from Cottage Confections, the fabulous cake shop conveniently located four doors down. Kim, the owner, and I became instant friends as soon as she welcomed me to the downtown with six chocolate cupcakes. We'll be referring each other lots. Andreas arranges the napkins, sets out a beautiful notebook so people can write down their emails.

To advertise my skills, the showroom is furnished with dress forms adorned with finished gowns in each of the classic shapes—A-line, mini, modified A-line, trumpet, mermaid, sheath, tea-length and, most popular of all these days, ball gown. The forms stand around Bliss like a beautiful army, shimmering in the pinkish lights of the store, the crystals from the ball gown catching the light and casting tiny rainbows, the satin of the tea-length glowing.

I fluff the cathedral train on the Grace Kelly–inspired dress, fingering the silk mikado. Bliss is not the type of shop that has ready-to-wear dresses. I'm not a salesperson; I'm a designer. But I do keep a few dresses on hand for the women who want to play dress-up.

Another section of the showroom features accessories—veils, belts, headpieces, gloves, garters. I'll have to make sure my nieces don't get into too much trouble over there. They tend to view my workplace as their personal playland.

Hung on the brick walls are a huge selling tool—pictures of my brides in their dresses, each one a black-and-white photo, hung at precise intervals. One picture is bigger than the others: Rachel, wearing the most beautiful dress I've ever made.

The back half of the shop is where the work really happens. Of course, there's the dressing room with its apricot-painted walls and dais with three-way mirror, as well as a couch and three upholstered chairs, a coffee table with a photo album of my work. That's where I'll do consultations and fittings, where the bride shows me pictures of dresses she likes, where I'll ask all the questions they love to answer—what's your vision for the day, do you have a theme, how do you want to look.

The workroom is across the hall, where Andreas and I painstakingly organized thousands of fabric samples: satin, silk, chiffon, organza, charmeuse, lace—I have more than a hundred samples of lace—and yards and yards of muslin, since I make a mock-up of every dress before cutting the dress fabric itself. In the center of the room is a huge oak table—my work space, complete with four different sewing machines.

Shelves hold tape measures and scissors and thousands of straight pins, dozens of types of appliques, lengths of crystal and beading and accents. I never understood how a designer could be unorganized. It makes me cringe on *Project Runway* when someone loses their fabric.

I love my job. I love weddings, all types. Me, I opted for a quickie wedding on the beach in Provincetown, a weekend when Owen and I seemed to be the only straight couple tying the knot. Rachel and Adam came, Mom, Owen's wonderful parents, Andreas and his boyfriend, a few friends from New York. We had lunch at a waterfront inn at the tip of P-town, and the sun shone, and we drank and laughed and ate. My dress was a flow-

ing empire-waist sheath with a pale violet sash that flut-
tered in the wind, and Owen wore a navy blue suit with
a lavender tie.

And look at us now.

The one thing I hate about the wedding industry
is that it focuses so much on the one day. People become obsessed with details, enraged with those they
love, worn out from planning a few hours of a day that
may not mean that much in the grand scheme of things.
Even as I'm designing a dress that will cost thousands
and thousands of dollars, I've always tried to work that
message in. *Don't forget that after this day comes thousands of other days. Be careful. Cherish each other.
Don't blow it.*

Even knowing all this, I blew it. I'd say Owen and I
blew it, but he's the happiest man on earth these days.

I take a pit stop in my little bathroom. I'm wearing
my work uniform, my straight, black hair pulled back
in a twist, red lipstick in place. I try to look as different
from a bride as possible—a little severe and simple, but
chic, too. Even though I'm on my feet a lot, I love my
fabulous shoes. A talent is a talent, and wearing heels
for ten hours a day is one of mine.

"Showtime!" I say, opening the door. "Welcome to
Bliss. Hi, Mom."

Most of the people here aren't really shopping for
wedding dresses. Not yet. Some of them are too young,
some aren't engaged, some just want to play dress-up,
which we won't be doing today. But they're all welcome,
because you never know.

"Oh, my God, this looks like Kate Middleton's
gown!" one young woman exclaims. Brides will be emu-
lating that dress until little Prince George gets married.

"This one looks like a cloud," says another, pointing to a tulle-skirted masterpiece. I smile and murmur thanks, then tell her a little bit about the construction. Someone from the local newspaper takes my picture. I can hear my mother discussing the details of my father's death.

The door opens, and in come my three little nieces. "Auntie, Auntie!" they clamor, reaching up with their delicious little arms.

"Hello, my sugarplums," I say, bending down to smooch them all. "You're so beautiful!" There's an audible sigh from the customers. Charlotte, Rose and Grace are dressed like flower girls, in tiny pink tulle dresses with long pink ribbons—made by yours truly, of course. Hey, those girls are excellent marketing tools—who wouldn't want them walking down the aisle, scattering rose petals?

"We're fancy," Grace says.

"You sure are." I give them each a basket full of cookies. "Would you share these with the nice people?" I say, and off they go. Rose eats one, but that just adds to the charm.

Then I stand up, see my sister, and it's a punch to the heart.

Adam must've told her. She knows. Oh, God.

"Hey," I breathe, and my voice is already shaking.

"It's okay," she says. "We'll talk later. But I'm fine. I don't want Mom to hear anything."

No, of course not. And Rachel *does* look fine. She's nicely dressed, as always, and as always, she has one eye on the girls. She gives me a little smile. But she looks so old! Rachel, who still gets carded when we go out, suddenly has lines around her eyes and a general droop to her face. Tears flood my eyes.

"No, no," she says. "This is your day. Jenny, I'm so proud of you. Daddy would be so proud of you. This is simply beautiful."

Dad would be proud of *her*, I'm thinking, keeping her shit together, being so generous and strong to come to a public event just for my sake. Then again, his feelings would be mixed, wouldn't they?

"Speaking of beautiful, hi, Rachel," Andreas says. He hands her a glass of sparkling wine. "What do you think?"

"I think my sister and you are both geniuses," she says. She glances at me, then drops her eyes.

Shy. She's being shy because of me, the only person she's never shy around—except for her daughters. Shy of me because I *know*.

That fucking Adam.

"Well, I can't speak for Andreas, but yes, I'm a genius," I say, my voice firm and fake.

"I'm just the power behind the throne," Andreas says.

"Hi," says Charlotte, attaching herself to his leg.

"Oh, God, get it off me," he says, making Charlotte dissolve into giggles. "Go away, little octopus." He shakes his leg, which makes Grace zoom over and latch on to the other one. Rose is too busy sitting under a table, powering through her basket of cookies.

Poor Rachel. I knew it, but I didn't want to be right. I never wanted to be wrong more.

"Andreas, would you watch the girls for a second?" I ask.

"No. Don't leave me."

I ignore him. "Come on, Rach, let's talk in the back,"

I say, taking her hand and towing her through the crowd. "Hello. Thank you for coming."

"No, Jenny, I—"

"Rach, we're going to talk. Jesus."

We get to my office, and I close the door. I wait a second, then open the door a crack to see if Mom tailed us. She didn't. I close the door once more. "What happened?"

"I went to his office, and…I saw this woman. She came in, and I just knew." A fine tremor runs across her face. "And he didn't deny it this time."

"Oh, Rachel. Oh, honey." I move to hug her, but she steps back.

"I can't," she whispers. "Don't be nice to me right now, or I'll lose it."

"Did he… Is it still… What did he say? Who is it? Do you know her?"

"Emmanuelle St. Pierre. A litigator."

"What a whorish name."

"Please don't make jokes."

I cringe. "I'm sorry."

"He said the sex is amazing. He might be in love with her. But he doesn't want a divorce, because he loves me, too."

A blue-black cloud of curses churns in my mouth. That bastard. So, he'll keep Rachel as his perfect wife, and then go have dirty sex with Emmanuelle? Sure. Why not?

"Would it be wrong for me to want to strangle him?" I ask, my fists clenched.

"Don't. Look. I… We're working on things. Um… we have a family. We have to do things the right way. It's complicated."

"It's not complicated!" I hiss. "He's a complete shit-head, Rachel!"

"Stop. You're not helping."

"What are you going to do?" I ask.

"I don't know," she whispers, and that tremor quakes through her face once more. "It means we have to go slowly. We have to think of the girls. And I don't want to talk about it here."

"Right, of course," I whisper back. "But let's talk, Rachel. Come over tonight. Or I can come over there."

"No. I need to be with Adam. We have a lot to work through." She sighs. "Look. I didn't want to tell you today. This is your grand opening. Let's get back out there."

"Rachel, you're much more important—"

"I'm really fine," she says, and there's that brittle-ness again. "Weren't you going to say something about the store? Let's go."

My God. If I feel like the world has tilted off center, how must she feel?

Back in the showroom, Rachel goes to Grace, who's trying on tiaras. She forces a smile toward me, then turns her attention to her daughter.

My hands are shaking. Nevertheless, I give Andreas a nod, and he taps a champagne glass. The murmur dies down.

"Thank you all so much for coming to Bliss," I say with a big smile. I wonder how my face looks. "I'm Jenny Tate, and our token male today is Andreas Calderi, my assistant." There's a laugh, and Andreas raises a perfectly waxed eyebrow. "At Bliss, you're going to get a one-of-a-kind dress made just for you. I'll never make another dress exactly like it, so you can rest assured that your dress will be unique."

There's an appreciative murmur from a few young women. Yes, God forbid they have a dress that looks like someone else's. I recognize the irony of my cynicism.

"I can also modify existing dresses, so if you want to wear your mom's dress but have an updated look, or if you've already bought a dress but want some changes, that's not a problem. If you're a bride who has a hard time with traditional sizes, I'm your girl." There are a few plus-size women in the shop who brighten at this. "If you have any questions, feel free to ask. I'm here all afternoon. Look around, drink some champagne and contact Andreas if you'd like to make an appointment. Your first consultation is free. Thanks again for coming!"

For the next half hour, I take questions, get complimented on my shoes, escort Charlotte to the bathroom, get hired to make a mother-of-the-bride dress for next winter and sell the tulle ball gown. I keep an eye on Rachel, who seems shockingly normal, mostly lingering in the back with Andreas or digging in her giant mommy bag for crayons, a Wet-Nap and a book or two. Grace, armed with a Hello Kitty notebook, pretends to take dress orders from customers, who are enchanted with her cute solemnity. Rose has curled up in the upholstered chair and looks like an angel sleeping there, and Charlotte is sitting under the drinks table, playing with Andreas's shoelaces.

Someday, maybe my daughter will be here. The image of her is so strong and clear that I feel her, my heart swelling with fierce love—my little black-haired daughter, playing dress-up with her cousins, sitting on the floor to show off her sparkly little shoes.

"I can't believe people will pay so much for a dress," Mom says.

"Can you keep that sentiment to yourself, please?" I whisper.

She sighs. "Well, fine. But I can't believe it."

"Yeah. You've told me a thousand times or so. Go drink champagne. Or better yet, help Rachel with the girls, okay?" Celebrating her children's accomplishments isn't one of her strengths.

The door opens, and like salt in a wound, in come Owen, Ana-Sofia and their baby, who's sleeping in a sling, making Ana look like a very posh Native American. My mother's face lights up. Drama. So much fun for her.

Owen comes right up to me, takes both my hands and kisses me on the cheek. "Jenny. This. Is. Amazing."

"He's right, Jenny," Ana-Sofia seconds. "Oh, what a shop! It makes me want to get married again." Then, realizing what she's just said, she freezes.

"Me, too," I say to break the awkwardness. "Hello there, Natalia!"

She's even more beautiful than last week. Long, straight eyelashes, elegant eyebrows, a tiny pink rosebud mouth. Her lips move as if blowing kisses.

The ache in my chest is painful now.

"Jenny, I'm sorry to interrupt," my sister says. "Owen. Ana." Her voice hardens, bless her. "Nice to see you. Your baby is just beautiful. Jenny, so sorry. Mrs. Brewster's here, and she's got a slight emergency with Jared's wedding. I told her you could help."

"Look around, guys," I say. "And thank you so much for coming. It means a lot." As Rach leads me through the crowd, I whisper, "And thank *you* for rescuing me."

"Why are they here?" Rachel whispers back. "Can't they leave you alone? Do they have to force-feed you their perfect life?" Nice to see some fire in her. Of course, it's always easier to be mad on behalf of someone you love, rather than deal with your own problems.

"It's not like that," I tell her. "We're all friends."

She gives me a cynical look. "Mrs. Brewster," she says, "you remember Jenny, don't you?"

"I suppose I do. Yes."

"Thank you so much for coming, Mrs. Brewster. How are you?"

"I've been better," she says.

When we were kids, the Brewsters lived up the hill from us in this glorious old house where we were told not to run, not to eat and not to laugh. Mrs. Brewster is the president of the chapter of the Daughters of the American Revolution, the COH Garden Club, the Women's Committee (which seems to exist to sell pies), and the COH Lawn Club board of trustees. Her husband is the pastor of the Cambry-on-Hudson Congregational Church. *He's* actually quite nice.

It would be a coup to make the wedding dress for Jared Brewster's wife. The ceremony will take place at Mr. Brewster's enormous and beautiful church, and with a venue like that, the dress is usually big and memorable—and expensive. The reception will be at the country club, and Mrs. Brewster says it will be featured in *Town & Country* and *Hudson Bride*, glossy magazines geared toward the one percent.

I could use that kind of business. Up here, it's commonplace to rent a limo and head to the city, to Kleinfeld's and Vera Wang, to find the dress of dresses—and possibly appear on a TV show. I need those clients to come to me. Moving here was a risk, and the blessing of the blue-blooded Brewsters would go a long way. A lot of mothers of brides will urge their daughters to go where Eleanor Hale Brewster tells them to.

"Excuse me, I need to help Charlotte. So nice to see you, Mrs. Brewster." My sister zips away, her girls always good for the perfect escape hatch.

I notice that Ana-Sofia has knelt down so Grace can inspect her baby. My niece looks up at Owen. "Your baby is pretty, Uncle Owen," she pronounces solemnly.

The title is like a shard of glass in my heart.

"So what can I help you with, Mrs. Brewster?" I ask. "I know Jared is getting married this summer." Time to focus on business.

"That woman picked out a ridiculous dress," she says. "We need something suitable."

That woman, huh? An entire relationship explained in two words. "Well, my lead time is generally closer to a year, but for an old family friend, of course."

She gives me a look as if she's trying to remember my name. Message received: *Your people were never friends with my people.* "Of course, we can afford a rush charge or any other extra fees you see fit to add." Message: *You working-class types will do anything to pad your purses.* She looks down her bony nose at me. "I don't think…Kimber…understands just what it means to be marrying into the Hale-Brewster family."

You'd think that this type of snobbery would've died out a century or so ago. You'd be wrong. "Well, I'd love to work with her."

"You'd be working with me."

"I'd love that, too." I smile firmly. I'm used to the

myriad emotions and egos involved in weddings, of course.

My husband—ex-husband—is now holding Charlotte so she can see the baby, too. Mom has joined the circle of admirers, too. Sigh.

Mrs. Brewster is still talking about Jared's fiancée, whom I haven't met. The words *inappropriate*, *unsuitable* and *unbefitting* are all used more than once. Not a surprise from the WASP Queen. Rachel's told me that Kimber is quite nice.

Jared was more of Rachel's friend, being the same age, but he never minded me tagging along with them back in the day. Every time I've seen him over the years, he's always been warm and funny and nice. Kind of an all-around peach, that guy. I always appreciated how he stayed friends with Rachel.

I wish she'd married someone like him.

A hot knife of rage stabs me in the heart. I used to love Adam, and it's quite easy to say that at this moment, I hate him more than I've ever hated anyone.

Just then, a veritable rainbow of a woman comes in. Short black skirt, engineer boots, black fishnet stockings, denim jacket and a tattoo that circles her neck with roses. Her hair is pink. I like her immediately. She comes right up to us. "Hi. Sorry I'm late. Um, I'm Kimber Allegretti?" Her eyes bounce from me to Mrs. Brewster.

"Don't say it like it's a question," Mrs. Brewster snaps. "Are you or are you not?"

"Yeah. I am," Kimber says, flushing.

"I'm Jenny, Rachel's sister," I say. Kimber looks about twenty-five. And Jared is forty, or close to it. "It's so good to meet you. Rachel's told me a lot about you. Said she liked you right away."

"For reals?" Kimber beams.

I swear, Mrs. Brewster growls. "Jennifer has agreed to throw together a dress that's more appropriate than that joke you showed me before. You can't really have planned to wear that in a house of worship."

Kimber bites her very full bottom lip. "I guess I didn't really think it through," she murmurs.

"I should say not."

"Well, I'm sure we can come up with something stunning that you both like," I say. "It will be beautiful, Kimber. And I don't *throw together* anything, Mrs. Brewster." I smile firmly. "I have a master's degree from Parsons Institute of Design. It will be incredible, not to worry."

"So long as it covers those tattoos," she says. "Honestly, young people today."

I give Kimber a wink, and while I'd like to, oh, I don't know…duct tape Mrs. Brewster's mouth shut, I know it won't help the situation. Part of my job is to be a family therapist and teach the art of the compromise. A woman who wants a low-cut, supersexy wedding dress goes up against her mother, who tells her she'll look like a tramp. Hateful bridesmaids, who find fault with every aspect of the dress, seething with jealousy that they're not the ones standing on the pedestal in front of the mirror.

And there are those brides who'd rather wear the ugliest dress on earth than upset a relative.

My job is to make everyone happy, to have a bride who cries at her own reflection, a mother who says she can't believe her baby is all grown-up, a dad who bawls all the way down the aisle and a groom who can't contain his surprise and awe at that first glimpse of his soon-to-be wife.

The dress symbolizes everything about the couple. Hope, love, beauty, promise, commitment.

I glance over at the photo of Rachel.

Shit.

"Well," I say, clearing my throat, "let's find a time for a consultation."

"Tomorrow at eleven," Mrs. Brewster says.

"Let me check my calendar," I answer patiently. I know I'm free, but I don't want to be treated like an indentured servant, either. "Is there anyone else you'd like to have with you, Kimber? A bridesmaid or your mom, maybe?"

"Um, no, just Mrs. Brewster," she says, picking at her thumbnail.

"Sometimes the groom comes, too, you know," I suggest. This girl is going to need an ally.

"Really?" Kimber's face brightens.

"I hardly think Jared should be here," Mrs. Brewster says.

"Mrs. Brewster, why don't you look around and see if there's anything that sparks your interest?" I suggest. "Have some champagne. Andreas? Would you show Mrs. Brewster around?"

My lovely assistant comes over and ushers her away. "Mrs. Brewster! Such an honor to have you join us today!" He just earned a raise.

"So how did you and Jared meet?" I ask Kimber.

"Well, I sing in a bar sometimes? Miller's, down by the river?"

"Sure. I used to sneak in there when I was underage," I say with a smile.

"Really? You seem so classy."

"It's the shoes. Don't be fooled. So you were singing?"

"Yeah, 'Son of a Preacher Man'? And Jared, he came over after and he said, 'You know, I actually *am* the son of a preacher man,' and he asked me out."

"What a great story! He's such a nice guy. I've known him a long time."

"I love him," she blurts, then grimaces. "I mean, duh, right?"

"No, it's great! I'll see you tomorrow. Hey, bring the dress you already bought, okay? You can tell me what you liked about it, and maybe we can incorporate some of the same elements."

"Mrs. Brewster had me return it."

"Ah. Okay. Well, I'll see you tomorrow, and we can start fresh."

"Thanks, Jenny," she says with another wide smile. She may have a tongue piercing, since she has a little lisp. "It was nice to meet you."

"You, too."

My eyes find Rachel again. She's got Charlotte on one hip and is tucking her daughter's hair behind her ear.

I go over. "Lottie," I say, "Andreas can do a magic trick. Go see!" My niece wiggles out of Rachel's arms and bolts over to my child-fearing assistant.

"I should get going," Rachel says.

"Want me to come over later?" Not that I want to see my asshole brother-in-law, but Rachel might need the support. She looks exhausted. Then again, if I see Adam, I can accidentally stab him in an artery. Bet my sewing shears would snip right through his penis, come to think of it. "Or you can come to my place. I'm all unpacked. I have wine, and if you wanted to vent—"

"No. I need to be with Adam."

I wonder if he's sexting his mistress. If Rachel's afraid to leave him alone for long. If he's with Emmanuelle right now, having porno sex. "Okay," I say.

"Don't judge, Jenny." Her voice is already resigned.

"I'm not! Rachel, I'm not. I just want to help."

"You can't." She sighs. "Look, I'm sorry. The shop is gorgeous. I'm proud of you." Her expression is shell-shocked, as if she just came out of the London Underground after the Blitz.

"Can we have coffee tomorrow?" I ask.

"I don't know."

My eyes fill again, and my sister gives me a sad smile. "I'll talk to you later," she says. "Love you."

"I love you, too. Thank you so, so much for coming."

I help her herd the girls to the car, scooping up Grace, holding Rose's hand, and buckle them into their car seats. I give Rachel a hug, and she squeezes me back.

"All I ever wanted was for Adam and me to have what Mom and Dad did," she whispers, then lets go of me and gets into the car. "Bye. Talk to you soon."

There are tears in her eyes.

I watch her drive away.

She's got more in common with our parents than she knows.

WHEN I GET home that night, my feet are telling me that wearing four-inch heels all day long is a life skill with an expiration date, and mine is just around the corner. I start up the front steps, then freeze.

I hear music.

In the two weeks I've lived here, I haven't heard any-thing other than those horrendous, repetitive *Teaching*

Little Fingers to Play songs. One would think that living above a Juilliard-trained pianist would at least get me a little free music, but Leo's usually just welded to that lawn chair when I come home, drinking a beer, his stinky, ill-tempered dog by his side.

But right now, there's music. At first hesitant, and sad, and familiar. The melody rises gently, and my heart hurts, it's so sad and beautiful. Goose bumps break out on my arms.

My God.

In a little bit of a trance, I go through Leo's gate, tiptoeing so my heels won't tap on the slate, and sink down in his doorway, not wanting him to know I'm here. The music twines around me, a little faster now, less sad, but then changing, a hint of darkness and sorrow, then back to the wistful strains I first heard, and good Lord, if I could play like this, I'd never stop.

Since I moved in, I've seen Leo almost every day. He's been up to not fix things three times so far, and ended up staying for more than an hour each time, drinking beer and insulting me. I've managed to pry some personal details from him—he doesn't have a steady girlfriend, he isn't gay, and his favorite food is Kentucky Fried Chicken, which is inexplicable. He seems to be the epitome of the happy slacker.

To think that he has *this* inside him is breathtaking. I lean against the door and close my eyes.

Then the door opens, and I fall backward.

"Jenny," Leo says, stepping aside. The music continues.

I scramble to my feet. "I thought you were playing."

"That's one of my students. I'm not the only person on earth who can play, believe it or not. Come on in."

A little boy is sitting at the upright piano. He stops when he sees me and folds his hands neatly in his lap.

"Evander," Leo says, "this is my friend Jenny. Jenny, meet Evander James."

"You're wonderful, sweetheart," I say.

"Thank you," he answers, not looking at me.

"What was that piece?"

Evander looks at Leo. "Chopin's Étude Number Three in E Major, Opus Ten, better known as *Tristesse*, which means *sadness* in French," Leo says.

"It was beautiful," I murmur, and my voice is husky. Leo's mouth tugs a little.

"I can't play the hard part," the boy says.

"Not yet," Leo says. "Give yourself a week."

There's a knock on the door, and Evander scrambles off the bench and stands next to the piano, his hand on it as if he can't quite bring himself to leave it. "Thank you, Mr. Killian," he says. His gaze is on the floor.

"You're welcome, buddy. And call me Leo." He answers the door, and a woman about my age comes into the room. "Mrs. James," he says, "I'd love to teach Evander. He's very talented."

"Thank you. I'm afraid we really don't have money for that. But I appreciate today." She's dressed in scrubs and wears Crocs. Seeing me standing there, she gives a little nod.

"There's a grant that lets me offer lessons to promising students," Leo says. "I'd like to use it for Evander. No cost to you."

She hesitates. "His father works the night shift, and I'm on days. I don't know if I can get him here."

"Can he take the school bus here on Thursdays?"

"Well, yes, but I don't know how he'd get home."

"He can stay here until you can pick him up. Or I could put him in a cab. There's plenty of money in the grant, and someone with Evander's talent only comes along once in a while."

I have to say, I'm a little surprised. While I've seen Leo here and there with his students, he's always pretty casual. This hard sell seems like a different side of his teacher persona.

"Really?" she says.

Leo nods. "Juilliard can give my references. So can Elmsbrook School—they did a background check on me before I played there this past February. And I can give you the names of the parents of my other students."

"Um…well, let me talk to my husband," Mrs. James says.

"Please, Mom," Evander whispers.

"We'll see, sweetheart. Thank you, Mr. Killian."

"Leo. You did great, kid." He winks at Evander, who gives a sweetly shy smile back. "I'll check in with you in a couple of days, how's that?"

"That's very nice of you. Thank you." The mom looks at me and smiles.

"Your son is very gifted," I say, like I know anything.

"He is," she says, smiling down on the boy. "He's been blessed." Loki's stumpy tail wags as they leave; the dog seems to hate only me.

When the door closes behind him, I sit on Leo's couch. "So that's what you call a prodigy, huh?" I ask.

"Yep."

"And this grant of yours… Does it exist?"

"Nope." He smiles. "Want some wine, irritating tenant?"

"I would love some, grossly under-qualified super. By the way, thanks for coming by today."

"Coming by where?"

"To the grand opening of my store. I invited you, remember?"

"I'm not in the market for wedding cakes, Jenny."

"Dresses."

"Those, either. So how was it?"

"Well, let's see. My mom told at least nine people how wretched she's been since my father died twenty-five years ago, my ex-husband, his beautiful wife and perfect baby showed up, and my sister's husband confirmed that he's having amazing sex with someone else."

"Shit. Now I wish I'd gone." He sits down in the chair across from me. "I'm sorry about Rachel."

"Me, too." Not wanting to think about my sister and all the ugly thoughts her situation inspires, I ask, "How did you find a kid like Evander?"

"The music teacher at Elmsbrook gave me a call. Evander's been playing piano since he was three, all by ear, and the teacher taught him to read music, but she's kind of out of her depth. He plays better than she does."

"Wow." I take a sip of wine. "So you're new to Cambry-on-Hudson, but you have all these students. How did that happen?"

"I gave a concert at the elementary school. When the straight mothers and gay fathers saw how good-looking I am, not to mention how incredibly talented, they stampeded to my door."

"And still I haven't heard you play. I thought that was you, when Evander was playing."

"I'm a better teacher than performer."

"So you say. And yet you also claim to be incredibly talented."

"All Juilliard students are incredibly talented, my dear. But we're not all Emanuel Ax, either."

"Who's that?"

"Get out." He gives me that killer smile, and my heart moves in my chest.

"So what makes a kid like Evander so special, aside from clever fingers?"

Leo tilts his head and looks at me, and there it is, that irritating and wonderful tug of attraction. "Women sit in doorways to listen." He grins. "There's technical ability, which is easy enough to learn. Virtually anyone can become proficient if they're dedicated enough. What you can't teach is interpretation. How to express the notes, not just which keys to hit."

"So when you were at Juilliard, did the great ones really stand out?"

"God, yes. All of us in the performance program grew up playing and listening. Being able to play Beethoven's *Moonlight Sonata* is no big deal. But someone playing it so that it feels like you've never heard it before, so that great, overplayed warhorse fills you up with light… That's greatness."

"Ah. How poetic you are tonight."

"It's the wine. When you were at wedding dress school—"

"Parsons Institute of Design, thank you very much. The Juilliard of the design world."

He raises an eyebrow. "When you were at Parsons, could you tell the great ones?"

I smile. "I see your point. Yes. The great ones made you gasp at how beautiful their pieces were."

"So just as it takes more than understanding how to sew to be a great designer, it takes more than knowing how to play to be a great performer. Evander is eleven years old, but already he plays with his whole self. Most of my students sit there like lumps with arms, but he becomes part of the piano. Did you see how he touched it when he was done?"

"I did. Like it was his friend."

Leo puts his feet on the coffee table. "Exactly." He finishes his wine and pours more, looks at my glass to see if I need a refill. I don't, since I haven't chugged mine quite as fast as he's done his. "Are you a great designer, Jenny?"

"Come by my shop and see for yourself."

"Maybe I will." His dog wanders over to him, curls his lip at me and sits at Leo's feet.

"Did you visit your mom today?" It's Sunday, after all.

"Yes." His smile drops so suddenly it's as if there's a different person in his place, and the...the *tragedy* there causes dread to flash through me.

"How was that?"

"It wasn't a good day," he says, stroking Loki's head and not looking at me. "She has dementia."

"Oh, Leo, I'm sorry."

He nods, his eyes still on the dog. "Thanks."

"Do you have other family around?"

"No. I'm the only one." He doesn't say anything for a minute, just takes a sip of wine, his long fingers cradling the glass with unconscious grace. "She went downhill pretty fast and had to move into a facility. And that was...tough."

"What about your dad?"

"Not in the picture."

I've learned more about Leo in the past minute than I have in the past three weeks.

He sighs. "So now I'm the keeper of the memories. My… Our family, the people who died… Most of the time, she forgets that they even lived. And when she forgets, it's like they're a little more gone." His eyes drop again to the dog, who looks up at him worshipfully.

"I'm so sorry," I say again.

He nods, then suddenly sits up, all interest and energy. "So! You're looking for a man, right?"

"Um…well, yes. I mean, yes, I would love to be married again. And have kids."

"Why?"

"I just do, Leo." I hate that question. *Because I believe in love. Because I never saw myself not having children.*

"So your sister's husband is cheating on her, your own husband dumped you, your mom's a lonely widow, but you believe in love with a capital *L* and hearts and butterflies."

"Don't forget bluebirds and rainbows. And yes, I do. It's the cornerstone of my business."

"I thought the cornerstone of your business would be bilking brides of every last dollar for a dress meant to make their friends jealous."

"You'd be wrong."

That smile flashes. "Want me to ask around? See if I can scare up a man for you?"

"You're getting on my nerves now. And I don't need your help. Believe it or not, men like me, Leo."

"Oh, yeah? Anyone promising?"

"Yes. I have a date Tuesday, actually." Before she was dealing with all her own crap, Rachel had fixed me up with a divorced dad whose son goes to the same nursery school as my nieces.

Leo sits back against the couch cushion. "Well. Make sure you report back to Uncle Leo. I want to hear all about it." He winks.

For some reason, that stings. "Thanks for the wine."

"You're welcome." He doesn't stand up.

As I go through the little courtyard to my front steps, I can't help glancing in his window.

He's still there on the couch, and gone is his irreverent, mischievous gleam. In its place is... Shit. Complete and utter loneliness. Someone should warn him, because it looks as if all the heartache in the world is written in the slant of his brows, the line of his mouth, the confusion in his eyes.

Leo Killian needs to be loved.

And there we go. As stupid a sentiment as exists in the universe. Leo has told me he's not interested in me. I'd be stupid not to believe him.

But he likes you, says the little whiny voice in my head.

Owen liked me, too, and we all know where that got me. Adam *loves* Rachel, and he's rubbing her heart on a cheese grater.

And my father loved Mom. Her image of him is suspended in amber, where he can't be touched by reality.

I wonder if it's time to tell my sister that, like her husband, our father was a cheater, too.

Rachel

------- ❖ -------

IT'S NOT EVERY day that I get checked for herpes. Nope. This is a first. No wonder I'm wearing new underwear.

I seem to have become a stand-up comedian in my own head, ever since finding out that Adam is/was cheating on me. It beats hysteria and/or murder. Ba-dum-ching!

I hustle the girls into the minivan and drive to nursery school, saying goodbye with fast hugs. This, of course, is the day that everyone wants to talk to me. Four or five mothers stand in a well-dressed knot outside the doors, and I have to weave between them.

"Rachel, come to Blessed Bean with us," Elle says. She's wearing a top so tight it's a wonder she can draw breath to speak.

"Yeah, Rachel. You never come," Claudia says, twisting her most recent diamond ring.

"I'm sorry. I have an errand to run," I say.

"Meeting someone?" Mean Debbie suggests slyly. She gives me an arch look. "So dressed up, Rachel."

Yes, I have dressed up. To make a good impression on my syphilis or chlamydia or whatever I may have. *Hi! Take it easy on me, because as you can see from this adorable dress, I'm supernice!*

"I gotta run, too," Kathleen says, though technically they haven't invited her to go out for coffee. She's older than the rest of us, and the one time she did come along, she ordered a full breakfast, while Claudia, Debbie and Elle watched with the same horrified fascination as if she'd been shooting heroin. Ba-dum-ching! "Come on, Rach, we can walk to our cars together." When we're a safe distance away, she whispers, "Everything okay?"

"Mmm-hmm. Thanks for asking, though." I can't look at her, because I can feel tears rising behind my eyes, and if I see any kindness in her expression, I'm likely to fall apart, which would make Mean Debbie and Claudia and Elle incredibly excited.

"Give me a call later if you want," Kathleen says. "I'm gonna just come out and say this. I hate those bitches back there. You're the only genuine person I've met since we moved here, and I'd love to be friends if you're as nice as you seem."

My mouth falls open. "Oh, Kathleen! Thank you. I feel the same way. I mean…they're not really that bad. But you seem really nice, too." My cheeks prickle with a blush, but it's wonderfully awkward.

In a flash, I see her coming over to my house, sitting in the kitchen, eating those lemon cookies I baked last night. "Do you want to— Oh, wait. I really do have an errand. Maybe…"

"Another time, then?"

"Yeah. Absolutely." I hesitate, then force out the words. "I have some personal things going on. It might be a while, but I'd really like to get to know you better." It's mortifying. I hate being shy. I hate it.

"Great. I mean, shit on the personal things, but let me

know if I can help." She smiles then gets into her mini-van, which is cluttered and filthy and smells like boy.

"Thank you," I say. "Thanks." I swallow hard and get into my car.

A few minutes later, I'm standing at the reception-ist's window at my doctor's office. "Rachel Carver to see Dr. Ramanian," I say.

"Insurance card, please," drones the extremely young woman. She looks as if death by boredom is imminent. I hand over my card. She glances at it and types. And types. And types. "What is the reason for your visit?"

Horror flashes like weak lightning. Do I have to ac-tually say this out loud? "Um…a checkup?"

"You just had a checkup four months ago," she says, staring at her computer screen.

I bite my lip. "I…I know. I need another one. I have an appointment."

"Well, your insurance isn't gonna cover this. Are you sick?" Her voice is all too loud. My face feels as if it's bubbling, I'm blushing so hard.

"Um…"

My husband is cheating on me. I need to make sure he didn't give me anything.

"Hello? I need to fill in this form." She looks *so* bored. And beautiful. And so damn young, chewing on her gum, all those silver bracelets, a Chinese character tattoo on her hand…

"It's none of your business," I say in a hard voice. "I'll tell the doctor. I have an appointment, so just get me in there."

Wow. This new Rachel…she kind of kicks ass.

The girl is not impressed. "Fine. Have a seat."

Like all doctors' offices, this one features uncomfortable chairs with itchy upholstery, travel magazines and outdated editions of *Entertainment Weekly*. I pick up an issue of something and pretend to read, but my heart is thudding.

Napoleon Bonaparte died of syphilis, didn't he? Or was that Al Capone? Or both?

Good God. What if I have something? It's utterly surreal. Adam, too, is being tested, but somehow, I doubt he's suffering the way I am. In fact, I picture him going into his doctor's office saying, "Here for another screen, dude! Been fucking around on my wife, and, boy, is this other woman *hot*!" and the doctor says, "Yeah, you go, Adam, you da *man*!" and they high-five and—

"Rachel? Oh, it *is* you! How are you?"

My heart sinks. It's Mrs. Donovan, who lived next door to us when I was a kid. It's not that I don't like her; it's just that I'm here for such nasty purposes. I try to get up, but she's standing too close, and I don't want to knock her over. "Mrs. Donovan! Hi." I smile up at her, sort of, and squeeze her free hand. The other holds her cane and a huge quilted purse that looks like it could hold an eight-year-old child.

"How are those beautiful girls of yours?" she asks.

"They're great," I tell her. "Want to see a picture?" I pull out my phone, but she waves it away.

"I hate those cell phone thingies," she says. "Do you have a real photo?"

"I don't. I'm sorry."

"Why are you here, dear? You're not sick, are you?" *I better not be.* "Oh, just a checkup. How about you?"

"I have the worst itching!" she crows. "And discharge! In the strangest place, too!"

Oh, God. Maybe she has an STD, too. I try to keep

my face from morphing into a silent scream of horror, but I have no idea if it's working.

"Look," she says, pulling up her World's Best Grandma T-shirt. "Look at my belly button. See that oozing?"

I try not to gag. First of all, it's a wrinkly, elephantine stomach, and it's about an inch from my face. Secondly, she's got such an outie that it looks like a snout, like some sort of alien pig baby is trying to push its way out of her.

And yes, there's discharge.

"I've been using these hemorrhoid wipes on it," she continues in that blithely unselfconscious way old people sometimes have when discussing hideous medical issues. "But it's just getting worse. It's thicker now, and if I squeeze—"

"Rachel Carver?" A nurse opens the door and I fly across the room.

"Good luck, Mrs. Donovan!" I call over my shoulder.

A few minutes later, I'm in my johnny coat, waiting for the doctor to come in. I shaved my legs for this appointment. Definitely want to make a good impression as a cuckolded wife. I've seen Dr. Ramanian for about ten years. I feel like we're almost friends, in that sense that she's seen parts of me *I've* never seen, knew about my struggles to get pregnant and came to see the girls when they were in the hospital, just because she's nice. I always wanted to ask her out for coffee or a drink, but that effortless way some people (like Jenny) have of making friends has always eluded me, and now the window has shut. I can't just say, "Hey, about nine, ten years ago, I meant to ask you if you wanted to be friends, but I couldn't get the words out. How about now? Does now work?"

A brisk knock comes on the door. "Come in," I say.

"Hello, Rachel," she says, walking in, eyes on my chart. "How are you?"

"Fine, thanks, how are you?" I answer automatically.

"Very good. What can I do for you today?"

I practiced what I'd say in the car ride over here, but my heart pounds against my ribs like a bird trying to get out of a house. I clear my throat. "I seem to need an STD panel," I manage to say, and I don't cry, though my freshly shaven and moisturized legs are shaking.

Dr. Ramanian's face changes, melting in sympathy. Not really a mystery who cheated, I guess. "All right, then," she says. "Let's check you out."

So I scooch onto the exam table and let her probe my cervix and try to breathe deeply. I'm brave, after all. I had triplets. During my infertility workups, I've been probed and prodded and squished a hundred times.

There never was anything wrong with me, by the way. Adam has a low sperm count. Yet I was the one who had to take fertility drugs so the swimmers he did have had a better chance to home in on something.

Dr. Ramanian is fast and gentle and tells me to sit up. She draws blood herself, and gives me a cup to pee in. "It won't take long to get the results," she says. "I'll call you myself."

"Thank you," I say briskly, all New Rachel as I pull on my clothes without even waiting for her to leave. "I appreciate that."

Because Old Rachel really couldn't take this. Old Rachel would be sobbing on this woman's shoulder.

New Rachel is thinking about how satisfying it would be to kill her husband right about now.

Jenny

WHEN I WAS eleven and Rachel was fourteen, our father was shot and killed when two teenagers robbed the Auto-Mart.

Dad's guilty pleasure was those nasty frozen drinks guaranteed to rot your teeth. Hey. Gotta relax somehow, right? We always got a kick out of it, our father, the high priest of flossing, stopping in a 7-Eleven or a Stewart's for a drink made of sugar, corn syrup and God knows what else.

On the night of July 11, Dad decided he had to have a Green Watermelon Brain Freeze, his favorite flavor. The video surveillance showed him at the self-serve slushie counter, filling a barrel-sized foam cup. At the same time he was thus engrossed, two boys came in, nylon stockings over their faces. Jittery, nervous, druggies…the worst kind of criminal. They pointed a gun at the clerk and ordered him to open the safe.

My father capped his drink, still oblivious, and reached for his wallet, his last act on this earth, because that was when the clerk reached for his own shotgun, the kids fired, the clerk fired, and Dad, who stood there with his hands up, was dead.

The whole thing took less than fifteen seconds. I

know, because when I turned eighteen, I got the video from the police. It wasn't gruesome; Dad just fell back, out of the screen except for his shoes. I don't know what I was hoping the video would show me, but I felt compelled to see everything that happened.

Until three months before that horrible day, my life had been charmed.

My parents were wonderfully safe and normal. Dad loved being a dentist, and Mom taught art therapy at a nursing home. Part-time work for Mom, the perfect kind of job for her, a little artsy, a little holy, with just enough hours that she could do something unrelated to us girls while still going all-out for the title of mother of the year. She came to every recital, every concert, every horse show. She baked cookies, came up with themes for our birthday parties, gave out the best candy at Halloween—as well as a toothbrush, of course. Mom French-braided our hair, baked chocolate chip cookies from scratch and put in the requisite hours volunteering in our schools.

Every once in a while, she'd give us a little flash of adventure—careening too fast into the driveway, making us scream with fear and delight, or, if Dad was at a dentists' convention, letting us have ice-cream sundaes for dinner and telling us we didn't even have to brush afterward (though Rachel did, for the record).

We assumed all families were like ours. Our parents were happily—very happily—married, our house was big but not fancy, Dad made enough that we were quite comfortable, though not rich. We didn't own a horse, but we took riding lessons. There was a new car every five years or so. We took vacations each summer, renting a house on a lake in New Hampshire or visiting the Grand Canyon. We went to the movies together and played board games—bored games, I used to call them, quite delighted with my sophisticated wit.

Mom and Dad made adult life look incredibly desirable, and both Rachel and I couldn't wait to grow up. On date nights, which happened every weekend, Mom wore a dress and panty hose, heels and perfume. They went to benefit balls and country-club dances and dinner parties at their friends' homes, and when it was their turn to host, Rachel and I would take coats and serve hors d'oeuvres and spy from the stairs landing before going upstairs to watch TV.

Mom was great.

But Dad was better.

He was, I realize now, incredibly good-looking. But dads are dads; of course we thought he was handsome. As I got older, I noticed women talking to him, laughing, laying a hand on his arm or chatting to him for too long after he'd cleaned their teeth. Kids skipped into his office and ran up to him at school events to show him a loose tooth or just to say hi. He played golf with his buddies once in a while, went to a Yankees game once a year with his brother, but really, he was all about Mom and Rachel and me. His girls. He adored us.

Mom was a really good mother. Dad was perfect.

Sometimes, Rachel or I would walk in on our parents kissing in the kitchen, a sight that Rachel adored and I pretended to find disgusting. It seemed to me that Mom was lucky to be married to the great man, the guy who made people love going to the dentist, the best father, the nicest person in the world. It was never the other way around.

Weekends were spent taking hikes along the Hudson, Sunday-night pizza at Louie's. At bedtime, Dad would sit in the chair between Rachel's and my beds and tell us long, absurd stories about renegade cats, or child armies defeating evil giants through cunning and homemade weapons. On Sunday mornings, he'd make chocolate chip pancakes, so long as we brushed extra long afterward.

Sometimes, I'd go to his office after school, skipping down the hall, the sound of drilling not at all disturbing to me. His staff was all women, and they seemed to swell with love, seeing Dad scoop up his daughters and introduce us to his patients. Dad would always have time to examine our teeth and give us the grave news: "It seems like I'll have to pull all your teeth, little girl. Every single one is black and rotten. Don't your parents make you brush?" He let Rachel and me pick out the posters that he tacked to the ceiling above the exam chairs— a kitten dangling from a branch with the caption Hang In There! or the unicorn standing under a rainbow and the words Don't Stop Believing! There was a treasure chest filled with little toys for kids once they'd endured their checkup, and Rachel and I got to pick out the loot.

Down the hall from Dad's office suite was a storage room, not much bigger than a closet, filled with dental supplies—boxes and boxes of toothpaste, floss and toothbrushes, canisters of nitrous oxide, extra scrubs and boxes of masks and latex gloves, syringe tips and bib clips, plastic chair covers and Dixie cups. Rachel and I loved to play in there, tucking notes for Daddy in between boxes of his supplies, or just hiding.

Lena, his younger hygienist, got engaged right there in the office, and Dad was in on the whole thing. Lena's father had died years before, and she asked Dad to walk her down the aisle. Rachel and I got to go to the wedding, and it filled us with pride, Dad being acknowledged like this. "I can't wait to get married," Rachel whispered to me, even though she was only fourteen at the time. "I want it to be just like Mommy and Daddy." I didn't share the same sentiment, not yet—I was eleven and still in love with horses. But I knew what she meant, even if at that time, my vision of adult life entailed living next door to my parents and owning a lot of cats.

Rachel was Mommy's girl; they both loved the domestic arts of decorating and baking and gardening. Me, I liked to think of myself as more like Dad. I'd sit next to him in his big chair, his strong arm around me, and breathe in his comforting dad smell—Dial soap, freshly cut grass and Crest toothpaste, the original mint flavor.

So you see, life was both normal and remarkable, banal and utterly happy, and more than anything, safe. Our parents loved us and each other, my sister was my best friend and we had plenty of everything a child never knows she needs until it's gone.

Then, two things happened. Dad's practice was thriving to the point where he hired another dentist. Dr. Dan Wallace, my first crush. He looked like Johnny Castle from *Dirty Dancing*, and what girl didn't love Johnny? Dr. Dan was just out of dental school, funny and wore an engraved silver ring on his right hand. I had never met a man who wore a ring that was purely ornamental, and it made Dr. Dan seem unbearably hip.

I wasn't the only one who thought so; Rachel couldn't go into the office without being struck dumb and blushing the entire time, and God help her if Dr. Dan spoke to her. Mom would invite him over for dinner, and it was an agony of pleasure and mortification, having him see us in our natural habitat, me trying to seem more interesting and exotic than I actually was, Rachel almost paralyzed with shyness, our father chuckling at both of us, Mom rolling her eyes but making sure she served an extra-complicated and delicious dessert.

I did manage to talk to Dr. Dan about school and playing the clarinet, as he had when he was my age. Finally, at the advanced age of eleven, I had found a man I could picture marrying; move over, Bono, and hello, Dr. Dan. At night, I'd picture our life—I'd be a full-fledged adult at twenty-one, a mere ten years from now, and we'd do a lot of hugging and hand-holding, a few chaste kisses on the lips—sex to an eleven-year-old was still incredibly disgusting. We'd host glamorous parties and go sailing and take trips to Paris to see the Eiffel Tower.

It was right around that time that Dad seemed to change a little. One Saturday afternoon, he and I went to the pharmacy so I could buy maxi pads for Rachel, who was unable to face the humiliation of buying them herself—or even being in the store when they were purchased. I got the brand she requested—two giant packages to stockpile—and went through the aisles looking for my dad.

There he was in the skin care section, studying a jar of moisturizer.

"Dad. That's for women," I said patiently.

He flushed and put the box back. "Right, right," he said. "My skin's been a little dry, that's all. You all set?" He headed up to the register.

I looked at the box he'd put back. Age-Defying Overnight Serum.

And when we got in the car, Dad told me he'd forgotten to get razors, ran back into the store and came back out with a bag that clearly contained more than razors.

I didn't say anything, but later on, I checked in my parents' medicine cabinet. The serum wasn't there. I found it under the sink, hidden behind a package of toilet paper. Not only that, he had hair dye. Hair dye! For men! How embarrassing! Why would Dad care about defying age? He was old. He knew that.

Then Lena the hygienist had a baby and went out on maternity leave, and Dad hired someone to take her place.

I barely noticed Dorothy, too busy being sophisticated around Dr. Dan when I went to the office. But her name began cropping up at the dinner table, and my antennae twitched, because something else was happening, too— my mother was irritated.

Dorothy hadn't been able to find a steady job as a hygienist, Dad said. "What does that tell you?" Mom said, uncharacteristically judgmental. Dorothy was widowed and struggled financially. "Is she already nosing around for a raise?" When Dad suggested that they fix Dorothy up with my uncle Greg, Mom said, "Rob. Be serious. Greg's not going to date a dental hygienist." Even at age eleven, I recognized the put-down in my mother's voice. She did tend to worship her little brother, who went on to marry an unemployed stripper, for the record.

Talk of Dorothy continued, almost as if Dad couldn't resist mentioning her. I didn't know why. She sounded pathetic to me. Dorothy had a daughter a few years younger than I was. The two of them lived in the grittier town of Brooks Mill, in an apartment. No one I knew lived in an apartment—just in houses.

"I thought we could give her some of the girls' clothes. Stuff that they've outgrown," Dad suggested. I looked up sharply, not sure if I wanted to part with anything, especially to an unknown stranger.

"How old is she again?" Rachel asked.

"She's six," Dad answered. "First grade." The fact that he knew that made me jealous. Dad had two daughters. He shouldn't care what grade someone else's daughter was in.

"She can have my yellow dress with the daisies on it," Rachel said. "That was a pretty one. Remember, Mom? I wore it to Science Night when I had Mrs. Norton. And those overalls with the pretty pockets. Oh, and that red velvet dress! I loved that dress!"

Thus shamed by Rachel's kindness—as was often the case—I went up to the attic and dug out some of my clothes for this poor and mysterious child and added a few stuffed animals and books, too.

Summer turned to fall, that season of golden leaves and gray skies. I played soccer; Rachel was in high school and getting pretty good at horseback riding, showing on the weekends, bringing home ribbons. Mom had been promoted to a full-time position as activities director at the nursing home, and she got home just before dinner, stressed and moving at a hundred miles an hour, trying to throw dinner together and arrange a car pool for Rachel and make cookies to show that she was still that kind of mom.

She loved her new job and had a lot of stories to share, which was different—before, she'd talk only about her clients, whom I viewed as tragically old. Now she had stories about the haughty yoga instructor, or the wardrobe consultant who cried when Mr. Zeigler flashed her, or the kids who came up to play violin and piano or sing for the residents. For the first time, it seemed that Mom was suddenly the more interesting parent. We knew Dad's staff and clients…but Mom had a whole new cast. Not that I still didn't love him best, of course. He was just a little…predictable.

One Friday night, it was just Dad and me, that rarest of treats, and he said he had to make a quick phone call before we could watch our movie. He went into the den, and I waited in the living room, patiently at first, then not so much. Our movie was *Edward Scissorhands*, and Lisa, my best friend, had seen it twice already, and said I'd love Edward because he was so beautiful and strange, and I'd had the movie on the waiting list at the library for months, and finally, finally, it was here.

So I sighed hugely and agreed to wait. "Ten minutes, honeybun," Dad said.

After twenty, I went down the hall.

"I know, I do…Well, it wasn't quite the same, but… Yes! Exactly…Really? You did?" He chuckled, that low, wonderful sound, and I felt an instinctive flash of jealousy.

"Daddy," I said loudly. "Are you gonna be much longer?"

He looked up. "Oh! Hi, honey," he said to me. He held up a finger. "Listen," he said, "I should go. My princess and I are watching a movie. Edward Something."

"Scissorhands!" I said. How could he forget the title…

"Scissorhands…I don't know. I'll ask." He looked up at me. "Think a six-year-old would like it?" he asked.

"No. It's too sophisticated."

"Oh," he said with a wink. "You hear that? Too sophisticated…Okay." He laughed again. "Bye. See you Monday." He hung up. "Want popcorn?"

"Who was that?" I asked.

"Dorothy. From the office."

"It's the *weekend*, Dad," I said.

"I know, honey. But she's lonely. She only has her little girl for company."

"So?" I said. "She could get married if she wants. Maybe she likes it being just her and her daughter."

"Maybe so," he said. "Come on, let's have popcorn. As long as you floss afterward."

NOT LONG AFTER that came the day that changed everything. My soccer practice had been canceled due to rain, and I was looking forward to being in the house by myself. Rachel was at her riding lesson—she took a different bus on Tuesdays to get to the stable—and Mom was still at work.

But the spare house key wasn't in the fake rock in our flower bed; the little space was empty, which meant whoever had used it last hadn't put it back.

Feeling deliciously aggrieved and martyred, poor latchkey child that I was, without so much as a key, I walked around the house and tried the windows. All locked. Our neighbors had a key, but I didn't want to go there. Mrs. Donovan was very nice, but Richie, her son, had just turned nine and asked if I was wearing a bra every time he saw me on the school bus.

I decided to walk downtown to Dad's office, the better to martyr myself on the cross of adolescent suffering. It was quite possible that Dad would take me to the Corner Café and buy me a hot cocoa to make up for this sorry state. Even better, maybe he'd make Dr. Dan take me! Not that this had ever happened, but it could, at least in my imagination. Also, I might trip on our way there, coming dangerously close to an oncoming car, and Dr. Dan would grab my arm, pulling me out of harm's way, saving my very life, and his hand would rest on my shoulder, warm and strong and comforting…

Of course, nothing would happen; that would be so gross. No, he'd just say something about how ten years could fly by, and he wasn't going anywhere and he hoped that I'd come down to the office every week for cocoa, so we could talk. He'd smile at me, then go back to his lonely house—where we'd live someday as a married couple—and wait out the years.

Filled with this lovely dream, I walked in the cool rain toward downtown. My dad's office was housed in the tallest building in Cambry, and the thrill of riding in an elevator had never left me. I pushed the button for the eighth floor and mentally reviewed stories I could tell Dr. Dan to entertain him and show him I was mature and insightful. Caleb Johnson's spoiled tuna fish sandwich? No, too disgusting. Sydney Dane dating a ninth grader? No, because that might make me look a little young. Oh! Mr. Heisman's limp, a subject of great speculation today at lunch. I could express my compassion for those less fortunate. "I think it's a war injury," I could say to Dr. Dan. "But he doesn't like to talk about it. Understandable, of course." As it turned out, Mr. Heisman sprained his knee while in a bouncy house with his daughter, but I didn't know that then.

I got off the elevator and went down the hall into my dad's suite. Dr. Dan was right there in the reception area, leaning on the counter where Lizzie the receptionist sat, a *very* handsome smile on his Swayze-esque face. "I'd go wherever you wanted," he was saying. "Le Monde is fine with me, if that's where you want to eat."

Le Monde was a fancy restaurant on the Hudson River. My parents went there for their anniversary.

I felt the burning prickle of humiliation in my face before I completely understood that he was asking Lizzie on a date.

"Hey, kiddo," Dr. Dan said, turning to me. "How's it going?"

Kiddo? *Kiddo?* Not what you'd call the girl you were going to wait for. A spear of pain slammed through my chest, snapping ribs, crushing my heart. Even worse, I felt the burn of tears in my eyes. In a second, I'd be crying, and Dr. Dan would *know*. And so would Lizzie. And so would *everyone*.

"Is my dad here?" I blurted. "I—I have an emergency."

"Are you okay?" he asked, frowning.

"Where's my dad?"

"I think he's in the storage room, honey," Lizzie said.

The storage room was down the hall, back toward the elevators. I pushed through the doors and ran, my wet jeans flopping against my skin, which felt raw and cold. Stupid, stupid, *stupid*, imagining someone like Dr. Dan would think I was interesting. That he would wait ten years for me! I was an idiot.

I burst into the storage room and saw a man and a woman kissing, their arms twined around each other. At my entrance, they jumped apart.

The man was my father.

The rush of my heartbeat thrummed through my ears.

One second. Two seconds. Three. The silence spread like melting tar. Dorothy—Dorothy? He liked *Doro-*

thy?—twisted the hem of her jacket in her fingers, biting her lip.

"Pumpkin!" my father said, far, far too late. "What a nice surprise! Is, uh, is school over? Why are you all wet?"

"It's *raining*," I said. My eyes felt hard and dry.

"Of course, of course it is. Um, Dorothy, did you find what you needed?"

"Yes, Dr. Tate," she said, then slithered around us and out the door.

"Soccer practice was canceled," I said, accusation knifing through my tone.

"Sure, honey. Come on. Let's go get a hot chocolate. My poor Jenny! You're soaked! You must be freezing!" He almost made me feel better.

"You were kissing her."

His face wriggled as he searched for an answer. "She…she was upset. That's all."

"You were kissing her."

Dad sighed and crouched down to my eye level. "Yes. I was. Because she was upset. But I love Mommy and you girls, and if you tell your mother or sister, they'll just be upset. Don't give it another thought, Jenny. It was nothing."

Except I knew. There was no *nothing* about it, and the wrongness shimmered in the air. Dr. Dan's betrayal evaporated in the heat of that wrongness.

"Let me buy you a hot chocolate, sweetheart," he said, and his voice, his dad voice, was the same as always, warm and low and loving, and I hated him in that moment.

But I went with him, and I drank my hot chocolate and ate two madeleine cookies, and when Mom harped on me that night for not eating my dinner, he told her to go easy on me.

I didn't forgive him. I knew. He *liked* that Dorothy. How dared he?

From that day on, true adolescence in all its sulky, consuming power burst out of every pore, seeped into the air around me. I didn't speak to Rachel when she asked in her gentle, sweet voice if something was wrong. My mother muttered something about another menstruating female in the house, and I stormed out of the kitchen. When Dad asked if I wanted to go for a bike ride that weekend, I said no and stayed in my room, furious that he'd then asked Rachel and actually gone and had fun. The *nerve*. The betrayal.

The next week, Mom asked Dad how Lena and the baby were doing. They were great, he said. Lena would be back next week.

"What about Dorothy?" Mom didn't look up from her plate.

His eyes cut to me. "Well, I don't need another hygienist. I'll give her a good recommendation, though."

He took another bite of potatoes and chewed. The skin on his throat was lax and swaying with the motion of his jaw. Funny, how I'd never noticed that before.

My father was getting old.

Of course, to a sixth grader, "old" is anything north of eighteen. But in that moment, I felt two things—a savage, hot triumph that Dorothy was out of our lives, and an overwhelming disgust for my father. Just because she was gone didn't mean I was going to forgive him.

And then, three months later, my father was shot in the face and killed, and he never got a day past fortyfour years, six months and one day.

DEATH AFFECTS EVERYONE differently. For me, I became more protective of my sister. Rachel had always struggled, too tender, too giving. After Dad died, she became even sweeter, and more shy.

Mom became someone entirely different. She was now a professional widow. Gone was the busy-bee mother, the art therapist, the committee chair for every committee that ever existed. Instead of World's Best Mother, Mom became World's Most Grief-Stricken Wife.

A creeping dread—and disgust, I'll admit—grew in me like mildew as my brisk, capable mother devolved into someone who fell asleep in her chair every night, clutching a picture of Dad and her on their wedding day. She stopped coloring her hair, gained weight, started wearing Dad's clothes. Work, which she'd so loved the past year, became too much, and she demoted herself back to art therapist, then cut her hours back to just a few a week. "I can't bear being around all those old people," she'd say. "Why was Rob taken so young? Why not one of them instead?"

All she could talk about was how happy they'd been, how *blessed*, a word I'd never before heard her say. "I wish it had been me," she said one night, her tone sticky with self-pity. "You girls would've been better off if it had been me instead of Rob."

That was another thing. There was no more *Daddy*, or *Dad*, or even *your father* when Mom spoke. There was only Rob, her husband. She was a pale comfort to us in our grief, but "at least you two have each other." Meaning she was suffering much more than we were. And maybe she was, but it didn't seem fair for one of us to burst into tears and then have Mom cry harder, and longer, and louder.

That's how I changed. I became cynical and tougher, though really, the change had started in the dental supply room.

A conglomerate bought Dad's practice, and Tate Dental Offices became Oak Hill Dental. The hygienists stayed on, a sixtysomething-year-old woman who didn't believe in nitrous oxide was hired, and Dr. Dan moved down South a couple of years after Dad died.

Every once in a while, I thought about Dorothy…wondering if she knew about Dad. If she was sad.

And then one night, I bolted awake and decided something.

I had seen wrong.

They *hadn't* been kissing. Hugging, yeah, maybe, but not kissing. Dad would never cheat on Mom. It was me. I was wrong. My romantic fantasies about Dr. Dan had infused my little brain with all sorts of tawdry soap-opera images. That was all.

I needed to mourn my father, that wonderful, sweet, gentle man. He couldn't be a cheater anymore. I mean, he never was, anyway! Right? With my mother an abject wreck, I had to love my father again, think of him as that nearly perfect guy. It was too hard to fight, even silently, against Rachel and Mom and their unadulterated grief.

During my freshman year of high school, I took an elective called Design Basics, and suddenly, finally, I had something to do at home to distract me from our house of mourning. I asked for sewing lessons for my birthday, and a tiny Italian woman taught me how to make French seams and rolled hems, gussets and buttonholes. Rachel went to college for graphic design; she was also artsy, and she stayed close by, going to college in New Paltz.

When it was my turn, I headed for the city, to Parsons. To anyone in the Empire State, Manhattan is the shining star, shimmering at the mouth of the Hudson like Oz. Within a week, I knew the subway systems, the best place for Thai food and had already introduced myself to every one of my professors. I became a clichéd New York City college student, wearing black clothes and ugly, heavy shoes, carrying my sketch pad with me wherever I went, proudly living in a refrigerator-sized apartment with three other students. I went home often but briefly, grateful to slip back to the city, *the* city, where already I was distinguishing myself. Every guy I dated, I imagined marrying, but nothing stuck, and I had my heart broken more than a couple times.

Then, between my undergraduate and master's degrees, I headed for Sydney for a six-month internship at Chanel Australia. There was a huge snowstorm, and my flight was delayed by nineteen hours, give or take. Rather than crash on a friend's floor or go home to Cambry-on-Hudson, I decided to tough it out at JFK, wandering with the throngs of fellow strandees and airport staff as the leaden skies pelted us with fist-sized snowflakes. I sketched four dresses and a suit, entertained a little Korean boy by drawing him anime characters, then got up, my ass numb from sitting on the floor for so long.

I wandered through the vast terminals, watching people, checking in with my mom and sister to assure them that I was fine and didn't want to come home, that I'd be on my way soon enough. The sun-drenched glory and good cheer of Sydney seemed as far as Pluto, and my eyes grew gritty with fatigue and filtered air.

And then I saw him.

Dr. Dan Wallace, DDS, my father's old partner, sitting at one of the many crowded bars. Still looked like Patrick Swayze, too. When I tapped him on the shoulder and told him who I was, a smile sliced his face, and he hugged me tight, smelling of whiskey and Irish Spring. When he pulled back, he was a little teary-eyed. "Join me for a drink," he said, and I realized with some degree of affection that he was half in the bag.

"Have you been stuck here long?" I asked.

"Twenty..." He looked at his watch. "Twenty-seven hours, more or less. Bartender, a drink for my friend here. Hang on, Jenny, are you old enough to drink?"

"I am," I said, ordering a glass of merlot. "I'm twenty-two now."

"No!" Dr. Dan exclaimed. "That doesn't seem possible. Oh, Jenny! You've gotten so pretty! Well, you always were a beautiful girl."

He had an impressive memory, given that he'd worked for my dad for such a short time. I told him about Rachel, her graduate degree in graphic design, her work for an online start-up. Mom was happy, I lied. Doing well. And how about himself?

"Oh, I'm married, very happily," he said. "Got two kids, a girl and a boy." He pulled out his wallet to show me pictures, and they were awfully cute. His wife was lovely. It dawned on me that Dr. Dan wasn't even forty. Not really that old at all, now that he and I were both adults. He lived in Macon, Georgia, though he remained a Yankee at heart.

"Your father was the greatest guy," Dr. Dan said, slurring the slightest bit. "He really took me under his wing. Gave me a chance."

"I know he liked you so much," I said.

"Well, I looked up to him, that's for sure. He was everything I wanted to be. The original family man. Beautiful wife, you girls, that gorgeous house... You know, I was so glad when he gave up that woman. 'Rob,' I told him, 'you have everything. Don't shit where you eat, even if it's not my place to say so. Is she worth ruining your marriage?' And see, even though I wasn't married at the time, I *knew*. He and your mom, they were the real deal."

The bartender met my eye, and I stared back. What? What did he want? Oh. He was asking if I needed a refill. I nudged my glass a little closer, and more red wine flowed. He had a tattoo on his wrist. The wine was Yellow Tail. There was a maraschino cherry on the floor, and he was just about to step on it. My legs were shaking.

Dr. Dan was still talking.

"Dorothy?" I interrupted. "Was that her name?"

"Dorothy. Yeah, I think so. Lizzie hated her. Oh, man, Lizzie—remember her?—she and I dated a couple times. She was all right, that Lizzie."

He kept up in that vein, talking and talking and talking, the subject drifting from his days in COH to his migration south, how he met his wife. I stopped listening. I nodded in the right places, then checked my watch and pretended my flight was boarding in ten minutes. Kissed him on the cheek, thanked him for the wine and left.

Dorothy.

I could see her face as if she'd been standing in front of me. Blond hair, black roots, that full-lipped mouth. Blue eyes. Big nose, but it worked.

So it was true after all. My father had indeed been kissing Dorothy. In fact, he'd had an affair.

I was so glad when he gave up that woman.

That didn't even sound like a one-night stand.

A middle-aged man, confronted with his fading youth in the face of Dr. Dan, a wife who's suddenly in love with her career, two daughters who didn't leap into his arms at night anymore…and a damsel in distress in the form of a single mom who struggled to pay the bills.

I remembered Mom's flashes of jealousy, her easy dismissal of Dorothy's problems. But I also knew Mom well enough to understand that if she had known Dad was sleeping with someone else, she'd never have been able to hide it.

Mom didn't know.

Rachel didn't know.

Six hours later, my flight really did board, and I fell into a coma-like sleep the second we taxied down the snowy runway. When I woke up somewhere over the Pacific, I was resolved.

I'd never tell. It was too late.

The hot chocolate and madeleines hadn't fooled me back then, that rainy day when I was eleven. I had *known*. I gave him the benefit of the doubt that night when I decided I'd imagined the whole thing, and I was wrong to do it. For the past twelve years, I'd been pretending Dad wasn't the cheater he was.

I should've told Mom when there was still time. She could've confronted him. Gotten counseling. Could've divorced him. She could've separated, at least, and when he died, she at least might've been on the road to some other form of happiness.

And maybe…just maybe, if he'd been the guilty man who had to make amends for his affair, he wouldn't have gone for that stupid Green Watermelon Brain Freeze. If he'd been living in some pathetic apartment, wondering how he was going to pay alimony and child support, maybe he wouldn't have stopped to indulge his sweet tooth.

Maybe, if I'd told, he'd be alive today.

Rachel

❖

My STD PANEL came back clear.

There have been moments in the past two weeks when I've been able to forget my husband had an affair. During the days when the girls don't have school, for example, when we're elbow-deep in organic clay or paint or dirt, I forget.

I dug out part of the backyard to make the girls their own garden, and they're so beautiful out there that I take dozens of pictures... Grace sprinkling the pink impatiens with one of the three tiny watering cans we painted; Rose, laughing and filthy, clutching a seedling in each fist; Charlotte lying in the dirt, singing to her "pupple plant." I'll mat and frame a photo of each girl, and hang the photos in their room. My love for them still fills me with such light and joy my feet almost leave the ground sometimes, and when they snuggle against me, or pick me a flower or leaf, when they draw a picture of me with a big red slash of a smile, I know who I am.

Everywhere else, though, I'm muddled. Three weeks ago, I was a happy, *happy* wife in love with her husband. Now, hatred flashes like corrosive acid, spurting out of me at the very thought or sight of Adam. I hate myself as well, that stupid, *happy* woman who thought that making inventive dinners and wearing pretty clothes would keep this wolf from my door. I never knew I had hate like this in me, and it horrifies me, a consuming monster that leaps and claws at the love I had for him, and for us.

And then sometimes he'll just call to see if I need anything before he comes home, and I forget that he had sex with someone else, and I love him again. Until I remember.

I've called the Tribeca Grand four times this week. The poor woman at the reservations desk is starting to smell a fake, I'm pretty sure, but she's been so kind, as if she knows exactly who I am and how I'll never stay in a hotel like that, certainly not on my own. I've noticed they've updated the pictures. There's a bar in the suite, and in the lobby, for that matter. A long curving couch with pink pillows. That ocean-size white bed. What would I do there? Sit? Cry? Drink pinot grigio and watch *Say Yes to the Dress*?

I bet Emmanuelle would be right at home in that suite.

In the past seventeen days, I've read dozens of articles about infidelity, and we all have the same question, we stupid wives: What does she have that I don't?

In Emmanuelle's case, the answer is pretty clear. Confidence. Style. Amorality. A Brazilian.

I can't think of her. Just can't go there without the rage monster clawing its way right through my rib cage.

My phone dings with a text. Jenny.

She's been collateral damage in this mess. For the first time in my life, it's been hard to talk to my sister. She came over the other afternoon to play with the girls and visit, though we can't talk about *It* with the kids around. I know she wants to help, but what can she do?

I can barely look her in the eye, because then I'll see all the love she has for me there, and I'll lose it.

Tonight, however, she's babysitting, because Adam and I are going to a marriage counselor.

It was one of my ultimatums. That, and me sleeping in the guest room. The girls wanted to know why, so I told them that I had a little cold, which was why my eyes have been wet. They've already adapted, running into my room in the morning and climbing in bed with me, smelling of sweat and, in Charlotte's case, faintly of pee, since she still has to wear a diaper at night. Adam appears in the doorway, looking rested (how dare he sleep so damn well?) and hopeful and slightly sad, making me wonder if he practices that look in the mirror. The girls leap and bounce and beg to be held by their daddy. Whose tongue has been in places I don't want to think about.

And so, my list of ultimatums, trying to prove to myself that Rachel Is a Strong Woman.

Once, I thought I knew exactly what I'd do in the ugly face of infidelity. It was so clear back then. If I couldn't have what my parents had, then I'd rather be single. Divorced. I knew what I deserved, and I wouldn't be one of those pathetic women who settled, who ate or drank or starved herself in her misery, who carries anger like a switchblade, always ready to slice into someone else's happiness.

But I guess I don't know anything anymore.

JENNY COMES OVER at 6:30 p.m. "Hello, my little giraffe babies!" she calls, and the girls wriggle and squeal in delight, wrapping themselves around her.

"Auntie, I'm not a giraffe," Grace says.

"Are you sure?" Jenny asks.

"I am! I'm a giraffe!" Charlotte says, detaching from Jenny's leg and running around the house, whinnying. Rose follows, and Jenny picks Grace up and snuggles her.

Then Adam comes downstairs. "Hey, Jen," he says, and my sister's face hardens.

He ignores that. "Babe, you ready to go?"

As if it's a date. As if we're going to dinner and a movie. As if he's done nothing wrong.

"See you later," I say to my sister. "Bye, girls! I love you!"

I used to say *we* love you, but Adam's on his own tonight. He doesn't get included.

"Love you, princesses!" he says, then holds the door for me.

TWENTY MINUTES LATER, we're in the office of Laney Shields, who has a bunch of letters after her name. I found her by Googling "marriage counselors." She was covered by our insurance, and on her website, certain reassuring words leaped out: *brief, focused, solutions.* And, God, I want a solution.

Laney's office is a building in the backyard of her house—a tiny little playhouse, almost, with three couches and a chair, bookcases and end tables. Lots of boxes of tissues, the good kind with lotion. That strikes me as ominous.

"Come in, come in," she says warmly. I sit on the flowered couch, and to my annoyance, Adam sits next to me, like he's already trying to show what a loving husband he is.

Laney takes the chair across from us. She's in her

fifties with flyaway graying hair and a pleasant face. Wonderful crow's-feet.

"A few things before we start," she says. "You can only come here for scheduled appointments—if you need to reach me urgently, you must call. If I see you on the property without an appointment, the police will be called."

"Jesus," Adam says.

"Well, I had one client appear with a gun several years ago," she says calmly. "There are surveillance cameras all over the property, as well as a state-of-the-art alarm system. I'm sure you're not the types, but it's my policy to inform clients up front."

"Understandable," I murmur.

"Also," she says, "this building is soundproof, because emotions can run high. You don't have to worry about crying or yelling—no one will hear you outside of these walls. However, I have a panic button right here—" she points to the underside of the arm of her chair "—in case things turn physical, and the police will be here in under two minutes."

I *love* her. She's prepared. And clearly, we're not the worst couple she's ever had. We're not going to need the police! We're probably pretty run-of-the-mill for her. Just a cheating husband and his weepy wife. I bet she can fix us in two sessions.

I feel oddly cheered. Adam, on the other hand, is already uncomfortable, shifting next to me. I inch away. He should've gotten his own couch. He's not wanted here.

"Things tend to move faster if you're both honest," she continues. "It can be very painful, but think of it as lancing a boil. Unless you get to the heart of the infection, it won't clear up. It may be hard to hear what the other says, but that's what you're here for."

I liked her more when she was talking about the panic button. Painful boils aren't nearly as fun.

"So tell me what brings you here," Laney says.

Adam and I look at each other. He says nothing. *Asshat.* That's one of Jenny's favorite words, and it's becoming one of mine, too. I wait him out, staring steadily, wondering if he can feel the poison seeping out of my heart.

"Rachel thought we should see someone," he says finally. "We've had some difficulties lately."

"And what do you mean by that?"

He doesn't answer.

"He had an affair," I say. "With a coworker."

"And is this affair still ongoing?" Laney asks.

"No," Adam says.

She nods. "As of right now, do you both feel like you want to stay married? Your answer may change later, but right now, what would you say?"

"Why do you think we're here?" he snaps.

She's unaffected. "Adam, let me state up front that I'm here for both of you. I'm not going to side with Rachel just because you had the affair. It's not my job to make you feel bad about yourself."

That's a shame. Adam's been adored for too long.

"I also think it's important to understand *why* you had the affair. And, Rachel, I don't want you to think of yourself as a victim. You have all the right in the world to be upset and hurt, and you have a vast array of choices to make. The affair has happened, and our goal is to move past that initial hurt and see what kind of solutions will work best for you both. This is focused

counseling with an end goal in mind. It's up to both of
you to decide what that goal is."

"Right," Adam says.

Laney sits back in her chair. "Adam, why don't you
tell me how this affair got started. Rachel? Can you handle hearing about that?"

"Sure," I chirp. But my legs buzz and twitch, like they
want to carry me out of this little playhouse, and fast.

Adam sighs. "Well, Rachel's perfect. Everyone knows
that. Perfect housewife, perfect mother."

"How old are your children?"

"Three and a half," he says. "Girls. Triplets."

"Go on."

"And I guess things got a little boring," he says, and
I actually jump. God, I didn't expect that at all! Boring?
That word sledgehammers me in the chest, and tears
flood my eyes. "I'm sorry!" he says. "Look, it's just…
All we talk about is the girls."

"That's *not* true. I always ask about work, and you—"

"Let him talk, Rachel. Your turn is coming." Laney
smiles kindly, pushes the tissue toward me and nods at
Adam.

"Yeah, so, you know. We've been married for ten
years—" it's nine years "—and she became Holly Haus-
frau, and I just kind of felt myself…losing interest."

Fucking fuckety fuckster. How *dare* he. I wear match-
ing underwear! Lace, even if it itches! Last month, I
read a *Cosmo* article on new techniques in the world of
blow jobs, and I put those techniques to good use! Me!
A mother! And yes, the whole time I worried the girls
would wander in. We don't have locks on our doors.

"Emmanuelle is a woman I work with. Razor-sharp,

incredibly smart, takes no shit from anyone, and she was blatant about wanting it."

"And by *it*, what do you mean?" Laney asks.

"Sex. Fucking. Me." The words are like punches. "At first, I told her I was happily married."

"Did you consider yourself that way?" she asks.

"Yes!" He sounds surprised. He looks at me, sees my stupid, hated tears, and his face changes. He grabs the tissue box and hands it to me. "Oh, babe. Yeah. Just… I don't know. It's not even that I was bored, honey," he says. "That was a poor choice of words. It was…routine, I guess. And Emmanuelle, she…she's like a fantasy. It was porn sex."

"And what do you mean by that, Adam?" Laney asks. I shoot her a dark look, because I for one don't want to know.

"She was really aggressive and, ah, adventurous. And her body is amazing." I can see why Laney Shields has a panic button. The image of me punching Adam in the throat is deeply, deeply satisfying right about now.

He must read my expression. "I mean, your body's great, too, Rach. But…well, you know what I mean."

"You mean I bore your daughters in the three-for-one special because you had a low sperm count, and it took a toll on my body."

"Right. Blame me for the infertility. Dr. Shields, I have a low sperm count. Apparently, my wife wants the world to know."

"I just think it's unfair of you to talk about Emmanuelle's perfect body when having our children made mine less than perfect," I bite out.

"Let Adam talk, Rachel," Laney says calmly.

Adam shoots me a triumphant look, like the teacher

just sided with him. "I guess that's it. Emmanuelle, she's like a porno movie. Rachel is like a wife."

"Probably because I *am* a wife," I snap.

This is the new me, courtesy of my cheating husband. Angry. Curt. Hostile. All things I'm entitled to be, and all things I hate.

"How did you end things with Emmanuelle?" Laney asks.

Adam sits up straighter and looks Laney in the eye. "I told her that I could not keep up an affair with a co-worker when I love my wife. Because I do love Rachel. She's everything to me."

"Except a porno movie," I say.

"Do you have feelings for Emmanuelle?" Laney asks.

He shifts. "Well, yeah. I mean…not love, but…lust. She's funny. She's smart. We operate in the same world."

"How did she take you telling her it was over?" Laney asks.

"She was fine with it," he mumbles. "I think she hoped for more, but—" his voice changes into his country-club voice, firmer and louder "—I would never leave Rachel and the girls." *See what a great guy I am?*

"Why not?" Laney asks.

"Because…" His voice breaks. "Because I love them. I love you, Rachel. You're everything to me. And the girls are, too. I just screwed up. I thought it wouldn't hurt anyone, because…because I didn't think you'd find out. It was never going to be long-term. I was stupid, I know. A kid who wants all the toys." His face scrunches up, and he looks so much like Grace in that moment that my heart gives an unwilling tug. "I love you," he whispers.

"Yay me," I say, and we both laugh for a second, identical, surprised snorts.

"Okay, Rachel, why don't you tell me how you're feeling."

"Well," I say, and suddenly I feel more like my old self. Shy. Embarrassed at having to talk to a stranger. Horrified at the tides of anger and grief and shame that surge without my permission or control.

Grateful for Adam saying what he just did. Grateful and limp with relief.

He loves me. He's staying with me. She was just a fling.

Yeah. Right. And he said you were boring and Emmanuelle is razor-sharp. No one has called you razor-sharp before.

I stiffen. "I'm very angry," I say, and Laney nods and smiles sympathetically. "I…I don't trust him, because the first time I asked about this, he lied. He wanted to have porno sex with Emmanuelle, so he did. I had to get an STD screening last week. That definitely wasn't on my list of things to do. I told the babysitter I was getting a pedicure."

"But you *don't* have an STD. I would never endanger you," Adam says.

"You want a medal?" I look back at Laney. "It's hard to accept that screwing his porno dream was more important than nine years of marriage and three daughters and this precious, beautiful life we've built—"

"You mean, *you've* built," Adam interjects. "Your life. Your vision of precious and beautiful."

"Really? When did you *ever* want anything else before Emmanuelle and her vagina came along? Huh? *You* told me you wanted at least two kids. *You* were all for me being a stay-at-home mom. *You* bought our *house* without even consulting me! So don't give me this 'You've stifled my dreams' bullshit!"

I seem to be yelling. Adam looks stunned, and my face burns, and my legs are shaking, and I can't sit next to him another second. I bolt to the other couch and can't bear to look at my husband.

How did things get so, so wretched?

Laney leans forward. "Do you want to stay married, Rachel? Even knowing that Adam's been unfaithful?"

"I don't know," I whisper. Grabbing a tissue, I press it against my eyes. "I don't know. I kind of hate him right now."

"Well, I love you," Adam says impatiently. "Sex and love are different."

"Fuck you," I say.

"Nice. You sound like your sister."

"Don't you dare talk about my sister."

"Okay," Laney says. "Adam, I want you to do something right now. Look at Rachel and tell her you're sorry."

"I've told her that a hundred times since this happened."

"Since I found out, you mean. You actually tried to guilt-trip me the first time I asked."

"Tell her again, Adam. Really look at her."

He turns to me, and after a second, his caramel eyes soften from irritable to...to love. "I'm so sorry," he whispers. "I really am, Rach."

This is the hard part. The love. I stare back, feeling older than I ever have before.

"That's all we have time for this week," Laney says. "But we're off to a good, solid start, you two."

FOR NO REASON that I can fathom, Adam is chipper in the car. "That went well. I had my doubts, but that went well."

I don't answer. My head is killing me.

"Think I can have my wife back?" he asks, giving me a sidelong smile.

"What?"

"Can we sleep together tonight? I miss you."

"I don't think so, Adam."

He sighs. Taps a finger on the steering wheel. "Then when?"

"Whenever I feel like it. Which I don't." Listen to me. I do kind of sound like Jenny, who's always so quick and sharp.

I miss the old me.

"I meant what I said, sweetheart." Adam's voice is gentle.

"About me being boring, or about you being so sorry?"

"I *am* sorry. Do I have to chant it over and over?"

"Maybe."

"Then I will. I'm sorry. I'm sorry. I love you. Forgive me." His voice holds a hint of amusement, and I'm too tired to be angry about it.

The window is cool against my forehead. A soft rain taps against the windshield. The lovely homes of COH pass by in their tasteful colors, gray and white and yellow, dark green and Colonial red. Pots of pansies and wreaths of forsythia grace doorways, and the lawns are lush and thick.

"Would you mind driving me to the cemetery?" I ask.

"Sure, baby," Adam says. He's back to Considerate Adam, the Adam I love.

He pulls into Eden Hills, the vast, rolling cemetery that serves COH and three other towns. I've always loved coming here. It's only a mile from home. My mother finds it agonizing, and Jenny hasn't come in years, but I visit a couple of times a month and tend Daddy's grave. Just last week, the girls and I were here. They know their grandfather is in heaven, but they haven't asked the difficult question yet—how did Grandpa die. Grace will be the first, I'm sure.

"I'll walk home," I say as Adam pulls up to the gentle hillside where Dad lies.

"You sure, sweetheart? It's raining. Well, you like the rain." He gives me a sad smile.

"I do love you," I tell him. I can't help it. I do, and as Laney said, being honest is going to help. I was honest about the anger; I can be honest about this, as well.

"I love you, too." His eyes get teary again, and it's reassuring. And sad. "Take your time," he adds, clearing his throat. "I'll make sure the girls are tucked in."

"Be nice to Jenny." I open the car door.

"I will. Here. Take my jacket." He reaches back and hands me his windbreaker. "In case you get cold."

I take the coat up to Dad's grave and watch Adam pull away, then spread out his jacket and sit on the wet grass, the coppery smell of rain against granite oddly reassuring. Some of the graves here date back to pre–Revolutionary War days; Mrs. Brewster's family, the Hales—as in Nathan—have a mausoleum, in fact. There are different sections connected by twisting roads, huge old trees, statues of angels. The entire cemetery is enclosed by an iron fence. When the girls are older, I'll bring them here to learn to ride their bikes.

If we're still living in our house, that is.

I brush off a few maple seed pods that have fallen on Daddy's headstone.

I'm fairly sure my father would have been furious by all this; he would've punched Adam right in the face when he heard. Dad and Mom were that magical couple who never lost interest in each other, who still exchanged those private, smiling looks when they thought Jenny and I weren't watching, the ultimate united front. All I ever wanted in a relationship was to emulate my parents. To be as good a mother as my mom was before the shooting, to find a man who'd never tire of me.

Mom and Dad were married for seventeen years, together for twenty. Twenty years together seems like an eternity to me right now.

It sure would be nice to have my father right now. To get a hug from your dad makes you feel safer than just about anything in the world, and in his arms, you don't have to be brave or strong or selfless. You're daddy's little girl again, and just knowing he's there makes everything a little better, even if it doesn't really change anything.

I hear a hissing sound and look up. A man is riding a bicycle down the cemetery lane, the wheels slicing through puddles. It's Leo, Jenny's super, who was so nice to me that night.

"Hey," he says, slowing to a stop.

"Hi, Leo. Kind of a wet night for a bike ride, isn't it?"

"It's not so bad." He gets off his bike, puts down the kickstand and comes up to join me. Reads the headstone, which says Robert James Tate, Beloved Husband, Adored Father.

"I'm sorry," he says, sitting next to me on Adam's jacket. I haven't been this close to a man other than

Adam since... Heck. Since my obstetrician, and not counting him, since work, when Gus Fletcher, who had smiley eyes and flirted with every woman in the entire building, would lean down next to my computer and ask me to tweak a design.

"Thanks," I say belatedly. "He was a great father."

Leo nods. "Everything okay with you?" He gives me a sidelong glance. "Stupid question. Sorry."

"I guess Jenny told you."

"I kind of figured it out. How are your girls?"

"They're fine. They're wonderful."

"I hope to meet them sometime."

"You're great with kids, I hear."

His mouth pulls up. He has one of those faces that's not quite handsome—he's a little too angular—but is all the more appealing because of it. "I like kids."

"Do you have any of your own?" I ask.

"No."

"And you're not married."

"Nope. Don't fix me up with your sister, though. She's already half in love with me." He grins full-on, and I find that I'm laughing.

"Why would that be a bad thing?" I ask.

"Oh, I don't know. I'm not the most stable or serious of men."

"Sounds like a line."

"It is. But a sincere line just the same." He runs a hand through his hair, which is soaked. No helmet. Tsk.

"Can I ask you a question, Leo?"

"Sure."

"Will you be really honest?"

"You bet."

"How pretty am I?"

His eyebrows pop up. "Um…very."

"On a scale of one to ten?"

"At the moment, 8.75. When you're dry, 9.25. Your hair isn't great in the rain."

I push the wet hair back. "True. That's generous of you."

"No. Just accurate."

"Where would Jenny fall on that scale?"

"Three."

"Oh, please. She's a ten." He shrugs, rather adorably. "You sure you don't want to date her?"

"I don't want to date anyone. But thank you." He glances toward the gate. "Can I walk you home?"

"No, thanks. I could use a little alone time." Alone time. It sounds so juvenile. *Mommy needs some alone time*, I often say to the girls when I'm in the bathroom, but they push right in and play happily at my feet as I do my thing. The bathroom has become very communal.

"Okay, then." Leo stands up and offers me his hand.

It's a nice hand, very big and warm, those long pianist fingers. "Jenny says you went to Juilliard," I say.

"Yes. Piano performance and composition."

"I'd love to hear you play sometime."

"I'm really out of practice." He smiles a little, and I find that I like him a lot, even without knowing him. And I'm comfortable with him, which hardly ever happens with me and a man.

Leo walks with me to the cemetery gate, asks me again if I don't want an escort on the mean streets of Cambry-on-Hudson. "I'm fine. But it was nice to see you," I tell him honestly.

"You, too, Rachel." He gets on his bike and starts off. "Nine-point-two-five," he calls over his shoulder.

"Wear a helmet next time," I call back. The mother in me.

"Eight-point-seven-five in the rain," I murmur. Not bad for someone who'll turn forty soon. Yes, my sister is a ten with her shiny hair and well-deep eyes, that wry smile always ready to spring, her perfect skin.

And that whore Emmanuelle, also a ten, though in a very different, more blatant way. She reminds me of a model in the *New York Times* magazine—slightly terrifying, perfectly beautiful, angles and spareness everywhere except for her big, juicy, hungry mouth.

I don't hurry home. I want my alone time to last a little longer.

Jenny

❖━━━◆━━━❖

"DON'T JUDGE ME," Rachel says as soon as I pick up the phone. It's Monday morning, my day off.

"I hate when people say that. It's like saying, 'No offense, but you're so ugly' or something."

I'm drinking coffee by the sink and spying on Leo, who's got a pile of wood and a saw that he barely seems to know how to hold. "Hang on, Rach." I mute the phone a second and bang on the window. "Stop before you lose a finger!" He drops the saw instantly and smiles up at me, as if he was waiting for me to intervene.

"I'm back," I tell my sister.

"I need you to come with me somewhere," Rachel says. "But don't try to talk me out of it, okay? I'll be over in twenty minutes." She hangs up, knowing I'll agree. I admit, I'm curious. She's not usually so bossy. It's kind of refreshing.

I go down my front steps and into Leo's courtyard. "Why are you trying to mutilate yourself?" I ask. "Wouldn't that hurt your career and all?"

"Good morning, Jenny."

Damn. He's just so...deliciously adorable. I want to feed him. I want to cuddle him. I want to kiss him for hours.

The knowing eyebrow rises.

"Just because you *are* a tool doesn't mean you should use one," I say before he can whip out the old "eye-fucking" line.

"That's a good one." He's wearing what he wears most days, except when he goes to see his mom—jeans and a T-shirt. He has quite an array of T-shirts. This one is faded gray with faint blue letters spelling out Starfleet Academy. Such a dork. Then again, I know exactly what Starfleet Academy is, so I'm in the same dork boat.

"What are you making? Or, more aptly, what aren't you making?" Upon closer inspection, the pile of wood resembles a triangle. A crooked, timid triangle.

"It's a ramp for Loki."

I glance at the dog, who appears to be dead. "A ramp to…heaven?" I suggest.

"To my bed, which is kind of the same thing." Leo winks. "Or so they tell me."

"And by *they*, you mean foul-tempered dogs?" I put my foot on the "ramp." It collapses.

"I flunked wood shop," Leo says.

"You don't say. Why can't you just lift him up on the bed?" I ask.

Leo hesitates. "He has arthritis, and it hurts him if I pick him up." He looks away from me.

I get it. He doesn't want to put the dog to sleep, even if Loki is circling the drain as it is. I try to think of something nice to say about the dog and come up empty, so I crouch down and pet his ear. He growls at me. "He's quite a character," I manage.

"He's the best."

Yeah. Well, I can't go that far, but it's kind of sweet,

Leo's devotion to Old Yeller here. "My sister and I have plans today. Can I fix this later?" I ask.

"That'd be great, Jenny." For once, he's not flirting or tragic, his two resting states. "Tell your sister I said hi."

On cue, Rachel pulls up, waves, and off I go. "How bad is the crush on him?" she asks as I buckle in.

"Oh, pretty bad," I say. "He's unfairly attractive."

"I saw him at the cemetery the other night. Did he tell you? He was out for a bike ride."

I've seen Leo go out on his bike. I haven't seen him drive, oddly enough. Then again, he may well go out when I'm at work, and when I'm home, he's got his students, tormenting me with "Three Blind Mice" and "Pop Goes the Weasel" and "Let It Go." He's already warned me that around Christmastime, I may want to buy some swords for seppuku.

"So where are we going, Rach?" I ask.

To hell, she doesn't say, but ten minutes later, I'm in hell. Or, as it's known, Monarca MedAesthetics & Youth Restoration LLC, part of a beautiful shopping complex on the edge of Cambry-on-Hudson.

"You do not need this," I say firmly. "Rachel. Don't let Adam make you feel unattractive. Is that what this is?"

"Don't judge me," she answers blithely, closing the minivan door. "I'm only here for a consultation."

"You're perfect! You're beautiful! Rachel, you get carded when we go out! Everyone thinks I'm the older sister."

"I'm feeling a little…frumpy, that's all."

"So buy some green nail polish. You don't need anything done to yourself."

She turns to me, and her face is unexpectedly furious. "I want to see the plastic surgeon. Okay? I thought it would be easier with you here, but if you're going to be a pain, then leave."

Yikes. "I'm sorry. It's just that I love you and think you're beautiful."

"I know. Thank you." She takes a deep breath, shoots me an apologetic glance. "Look. Obviously, my ego has taken a hit. I'm just…curious. My friend Elle had a little work done—"

"She had some big work done. Those things are like cannonballs."

"—and even before this, I noticed I was looking a little tired. I've been thinking about it."

"Really? Since when?"

"Jenny, I'm allowed to have thoughts without immediately picking up the phone and calling you. Are you going to be a pain here? Or are you going to be supportive?"

"Uh…supportive. Sorry. Let's go!" I fake a smile.

Rachel has told me just about everything since finding that picture on Adam's phone. I know about the counseling session. I know she told him to ask Emmanuelle to get transferred, and he said he couldn't do that. I know she called AT&T, Verizon and Comcast to see if he has another phone. I know she broke their wedding picture, and got it reframed. I know she got a clean result from the STD panel. I know she deliberately oversalted his dinner the other night, and he ate it anyway.

But she's never once brought up plastic surgery.

The doctor's office is as dark as a cave. The windows are frosted, and there's a code to punch in. It feels more like we're going into witness protection than a doctor's office. When my eyes adjust, I can see that it's actually quite lovely in here. There's a huge dispenser of lemon-and-cucumber water and some hot water for tea, several tasteful black couches and cube end tables. Birdsong twitters from unseen speakers. A faux waterfall gushes behind the reception desk, reminding me that I had three cups of coffee this morning.

Rachel whispers to the receptionist, her shoulders tight, smiling hard to counter her shyness...and maybe the humiliation she feels at being here. It's hardly original, is it? Husband has affair, wife decides to get some work done. Except Rachel isn't the plastic-surgery type.

The soft-voiced and beautiful young woman checks Rachel in, and we take our seats. "Hi," says a woman next to me. I recoil, then scratch my nose to cover. She looks like someone took a baseball bat to her. Her face is swollen and plum-colored; her hair is matted. She's wearing pajamas and slippers. One of her feet is hugely swollen, and tubes snake out of the bottom of her shirt.

"Hi," I say, remembering to speak. Rach is staring at a *Martha Stewart* magazine, pretending to be invisible.

"Are you getting work done?" the poor, poor woman asks.

"No! Nope. Not yet. Maybe. Someday. I don't know."

"Well, Dr. L. is great," she says. "I'm just sorry I waited this long."

"How...how long?"

"I should've done this when I was sixty," she says, ventriloquist-like in her ability not to move her lips. "I'm eighty-two, can you believe it?"

She's actually ageless, given that her purple face is stretched tighter than an eggplant.

"So what did you have done?" I ask, unable to help myself.

"The whole package," she says. "Got my eyelids done, some Botox, a little filler, chin implant, cheekbones, got my lips done, neck lift, breast implants, tummy tuck, ass lift."

"Oh…wow," I whisper. I can't imagine the *pain*—let alone the cost—of all those procedures. I think she might be smiling at me. Or grimacing. An ass lift? At eighty-two? I plan on proudly letting my ass drag when I'm eighty-two. I sure as hell wouldn't—

"I say go for the whole package. No need in coming back ten or twelve times. Just have them knock you out and go for it."

"So are you in a lot of pain?" I ask my new best friend.

"Agonizing," she answers. "I won't lie. I was hit by a car when I was sixteen. This hurts more. I was begging for morphine the first three weeks."

My eyelids flutter. I've never been brave with pain.

"Rachel Carver?" a nurse calls.

Rach puts down the magazine and stands up, running her hands over the front of her dress.

I scramble up after her. "Did you *hear* that?" I hiss. "She was begging for morphine!"

"Can you just relax, please?"

"Rachel, that woman looked like she was attacked by gorillas."

She doesn't answer. I'm being an ass, but come on! My sister does not want this, I'm almost positive.

The nurse shows us into a spacious exam room, much nicer than the regular doctor's office, where you practically need to sit on each other's laps. Rachel is given a soft terry-cloth robe, and when she's changed, the doctor comes in, a very normal-looking woman, which I find reassuring. Maybe around sixty, a pleasantly big nose, bags under her eyes. "Hi, I'm Dr. Louper," she says. "Rachel, right? So nice to meet you. So you're interested in the Mommy Makeover?"

"Mmm-hmm," my sister says.

"And why now?"

Why indeed.

"Well, I'll be forty in a couple weeks," Rachel says, her voice shaking a little.

"You look great for forty!" The double-edged compliment—*forty is when you look old and haggard and flaccid, but you hardly do!* "The most important thing to remember is that this should be for you. If it makes you feel better about yourself, why not go ahead, right? You have three daughters, it says here, so like most women, I bet you put yourself last." She smiles kindly. "This would be something just for you to enjoy for years to come."

Rachel looks reassured. I don't roll my eyes. But I want to.

"Let's have a look, then," Dr. Louper says.

For the next fifteen minutes, Rachel is examined as if Dr. Louper is about to buy a racehorse. I'm surprised she doesn't ask Rachel to turn her head and cough, frankly. My sister's stomach, breasts, thighs, ass are pinched and poked and lifted. "So we've got sagging here, a little drooping here, some cellulite here. And of course, the loose skin here—you had triplets, so no wonder! You're a superhero!"

"She is indeed," I say.

Dr. Louper smiles. "We can do a little tummy tuck and get rid of that little bit of extra skin, move your belly button up to here, tighten everything up so you look like a teenager, because honestly, you don't have that much extra weight."

"She has *no* extra weight," I say, unable to stop myself.

"Your sister's right. And then for your breasts, I'd recommend a breast lift to get the girls back where they were, maybe some subtle implants if you'd like to go a bit bigger." She smiles reassuringly, but I can't get Eggplant Woman out of my mind. "And while we've got you on the table, we can do a little lipo on the thighs. You barely need anything. But a lot of women these days are doing that and then having some of the fat injected into their labia to plump things up down there."

Yes. So Rachel can enjoy that for years to come, because what woman doesn't fret over this? After all, don't we all walk around with mirrors in our panties, making sure our labia looks plump enough? I try to fix my face, but I'm fairly sure my disgust shows.

"We can even do a little vaginal tightening to enhance sexual pleasure for both you and your husband."

My sister bursts into tears.

Thank *God*.

"Please give us a few minutes," I say, taking my sister in my arms. The doctor looks confused, but takes her evil clipboard and leaves.

"Rachel," I say, hugging her tight. "Oh, my poor honeybun."

She's really sobbing now.

"You don't need anything changed about you," I say, my voice shaking.

"I know," she whispers. "I just can't... I can't help... I hate myself for coming here, but I can't help it! Emmanuelle is so *beautiful*, Jenny! She's so scary beautiful! She's Maleficent beautiful."

I want to say *so what* or *who cares* or *that shouldn't matter*. But of course it does matter to my sister. "I bet she's not that beautiful."

"She is," my sister says.

"Well, she has a very ugly vagina," I say, and my sister bursts into that mixture of laughter and crying. "And she's a whore," I add.

My sister gives me a watery smile. "I'm so glad you say all the things I can't," she says, wiping her eyes.

Dr. Louper opens the door. "Is everything okay?" she asks.

"Yes," Rachel says. "I'm sorry. I'm just not ready for this."

"That's completely understandable. You have to do this for the right reasons," the doctor says kindly. "Come back if you ever change your mind."

I TAKE MY sister out for an early lunch and tell her about some of my clients—the Russian girl who wants to wear a dress completely covered in Swarovski crystals, no matter that it will be so heavy she'll barely be able to walk in it; the bride with the EE bra size who wept when I told her it would be no problem to make her a dress.

"And Kimber? How did that go?" Rach asks.

"Oh, interesting appointment, that one. Mrs. Brewster wants her in a long-sleeved, high-necked ball gown. Not a centimeter of skin showing anywhere. The pictures she brought in were so ugly my eyes bled. Kimber is being an incredible sport about it, but I doubt very much it's her dream gown."

"Jared is really crazy about her. Kimber, that is."

"Well, she lights up every time she says his name."

"Think they'll last?" Rachel says, toying with a lettuce leaf.

"I do, actually." After so many brides, I have a good sense about these things.

"Do you think Adam and I will last?" she asks.

"I...I don't know. Do you think so?"

"I have to give him a chance," she says. "Right?"

I think of her tears an hour ago. Of the STD panel and the five days it took for the results to come in. "No, Rachel. You don't. You deserve better."

Gratitude flickers across her face, fast as a hummingbird, and then is gone. "I love my life," she says, her voice so soft I can barely hear her, and it just breaks my heart.

Then she perks up, or fakes perking up, more accurately. "You have a date tonight! Jimmy Grant, right?"

"Right. He'd better be normal, Rach, or you'll pay."

She grins, and it's almost sincere. Jimmy is the divorced dad whose kid goes to the same nursery school as the girls. "He's very normal. And he's pretty cute, too. Could be the one."

That's my sister. Her life is in the shitter, but she still wants me to find a happily ever after.

RACHEL AND I pick up the girls, and I spend an hour playing bucking bronco with all three of them (and probably rupturing a few disks). Then I head for home. I don't want to run into Adam, who's been coming home early, Rachel says, and I did promise Leo I'd make that ramp. And, of course, there is the date.

I went back to Manhattan the other day for the final fitting on a lovely woman who viewed her wedding dress with the perfect blend of joy and deprecation. I'd had to let out the seams a little bit to accommodate her growing belly—three months along, but already showing. She's forty-three. She and her fiancé are thrilled about the baby. See? It's not too late for me, seven years younger.

Anyway, the thing that surprised me was how the city—The City—felt both foreign and familiar. I knew to get off the West Side Highway before Fourteenth Street; I knew where to find a parking space on Greene Street. I knew to stop at Benny's Burritos to pick up dinner, because lukewarm Benny's is still better than anything you can get in a hundred-mile radius.

But in less than a month, New York is no longer mine. The city always seemed alive to me, a great, jagged dragon sitting on its jewels—the unexpected alley garden on the Upper West Side, welcoming you to sit and rest; the homeless man on Madison Avenue who offered critiques of your outfits for five bucks; the brownstone on East Eighty-first street where no one lived, but which could be accessed by the garden door, so you could wander the empty rooms as if you owned the place. Central Park at sunrise in June, a golden paradise filled with birdsong against the reassuring sound of fire sirens…reassuring because New York's Bravest were on their way.

What I didn't quite expect was that as soon as I left Manhattan behind, the beneficent, regal creature forgot me. It tolerated me when I was a student of eighteen, it gave me my chance, it celebrated me when I made it, and it forgot me the second I drove over the Henry Hudson Bridge. You're always just a foster child in the city that never sleeps. The second you go, someone else takes your room.

And though it was hard to picture, I'm glad. It's an

almost shameful confession. I love my hometown more than I thought I would. I love the buildings and the old trees, the little alleys between houses, the tiny backyards. I know where the tree roots buckle the sidewalk, and I know that the middle Ortega girl has a beautiful voice, that the cat who climbs the tree outside my bedroom window belongs to the Capistranos. I know the old guys who sit outside the barbershop downtown playing chess—Miles and Ben—and I know that Luciano's has better takeout eggplant parm than Firenze, which is three times more expensive.

I know that if impressive music seeps out of Number 11 Magnolia, as it does now, Evander James has a lesson. Leo has some fairly proficient students, and he has some abject beginners, and then he has Evander.

Heavy, ominous notes crash from inside Leo's apartment. I stand at the gate and watch the boy as his hands fly across the keyboard, his entire body playing, arms, shoulders, body moving with the sounds. His face drawn with intensity and fervor. It's like watching a force of nature, like watching an electrical current move through him.

Even I can see that he's special.

Leo sits behind him and to one side, his arms folded, watching his pupil's hands, a slight frown of concentration. He glances up to me, winks, then looks back at Evander.

The music stops, and the boy sits there for a minute, reverent and silent, then turns to Leo, who leans forward and says something, pointing to the music. Then they both get up, and a second later come out into the courtyard.

"Hello, Harriet the Spy," Leo says.

"Hello, Maestro," I say to Evander.

"*He's* the maestro," Evander says in a near whisper.

"Is he? He looks like Voldemort to me." Evander smiles at this. Leo, too, and there's that delicious tug in my uterus.

"Evander's gonna hang around for a while," Leo says, glancing up as a mother and child approach.

"Leo! Hello! So good to see you!" It's one of the Hungry Moms, as I've come to think of them—they who always carry food and look at Leo with voracious eyes. (Hey. At least I've never offered him food.) Hungry Mom is dragging along little Sansa or Renfield, a miserable-looking girl of about ten, and carries an expensive-looking picnic basket in one hand. She cuts me a cursory look, then decides I don't exist. "Listen," she purrs up at Leo, "don't say a word, but I made too much for dinner, so I brought some over for you. In fact, Renley here—" that's it, Renley, not Renfield "—is dying for you to come over for dinner one night! And not to brag, but I have taken quite a few courses from the Culinary Institute!"

Renley looks close to death by boredom.

"Hi, Renley. Did you practice this week?" Leo asks.

"No." She glares at Evander. "What's *he* doing here? He's *poor*. He can't afford lessons."

Evander looks at the ground.

"He's my star pupil," Leo says, his voice hard. "The best student I've ever had and probably ever will have."

"Now, Leo," Hungry Mom says, "it's not really fair of you to tell Renley that she's not as good as—"

"But she's not," Leo says. "Renley, you will never, ever be as good as Evander. I could lie to you and say you have talent and you just need to keep at it, but the truth is, you don't. Evander, on the other hand, can already play Bach and Chopin and Debussy, and you're still hacking your way through 'Ragtime Raggler' after three months. So show some respect, or find another teacher."

Well, if there was any doubt I was half in love with Leo, it's gone now. Evander's eyes are wide.

Renley looks at Evander. "I'm sorry." She sounds as if she means it.

"You can't talk to my daughter like that!" Hungry Mom yelps.

"I just did," Leo says.

"We're done here," she says frostily. "Renley, let's go!"

"Yay! Thank you, Mr. Killian! No offense, but I only took piano because my mom said I had to. Bye, Evander!"

Evander looks confused.

They leave, the mother hissing, Renley skipping. "There goes dinner," Leo says. "Well. Want to play some more, kid? Miss Jenny and I have a dog ramp to build."

"Can I help?" the boy asks.

"Sure," I say. "You can make sure Leo doesn't cut off any important parts."

Leo has left the supplies where they are. The pieces of wood are equal and make sense: four two-by-fours for the frame, a piece of plywood and four strips of lighter wood so Loki won't slide. A gangplank.

"Who cut these for you?" I ask.

"The woman at the hardware store," Leo says.

"I could tell it wasn't you." He smiles. "Evander, hold on to this, honey," I say, handing him a strip of wood and picking up the hammer. "I'm going to nail this one in, and then you can have a turn."

The boy is just beautiful, ridiculously curly lashes, the green eyes of Derek Jeter. He'll be a heartbreaker someday. All that and a prodigy, too.

"How come you know how to do this and Mr. Killian doesn't?" he asks.

"Some of us are geniuses in other ways, Evander," Leo says, sitting in his lounge chair and stretching out his long legs. "Cut me some slack." Loki collapses beside him. I check to make sure his furry chest is still moving.

"My job is all about putting things together," I tell Evander. "I'm a dress designer. Wedding dresses, mostly."

Evander flicks a look at me. He's still very shy, even though I've seen him four or five times now. I hammer in the nail, then hold the hammer out. "Your turn."

He takes the hammer carefully and gives the nail a tentative tap, then another. "Doing great," I confirm. *Tap tap tap.* He seems unwilling to give the nail a good smack. Fifty or so taps later, the nail is in. "Good job."

"Thank you," he says, a little smile lifting his lips.

"Can I ask you a question?"

"No, I'm sorry, I won't marry you," Leo says. "And Evander's a little young yet, right, pal?"

This gets a full-fledged smile from the boy. I give Leo a tolerant look, then hammer in another nail. "What does it feel like to be able to play the way you do?"

Evander doesn't say anything for a minute, just looks at the ground. Then he lifts his eyes to me. "I can feel the music inside me," he says in such a soft voice I can hardly hear him. "It gets bigger and bigger, and then it comes into my chest and down my arms and it gets out through my fingers."

I glance at Leo, who's listening closely.

"Does it hurt?" I ask.

Evander laughs. "No. It's my friend. My best friend."

"Do you play a lot?"

"Not really," he says. "Maybe five or six hours a day. I wish I didn't have to go to school, because the music quiets down then."

There were days for me like that, when I was learning design, days when I opted to stay up till four in the morning rather than stop sewing, when my back would audibly creak when I stood up.

Lately, not so much. Maybe it's just that I've been at it awhile and the thrill isn't new anymore.

I take the hammer again and show Evander the next step.

A half hour later, Evander's mom pulls up in a battered Honda, a dent in the front fender, a few rust spots near the wheels. "Hey, there, baby," she says, and Evander's face lights up. He runs inside to get his stuff, and Leo unfolds from the chair—the man is tall—and goes to speak to her. I don't hear what they say, but Mrs. James smiles and when Evander flies past me with a "Bye, Miss Jenny," I can't help the familiar ache of love and envy and longing.

Yes, I want a child. A little boy like Evander, shy and a little strange and solitary and lovely. A girl like serious, smart Grace, or ebullient Rose, or gentle Charlotte. Even a girl like Renley. I could whip her into shape in a matter of days, I think. Teach her manners and kindness. I'd be a loving, firm, fun mom. I'd teach my kids that of course they're special, but no more special than any

other child. My kids would go to bed early. They'd eat
vegetables. We'd cuddle and read together, right in the
second bedroom where the light comes in each morning
like a blessing and my husband would bring me a cup
of coffee, and he'd—

"Jenny."

"What?" I snap out of my reverie.

Mrs. James is gone, and Leo stands in front of me.
The fact that I'm on my knees makes things a wee bit
awkward, since I'm staring right at his groin, so I clam-
ber up.

"You almost done?" he asks. "I have to go out."

"Me, too, actually. And yes. All done." His eyes look
gray today rather than blue. A reflection of the sky, probably.

"You have that date," he says.

"I do. Yep." He doesn't say anything. "My sister fixed
me up with a friend of theirs. We're going to St. Arpad's
in Ossining." It was Jimmy's suggestion; he lives there,
though his ex-wife and kids live here in COH.

"St. Arpad's?" Leo asks.

"Yeah. It's Hungarian."

"I know. That's where I'm going, too."

"Really! Do you have a date, Mr. Recreation Only? I
thought you were more of the booty-call type. A date!"
Yeah, yeah, I'm jealous. "Great! I can check her out.
Or we can double, how's that? Want to drive together?
Maybe we should have a code word if things go south."
I may be trying a little too hard here.

Leo is not amused. "It's not a date. Just someone I
used to know." He's not looking at me. "Listen, do me
a favor, okay? Don't talk to me at the restaurant. And
don't wave, okay?"

My head jerks back. "Wow. Nice, Leo."

"She's kind of…difficult. If you could pretend not to know me, that'd be great."

"Sure. I won't make direct eye contact, either. And I'll back out of the room, bowing. And maybe I can scrub your toilet for you, since the dog ramp is already built."

"It's complicated. I just don't want you to meet her."

"Oh, shut up." I drop the hammer on the flagstone and stomp up my stairs. Slam the door to emphasize my point.

Don't talk to me. Why would he say that, huh? I'm a tenant in the building he manages—badly, I might add. He hasn't fixed a damn thing here, and the water in my shower is still either scalding or ice-cold. I *thought*, given the number of times he's dropped in, the number of times we've talked this past month, that we were kinda sorta friends.

I guess not. Not if I'm not allowed to wave.

St. Arpad's is dark and muted and old-world, with stooped, white-haired waiters in three-piece suits muttering in Hungarian (I assume), shuffling silently past with fragrant trays of food. Jimmy and I are already in a banquette booth, and he kissed me on the cheek in the foyer. He's quite good-looking, which I already knew, thanks to Twitter, Facebook and Google. But in person, he's even better. Brown hair, blue eyes, medium height. He smells nice, too. Armani, I think. His hands are clean.

That being said, I'm not sure I could pick him out of a lineup, because five tables away is Leo, deep in conversation with a woman whose hair is beautiful and straight and blond. She's quite pretty, I noted as I walked past, and she's wearing red. *Someone I used to know,* my ass. Red is *such* a date color. Otherwise, I can't see much, thanks to the fat guy with the shiny bald head who blocks my view of her, but not of Leo, who is facing me—but not making eye contact, of course. That might intimate that I matter.

He looks wretched. Even when he smiles, he looks like his dog just died. And even though I've been forbidden to acknowledge him, that stupid sad beautiful face *does* something to me.

The tiny waiter, who looks to be about ninety-seven years old, comes over and wheezes through what I assume are the specials. *Szabolcs*, his nametag says. I can't understand a word he says. He may be telling me that his great-great-grandchildren are in the kitchen being gnawed on by a pack of wolves. I nod and smile. "I'll have the chicken," I say. Szabolcs asks something that has a lot of *sht* and *tsz* and *ejht* sounds in it. "Sounds good," I tell him. This is how people end up eating cats, I believe.

"Goulash for me," Jimmy says.

Szabolcs creeps away. I'd offer to carry him, but I don't want to make a scene.

"So you're divorced," Jimmy says.

"Yes. Yep. About a year and a half now."

"Sucks." He pours himself more wine; I've barely touched mine. We ordered a bottle. It was cheaper, Jimmy said.

"No, it was all very civilized. But thank you." I smile awkwardly.

Jimmy reaches across the table and takes my hand. "Something incredibly sympathetic and sensitive yet masculine," he says—forgive me, my imagination isn't really having its best night. *The touch of his hand sends a tingle down my arm. "I feel the exact same way," I answer, and for the rest of the night, we can't look away from each other, and we laugh and he walks me home and says he can't believe we hit it off like this, and—*

Nope. It's not working. Not with Leo sitting across the way.

All of a sudden, I miss Owen so much it's like a knife wound. Somehow, I haven't thought of him in a day or two, not consciously, and I *ache* for him, his funny, boyish hair, his sweet smile. Yearning for my old life reaches up and slaps me hard.

I wonder what he and Ana-Sofia are doing right now. Owen was—is—a great cook. He's probably making dinner while his wife nurses Natalia, who undoubtedly hasn't cried once since her birth and is in fact mastering her third language. Because Ana-Sofia is from a country less constipated than my own, she'll accept a glass of wine—so funny that these provincial Americans think everything is bad for you!—and Owen will kiss her gently upon the lips.

When we met, Owen wasn't that great a kisser. I taught him a thing or two.

Jimmy drinks. I grope around for first-date conversation and come up empty. "Nice place," I say.

"Mmm," Jimmy answers.

Leo coughs. I don't look over.

Eventually, Szabolcs brings our dinners, and lo and behold, mine smells like heaven, chicken swimming in a golden gravy, heavily sprinkled with cheerful paprika, a mountain of mashed potatoes to one side like an island. Jimmy digs right in to his goulash.

Thus, cheered by food, as always, I have a burst of

conversational energy. "And what about you, Jimmy? You're also divorced, right?"

"Yes." He says nothing more, just washes down a mouthful of stew with his wine. That's his entire answer. I sigh and take a bite of the chicken dish, which is unbelievably rich and succulent and delicious. I wonder if I could somehow drink the gravy. I wonder if Jimmy would notice if I did.

I ask if he likes to read. No. (Seriously? And he admits that?) I ask if he watches TV. Yes, mixed martial arts. He doesn't ask what I watch. I ask if he has siblings. Yes. Does he like any sports, I ask? He guesses so.

Shit.

Meanwhile, I can't stop looking at Leo. It's not my fault! He's right in my line of vision. Short of holding up my hand to block him, I almost have to see him.

His hair looks beautiful. It's ridiculous that a man can have hair as beautiful as his, golden brown with the close-cropped curls, like a Roman emperor or something. It grows straight off his forehead, and he keeps it short. If he let it grow, he'd have Disney princess hair, I swear to God. He's not eating much. Doesn't seem to be drinking, either, just listening to the woman in the red dress and nodding occasionally.

Jimmy, on the other hand, has just poured the last of the wine into his glass. "You gonna drink that?" he asks me.

"Yeah," I say, moving the glass closer to me.

"Figures." He chugs half of his wine. "So your sister's the one with the triplets, right?" he asks, his voice a little loud. Will have to make sure he's not driving. Sigh.

"Yes. Three girls. They're the light of my life." I smile pleasantly.

"Oh, great."

"How about you? Any nieces or nephews?"

"No, I mean great, *another* woman who wants kids. I mean, isn't that why you're here?"

"Um…excuse me?" I glance around, aware that several tables of diners have gone silent.

"You want kids?"

"Well, I… Yes. I do. Yep. But that's not why—"

"Fucking A." Jimmy hiccups. "So. You want me for my fluids, is that it?"

"What? Um…no!"

"Yes, you do! You want me for sperm!"

"Can you keep your voice down, Jimmy?"

"You know what? I'm a person, okay? A flesh-and-blood person!"

"I'm aware of that."

"Are you? Because it sounds like you just want me for my *sperm*. You've been on my Facebook page, haven't you?"

"No!" I mean, I *have*, but there was nothing about sperm, for the love of God.

"How about a little romance first, huh? Can we at least learn each other's last names before you ask for a genetics workup?"

It appears I've hit a nerve. Or, more likely, Jimmy is both drunk and an ass. "Okay." I stand up. "Lovely meeting you. I'll leave my half for dinner with the maître d'."

"And I'll leave *you* a tissue sample so you can see if I've got what you're looking for."

"You don't," I say. It's a good line, but he's still ranting, so no one gets to hear it. Too bad.

I walk to the front of the restaurant. One of the busboys wiggles his eyebrows at me. Great. I am now *that woman who wants sperm.* Indeed, there is a murmuring as I walk past. Leo, however, fails to acknowledge me. He certainly doesn't come to my rescue. Not that I need rescuing, but if he jumped up and said, "Hey, Jenny!" and kissed my cheek, that would sure be nice.

The maître d' isn't at his station. I wait, feeling the eyes of the entire restaurant on me. Ah. Here comes someone. Zoltan, the nametag says. He makes my waiter look like an adolescent.

"Everything delicious, yes?" he wheezes.

"Yes. Thank you. I just need to pay for my half of our bill."

He sighs. "Your waiter? Who?"

I have no freakin' idea how to pronounce my waiter's name. Indeed, trying to picture his nametag just results in a blur of consonants. "I'm not sure. His name had a *C* in it. And an *S*. And a *Z*."

Meanwhile, Jimmy is delivering a fiery speech on how men are no longer needed or valued in society except for their tiny little swimmers, and how if women had their way, all men would be chained in cells and only taken out when a woman was ovulating. Which actually sounds pretty good about now.

"How about if I leave sixty bucks?" I suggest. "Will that cover it?"

"I come back soon," Zoltan whispers, then shuffles away.

Yeah. I forgot how bad dating sucked.

And now Leo and Red Dress are approaching. I stare stonily ahead, hoping Leo can read the "piss off" message I'm trying so hard to convey. I scratch my nose with my middle finger in case he misses the point.

"Well, it was so, so great to see you again," Red Dress says. "You look good."

"You, too," Leo says. "Uh, why don't I walk you to your car?" He darts me a look, which I pretend not to notice.

"Just go to a sperm bank, why don't you?" Jimmy shouts.

The blonde puts on her raincoat (Burberry, so boring, and does she have to be so damn pretty?). Then she takes Leo's face in her hands and I stiffen, bracing for their kiss.

They don't kiss. Leo takes her hands and sort of holds on to them, keeping her from moving in closer. She doesn't seem put off, just gazes at him. Tears fill her eyes.

"Leo—" she says.

"I know," he interrupts. "Thank you. Beth, thank you. Really. I'll walk you out." He gives me another look and holds the door for her. Who cares? I don't care.

"Get a turkey baster, bitch!" Jimmy shouts. Several elderly Hungarians have Jimmy by the arms and are slowly dragging him toward the back, where hopefully they'll beat him with rubber hoses or empty sour cream containers or whatever other weapons they may have at their disposal.

Szabolcs, my old friend, creeps up to the desk. "Dinner on house," he whispers.

"Okay. Great. Thank you." So standing in front of the entire restaurant, being shouted at, that was just for fun.

I go outside, where the rain cools my hot face. I take a few deep breaths, then get into my car.

You know what? A turkey baster is looking better and better.

I've been on five dates since my divorce. Two guys were very nice, said they'd love to see me again and failed to call. I waited the appropriate amount of time (six days, according to my dating books), then called (but didn't text) John, and then later, Marcus, and told them (again, according to the dating books) that there was (in John's case) an exhibition at the Museum of the City of New York on subway tunnels (male-friendly topic), and (in Marcus's case) a craft beer-tasting (same), and I was going to go (demonstration that I had interests outside of work), and would they like to come?

Both times, I got their voice mail. They never called back.

The other three dates consisted of a man who told me, in great detail, about the first time he saw his mother naked and how it made him feel—way, way too good, for the record. Guy #2 was nice enough, but our date took a nosedive when, right as we were finishing dinner, he found a *tooth* in his fettuccine. A human tooth. That was enough to have me dry heaving, but I had to give him credit. He was very cool about it, and the restaurant comped our meal—not that we were eating anymore— and even gave him a gift certificate for $250 to apologize. When we were about a block from the restaurant, my date started laughing and told me it was *his* tooth, and he did that all the time. He'd had a molar pulled and kept it for just this purpose. And Guy #3 came in, sat down, took a long hard look at me, then checked his phone and left.

And now we have Jimmy of the Fluids.

I have to wonder sometimes how I ever got Owen.

We met at a party; he was a resident, I'd just gotten hired by Vera Wang and was so buzzed on the fact that

Vera Wang hired me, I would've hit on Robert Downey Jr. I was feeling so confident and fabulous. There was Owen, handsome and funny and so cute, so normal, so kind! He listened when I talked, laughed at my jokes, called when he said he would, and I had no idea how rare and wonderful such a thing was.

I'm thirty-six years old. I was twenty-eight when I met Owen. Maybe it's that. My age.

At the moment, I don't even care.

Except, of course, I do.

Leo's lights are off when I get home. Fine. Good. Let him go get laid. Looking the way he does, he's not gonna be celibate. I get that. He's recreation only. He's not interested in me. Not like that. He's gay where I'm concerned.

And you know, that's great. Look at my sister. Look at me. Look at my mom. No one has a great marriage. No one.

Okay, yes, yes, my aunt Angela does. And so does my best friend from grammar school. And my neighbors in the Village, they were fantastic together.

But still. You know what I mean. No one is happy except those three.

I'll just adopt. Or, you know what? I'll go to the sperm bank and take a picture of myself there and send it to Jimmy Grant with a note: *Thanks for the great idea!*

It may be time to get a dog.

There's a knock on my door. I can see through the windows alongside the door that it's Leo. "I'm not home," I call.

"Oh. Okay." A second later, the door opens. "I have a key," he says apologetically. "I'm the super."

My throat tightens. It's not fair that he can be this

way and not want to sleep with me and marry me and father my babies, and I *know* this is stupid, but these are the thoughts that run through my head. "Well, you suck as a super."

"I know. I'm sorry."

"Take a class, why don't you? It's not rocket science."

"I'm sorry about tonight, I mean."

Damn. An apology. I'm back to my stupid crush. The juvenile hatred was easier.

Then he comes over to me and takes my hands, and my heart becomes gooey, warm caramel. "Jenny," he says, "trust me when I say you don't want to get involved with me. You're great, but—"

"Oh, shut up," I say, yanking my hands free. "I'd *love* to get involved with you. You're the one who's chicken."

He smiles, that sad, beautiful, happy contradiction. "Trust me."

"Why would I? I don't even like you anymore."

"Yes, you do. You have to. You're my only friend."

Then he kisses my forehead, and I feel the faint scrape of his five o'clock shadow, and I want to stab him in the heart and climb him like a tree at the same time.

And then he turns and goes out the front door, taking my dopey heart with him.

At 3:00 a.m., I decide to Google him.

I stalk Owen online. I'm not proud of it, but everyone needs a hobby, right? I've got Google alerts on both him and Ana-Sofia. I could dig around in Leo's past and see why he says he has no friends.

And then, I decide against it. For one, those damn Google alerts bring me no joy when I read again about how selfless and perfect Owen and Ana-Sofia are. For two, they don't exactly help the cause of me moving on.

And for three...for some reason, it feels as if Leo Killian deserves better.

Because I may be his only friend.

Rachel

———✦———

I'M SLEEPING WITH Adam again. Sleeping with. Not having sex with. It got too exhausting, all that righteous anger, all that "I'm still sleeping in here, because of *what you've done*." Laney has asked me what I'd like Adam to do to show me he's sincere. Be sincere, was my answer. "Forgiveness is difficult," she said, making me feel small-hearted and brittle. "You don't have to trust Adam again, not right away, but it does mean you have to accept what's happened and start to take steps away from the infidelity."

So once again, the burden is on me. Planning the wedding, though it was a genuine joy, was on me. Once we figured out why we couldn't get pregnant, the burden was on me, too, with those horrible shots that made me so hormonal I had to go into the bathroom at work and cry, and everyone knew and was so nice, which made me cry more. All Adam had to do was switch to wearing boxers and have more sex. The pregnancy—me again. I'm the one with a four-inch scar and a pooch of skin. The house decorating, painting, hiring people to overhaul the plumbing and electric…me. His mother's birthday—also mine to remember. Holidays, vacations, weekend plans, all mine.

And while I would never call my girls a burden, the huge responsibility of raising them is 99 percent mine.

And now the future of our marriage is on me. I have to forgive him. I have to accept his apology. I have to get past this. That first night, I lay stiffly next to him. He gave me a meaningful basset-hound look and said, "Thank you, Rachel," and it was all I could do not to flip him off. In that moment, I hated our bed. The bed in the guest room was unsullied and smaller, perfect for one.

But I have to take a step away from what happened. Otherwise, the fury will corrode me until I'm nothing.

I think about Emmanuelle instead, the hatred for her untainted by love. I picture my vengeance on her, pushing her down an escalator at the mall—I don't know why, it just pops into my head—the red soles of her Christian Louboutin heels flashing over and over as she falls. I picture slapping her. I imagine her peering from behind a tree as the five of us picnic in the park, Adam so in love with me again that he can't take his eyes off me, the girls giggling and singing, and Emmanuelle is filled with yearning and longing to have what I have. She's choking on the knowledge that she was just a *fuck* and I'm a *wife*, and tears stream from her eyes, her face ugly and smeared with drippy globs of mascara as she sees all that I am and have.

Sure. That could happen.

She's still working at Triple B. That was another sucker punch to the stomach. Adam has absolutely no power over that, he says. "I guess you can tell Jared and see if he can fire her," Adam told me. "He's always been your friend, not mine." Again, the burden is on me. And Adam knows I won't tell Jared.

So Adam and Emmanuelle still see each other. I

imagine they still talk. I asked him to send out his CV and start looking for another job, and he just laughed and asked if I knew what the market was for lawyers these days. "You want us to keep this house, Rach?" he asked. "You want the girls to stay in their expensive little preschool and take ballet next year? Then you want me to stay at Triple B."

There it was again, that faint threat. *Yes, I've been a bad boy, but don't push it.* I'll have to bring it up in counseling, though I swear to God, Laney likes him better than me.

Thank God it's book club night, because I need to get out of the house and think about something other than *this.* Book club consists of Elle Birkman, Claudia Parvost, Mean Debbie and Nice Kathleen. Elle is hosting, and Adam makes a big show of coming home early so I can shower and change. He makes the girls dinner. Macaroni and cheese from the box again.

"They need a vegetable," I tell him.

"No, Mommy!" Grace pronounces. "We do not."

"No, Mommy! No!" Rose and Charlotte second, and just like that, I'm the bad guy again. The burden of broccoli—on me.

"Mommy's right," Adam says, underscoring the *Mommy Is an Ogre* theme.

"Good night, sweethearts," I say. Grace stonily refuses to offer me her cheek, so I kiss her head.

"You smell pretty," Rose says, smiling at me.

"Thanks, angel."

"Why you going out, Mommy? I want you home!" Charlotte says.

"What?" Adam says. "I thought you *loved* Daddy Night! I guess if you don't love Daddy Night, we'll just have to have…Grizzly Bear Night!" The girls shriek and scream in terror and delight—Charlotte wets herself. I can already imagine them on the therapy couch twenty-five years from now. *Mommy was always going off to drink with her friends. At least Daddy was fun.*

Book club meets every other month or so. Besides marriage counseling and the very occasional night out with my sister, I'm home twenty-nine nights out of thirty, and still the girls resent me. Not once have they ever complained about Adam's late meetings—which may or may not have been booty calls for amazing porno sex. Me, I go out to my stupid book club, and I'm punished for it.

"Use Clorox Clean-Up on the pee," I tell Adam.

"Girls, I'll be right back," he says, following me into the mudroom. "You gonna tell them?" he asks, his voice low.

"Tell whom what, Adam?" I know what he wants to know. If I'm going to tell them about Emmanuelle.

"Look," he murmurs. "I know I have no right to ask you anything, but I'm asking anyway. The more people who know about this, the harder it will be to make things better. Put things back to normal."

"You should've thought about that, then."

"Baby, I know," he says. He looks at me a long minute, and irritation flickers across his face. I know this face well by now. This is the "I *said* I was sorry" face. The "what more do you want from me" face.

He must see something in *my* face. I'm pretty sure it's the "I hate you" face. A face that never existed until The Picture.

"Tell them if you need to," he says wearily.

"Daddy! Daddy! Come back!" Charlotte yells.

"Have fun," I tell him.

I won't tell. He knows it, and so do I.

AN HOUR LATER, we've moved from the "I'm still so insightful" portion of book club to the lion's share of our
nights—gossip. I listen with half an ear, consumed by
thoughts of Adam. Is he sexting with Emmanuelle? Is
he watching porn on the internet? Chatting with horny
eighteen-year-olds? A few weeks ago, those thoughts
wouldn't have even entered my blond little brain. Now
I can't stop wondering if coming tonight was a mistake.

"Here's the thing," Elle says. "I get that he wants her
for sex." My head snaps up. "I mean, she advertises a
certain bad-girl vibe. Guys like that."

"Who are you talking about?" I ask.

"Jared and his tattooed fiancée," Lucienne says.

"Harmon doesn't go for that type," Claudia says
proudly. "He only likes very classy women." Last month,
when Claudia wasn't here, Elle and Debbie discussed
Harmon's sexuality at length and found it to be lacking
in the hetero department.

"Rachel," Elle says, "you know them both. Tell us
about them!"

I swallow another mouthful of my red wine, which
will give me a headache later tonight. "They're really
in love," I say, eyeing the Brie. So fattening. I take a
healthy chunk and eat it.

"Kind of a Cinderella story, isn't it?" Kathleen asks.

"Her mother is a tattoo artist," Debbie says. "They're
white trash."

"No, Debbie, as usual, you're wrong," I say calmly.
"Her mother is a nurse. Put herself through school in
her forties, as a matter of fact."

"I hear your sister is making her dress," Kathleen says. "The shop is beautiful, by the way."

"Yes, she is," I answer. "And I'll tell her you think so."

"Oh, Bliss? That one?" Debbie asks. "So what's Kimber's dress like? Whorish, I bet. Total slut?"

"Debbie, don't be such a bitch," Kathleen snaps.

"My sister doesn't make whorish, total-slut dresses, Debbie," I say, my voice uncharacteristically hard to my own ears. "So if you ever need another wedding dress, you'll have to shop elsewhere."

"Oh! You just got served," Claudia crows in delight. She and Elle high-five each other.

"Rachel, honestly," Debbie says, laughing though her eyes are cold. "What's gotten into you?" I can tell she hopes it's something lurid and horrible. Cancer. That would make her day.

Of course, I won't tell them about Adam and Emmanuelle. They're not those types of friends. Kathleen could be, I guess, but not yet. Elle and Claudia, never. Forget Debbie; I knew her in high school, and she was mean as a snake then, too. No, they'd all side with the strongest social ties, and in my case, that's Adam. Look how many friends of Jenny's practically trampled her to be even better friends with Ana-Sofia. And Jenny's the type of person who knows how to be a *great* friend. Me, I've always been too shy. I have Jenny. I had Adam. I have Mom.

Maybe I need to make more friends. I look across at Kathleen, who smiles back, almost as if she knows something.

Talk between the other three has turned to Jared's wedding, which will be huge, and if they'll be invited, which they'd kill for. Who's doing the cake? Cottage

Confections, of course. Nothing but the best for Mrs.
Brewster.

"Is Adam a groomsman?" Elle asks.

Adam is fucking a woman at work, I almost say. Was
fucking. A technicality.

"No, he's not," I say. "I'm sorry, ladies, I have to go.
I forgot I have to make cupcakes for the nursery school
play tomorrow."

It's true. Never before have I forgotten such a monu-
mental and life-giving responsibility. Cupcakes. "Rachel, we need you!" the director of the preschool had
said. "No one else's cupcakes are gluten-free, nut-free
and still delicious!" At the moment, I'd been thrilled.
Validated. That's how pathetic I was.

I go out to my car, and Kathleen follows. "Hey. We
should have lunch or coffee sometime," she says.

"That'd be great." I smile, and for the first time tonight, it feels a little genuine.

"Everything okay, Rachel?" she asks.

I pause. It would be awfully nice to unload on someone other than Jenny. But Kathleen and I don't know
each other that well. "Yeah. Thanks, though."

"You bet." She sighs. "Well. Back to the great works
of literature." She rolls her eyes and goes back into Elle's.

I get into the car and head for home. Time to bake the
cupcakes and show the world who I am.

THE NEXT DAY, Adam surprises me by showing up at the
girls' play. A stir goes through the assembled parents
and grandparents... Sexism still reigns supreme at these
types of events, and most of the parents here are mothers, with the exception of Gil Baines, who's a firefighter
and has a flexible schedule, and Maury Benitz, who's

running for mayor again this fall and is here to remind people how wonderful he is.

Adam has never come to a nursery-school event before, unless it's after-hours, like the art show. But today, at ten-eleven in the morning, here he is.

"Oh, my God, you're so lucky," Claudia murmurs. "Adam! Hey! How are you?"

"Just here to see my little princesses," he says easily, sliding an arm around me. "And my queen, of course."

"You two are sickening." She smiles and looks at the stage.

"This is a surprise," I murmur, not quite looking at him.

"I want to do better," he whispers, kissing my neck. My skin either crawls or breaks out in gooseflesh. Or both. Miss Cathy, the girls' teacher, gives us a wave. *Look at the Carvers! Such a great couple!*

For the next half hour, we watch our daughters, who are each daisies, wriggle up from a brown blanket, demonstrating the growth cycle. They sing a song about sunshine and raindrops, and I feel my eyes watering, as they so often do at these kinds of things. The children are all so beautiful and innocent. Especially mine. I may be biased.

They deserve a happy family. I grew up in the safe, warm embrace of just that until the day my father died. My girls deserve that, too.

Adam hands me his handkerchief. He still carries one, every day. I should know. I wash and iron them. I wonder if he's ever had to give Emmanuelle one. Or why. I can't bring myself to use it. Picture her falling down the escalator again.

Except women like Emmanuelle don't fall. Even if

some spurned wife pushes them, they somehow make things work in their favor.

The girls are so happy to see their father after the play. They wrap their sweet arms around him and ask if he could hear them, and if he wants to meet Tyrion or Jennasys, their friends, then drag him to visit the bathroom, which is one of the highlights of nursery school, since the toilets are tiny.

"You're so lucky," Miss Cathy says. "What a wonderful guy."

"Yes," I say automatically.

"Not only is he gorgeous, he's here," Claudia murmurs. "If he's good in bed, I may have to kill you."

"It's so nice that your husband came, dear," says an older woman, a grandmother, judging from the fervor with which she shoved her way to the front to film the entire performance. "In my day, husbands never did things like that."

It's time to go; one of the frustrations about these special school events, of which there are at least three a month, is that they warrant early dismissal. No Me Time today. Good thing we pay thousands of dollars for the girls to come here.

No one mentions my cupcakes. I was up till three last night, finishing them, taking care to sterilize the counters, the muffin tins, the bowls, the mixer, the spatulas, so Aria Temkowsi wouldn't go into anaphylactic shock, so Cash Boreas wouldn't get a rash. I frosted them in a swirl using my special Williams-Sonoma set, and they're beautiful, these damn cupcakes.

But all anyone can do is make cow eyes at Adam in a rush of good-daddy hormones.

"I have to run," he says as we go into the parking lot. "Girls, you were so wonderful!"

"Who was best, Daddy?" Rose asks. This is something she's picked up recently. Competition. I wonder if she senses something from me, and my resentment toward Emmanuelle.

"You're all my favorites," he says. "You're all the best." He kneels down and kisses and hugs them.

He *is* a good father. I know that.

"See you at home," he murmurs. Then he kisses me, gently, on the lips. "Love you."

"See you later." His eyes flash disappointment that I didn't say the words back. Words I used to tell him four or ten times a day.

His patience isn't going to last long. The thought hums like a tuning fork next to my ear.

I buckle the girls into their seats, and get into the driver's seat. "Wait!" Grace bellows. "We didn't get cupcakes! Where are cupcakes!"

"Nooo!" Rose wails.

"Mommy! No!" Charlotte adds.

There's no way I'm going back inside that building to hear more about how wonderful Adam is. "You know what?" I tell them. "We're getting ice cream instead! Who wants ice cream? I know I do! And guess what else? You can get whatever you want on top!"

This stuns them into silence. "Really?" Grace asks.

"Yes. Whatever you want. Two things, even!"

They go a little crazy at Ben & Jerry's. Chunky Monkey with gummy bears and broken Oreos for Charlotte. Phish Food for Grace with chocolate-covered almonds and graham crackers. Cotton Candy for Rose, topped with rainbow sprinkles and more gummy bears.

I ask them questions and say silly things while they eat, and they're clearly delighted with me, *not* wiping their hands or faces, *not* telling them to slow down—though it's a physical battle to stifle the words. No, *I'm* the fun parent now, that's for sure. Who cares about vegetables?

We get back in the car after gleefully using way too much soap in the Ben & Jerry's bathroom, because Ben & Jerry's soap is much more fun than the soap from home. No need for lunch. I'll just run them around the yard a little bit, and you know what? It may be time for a puppy. I'll be the one to tell them that, and to take them to the pet store to pick one out—or three, so they can each have one—and I get to be the fun parent, thank you very much.

And then, nap time. Me time. And today, maybe I'll actually do something for me. I'll order stuff online. Watch *The Avengers* for the eye candy. I'm almost forty. I'm not dead.

"Mommy?" comes Charlotte's voice. "I don't feel good."

And then comes the sound that every mother knows.

The sound of a little stomach expelling its contents.

They puke like falling dominoes, three in a row, bing, bang, boom.

"Mommy! Charlotte threwed up and me, too!" Rose says, outraged. She gacks again.

"Mommy! Mommy, help!" Grace commands. "Mommy! Make it stop!" Another *very* juicy-sounding vomit.

I pull over as soon as I can, but I'm already dry-heaving myself. God, the smell, so thick I can taste it. Sour dairy and sugar and who knows what else, oh, yes, oat-

meal for breakfast and flecks of the carrot sticks, along
with the hummus I packed for snack.

"Oh, babies, Mommy is so sorry!" I say, leaning into
the backseat. Grace vomits on my chest, almost on purpose, it seems.

"Mommy!" she demands, outraged at the indignity.

"Mommy! I sick!" Rose says.

"Mommymommymommy," Charlotte moans, not to
be outdone. She retches again, as if knowing I doubt
her sincerity.

I carry Wet-Naps at all times, so I mop up the girls.
Rose is crying because she threw up on her favorite
dress, and Grace is crying with rage because she's got
puke in her lap and "it's too hot, Mommy!" and Charlotte is crying because one of her gummy bears came
up whole, and this is freaking her out.

"I'm so sorry, sweeties," I say, struggling not to cry
myself. "We'll get home as soon as we can, okay?"

I slide their door shut, and then I'm bawling, that
dreadful *Eh-heh-heh-hegggghhh* kind of crying, and
luckily, the girls can't hear me because they're still wailing, but I'm sobbing, my hands are shaking and I can't
stop crying. Me, in a meltdown, covered with vomit on
the side of Route 9. I can't drive like this. I think I may
actually be hysterical, and the noises coming from my
mouth and throat are horrible. My God, listen to me!

I want things to be the way they were before. I miss
Adam. I miss loving my husband. I can't deal with this.
It's too hard. It's just too hard.

Then a car pulls over, and a man gets out. "Rachel?"
he says, coming closer.

I'm still crying, so it takes me a minute to figure out

who he is. Then he smiles, his eyes turning into merry little arcs, and I do know.

"Gus… Hi," I sob. "It's so nice to see you. How've you been?"

The girls' volume inside the van has risen to shrieks of rage.

"I'm…I'm great," he says. "But you're not, I'm guessing? Unless you always wear vomit."

"My girls… I gave them too…too much ice cream, and they…they threw up." My sobbing intensifies.

He grimaces. "Nasty."

I nod and try to control myself. I sound like a cat being slowly strangled to death.

"Want some help?"

"What?"

"Want me to help? It sounds like you have rabid weasels in there."

"Um…no. I mean, no, I've got it."

"Can I open the van door?" he asks.

I nod. He slides it open, and the girls all fall silent immediately at the sight of a stranger.

"You must be the Puke Sisters," he says.

"You not funny," Rose says, and her own comment makes her laugh, then puke again.

"You're gross," Gus says. He reaches in the back for something—Rose's backpack, opens it up and takes out her lunch box. "If you need to puke again," he says, "do it in here. Okay? You, too, Princess Pukey." Charlotte accepts her Hello Kitty lunch box from him, and I grab Grace's backpack and give her hers—Matchbox cars… She's not the girliest girl.

"Mommy, why you crying?" Rose asks.

"Oh, honey," I say, not aware that I still was, "I'm just

sorry I let you have all that ice cream. I shouldn't have. I'm so sorry you feel bad."

"It okay," she says kindly, and my tears surge hotter and harder.

"Tell you what," Gus says. "I'm gonna follow you home."

"No, that's—"

"Oh, come on. How could I live with myself if I didn't?"

AN HOUR LATER, the girls and I are clean again. I've given the girls a bath, put them in their jammies and tucked them into bed for nap time. "We love you," Grace says sleepily, speaking for her sisters as she often does.

"I love you, too, my little angels. So, so much."

I go into my room and change into jeans and a sweater. I washed up while the girls were splashing in the tub. No makeup. My hair seems to have been spared the puke-a-thon, but I brush it and put it in a ponytail, then head downstairs.

Gus is just coming in, a bucket and some laundry detergent in his hands. "I cleaned up as best I could," he says, "but, good God, woman. It's terrifying in there. You probably need to get the car detailed. Or just set fire to it." He smiles, his eyes all but disappearing.

"Would you like some coffee?" I ask. "Or do you have to get back to work?"

"I'd love some." He washes his hands at the kitchen sink, and I make the coffee. Put out some cookies, too—organic oatmeal with fair-trade, locally grown organic cranberries—and we sit at the kitchen table.

"How's work?" I ask.

Gus is still at Celery Stalk Media, the company where

I worked for seven years before I left in my sixth month of pregnancy, an act of mercy for my boss, Adele, who was terrified the girls would slide out at any minute. It was—is—a lovely company, fifteen or so employees, a casual, happy place, as you'd hope it would be. We designed children's educational software, after all—lessons masquerading as games. I haven't kept up much; some of the women came over to visit when the girls were a few months old, a blurry, exhausting time that I barely remember. I send a Christmas card, the photo-montage type, and always get a few emails about how beautiful and big the girls are.

A lot of the women at Celery Stalk had a crush on Gus, who is so nice it's hard to believe he's genuine. He's cute rather than handsome; he has a round face and a slightly receding hairline which he doesn't try to hide; his hair is in a crew cut. He's only five-eight or so. Adele, our boss, once asked him what his ethnic background was. Italian, he said, with an Inuit great-grandmother, which explained those happy eyes. I think the quality that makes him so popular with women is simply his happiness.

He asked me out once, two days after my first date with Adam. Something casual, like "Want to get a drink sometime?" and I was taken aback; we'd worked together for more than two years, and he'd never shown any special interest toward me. I blushed so hard my face hurt and mumbled something about not being a drinker, really, but maybe a bunch of us could go out for happy hour sometime, I know Eliza had mentioned a new place she'd been wanting to try.

He got the message. Didn't seem to hold it against me. And truthfully, I forgot about it, caught up in the romance of Adam, who was tall and so handsome and sent me flowers the very next day with a card that said, "I like you a lot, Rachel Tate." I still have that card, in our photo album, along with a pressed rose from the arrangement.

"Are you seeing anyone, Gus?" I ask now, strangely at ease. Once a guy's seen you covered in puke, sobbing on the side of a highway...

"No," he answers. "I was, for a while. A nice woman named Alice. We lived together for a while, but..." He shrugs.

"So no heartbreak?" I ask.

"I didn't say that." He smiles a little. "She's a good person. We just weren't right for each other. We're still friends."

"My sister and her ex are still friends," I say. "I don't really understand how that works."

"It has its awkward moments." He pauses, but it's still there, the happiness that we all so loved back in the day. The notion that Gus Fletcher never had a bad day in his life. Naive, but reassuring. "Your daughters are beautiful, by the way. Even when they're snarling."

"Sorry Grace bit you," I say, feeling a smile start.

"It was a first. I'll be Tweeting it later." He takes a sip of coffee, his eyes still merry.

"So my husband had an affair," I say.

"Ah, shit." His smile drops.

And then I'm telling him everything. The Picture, the denial, the guilt over what I thought, how I just knew when I saw them in the same room. The rage, the fear, the awful, unbearable hurt, the escalator fantasy, which actually makes him laugh. Me, too.

I don't cry. I just talk. And Gus lets me. I talk for

forty-five minutes, according to the clock. And when I'm done, he covers my hand with his, gives it a squeeze and takes it back. "I'm so sorry" is all he says, and those smiley eyes are kind.

"I'm sorry I unloaded on you."

"I'm not sorry about that."

He has such a nice face. I wonder what would've happened if he'd asked me out a week before he did. Of all my coworkers, I had always liked Gus the best.

Well. No point in going there.

Fifteen minutes later, Gus leaves. "Thank you for everything," I say, and my voice breaks a little, because the magnitude of his loveliness today, his helpfulness and kindness, hits me in a warm wave.

"I'm really glad I was driving by," he says, and I can tell he means it. "Tell the girls thanks for exploding like that." Another smile flashes. "Call me if you ever need your car cleaned again."

Then he leaves, and that night, around nine, when Adam is watching the Yankees and I'm looking at Pinterest, thinking about repainting our bedroom, I get an email.

It's from Gus. His phone number, and the words It really was great to see you.

Jenny

❖ ─── ◆ ─── ❖

SINCE OPENING BLISS, I've booked eleven brides. I've also
made the decision to sell a few of the sample dresses.
I never had a storefront before, and now it seems silly
to have eight dresses in the shop that aren't for sale. As
Andreas so wisely pointed out—between writing chap-
ters of his lurid urban fantasy/gay erotica—the impulse
buy ain't gonna hurt.

And so I've designed a few more dresses, and the
two of us have been sewing till our eyes bleed, more or
less. We spend many happy hours discussing whether
our celebrity crushes are gay or straight and how they'd
be in bed. He tells me about his novel, his boyfriend and
how he wishes he knew a straight man or two for me.

The extra work helps keep my mind off Rachel, too.
It's been tooth-grinding, not being able to help her out
of her misery. I can't tell you how many times I've plot-
ted my brother-in-law's death. Then I'm filled with guilt
and remorse, because until very recently, I loved Adam.
He made my sister so happy.

Now she's dodging my calls.

"What's wrong with Rachel?" Mom asks one day
when I can't find a reason for her not to come to the
store. She wanders around, idly fingering material,

clucking disapprovingly here and there. Andreas, who confuses her—A man? In bridal wear? But why?—has brought her a cup of coffee and leans against the counter, drinking it all in for his novel. He's basing a character on her.

"I don't know," I lie. "She seems fine to me. We had so much fun with the girls the other day." In fact, I was babysitting; Rachel barely said a word to me, so distracted and pale. "They came to my apartment, and I made them a pillow fort, and Rose—"

"Do you think Grace is autistic?"

This is my mother. Able to suck joy from the conversation in under one second.

"No," I say firmly.

"Well, *something's* going on with your sister. God knows what she has to complain about. She has a perfect life. She shouldn't take anything for granted. I had a perfect life, too, once, and then it was gone in an instant. I told her to get over her little snit, whatever it is, and be grateful."

I take a cleansing breath at that. Andreas practically skips into the workroom to his laptop, inspired.

"Maybe you just don't remember what it was really like, Mom," I say mildly, though my stomach burns. "Maybe it wasn't quite so perfect, and you've just—"

"Oh, please. Your father and I were madly in love. We couldn't keep our hands off each other."

First of all, yuck. What kid wants to hear about their parents' sex life, even—or especially—as an adult? Secondly, because I just can't stand this kind of revisionist history, I say, "Yeah, but remember that last year? You were working so much, and Dad—"

"Are you jealous? Is that it, honey? Because of Owen and Ana-Sofia and how happy they are?"

Better to have her focused on me than on Rachel. It still cuts, though, my mom's constant need to win, to have had a better life, a better marriage, a bigger, truer love than her daughters. I honestly think Rachel's having triplets made Mom feel outdone. After all, Rachel has a third more daughters than Mom managed. Add to that my sister's glowing happiness, and that sweet, innocent sense that emanates—*emanated*—from her, and Mom always has to slip in a zinger. Her ease of getting pregnant. Two children being the perfect number, according to "studies I've read." Such studies could never be found, but she still claimed that that's what the experts said.

And of course, Saint Dad, perfect father, better husband.

Then, as always, irritating pity trickles in, mixing with the anger I feel. She loved my father. She'll never get over his death. "Come on, Mom," I tell her. "Let me take you to lunch. They redid Hudson's, and it's really cute now."

"You should eat at the new place in *my* town," she says. "Really top-notch. The best French food in the Northeast, the *Times* said."

"Yeah? What's it called?"

"Oh, I can't remember." She waves her hand dismissively. This is because if she did remember, I could Google the restaurant and thus disprove her claim on the *Times* review. "Betty and I had lunch there. The chef came out to greet us and made us a special appetizer. It really was amazing. Completely unique."

"I get it, Mom. Whatever Hudson's has won't be as

good as what's in Hedgefield. Would you like to go out with me, anyway? My treat?"

"Fine," she says, adopting a wounded look. "I just thought you'd be interested in a nice place. No need to get so touchy."

Two hours later, Mom kisses my cheek goodbye. I text Rachel to warn her that our mother may well stop by, and Rach gives the preemptive phone call, pretending to check in from a doctor's appointment. Mom warns her about vaccines, both pro and con, essentially saying that the girls are doomed whatever choice Rachel makes.

I wonder if Mom would be happier in some odd way, knowing that Dad wasn't perfect. If she might have moved on. Mourned less somehow.

It wouldn't be fair to tell her now. I'm almost positive. In her odd way, she's happy in her misery.

But I wonder if I *should* tell Rachel. Then again, maybe it would devastate her, knowing our dad had strayed. Or maybe it would reassure her to know that Dad did love Mom, tremendously, and an affair doesn't necessarily mean the end of happiness.

I don't know. The last thing I want to do is make things worse.

"Mind if I go home early today?" Andreas asks, sticking his head into my office, where I'm sketching a mermaid gown for one of my new clients. "Seth and I have a date."

"Fine," I say. "Rub my face in it. Why can't Seth have a straight brother, huh?"

"He has a lesbian sister. Want to give it a shot?"

"Some days, I do," I say. "It'd be easier than dealing with men."

"Tell me about it," Andreas says.

Alone in my shop.

I have plenty of work, but… I don't know. Something's still missing. I'm on autopilot these days. I still love making dresses, but I haven't been truly electrified in a long time. I'd hoped that owning my own shop would reinvigorate me, but so far, I feel horribly like I'm phoning it in. The dresses are still gorgeous, my brides are still thrilled; I'm probably the only one who knows something's amiss.

I look at one of the display dresses—this gorgeous, sweet hippie-vibe confection with off-the-shoulder sleeves and empire waist. I loved making that dress. The bride called off the wedding; hence the reason I still have the dress, but it suited her perfectly, and she adored it. The guy was the problem, not the gown.

The bell over the door rings, and in comes my afternoon appointment. Kimber, in to see the muslin dress I made, based on the sketches she (and Mrs. Brewster) approved.

Unfortunately, the Dragon Lady is here, too, her iron-gray hair sprayed into its fiercely chic helmet, her face set in those frigid lines.

"Hello!" I say, hugging Kimber, who beams at me. "So nice to see you both! Come on in to the dressing room. Can I get you coffee or tea?"

"Let's get this over with," Mrs. Brewster says. Kimber's smile twitches, then dies.

"Sure," I say, ever chipper with my clients. "Now, the dress is obviously going to be in that gorgeous silk we picked out last time. This is just for fit and to give you an idea of how it will look on. I'll show you the lace choices, and we can get to work making it really special."

"I can't wait," Kimber says, clapping her hands.

Because covering the tattoos was deemed critical by Mrs. Brewster—and because Kimber dutifully agreed—I've come up with a very elegant, fitted dress with a sweetheart neckline and a graceful, draped skirt. Three-quarter lace sleeves and lace over the bodice will camouflage most of her colorful tattoos. The back is also lace. The material will be ivory silk and with a very delicate, sheer lace—the wedding's in July, after all—and with Kimber's figure and olive skin, she'll look amazing in it.

"Let me help you get dressed, and then we'll show you, Mrs. Brewster."

Mrs. B.'s response is to glance at her watch.

In the changing room, Kimber strips down to her bra and panties, both shocking pink. Her tattoos are rose vines, climbing from her hip bone up her side to twine her neck. She also has angel wings between her shoulder blades and the full-sleeve tattoo. I wouldn't want a tattoo myself, but I don't mind them. And they suit Kimber, with her pink hair and studded ears. She has such an innocence about her; she looks like a rock 'n' roll angel.

"This is so much fun!" she whispers. "I hope Mrs. B. likes it! I really want us to be friends."

The admission is so honest and sweet. "If Jared loves you, I'm sure she already does. And not to toot my own horn, but this dress is perfect. You'll look beautiful," I say. "Here, just slide this over your head. Don't look. Now, let me zip you up. You'll have buttons on the real dress, but this can give you an idea."

Kimber closes her eyes and lets me do my thing.

The dress fits her perfectly, and that figure… Glory be. She's built like Scarlett Johansson.

"My tatts will still show," Kimber says.

"I know," I say. "This is the under-dress…just the

bodice and skirt, see? Now, this isn't your lace—we'll pick that out today—but I made you a little jacket to give you an idea of how it will look."

She slides her arms into the sleeves and lets me button the makeshift jacket. "You can pick whatever pattern of lace you want," I tell her. "It can be a corded lace, which is heavier, or you can go with something really light and airy. I think light would work best, personally, but it's up to you. And it can be beaded, too, if you want a little sparkle."

"Oh! Sparkle sounds great!"

I finish the last button. "Open your eyes."

She opens her eyes, and her lips part, her face at once dreamy and stunned. "Is that really me?" she asks.

"Sure is. You look amazing. Shall we show her?"

We go out to where Mrs. Brewster waits, looking pinched. Her face doesn't change, though Kimber is beaming.

"What do you think?" I ask.

"I can still see those ridiculous tattoos," she snaps. "I thought you understood our problem."

"This lace pattern is only for demonstration," I say calmly. "We can pick out something with a denser pattern if—"

"No," Mrs. Brewster says. "The lace won't work. No tattoos should be showing at *all*. This is a church wedding, not some civil ceremony. Jared's father is the minister of the congregation. His son can't seem to be marrying a…prostitute."

Holy shit.

Kimber swallows hard. Her eyes are shiny with tears.

"I'm sure no one would think that, Mrs. Brewster,"

I say, earning an icy glare. "Kimber, this is your day. What do you think?"

She looks at Mrs. Brewster. "Um… I guess more, um, opaque? Because I get what Mrs. Brewster's saying. It's kind of a formal day. So maybe no lace. What else could we do? I mean, I love the shape. It'll be beautiful in anything. Right?"

"It's hardly modest," Mrs. Brewster says. "Her…rump is far too obvious. What about a higher waist? A ball gown would be more appropriate for a church wedding."

Kimber's one request was anything *but* a ball gown. Which Mrs. Brewster, she and I had discussed in our first and second appointments.

"I could try a ball gown," Kimber says meekly.

"Good. Jennifer—"

"It's Jenny, actually. I was never Jennifer."

"Can you whip up a ball gown?"

I force a smile. "Yes, I can make a ball gown in time for the wedding. If that's what Kimber wants."

"Then let's pick out some fabric. Do you have any satin?" She stands up, breezes past Kimber and goes to the wall of sample fabrics.

Ten minutes later, Mrs. Brewster has chosen an antique satin—a heavy, lustrous fabric. Under her critical eye, I sketch out a classic, Cinderella ball gown. High-necked, long-sleeved, high-backed.

"This is going to be very warm, especially if you have a hot day," I say to the bride, who's biting her fingernail, standing behind Mrs. Brewster.

"Sew in some sweat shields," Mrs. Brewster says.

"Kimber? Anything you'd like to add, honey?"

She inches over and looks at the picture. "Um… maybe some bling? Just a little?"

"Sure. We can add some beading here, and maybe here, too—"

"No," Mrs. Brewster says. "That's so tacky."

"I have everything from Swarovski crystal to seed pearls to—"

"It should be modest. Unadorned. Simple, as mine was."

"Okay," Kimber agrees. "I like it plain, too."

"I did *not* say plain," Mrs. Brewster says through her teeth. It's the first time she's spoken directly to Kimber this entire appointment, and I can feel the hate coming off her in waves. "I said *unadorned*. There's a standard of class you need to embrace, Kimber, if you're going to be seen socially with my son."

Kind of hard to picture Kimber and Mrs. Brewster friends, no matter what the poor kid hopes.

I glance between them. Mrs. Brewster doesn't deign to look at me. "Let me double-check some measurements, then," I say, grabbing my tape measure. "Kimber, if you wouldn't mind coming back into the dressing room." When I get her there, I whisper, "Kimber, don't let her railroad you. This is your wedding."

"I…I just want her to approve," she whispers. "Once we're married, I'm sure she'll chill out a little. I don't want to get started off on the wrong foot. It's just a dress."

"You're right. But it's an important dress. You shouldn't hate it, either."

"I…I don't. I won't. I'm sure it'll be beautiful, Jenny."

Yep. A rock 'n' roll angel, a cherub with those wide blue eyes and perfect rosebud mouth. I give her a hug. "You and Jared are going to make beautiful babies," I tell her.

"Thanks," she says, blushing. "I can't wait. I love kids. Your sister's triplets? *O-M-G*, I love them!"

She gets dressed in her own clothes again, and Mrs. Brewster once again tells me her next available slot… not the other way around. But again, a referral from her in this town will mean a lot. If she blacklists me, that'll hurt. "Kimber, I haven't even asked," I say. "What do you do for work? Or are you a professional singer?"

Mrs. Brewster snorts.

"I'm a nutritionist? Well, not really. Not yet? But I'm working for my associate's degree. I work at the middle school, making lunches. Trying to get the kids to like veggies, right?" She beams.

"That's nice. It must be great to work in a school."

"It is," she says. "I always wanted to—"

"Thank you for your time, Jenny," Mrs. Brewster interrupts. "Kimber, let's go. We have to talk to the caterer."

I sigh as they leave, then get busy closing up the shop. Poor Kimber. I wonder if Jared knows how his mother is bossing her around. Maybe I'll ask Rachel to say something to him. Then again, Rach has her own problems. I'll ask Kimber out, that's what I'll do. Rachel and she and I can have a girls' night out. I bet Rachel could use one, too.

I get home—no music from down below today—and am just about to pour myself a glass of wine when someone bangs on my door.

"Jenny! Shit, Jenny, are you home?"

I run to the door. "Leo! What— Oh, no."

Leo is holding Loki in his arms. The dog is shaking. "He's having a seizure. Can you drive me to the vet?"

"You bet." I grab my keys and run down the steps, open the back door for Leo, who gets in. "Which way?"

"The emergency clinic. It's in Poughkeepsie. Can you hurry?"

Of course I can hurry. I'm from New York. Speeding is the pace of my people. "Hang in there," I say, but he's crooning to the dog, who's still jerking, telling him what a good friend he is, asking him not to die, not to leave him.

There's a lump in my throat and tears in my eyes. Loki is old. I don't know how long that breed, whatever Loki is, is expected to live, but I find myself saying a little prayer that Leo doesn't lose him just yet. He loves that dog so much.

"It's on Manchester Road," Leo says tersely, and I glance in the rearview mirror. His face is so tragic, his eyes wide and unspeakably sad, and I can tell he's trying not to panic. It's a raw, horrible thing to see.

"I think I know the place," I say. A long time ago, Rachel hit a cat, and she and I drove the poor beastie to this same place. The cat made it, and Rachel visited him every day until he was adopted.

"Can you go any faster?" he asks, and his voice breaks a little. So does my heart.

I push the gas pedal a little harder.

When we pull into the parking lot, Leo barely waits for the car to stop fully, just gets out and runs inside. I run in after him. "I'm Leo Killian," he says to one of the women behind the counter. "I called."

"Come on back," she says, and Leo goes ahead. I start to follow, but the other woman stops me.

"We need some information," she says, handing me a clipboard.

"I...I just drove him here. I don't know too much."

"Well, maybe you can get it started, anyway," she says. "Name, address, that kind of thing."

I want to go back with Leo. "Can it wait?"

"No," she says. "We need a guarantee of payment and some basic information."

"Fine." I grab the clipboard, turn around to sit down. There's a woman there with a cockatoo, and something about her makes me freeze. At first I don't recognize her.

Then I do.

It's Dorothy.

My father's Dorothy is here.

Twenty-five years older, but I know it. My gut knows it. My face throbs as the blood rushes upward, and all I can think is *It's her, it's her, it's her*. Blond hair, black roots, still so pretty.

"Hi," she says, and of course she doesn't recognize me. I was her boss's kid. She worked for him for three months. She saw me maybe five times, and I was eleven years old.

"Hi," I say, sitting down.

Her bird makes a croaking noise. That in itself is so weird—Dorothy, my father's *mistress*, has an exotic bird as a pet.

"His name is Perry," she tells me.

"Oh. Um, he's beautiful."

"He started pulling out some feathers. I just wanted to be on the safe side, you know?"

"Yeah."

"What's wrong with your dog?"

"Uh...he had a seizure." I glance at the clipboard and start filling in what I can—Leo's name, address; Loki's age: fifteen; breed: Australian shepherd/mutt. But my heart is racing, and my face is hot. First of all, Leo may be in there, saying a final goodbye to his dog.

And secondly, Dorothy's *here*.

I bolt up to the counter. "Can I go back there?"

"He's already doing a little better," the woman says. "Seizures aren't uncommon in older dogs. We'll have you go back in a few minutes, okay?"

"Okay. Thank you."

I go back to my chair. Dorothy smiles. "He's a cute dog," she says, very nicely.

Shit.

I should tell her who I am. I could ask her why he did it, and if she loved him, and did she want to marry him, and was he going to leave my mother. I could call her a slut, tell her that she stained my memories of my father, my daddy, the man I loved best in the world, thanks a lot, whore.

I want to know *why*. I want to know how a woman can sleep with another woman's husband. I want to know how it started, how my father took that first step away from my mother. Did he stop loving Mom bit by bit, the way Owen stopped loving me? Or was it pure, carnal sex, like Adam described to my sister?

I hope Dorothy never found anyone. I hope she lay awake at night for years, thinking about the poor widow and daughters and how she tainted and polluted his last months on earth.

I'm Jenny Tate. Robert Tate's daughter. Great. I'd sound like an idiot. *My name is Inigo Montoya, and you slept with my father.* What if she says, *Big deal?* or *Who's Robert Tate?* What if I'm wrong and it's not really Dorothy?

I'm not wrong. Her face has been burned on my brain

for twenty-two years. You don't forget the woman you saw your father kissing.

But I just sit here like a lump, pretending to be totally engrossed in this form.

"Leo Killian's friend? You can come back now."

"Good luck," Dorothy says, and I remember that smile, that sweet smile. She looks so much younger than my mother. Still.

"You, too," I say, then I go through the swinging door with the vet, down the hall. "How's he doing?"

"We gave him some medicine, so he's groggy, but he'll be okay."

She opens the door to an exam room, and there's Leo, sitting on the floor with his dog, rubbing his belly.

Those blue eyes are wet, but he smiles.

"Hey," I whisper, and before I can stop myself, I bend over and kiss the top of Leo's head. "You all right?"

"Yeah."

I sit in the chair and listen to the vet explain that this, while upsetting, isn't that uncommon, and for the most part, a seizure will pass on its own. Loki is an old guy, but he's in great shape, and obviously Leo takes good care of him. She gives Leo some medicine that should help Loki feel more energetic, then reaches down and pets Loki herself. "You're all set. Just see Gina on the way out."

"Thank you," Leo and I both say. We sit there a minute, me in the chair, Leo on the floor with his dog, until he looks up at me. "Let's go home."

"Okay."

When we go out to the waiting room, Dorothy is gone.

"Do you happen to know that lady's name?" I ask as

Leo pulls out his credit card. "The one with the cockatoo? I think I know her."

"Um, let me check," Gina says. "Dorothy Puchalski."

Dorothy Puchalski.

The name sits in my heart like a rock.

I DROP LEO and Loki at home, then run to Luciano's and get us some eggplant parm, garlic bread and salad. When I get back, I go right into Leo's. He's sitting next to Loki's doggy bed, petting the old guy. The dog is snoring.

"Everyone good here?" I ask.

"Much better."

I set our food on the table, then open a bottle of red wine and pour us both a big glass. Leo gets up. He looks older, the poor thing, not quite recovered from tonight's ordeal. God help him if he ever has a kid.

"So where'd you get this guy, anyway?" I ask.

Leo takes a sip of wine. "He came from a shelter."

"Best place to get a dog, I hear."

"It is." His eyes flicker to mine, then back again, as if he's embarrassed at what I've seen tonight. "So who's Dorothy Puchalski?" he asks.

I jerk a little. I hadn't thought he was paying attention. "Um...someone my parents used to know."

"How did your father die?" he asks, and it's such a normal question. It's true—my father is dead. Leo knows this. He's even seen Dad's grave; Rachel told me how he sat with her that time. Me, I haven't been there in years.

"He was shot in a convenience store robbery," I say. "Buying a Green Watermelon Brain Freeze. He loved them."

Leo doesn't say anything, but his face... Crap, I've never seen a face that holds so *much* before in my life.

Maybe it's because I've seen Dorothy, or maybe it's the well of sympathy in Leo's eyes, but my throat tightens unexpectedly.

Over the years, I've told dozens of people how my father died. It's become part of my life story, another fact, same as having a sister, same as having black hair. I'm used to it.

But right now, I'm afraid to say anything else, because I haven't cried over my dad in a very long time. I didn't when I told Owen; horribly, I was almost glad to have something so unusual to talk about, to see the gentle sympathy in his dark, dark eyes.

But Leo... It's different. Owen was almost always gently sympathetic, now that I think of it. Dr. Perfect, all day, every day with everyone.

Sympathy from Leo somehow carries more weight.

I clear my throat. "So my ex-husband and his perfect wife have invited me to a dinner party in the city, in the same apartment where I used to live with him. Want to come? Should be a fun little freak show."

"Hell, yes." Leo smiles, and his face goes from tragic empathy to wicked, and I'm filled with relief. Back on safe land. "When is it? Doesn't matter. I'll clear my schedule. I'd miss dinner at the White House for this."

I get up to clear the table, and Leo rises, too. "So glad to entertain," I murmur. "Feel free to laugh at my personal heartbreak."

"You're not heartbroken," he says with a wink. "Not anymore."

"Is it hard, being a woman trapped in a man's body?" I ask. "Because you know so much about the female heart, I can only assume you're—"

He leans over and kisses me, just a warm press of his

lips against mine, lasting just a beat too long for it to be just friendly… A *kiss*, and it's over before I can figure out what to do with my hands or my mouth.

"Thank you for tonight, Jenny Tate," he says, and his eyes are warm. "You're a good friend."

"And thank *you*, Leo Killian, for just kissing me and confusing me and making me think you like me."

"I do like you."

"'Like me' as in 'want to sleep with me'?"

"Of course. I'm a guy."

"But you don't want a real relationship."

"Correct."

I throw my hands up in the air. "I hate men."

A delighted smile. "Get a cat."

"Maybe I will. See you around."

"Jenny."

His face is like New England weather, sunny one minute, rain the next. I've never seen a face change the way his does. Right now, that sorrow is scudding across his eyes like storm clouds, and I think he's about to tell me something real, something *more*, and the hair on the back of my neck lifts in anticipation.

"Yes?" I whisper.

He doesn't answer right away, and then his eyes drop to the floor. When they return to mine, I can see he's changed his mind. "Thank you again," is all he says, then opens the door for me to leave.

Rachel

———— ✦ ————

LATELY, ADAM IS being perfect, which makes me irritable. I don't know why. I'm not myself anymore. Thoughtful things he used to do—bringing me flowers, offering to pick up dinner for him and me to eat after the girls are asleep—everything is suspect, a bribe, a cover, an apology. We talked about this in therapy, our weekly Tuesday night appointment.

"I'm trying to do everything I can to show Rachel how much I want our marriage to work," Adam says. "Nothing makes a difference. I feel like I'll be punished for this forever."

That sounds about right, I think.

"What are your thoughts on that, Rachel?" Laney asks.

I look at my hands. "I feel like he's trying to prove he's husband of the year, and while I do think he should be groveling—" Jenny's word "—everything seems like it's for show."

Adam throws his hands up in the air. "Then, what? What can prove that I'm not being fake?"

I don't answer for a second. Nothing. The answer is nothing. "Adam, if I knew the answer, I'd tell you. You broke my trust. You cheated. When I asked you about it, you lied. You swore you'd be faithful to me in a church, and if you can't live up to that, what can you live up to? Why should I believe you now?"

"Like I'm the only man who's ever cheated. The only spouse," he hastily corrects.

"I guess the fact that you still see Emmanuelle every day is hard for me to get past," I say. "If there was one thing you could do, it'd be leave the firm."

He sighs hugely. "We've been over this, and over it, and over it." He looks at Laney, that tolerant "women are so irrational" look he's given me so many times. "I can't leave the firm," he says. "There's no way I could get a job that pays this much in this area. I could go work for the Public Defender's office and make a fifth of what I make now, but then Rachel would have to give up her house, and the private nursery school, and maybe you might actually have to get a job, too."

"Is that something you'd consider, Rachel?" Laney asks.

"Yes," I lie. Well, no, I'd consider it. I just haven't yet.

What I want most is my old life. My old self. I miss *me*, if such a thing is possible. I miss the way I looked at Adam, my wonderful, handsome, funny husband. I miss that sense of wonder and happiness that he picked me. I miss the utter joy I felt when the five of us did anything together. Even if the girls were fussy or knocked over their drink, whenever we were in public, I'd be smiling. It wasn't smugness. It was just happiness. Plain, simple happiness.

"So, Adam," Laney says, "why don't you at least try to see what else is out there?"

"Fine," he grumbles. Resentment rolls off him like a thick fog. "You know what I'd like to talk about? Just to change the subject from what a shit I am to something a little different."

"Go ahead," Laney says.

He turns to me. "You're angry because I had an affair, and I totally understand that. But did you ever think about the reason I did it?"

"Yes. I've thought about that a lot."

"You ever think that maybe I felt like you weren't interested in sex anymore?"

"What?" I shriek. "How dare you? We did it all the time! Much more than any other couple I know!"

"Yeah, but you didn't like it."

"What?"

"What do you mean, Adam? Why do you think that?" Laney asks.

He looks at her and crosses his legs. "She fell asleep. During. Not before. During." He says it with the same gravity and accusation as if he'd just found a crystal-meth lab in our basement.

My face prickles.

"You didn't even think I noticed, did you?" he says smugly, now the injured party. "So maybe I strayed because it was clear I was just burdening you with wanting a normal sex life."

"Rachel?" Laney says. "Would you like to respond?"

"I would," I say. "Yes, I fell asleep one time. The girls had had a stomach virus, I hadn't had a good night's sleep in a week, but I happen to *love* sex, and I've been very conscious of keeping it in our life together, and *one time* I fell asleep for *a second*."

"How do you think that made me feel?" Adam asks.

"How do you think *I* felt, Adam? I was exhausted! So what does this mean? I can't get tired or you have permission to fuck around?" There it is, the foul mouth that never existed before.

"Rachel, let me just ask you this. Why didn't you tell Adam you were too tired, and all you wanted was a good night's rest?"

I pause. "Because I didn't...I didn't want him to think of me like that."

"Like a human?" she says with a faint smile.

"Like a wife who's too tired for sex."

"But you *were* too tired. Just that one time, maybe, but probably more. You're not letting Adam see you as a regular person, which can be distancing."

"So...this is my fault? His affair is my fault?"

"No, no, not at all. Adam is the only one responsible for the affair. But true intimacy is more than just sex on regularly scheduled nights. He has to know how you feel. You're a very capable woman who's a wonderful mother and has created a lovely home."

"And that's bad?"

"No. But maybe Adam isn't sure what his role is."

"Exactly," he says.

I look at him. "So you would rather give me a back rub and take over making dinner a few nights a week, and clean the bathrooms on the weekend, because it'll make you feel more important, and therefore you won't be tempted to sleep with other women?"

His eyes flicker. "Yes," he lies.

"Let him be more a part of your world. You don't have to be perfect, Rachel," Laney says.

That's news to me.

"Our time is up, but I think we're moving forward," Laney says. "See you next week."

We get into the car without speaking and head through town, past the old folks' home and the park.

"Why don't we go out for a drink?" Adam says as we're paused at a stop sign. His voice is tense, but I know he's trying.

"Sure," I say, because Laney has said to be open to moments of intimacy, and not just sexual intimacy. Plus, I have to show that I'm trying, too.

"Want to go to Storm King?"

"Sure." I've never been there; it's for the new breed of Cambry-on-Hudson residents, the hipsters and artists and young PhD students from the university, still straddling the line between adulthood and perpetual student.

Inside, it's sleek and dark, white leather chairs at glass tables, the bar backlit with blue light. And suddenly, it seems fun. Jenny is babysitting; I text her that we'll be later than we thought, and she texts back, No hurry! We're having a blast. I appreciate the good cheer, because I know she hates Adam these days. I appreciate that, too...the solidarity.

"Feels like we're playing hooky," Adam says, and though I never did that before, I know what he means.

Instead of ordering my usual boring white wine, I ask for a dirty martini, very dry, three olives.

Adam raises an eyebrow. "Same for me," he says. We don't talk, just look around until the waiter brings our drinks. I take a big sip. Dear God, it's disgusting. But I smile at Adam. "Let's not talk about the Situation," I say, which has become our code word for his affair. "And let's not talk about the girls."

"Deal," he says, offering his hand, and I shake it and laugh. Then I lick my upper lip as if savoring the paint thinner I've just swallowed.

"I had a dream the other night," Adam says, his eyes on my mouth. "I'm not sure if I should tell you about it, though."

"Go ahead," I say, taking another swallow of martini.

"Well...I dreamed I was alone. I wasn't sure if you were away, or if we were divorced, but it was just me and the girls, and as the dream went on, I realized that you weren't coming back. At first I thought you left me. Then I realized it was because you...died."

He waits for my reaction. "I have those dreams about you all the time," I tell him. "Daydreams, I call them." And I laugh, and Adam gives me a bemused look, then laughs, too.

"No, you don't," he says.

"No, I *do*," I say. "I'm always checking to make sure your life insurance is paid up, because I'm going to be really comfortable. It's all very tragic and noble, because you'll die a horrible death. Also, I might get highlights, go a little blonder." I laugh, quite entertained by this person who speaks her mind in so entertaining a fashion.

"Jesus, listen to you," he says, but he's laughing, too. "Do you get remarried in this happy fantasy?"

"I do," I say. "He's wonderful. A firefighter, I think. Very brawny, with a tattoo on one shoulder."

"Shit. I guess the selfless thing for me to do here is sleep on the train tracks tonight."

"I'd appreciate that. I'll make sure the girls remember you. Fondly."

And we're flirting. I don't know how it happens, but we're flirting, and God, he's so attractive, so handsome and sexy, and yes, there are women in the bar looking at him, but he doesn't look away from me, and I suddenly feel like I can do this, I can get past his indiscretion. People get through these things. Our marriage can be better because of it. I'm not so naive anymore. I'm a woman of the world; I'm very European—sure, my husband had an affair, but it's so last month. And soon it will be so last year, and then last decade, and we'll barely remember it, except, ironically, almost as a joke. *Remember when you cheated on me? With what's-her-name?* and Adam will say, *Yeah, my head was really up my ass, wasn't it?*

We don't wait to get home. We do it in the backseat of the car, and it's dirty and fast and amazing, as if we're twenty years old. I come before he even gets his pants down, and I come again when he shoves into me, and the smell of his neck, the sounds he makes are so familiar and wonderful; they're a part of my life, and I don't want to give him away. I want us back. I'll get us back.

Adam wants porno sex, and he's getting it, by God.

FOR THE NEXT few days, I feel a little smug. It's easier to be happy, and while I'm not my old self, I'm not a bitter, hateful shrew, either.

I try to put this into words when I'm on the phone with Jenny during the girls' nap time. I'm baking oatmeal raisin cookies, Charlotte's favorite for this week. The girls just finished the Snickerdoodles—Grace's favorite—and next week, I'll go back to chocolate chip for Rose. Oatmeal is my favorite, too, and if there's a smell for love, it's warm oatmeal raisin cookies. Or the girls' heads when they first wake up from naps.

Or Adam in the morning, slightly salty and sweaty mixed with the smell of sun and fresh air from our line-dried sheets.

"I guess we turned a corner," I tell my sister.

"So you're sleeping together again?"

I feel my cheeks warm. We're *fucking*, is what we're doing. "Mmm-hmm."

"Condoms still?"

"Jenny! Can you give us a break, please?" The residual shame of that doctor's visit makes my stomach curl, and Jenny's reminder makes me both mortified and furious.

But yes. Just in case.

I add the raisins to the batter and stir them in. Jenny is still quiet.

She does this sometimes, just slips under like a submarine diving, following urgent orders for a top secret mission. Whatever she's about to say will be momentous, if it follows her pattern.

"You ever wonder about Mom and Dad?" she asks quietly.

"Wonder what?"

Another pause. "If their marriage was as good as Mom says."

I frown. "Jenny, we were there. It *was* good. They were so happy. Why would you even ask that?"

"It just seems a little too perfect when Mom talks about it."

"Well, first of all, it *was* pretty goddamned perfect." New Rachel, who fucks her husband, also swears with great relish. "And secondly, so what if she embellishes the past? That's all she has."

"She could have the present."

It's a familiar refrain. Jenny can be too judgmental. I can't count how many times she's told our mother to take a class, a trip, volunteer, get a job. I used to worry about what she'd think of me being a stay-at-home mom, but she's only ever told me how much she admires me for it. She's always seemed sincere.

"Mom's doing the best she can," I say. "Cut her some slack, Jenny. Her husband was killed in his prime."

"Twenty-five years ago."

"I know how long it's been." There's an edge in my voice. New Rachel is allowed to have an edge.

"Of course you do. I'm sorry. What did the girls do today?"

"We had Mommy and Me swimming. Rose finally went underwater for real."

"Hooray! I'll call her later and congratulate her, okay?"

"You bet. I have to go. Cookies to bake, laundry to fold."

"Okay, Martha Stewart. Love you."

"Love you, too."

I realize the question about the girls was a peace offering. Jenny does adore them, that's for sure.

My mind goes back to Mommy and Me swimming today. Elle complimented me on my weight loss and asked me which diet I was on. *Acid stomach*, I wanted to say. *You should try it. I can introduce your husband to Emmanuelle if you want.*

Still, the sight of my hip bones is strangely pleasing to me. And to Adam, who bit one last night when we were *fucking*.

A sudden wave of grief rocks me on my feet, a hard, fast rogue wave.

And then I hear the girls stir over the monitor, and I'm so glad they're awake I run up the stairs.

A FEW DAYS later, Jared calls and asks if I can have lunch with him. I arrange for Donna to pick up the girls from nursery school—Mom would, she said wearily when I asked her first, but she hates driving with the girls and can never figure out the car seats, and what if something happened? She is both jealous of Donna and grateful for her.

I leave the minivan with Donna and take Adam's fortieth birthday present to himself, a two-seat convertible Jaguar—red, of course. We take it on date nights and to country-club functions. I've never driven it, and I don't ask permission to take it today. What's mine is yours, after all.

I remember the joke someone made at Adam's fortieth—better a sports car than a mistress, ha ha ha.

New Rachel looks past that. New Rachel doesn't bother telling Adam she's going out to lunch with a male friend.

It takes me a minute to figure out how to start the car, but I manage. It's a gorgeous May day, and with the top down, I can smell the lilacs and apple blossoms. The minivan smells like apple juice and Goldfish crackers—*eau de maternité*. At least it no longer smells of vomit. Adam took the car to be detailed after the girls exploded that day.

I never did tell him about Gus and how he rescued me.

The truth is, I love having a secret from Adam. Gus and his smiling eyes are hardly Emmanuelle's vagina, but the memory of him is comforting and a tiny bit thrilling.

My hair whips around, so I shove my sunglasses on my head to keep the strands out of my face. Very New Rachel of me, driving the Jag. I pass Bliss, whose windows glow with the beauty of my sister's work. The latest display dress is a blush ball gown covered in tiny sparkles, and it looks as though it could float away, it's so light and airy.

The shop is the jewel of the downtown shopping district, the newspaper article said, and at the time, I felt a pang of jealousy. My sister's been here for a month, and already people are flocking to Bliss, standing in front of the windows. Rumor at Mommy and Me said that a Roosevelt descendant is going to have Jenny make her dress. She hadn't mentioned that to me.

In some ways, Jenny belongs to Cambry-on-Hudson more than I do. She knows the baristas at Blessed Bean by name, went to a gallery opening one night, joined a Zumba class at the rather gritty YMCA. One day when we went for a walk with the girls, she was called by name by the old black gentlemen who sit in front of the barbershop every day. I've never talked to them, which made me feel racist at that moment. But Jenny's always been like that, able to make friends just by walking into a room and saying hello. I also say hello, but my stupid, unavoidable shyness keeps me from actually making the kind of connection Jenny does.

I know the other moms. I know some of our old classmates, I know the country-club crowd. I know the children's librarian, but not the other adults who work there, even though I go in at least once a week.

It occurs to me that I'd like to have more friends.

I'll stop by Bliss after lunch, if I have time. Or not. I might do something else. Get a facial, maybe, at Vous, the day spa around the corner. Maybe I'll buy some new shoes, the kind that Jenny wears. Not flats. No way.

Or I'll just go home and plant the pansies the girls and I picked out the other day. That's what the old Rachel wants to do. But maybe it'd be good to have some true Me Time.

I go into Hudson's, the sweet little tavern that was formerly a dark and sticky bar patronized by hardcore alcoholics. There's Jared, waiting for me, a smile on his face. "Hey, Rach!" he says, and we sit down, getting a table by the window so we can admire the mighty river.

"Thanks for meeting me," he says.

"Of course!" I say. As always, Jared reminds me of the dogs his family used to have—golden retrievers, always happy, always wagging. Jared is like his dad, who's the minister of our church. Not like his mother, who has never once invited me to call her by her first name, never once acted happy to see me in town or at the club.

Jared makes up for it. He's one of the few people I feel really comfortable with.

"Got any new pictures of the girls?" he asks, and I comply, whipping out my phone so he can admire. The girls worship him; they call him Uncle Jared, and he always manages to find strange and wonderful presents at holidays and their birthday. "God, they're so cute!" he says. "Look at Charlotte. She looks just like you. And Grace is the spitting image of Adam, isn't she? Aw, look at Rose! Bet she enjoyed that... What is she eating, anyway? Mud?"

"Actually, no, Jared. It's pudding. Believe it or not, we don't feed the girls mud."

He grins, and we order lunch—a huge burger for him, fries and a milkshake; he's as skinny as can be, always has been. A salad with dressing on the side for me, so I can keep my hip bones. When the food comes, he reveals the true nature of this lunch. "So, Rach," he says,

"Kimber was wondering if you'd be in our wedding. Bridesmaid. What do you think?"

"Really? Of course! I'd love to." I take a sip of my water. "But, um, why didn't she ask me herself?"

"She was afraid you'd say no."

"Why would I do that? I mean, I'm a little old to be a bridesmaid, but it's a huge honor."

"I'm a little old to be getting married for the first time," he says, grinning.

"Nah. It just took you a while to find the right woman."

"She's great, isn't she?"

"I really like her. She's very...sincere."

"Yes! That's a perfect word for her." His smile drops a little. "The thing is, Rach, my mom kind of hates her. And Kimber's having a tough time. She had a really different upbringing than I did, and Mom's making sure she knows it. Kimber wants to fit in and stuff, but you can see she's not..."

"Typical."

"Exactly. Which is why I love her."

"Maybe she and Jenny and I can go out sometime."

He smiles hugely. "I was hoping you'd say that. You're the best, Rach. Hey, she's meeting me at the office at two. We have to do something wedding-related. Cake-tasting or something. Want to come and say hi? She'll be so happy you said yes to being in the wedding."

"Sure," I say. "That'd be nice." I pause, struck by a horrible thought. "Who else is in the wedding? Anyone I know? Anyone from work?" In a flash, I see myself posing for pictures with Emmanuelle. Maybe they're friends. Jared likes everyone, after all.

"No one from work. Her cousin, a couple of friends.

They all have tattoos. My mother is dying a thousand deaths." He keeps talking, a lot more informed than Adam was when we got married.

Since I found out about Emmanuelle, I've wanted to ask Jared about her. But I can't. It would give her legitimacy, somehow, if I had to tap my oldest friend for insider information. And to be honest, I was afraid Jared would know why I was asking, and our lifelong friendship would be tainted by pity. And then Adam's work relationship would suffer, because it's always been clear that while Jared and Adam get long just fine, Jared is *my* friend.

What you don't realize when your husband has an affair is how much lying you'll do, too. In the past month, I've lied to my mother for the first time. To my in-laws— thank God they live in Arizona. To Adam's sister, who lives in Portugal but emails often and sends the girls lovely gifts from her travels. I've lied to the nursery school teacher when she asked if everything was okay, and I've lied to my book club friends. I've even lied to Jenny. Lying has become a reflex. I don't even think about it anymore.

When we leave the restaurant, I get into the Jag. Jared grins. "Can't say I've ever seen you drive that thing," he says.

"Because I never have," I say. He gets into his BMW, and we head to Triple B. Kimber is waiting in the foyer, wearing a peasant blouse, rainbow skirt and leather vest. She has on dozens of bracelets that jingle and chime when she jumps up. Her face flushes pink at the sight of her honey.

"Hi, you guys," she says. "How was lunch and stuff?"

"It was great," I say. "Thank you so much for asking me to be in the wedding, Kimber! I can't wait."

"Seriously? Oh, Rachel, thanks! Really! I mean, like, of course you're Jared's oldest friend and stuff. I'm just so happy you'll do it." She gives me a sudden hug. "Thank you."

"My pleasure. Hey, I was saying to Jared that maybe you'd like to go out for drinks with my sister and me."

"Totally!" she exclaims.

"I'll call you, then." Her eagerness makes me happy, makes me feel like myself. My old self.

"Well, we have cake to eat," Jared says. "Shall we go, babe? Bye, Rachel. Thanks again." He gives me a kiss on the cheek, waves to Lydia, the receptionist, and off they go into the sunshine.

I hope they stay happy. I can't imagine Jared ever cheating on her. He's so loyal… I mean, who stays friends with the shy girl who rode the bus with you, even though you've met a thousand people since? Loyal people, that's who.

"Guess you want to see Adam, huh?" Lydia asks.

"What? Oh, yes. Yes, please."

She picks up the phone to let him know I'm here. "I'll just go, Lydia," I say. "No need to buzz him."

Because I have that feeling again, that prickling, sickening feeling in my knees and elbows. I walk down the hall, fast and quietly, hoping not to get pulled into a chat with any of the other lawyers, and get to Adam's office.

The door is closed.

I open it, fast, and there they are, kissing.

They leap apart. Emmanuelle's eye makeup is smeared, her lipstick is gone.

"Babe," Adam says, and I just stand there, frozen.

At least my outfit is better today. That's my first thought. Last time, I looked like a child. Today, I look pretty hot. Not as hot as she does, granted, but hot for me. Today, her dress is a very tight red knit with a slit in the front, a wide neckline, long sleeves. She's one of those women whose sexiness comes from what she doesn't show, not from what she does, apparently. Her red hair is in a high ponytail, and I remember a comment from Jake Golden at a country-club function once—redhead in a red dress equals instant erection. Jake Golden is an ass. That being said, yes, Adam seems to have an erection.

I should go. Clearly, this is the moment when the wife walks out, proudly, head high, shoulders back, and goes…um…where? Where does the wife go? Well, hey, I'm in a big-ass law firm. I should go to one of the family law attorneys, right? Or Jared. I could go to Jared's office—much bigger than Adam's, much more prestigious—but no, he's out tasting cakes. If my father were still alive, I'd go to him and cry on his shoulder till I was all cried out. Jenny's. I'll go to Jenny. Or home. Except the girls will sense I'm upset, and they'll act up because of it. Happens every time.

My hand is still on the doorknob.

"I'll go," Emmanuelle says. She grabs a tissue and wipes her eyes, then slips out of the office. Her hand brushes my bare arm, and I leap back as if she has leprosy.

"Rachel," Adam says in a low voice. "Come in. Close the door."

I obey, standing in front of the couch where he explains tax loopholes to his clients or confers with Bruce, his paralegal, or fucks his mistress.

"Have a seat," he says.

"No."

"This is not what it seems," he says. "She's having a hard time with…me ending things. She came in here, very upset, and threw herself at me. That's what you saw."

"How stupid do you think I am, Adam?"

"I don't think you're stupid."

"You're still sleeping with her."

"No! No, I am *not* sleeping with that woman."

"Save it. Enjoy single life."

I turn to leave, but he grabs my arm, and his face is suddenly furious. "You want a divorce? Do you *really* want a divorce, Rach? You want to get the girls every other week? You want them to have a stepmother? You want to move to some shitty apartment? Because last time I checked, I'm the one who pays the bills around here."

"So what does that mean? You get to screw around? You get to cheat on me, because I stay home to raise our children? You think a judge isn't going to squeeze every last dime out of you, Adam? You think Jared Brewster will let you keep working here?"

Something ugly flickers across his face. "Right. Too bad you couldn't marry him. All those years wasted, waiting for him to notice you."

I don't dignify that with a response. "I'm taking the girls to Jenny's. Have a wonderful weekend. I'm sure your slut will be thrilled that you're free."

And I *do* walk out, head held high, shoulders back. I make it to the car before I throw up. Right in the backseat.

Jenny

EVEN THOUGH I'VE seen Leo in a suit once before—sleeping in his ratty lawn chair—the sight of him clean-shaven, groomed and dressed to kill is a little...uh...wow.

Gray suit. Black shirt. Gray patterned tie. He looks like he stepped out of the pages of *GQ*, all tall and kind of thin, making me want to cook for him. His hair curls off his forehead, and his eyes are so... And those heartbreaking cheekbones...

"Close your mouth," he says. "Are you ready?"

"Oh. Yes. Uh-huh."

"Come on, Jenny. Snap out of it."

"You look... You're beautiful."

His brow wrinkles with an incredulous look. "Can we get this show on the road? You look nice, by the way."

I manage to close my mouth. "I better. I spent a fortune on this dress."

"Impressing the old boyfriend. A staple of the female psyche."

"It's more like 'impressing the ex-husband's wife,' but yes."

Tonight's the dinner at Owen and Ana-Sofia's, and of course I bought a new dress. I'm a clothing designer.

Clothes are maybe the one area in which I can claim a slight edge on Ana-Sofia. Not that it's a competition; she was crowned the victor a good while back. Whatever the case, I'm wearing a Catherine Deane white embroidered dress with leather trim and my suede gray-and-black leopard print Manolo shoes. Don't judge me. Whenever I buy an outfit that costs this much, I donate the same amount to a charity. Plus, I have to look gorgeous as part of my PR program for Bliss—or so I justify my clothes-whore ways to myself.

"You're driving, by the way," Leo says. "Hang on, I'll get Loki."

"What? No, you won't. Loki's not coming!"

"He is, or I'm not." He gives me a patient, pitying look. "Jenny, what if he has a seizure? I'm not leaving him."

"But I didn't tell them we were bringing a dog."

"So what? Throw them off their game a little. Fuck up their perfect little world. Maybe Loki will do you a favor and puke on the new wife."

"Okay, that *is* a pleasing image, I'll give you that. But if Loki sheds on my dress, I'm letting him out on the West Side Highway."

He leans in, and I practically swoon. "No, you wouldn't," he whispers. "You're too nice."

"It's hard to stop eye-fucking you when you flirt with me."

"Duly noted."

I get behind the wheel and wait as my date-who-is-not-a-date gets his dog and guides him into the backseat. Loki growls at me, but I'm used to it by now. The smell, however, is new. "You can wash dogs, I've heard," I say as Leo gets in the front seat.

"Yeah. Well, Loki doesn't like baths."

"Neither does my niece, but she gets them." I start the car and pull into the street.

Leo turns back to see if Loki is settled, and pets the foul-tempered (and smelling) dog. I do admire his devotion to the animal. It'd be nice if the animal could find it in his heart to like me a little. I see him almost every day, after all. Now that the weather is gorgeous and the days are longer, Leo is outside in his lounge chair more than ever. I've bribed both Leo and Loki with meat products, but it's only worked on Leo so far.

There have been no other kisses exchanged. Made me almost wish for Loki to have another seizure.

"So tell me about Mr. and Mrs. Perfect," Leo says.

"It's Dr. and Dr. Perfect. She has a PhD in something noble. He's a plastic surgeon, the type who fixes facial deformities, not the boob-job type. She runs a foundation that digs wells in third-world countries."

"I hate them both already."

"Thank you, loyal friend."

He grins, and I have to concentrate on not sideswiping the Hummer in the lane next to me.

"So what went wrong with you and Dr. Perfect the Male?"

"Owen. I don't really know."

"Oh, come on. Sure you do."

"The divorce was his call. I was very happy."

"Really? So you were completely stunned when he sat you down for the talk. No warning signs. Just blissful happiness and then he shot you in the heart."

"Yep."

"Jenny. You're not that dense, are you?"

My hands tighten on the steering wheel. Behind me,

Loki farts, and the smell is damn near toxic. I give Leo a look and roll down my window.

"I'd rather not analyze the failure of my marriage right now, okay?"

"What better time? I bet there were warning signs."

"Maybe there were. I just didn't see them as warnings. I thought it was just normal stuff."

"Like what?" He's turned in his seat to look at me, and there's something about his eyes that basically forces a person to talk. The interest, the kindness, the hint of humor—or mockery. "Tell Uncle Leo."

I sigh. "He wanted to travel more than I did. He did three weeks with Doctors Without Borders every year, and he wanted to do more. His workdays got longer and longer. He zoned out when I talked about my job." *The sex wasn't fabulous anymore. He stopped laughing at my jokes.*

He got bored with me.

Leo sighs. "Men suck."

"Preach it, brother." I put on the turn signal and take the exit that leads to my former home.

ANA-SOFIA GREETS ME at the door with her usual cry of joy. "Jenny! How wonderful to see you! And you look so beautiful!"

I'm horribly overdressed. Ana is wearing long wide-legged raw silk pants and a white asymmetrically cut, perfectly simple tank top. Eileen Fisher, fabulous on Ana's superslender tall figure. Bare feet, no makeup, no pedicure, her straight, long hair in a simple ponytail.

Damn. I got the clothes completely wrong tonight.

"And you're Leo," Ana-Sofia says, kissing Leo on both cheeks. "Come in, come in! Oh, you brought your dog! Hello, puppy!" Loki, that foul-breathed, gaseous cur, wags his stumpy little tail and lets Ana-Sofia stroke his ears. Traitor.

"Holy shit," Leo mutters. "You weren't lying about how beautiful she is."

"Not helping," I mutter back.

"Jenny." Owen gives me a big hug. "I've missed you! It's so good to see you. Hello, I'm Owen."

"Right, the ex-husband. I'm Leo Killian. Nice to meet you."

"Would you like a drink?" Owen says.

"Love one," Leo answers.

"Jenny?"

"You bet. Whatever you're having. Where's Natalia?"

"She's sleeping," Ana-Sofia says. "You haven't seen the nursery, have you, Jenny? Come, take a peek!"

She leads me down the hall—already hung with three black-and-white photos of the new family—to what was once my home office. It's been transformed into the most beautiful baby's room I've ever seen, soft peach walls with white trim, a series of Classic Pooh prints hanging in a row. Exotic mobiles and wall prints add color to the room, as does a bright red-and-orange printed rug. There's an entire wall filled with shelves of children's books in several languages and a hammock of stuffed animals—all made with organic wool, no doubt, hand-knit by nuns in the Swiss Alps.

But what gets me the most is this: in white paint, in the handwriting I recognize all too well, is written "Daddy loves you very much," and underneath that, in different handwriting, "Mommy does, too!" Natalia is sleeping on her back, her arms by her head. She's covered by the white satin quilt I made.

I love her. I can't help it. She's the child of the man I married, the child of a kind and generous woman, and I helped her into this world. I'm a schmuck, but I love this baby. My eyes mist over, and Ana-Sofia puts her hand on my back. "You are so kind to us," she says.

Oh, shut up, I want to say. I smile instead.

We go back into the living room, where two more couples have joined the party. Introductions are made—Felicia and Howard, Bitty and Evan.

What if I hadn't brought Leo? I'd be the odd woman out, surrounded by three married couples, like that horribly familiar scene in *Bridget Jones's Diary*. Or was Ana-Sofia going to dig through her list of eligible men and find me someone? And if she was, why hasn't she? Fixing up the lingering ex-wife would seem like a priority, wouldn't it? Why, for that matter, hasn't Owen introduced me to a wonderful doctor friend? "*Jenny, this is Alessandro, a cardiologist*—no, strike that, too many emergencies—*an ophthalmologist, and I knew you two would hit it off.*" *And I look into Alessandro's dark eyes—yes, he's from Italy. Venice—and there's a sparkle there, and when we kiss...*

I remember Leo's kiss. That not-quite-just-friends kiss. I look over at him, and he cocks an eyebrow. Yeah, yeah. I'm incredibly transparent. I know that.

The other couples are fine. They're *those* New Yorkers, the people who spend Thanksgiving morning at the soup kitchen, then stop by the package store to buy a three-hundred-dollar bottle of wine to bring to their friends' penthouse. They listen to NPR—and so do I, but only for the storytelling shows. The people who send you those petitions for your online signature to stop the killings in wherever killings are taking place. As if those signatures are really going to do anything.

Felicia Balewa, who's Nigerian, makes documentaries about social injustice. Her husband, Howard, is a movie producer—and also a Vanderbilt. Bitty Lamb, I know, is a gastroenterologist (hard to believe people choose that particular specialty). Her husband, Evan Allard (French), is a high-end fund-raiser for an organization that educates girls in India.

And the thing is, that's all fantastic. I'm glad they work at the soup kitchen and care about *their causes*. It's the self-congratulatory sense they have, so gravely discussing their commitment and level of knowledge.

I find myself doing it, too. *I haven't found the right volunteer opportunity just yet, but I'm still getting settled in. An apprenticeship program for sure, absolutely.* To my credit, I *have* actually thought of that idea... I just haven't done anything about it yet. *Yes, it's terrible about urban blight. Surely there's more we can do for those at-risk kids.* I hate the way I sound.

At least Leo isn't listening. He's surveying Owen and Ana's book collection, which are all glossy, important tomes and coffee-table books that raise awareness on subjects that matter.

Sigh.

The appetizer hour is endless, in which we eat organic sheep cheese flavored with locally grown organic herbs served on, yes, organic, gluten-free, fair-trade crackers. Ana-Sofia talks about the latest wells her foundation has funded. Felicia mentions her interview on CNN last week in reference to her latest documentary about a secret girls' school started by a friend of Malala. Bitty and Owen discuss Doctors Without Borders and where they're each interested in going next.

Wedding dresses don't really come up.

Owen must sense my discomfort, because he comes over and gives my shoulder a squeeze.

"Bitty's uncle was recently visiting," Evan says in his thick and gorgeous accent. "We took him to zee exhibit at zee Frick. So beautiful. They gave a private tour, of course, so he would not be recognized."

"Who's your uncle, Bitty?" I ask.

"I don't like to name-drop," she says, smiling down at her wineglass.

"I will give you clues, yes?" Evan offers. "My wife, her uncle is an author of some fame. He has been on that woman's show? *Oprah*?"

"*Wally* Lamb?" I say, feeling like I just got the right answer to Final Jeopardy. *See, gang? I, too, can read!* "Wally Lamb's your uncle?"

She shrugs and gives a small smile.

We observe a moment of silence for the great man, whose books I'm almost positive I've read. Well, I've read one or two. Probably just one. I make a mental note to read them all, because I feel really stupid right about now.

Then Loki rises from behind the couch, where he's been sleeping this past eternity, stretches and breaks wind in a long, poisonous hiss.

"Oh, no, is that a dog?" Felicia asks. "I'm afraid of dogs," she says.

"So stay away from him," Leo says mildly. He's not helping.

"Leo, your work, what is it that you do?" Evan asks.

"I'm a piano teacher."

"He's a Juilliard graduate," I offer. "Right, Leo?"

He gives me a dark look.

"We have a piano," Ana-Sofia offers, nodding at the baby grand. "How wonderful if you'd play for us, Leo."

"I don't play anymore," Leo says. "Sorry." He pours himself more wine.

"Dinner's ready," Owen says.

"You remembered I'm a vegan, right?" Bitty says. "I can't tolerate animal products of any kind."

"Makes me sorry I wore my bacon bra," I say. No one laughs but Owen, who puts his arm around my shoulders as we walk into the dining room. I'm grateful. Even if Owen's guests are not really my type, even if Leo isn't being a great date, Owen is still Owen, and still cares about me.

"I hear the baby," Ana-Sofia says. "Excuse me, please."

"I'll come with you," Felicia says. "I've been dying to hold her."

"Jenny, will you give me a hand?" Owen asks. His hand rests on the small of my back as we go into the kitchen. "Ana said to keep an eye on this couscous, but to be honest, I have no idea what I'm doing."

For the next few minutes, Owen and I work together in the sleek galley kitchen. Asparagus and couscous, sweet potatoes and quinoa. It's like old times, though we used to serve more basic foods when we were married—roast chicken and stew and lasagna, with the occasional Japanese meal when Owen felt like putting on a show. But we know the space well, and each other's rhythms. He slides behind me, I remind him where the serving spoons are kept. Guess he and Ana-Sofia never did rearrange the kitchen.

"So you and this Leo... Things serious?" Owen asks.

"We're friends," I say. "We met when I moved in." Owen nods at that. "How's fatherhood, Owen?"

His face changes, gentling and glowing at the same time. "Amazing," he says. "She smiled the other day, and I...I *felt* it, Jen. You know? In my heart." He wipes his eyes. "I'm so sorry I never thought I wanted kids. I was wrong."

What's the proper response to that? *Great! Then let's kill Ana-Sofia and raise the baby just us two.* Or how about *Bite me, and thanks for nothing.* "Well. A lot of people say that, I guess."

Natalia the Perfect Infant apparently goes back to sleep. Ana and Felicia return to the table, and talk turns to foreign films. Leo shoots me a pained look and pours himself more wine. Ana gives him a smile, as if she's apologizing.

"I always thought *The Seventh Seal* was Bergman's greatest work," Howard says.

"No! Are you kidding with me?" Evan exclaims. "But of course you have seen *The Virgin Spring*? It is so superior!"

"The Angelika had the most amazing retro documentary night last month," Bitty says. "*Deus e o Diablo na Terra do Sol.* You have to watch it without the subtitles for the full impact. As 1960s socioeconomic films go, that one has to be the best."

"I was just going to say that," Leo says.

"Were you!" Bitty coos.

"No."

Super. I think Leo may be a little drunk. Then again, if I wasn't driving tonight, I'd be right there with him.

But he's not being the world's best date, and he is being borderline rude, barely talking.

"I just watched *Citizen Kane* again," Howard says.

"For the twentieth time!" Felicia cheers.

"The message of corruption and innocence… So profound."

Then Ana-Sofia comes out from the bedroom, holding the perfect bundle that is Natalia, and hands her to me, and I breathe in that perfect baby scent, and then her warm little face is snuggled against my neck. "She missed her Aunt Jenny," Ana says.

Oh, *babies*. My whole body aches with the wonder and wanting of them, the sweet, trusting weight, the silken head of black hair. I close my eyes, love wrapping around me in a warm, soft squeeze.

Leo stands up. "I have to take Loki for a walk," he says. "Excuse me."

The baby is passed around while Leo is out. He's gone for a longer time than I'd like.

To make up for my date's lack of conversational input, I find myself trying harder. After all, these people aren't horrible. In fact, they're really sincere, if a little hard to take. Yes, they're wealthy. A lot of New Yorkers are. Owen is. I didn't do too badly, either. Still don't. So I chatter and listen and joke, getting uptight Felicia to admit she misses ham, telling stories about brides and Andreas. It's nice, too, because Owen chimes in here and there, saying, "Jenny, tell them about the Christmas when Andreas and your mother got lost in the Bronx," or "Oh, God, I remember that wedding!"

Natalia, however, is the star of the show—she's smiling and cooing. I can't take my eyes off her, and when Felicia gets to hold her, jealousy knifes through me. Felicia lives three blocks away. She can see Natalia all the time.

Leo finally comes back in, washes his hands in the kitchen and returns to the table. "Nice night," he says, sitting back in his seat as Loki trots off to collapse in the living room.

"Would you like to hold the baby?" Felicia asks, offering him Natalia as if she's a loaf of bread.

"No, thank you."

I don't see how he can resist petting the baby, or touching her adorable little foot, which she keeps kicking in his direction.

"Leo, do you have children?" Ana-Sofia asks.

"No."

There's an awkward silence. "Leo's great with older kids, though," I offer.

"It must be so rewarding, Leo, introducing children to music," Ana says.

"Sometimes."

"Tell them about Evander," I suggest.

He doesn't answer. Does pour himself more wine, though.

"Evander is an actual child prodigy," I say to cover. "Leo thinks he has great potential. You should *hear* this kid play. He's amazing. I get goose bumps, and I don't even like classical music." I smile. Leo does not smile back.

"Jenny, remember when I took you to the Met to hear *The Magic Flute*, and you fell asleep?" Owen says fondly.

"I don't remember the opera. I do remember that nice nap, though."

Talk turns to music, and I feel myself getting more

irritated with Leo. After all, he's probably more quali-
fied than anyone here to talk about that particular subject, but he doesn't say a word, just sips wine. Not very
slowly, either. Though the others try to bring him into
the conversation, his answers are curt.

I wish I hadn't brought him.

As Ana-Sofia starts to clear dessert dishes, I stand
up to help her—no one else does, I'm irritated to note.
"Jenny, please, you're our guest," she says gently.

"She wasn't always, though, was she?" Leo asks
mildly. "She was once the hostess. Probably still re-
members where everything goes."

The table falls silent, and my face burns.

Then we hear the unmistakable gacking of a dog
about to puke. *Ooah. Ooah. Ooaaah*… And puke Loki
does, right under the coffee table.

"I'll get that," I say, grateful—yes, grateful!—that I
can clean dog puke instead of sit there and fight the urge
to kick Leo in the shins. Ana-Sofia assures us it's fine,
the rug is nothing special, just something she picked up
in Syria a few years ago—probably a priceless gift from
a tribal lord, knowing Ana.

But I do remember where the paper towels are, and
she's holding the baby now, so yeah, I help clean it up,
trying not to dry-heave myself—dinner was *good*, and
leave it to Ana-Sofia to make vegan food not only pal-
atable but delicious.

Owen helps. Leo doesn't. Leo, the ass, has Loki's
leash out and the dynamic duo stands by the door. I assume we're leaving.

I wash my hands in the kitchen. "Jenny," Owen says,
"I don't know exactly what Leo meant, but I hope you

know how much Ana-Sofia and I love having you in our lives."

"No, I do. He's... He doesn't know what he's talking about."

Owen fixes me with a long look, then takes my hand. Being a surgeon, Owen has always taken very good care of his hands. They're smooth and immaculate, his nails trimmed perfectly. The gold band on his left hand still looks very new.

I always loved his hands. So gentle and perfect. He used to rub my shoulders almost every night, knowing that at least part of my day had been spent at a sewing machine or bent over a sketch pad, and he'd joke that it was good for his hands, too, to keep them strong for the long surgeries when he'd have to wield his instruments with such precision and care. My favorite part of sex with him was the way his hands would skim across my skin, so gentle and thorough.

"It's good to see you," he murmurs. "I miss talking every day."

My throat is suddenly tight. "Well," I whisper. "Me, too."

"Maybe we can have lunch or dinner sometime. Just us two. Really catch up."

"That'd be nice." I clear my throat. "I guess I should get going."

I say goodbye to the other guests, which is horribly awkward with Leo standing over by the door like a kid who can't wait to leave Grandma's. Ana and Owen walk me to where he stands, his face neutral. A weird energy is crackling off him. Dog stress, no doubt. "Thank you for a wonderful night," I say, kissing both of my hosts on the cheek.

"Very nice to have met you, Leo," Owen says.

"We hope we'll see you again," Ana-Sofia seconds.

"Nice to meet you, too," Leo manages.

"I'll call you about lunch, okay?" Owen says. He takes the baby from Ana-Sofia and makes her wave her tiny fist at me. It might be my imagination, but I think Natalia Genevieve just smiled at me. My heart clenches, and I force a smile, which drops the second the door is closed.

The dog won't get into the elevator, so Leo picks him up, getting a faint growl. I look at the dog, whose eyes are cloudy with cataracts. Poor thing. First the seizures, now the barfing. Leo probably should put him down. The dog burps at me. Just what I needed. The smell is disgusting.

The elevator doors open and Leo puts Loki down. I wave to the doorman—Steve, always so nice—and he nods back. Seems he's forgotten me.

Outside, the air is damp and coppery from a shower. The omnipresent song of the city—cab horns and fire sirens, air brakes and subway rumbling—plays around us. Leo gives me a look. "Ready to go, or do you want to genuflect a minute or two?"

"You know, Leo, you were a pretty shitty date tonight. I have to say, I thought you'd do better."

"Didn't I kiss enough ass? I'm sorry," he says.

"No ass-kissing required, Leo. Polite conversation would've been nice, though."

"Oh. So I should exploit Evander for dinner conversation? So those people can go back and say 'We know a little black child who's being taught piano for free! Isn't the world a wonderful place?'"

"No! We were talking about music, and Evander is interesting, that's all. Jeesh."

"Yeah, well, he's also a child."

"A child with great musical talent. What was the problem, Leo?"

"You! Trying to impress those jackasses, and I definitely include your ex-husband in that group."

Loki barks as a scruffy white dog is led past. The owner gives us a dirty look. "Fine, let's go," I say, fishing in my cute little bag for my keys. By the grace of the gods, we'd found parking just two blocks down. Leo's long legs outpace mine, hobbled in heels as I am, and I don't try to keep up.

Besides, I miss this neighborhood. The Upper West Side has all the glory when it comes to town houses and prewar buildings, but the Upper East has its jewels, too. I take my time, stopping to look up at a beautiful window or admire a doorway. The buildings are all like old friends, the old brownstones and oak doors, and even if I didn't know a lot of neighbors, I knew a few. This had been my home. Sort of.

On the drive down, Leo asked me if I'd seen any signs that my marriage was in trouble. One thing I could've mentioned was that throughout the entire course of my married life, I felt like I was playing grown-ups. *Look at this great apartment! Look at my husband, the doctor! We're going out with friends! I know Tim Gunn! No, I'm serious!*

That feeling was present tonight, too…this cool dinner party where I was a guest, where I talked with those sophisticated, educated people. The elegant food, the lovely wine, the intelligent—and sure, sometimes pretentious—conversation. So what if they like documentaries and Swedish films? Someone has to.

And I *can* hold my own. I'm not some hick with nothing going for her.

I get in the car in what I hope is frosty silence. Leo gets his smelly dog settled in the backseat, then buckles in. Neither of us says anything as I negotiate my way up to Ninety-seventh, across the Park and over to the West Side Highway.

"What I don't understand," Leo finally says, "is why you still want your ex to like you. He rejected you, he burned rubber finding someone else and he popped out a baby with her in record time, and you just can't get enough punishment."

"What *I* don't understand is why you want so much for Owen to be the bad guy here. He's not. He's a very nice man."

"Fuck him."

"Leo, you're a little drunk, I think."

"Not drunk enough."

"Well, you should stop talking, at any rate."

"You wanna know what I think?"

"No, I do not."

"I think your ex-husband and his wife keep you close because then they don't have to admit what they did."

"And what did they do, Leo? Huh?"

"He dumped you. He told you he didn't want kids, and within a year, he's a daddy. Why aren't you mad about that?"

"What would that serve? He didn't mean to fall out of love with me."

"Maybe he was never in love with you to begin with."

"Thanks. I feel better now."

"Why don't you tell him how you really feel? Say, 'Hey, Owen, I deserve more than the scraps you throw me, and I won't soothe your guilty conscience by coming to your pretentious fucking dinner parties. You broke my heart. Fuck you and your perfect wife, too.' That's what you should say. You can write that down if you want."

"I'll pass."

"I think he's an idiot. Love is a decision. It's not just a feeling."

"How profound," I snap. "And this coming from the man whose hobbies include lying on a lawn chair from 1975 and drinking too much. A commitment-phobic Juilliard grad who barely scrapes by because his ego is too fragile to play in front of anyone above the age of fourteen and literally cannot change a lightbulb in the building where he's allegedly the super."

"You don't know anything about me, Jenny."

"Yeah, you've made sure of that, haven't you?"

Loki contributes to the conversation by throwing up. Leo turns around. "You okay, boy?" he asks, petting him.

I sigh. "Leo, how much longer are you going to keep this dog around? Don't you think it's getting selfish?"

Shit.

Leo looks at me as if I've just ripped his heart out and taken a bite.

"I'm sorry," I say, looking back at the road. "That was uncalled-for. I'm really sorry."

He doesn't say anything back. Which doesn't seem fair; I said something unkind and apologized for it. He also said some unkind things, but he hasn't apologized.

"Do you think we should go to the vet clinic?" I ask. "Check if he's okay?"

Leo nods. "Thank you."

And so my Catherine Deane dress gets to be seen by the staff at the twenty-four-hour veterinary clinic. Loki is deemed "quite healthy for an old guy," despite his pukes, and we're sent home with some pills that should give him some pep and soothe his stomach at the same time.

When we get home, it's nearly 3:00 a.m. I have a bride who needs to be sewn into her dress in five hours. She broke my cardinal rule of weight gain after her final fitting, but what am I going to do? Let her walk down the aisle naked? My eyes are gritty, my feet hurt, my heart is achy.

"I didn't mean what I said about Loki," I say as Leo opens the gate to his courtyard. "You're really good to him. I know you're not selfish."

"No. I am."

He looks at me, and in the gentle pink light from the streetlamp, his eyes are so sad that my own fill with tears. "Leo, I'm really sorry."

Then he hugs me, letting go of Loki's leash, a two-armed, full, warm, horribly wonderful hug. I slip my arms around his back and hug him, too, and it feels like my heart goes right into his chest. He smells so nice, soap and shaving cream and red wine, and I wish we could stay like this all night. "I'm sorry, too," he murmurs.

Then he lets go of me and goes inside, and I climb the steps to my door, doing my damnedest not to cry.

Rachel

—◈—

MY SISTER ISN'T home when I get there, but I have a key.

I lug in the two giant duffel bags, then get the girls from the minivan. I took them to Chili's for supper, then ran them around the town park so they'd be good and tired. "Bath time!" I say, and they jump and clap, because Jenny has an old Victorian tub they find quite wonderful. After that, we read stories, and I tuck them into the queen-size bed in Jenny's guest room, the three of them lined up like little flowers against the "million pillows" Aunt Jenny has on the bed.

"Will Daddy come, too?" Grace asks. "For the sleepover?" She rubs her eyes, yawning.

"No," I say. "Daddy has to work a lot these days." With his mistress, no less.

It occurs to me that I'm giving him a whole lotta freedom, leaving like this. But what else am I going to do? Leash him? Put a lock on his stupid penis?

When the girls are asleep, I pour myself a glass of wine and watch TV. I don't text or call Jenny. She might be on a date, and I'm already interfering with her life as it is.

I doze off on her big red couch, waking up at the

sound of the door. My watch says quarter past three. Yikes.

Jenny comes in, looking beautiful, as always. "Hey," I say. She jumps a little.

"Hi! What…" She does the math. "Oh, honey."

Then I'm crying, it seems, and she takes me in her arms and hugs me. "I didn't want to leave a message," I say against her shoulder. "I had to get away. He's still… They were kissing today at work. I walked into his office, and they were kissing like it was their last day on earth, and I had to leave."

She lets me cry, murmuring and patting me, and God, she'd make the best mother. Better than our own, who'd only be more upset than I am.

Finally, I blow my nose, and Jenny gets up. She makes me some cocoa, padding around the small kitchen in her bare feet. I haven't spent enough time with her here, in this lovely new place, not when I've been afraid to leave my husband alone in our house for fear of what he'll do without my angry, punitive presence.

She sets a mug in front of me, and takes one for herself as well and sits across from me. "I'm really glad you're here," she says, and my eyes fill again.

"I think I have to divorce him," I whisper.

She nods and covers my hand with her own. "I think so, too. You deserve a husband who'd cut off his own dick before he'd cheat on you, Rach. You do."

"Maybe we can put that in my Match.com profile," I suggest, hiccuping on a sob.

"Definitely." She smiles, and I love her so much, my sister. God, what would I do without her? "I have an idea," she says.

"Good. Because coming here was my big play. I've got nothing else."

"Why don't you leave the girls with me this weekend and go somewhere? It's Friday…well, Saturday, now. Just get out of town? Go to… I don't know. Maine. Cape Cod. Somewhere away from the girls, away from Adam, and treat yourself. Read, get a facial or a massage or both, order expensive drinks, sleep in a bed by yourself. What do you think? Adam makes more money than God. Time to use it, don't you agree?"

I nod. I know exactly where to go.

And ten minutes later, the Penthouse Suite at the Tribeca Grand is booked for one.

WITHOUT THE GIRLS around, home seems like someone else's place. It's Saturday morning; Jenny had to run into the shop to fix a dress, then came back and shooed me out of her house. I suspect she's rescheduled brides for me. I'll have to think about how to pay her back.

I texted Adam and told him the girls were with Jenny this weekend, and I was going to a hotel to think, and I'd talk to him on Tuesday when I get back—yes, Tuesday. Jenny's shop is closed Mondays, and she insisted that I stay till Tuesday. I asked him not to be at the house when I went over to grab a few things, and he said, fine, take my time, and he was glad I was getting away, and he hoped I'd have a nice time.

He also left me three voice mails, which I'd only listened to after the texts.

He's contrite in every one.

You have to believe me, Rachel, she just threw herself at me. She doesn't want it to be over, but it is. I know how bad it looked, but that was a kiss goodbye.

Rachel, God, I'm so sorry for what I said. I love you, I love you so much, please call me.

And the one that got me the most:

Rachel—a long silence, and then his voice is husky. *I'll do anything to make this better.*

Well. I can think about that later.

I open my closet and take out a couple of dresses. Jenny will be sending me some restaurant recommendations later on. My nicest pajamas, the pink-and-white-striped silk pair that Adam gave me for Mother's Day last year. Black trousers and a white blouse, because Jenny says you can't go wrong if you have the right white blouse, and this one is a gift from her—crisp and sleek and something I've only worn once. The red suede booties with metallic heels.

I shower and blow my hair dry and put on makeup with more care than usual. Instead of my usual "just a little blush and mascara" mommy look, I go all out. Cat's eyes. Foundation. Lipstick.

When I get dressed and look at myself in the mirror, I look like another person, almost.

How strange that feels. Strange, and a little exciting.

An hour and a half later, the concierge of the Tribeca Grand, Sylvia, practically leaps when I give my name at the check-in counter.

"Ms. Carver! We've been so looking forward to having you!"

Sylvia is the woman who's taken so many calls from me in the past. And yes, she is Swiss, believe it or not.

She gestures to a bellboy, who takes my suitcase. I've also brought my laptop and three books. "I hope your stay here will be everything you hoped," she says.

"Please don't hesitate to contact me personally if there's anything at all you need."

"I appreciate that," I say. My voice is low and pleasant. I wonder who she thinks I am. An actress, maybe, someone she can't quite place? Yeah, right. Maybe a screenwriter or producer. An important novelist who needs to be alone with her craft. An executive. A famous lawyer who does guest stints on CNN.

Probably not a housewife with a cheating husband, pretending to be someone else.

We ride up in the elevator, and my heart is pounding. And yet my reflection shows a calm, attractive woman who is slim and tall—thanks to the booties—whose bag is expensive but understated.

No one would guess that I found a clot of dried hamburger in my bra when I got undressed this morning.

"And here we are," Sylvia says, waving her key at the keypad. She opens the door.

It's so… It's *beautiful*. The word doesn't do it justice. Even though I've seen it a dozen times in pictures, the penthouse is breathtaking. It's sophisticated and warm and quietly cheerful. Unusual lamps, interesting coffee tables and huge windows overlooking the jewel of lower Manhattan.

"Allow me to show you the amenities," Sylvia says, and proceeds to do just that. There are fresh flowers— last night at 3:43 a.m., the person who took my call had asked what my favorite flowers were. I said peonies, and there are no fewer than five flower arrangements throughout the suite, all featuring peonies with twigs of curling cherry branch. The curving brown leather couch would seat ten. There's an entire *bar*. Another sitting area. The bedroom is immaculate, the bed so perfectly made that I don't want to even set my purse on it.

And then there's the staircase to the rooftop deck. Up we go, and it's all I can do not to giggle. The deck features lounge chairs and couches and potted palms and the view, that heartbreaking vista of lower Manhattan, Liberty Tower gleaming in the sunshine. Just across the way is a town house, and I can see into the windows of the top-floor apartment. Are they looking back at me? Wondering who that lucky, fabulous woman is? *Is that the woman who won the Academy Award last year? No? Are you sure?*

Sylvia encourages me once again not to hesitate to contact her if there's anything I need, then leaves.

When I worked for Celery Stalk, I traveled a bit. Our company always booked with the Westin, hotels that were perfectly nice and extremely comfortable. Once a year, we'd all go to an educational software conference, and Adele would book a suite for herself (she founded the company, after all). She'd invite us all up for drinks, and lordy, it was fun! I loved those hotels, loved watching TV in bed, which was a luxury I never had unless I was on a business trip. I remember thinking about how amazing Adele's suite was, how much she deserved it and how I'd probably never stay in such a nice place.

But this… This is amazing.

I reach for my phone to call Adam to tell him about the hotel, the flowers, the bar, and then remember.

So, not Adam.

Well, Jenny, then.

"Hey!" she says. "So?"

"It's amazing. I love it. Jenny, I wish you could come down!"

"No, no. You need the time alone. Just forget your troubles. The girls are being angels—" I hear a crash and a scream "—except Rose, but don't worry, I can handle her. I'm having so much fun! I love them so much! God, I should've sent you away years ago so I could pretend they were mine. You don't mind if I tell people they are, right?"

I smile. My sister knows just what to say.

I promise her I won't hide in the hotel, and yes, I will stay until checkout on Tuesday. I promise to indulge myself. "You can call Donna if things get hairy," I tell her. "Or if you need to go into the shop. You have her number, right?"

"Yes, yes, you left it right here. Now go have fun. My daughters await me. Love you!"

"I love you, too." I hang up. Walk around the suite again, hang up my clothes, put my toiletries on the vast countertop in the vast bathroom. I make sure everything is tidy, because I don't want to ruin this experience with messiness. Having triplets means that messiness is a fact of life, no matter how hard I try. I'm going to enjoy this tidiness, damn it.

That all done, I look at my watch.

It's 11:22 a.m.

I'm starving.

I pick up the phone. "How can we assist you, Ms. Carver?" asks a voice.

They know my name! "Hello. I'd like to order lunch."

"Of course. What can our chef make for you today?"

I order a cheeseburger—well, an Angus burger— with bleu cheese and bacon, a side of truffle fries and a green salad. A bottle of... Scratch that, actually. The hibiscus martini, please?

Twenty minutes later—because I am so fabulous and inhabit the penthouse suite for the next couple of days—room service is delivered. "Would miss like to eat on the patio?" asks the waiter.

Miss would. And miss does.

I read my book, which is not a book club selection, but instead a wonderfully fun and engrossing novel about a female assassin in Victorian England. I remember to look up at the view often. To feel the comfort of the chaise longue supporting me so perfectly.

For an hour, I eat and drink and read and look and then, feeling a little buzzed, I go back down, go into my bedroom, and strip off every inch of clothing and climb into bed. I never sleep naked, but I will now.

These sheets must be sixteen-hundred count, I think, and then I'm asleep.

WHEN I WAKE up, I take a bath in the glorious tub—there's a special pillow for the back of my head!—read some more, then decide to go shopping. The hotel provides cheery blue bikes, and what the hell? I take one and head out, bumping along on the cobblestone streets. I've never ridden a bike in Manhattan before. It's terrifying and exhilarating. I make it to the bike path along the Hudson without dying and relax a little.

My head is pleasantly empty. The late-May sun bathes the city in gold and blue, the architectural miracle that is the Big Apple. I never wanted to live here, couldn't understand Jenny's desire to get out of Cambry-on-Hudson, but today, I can see it. I'd live in a little town house, maybe. Or a condo in one of those slick buildings. Get to know my neighbors. Work for Domani Studios, maybe, the top ad agency who once tried to recruit me.

Every once in a while, a wave of grief washes over me, but I push it back. Jenny's right. I'm going to enjoy myself.

But I wonder how Mom and Dad did it. I honestly can't remember a fight between them. Dad never even *looked* at another woman, and he had his chances, God knows. I remember spying on their parties from the stairs, remember how proud I'd feel that my parents were *the* couple, the happiest, the most affectionate. I can remember one couple who'd snipe at each other, and another who'd ignore each other, and even remember overhearing two women talking about another, who'd slept with someone else, and I was so, so grateful my parents were happy. It made my childhood safe.

God, I want that for my girls. But I can't do it alone.

I wonder if Adam has any idea what he's really done.

I turn my bike around and head for SoHo. Time for some new clothes. Time to be Julia Roberts in *Pretty Woman*, every woman's shopping fantasy. The money I spend is, I imagine, from the money Adam's been putting in his boat fund. Or maybe it's his whore fund. After all, I imagine they have to go to hotels to fuck. I imagine he's bought her a dinner or two. Maybe some jewelry. Definitely some sexy underwear. He has a thing for sexy underwear. Such a cliché.

So, too bad. *No boat for you, cheater. Armani for me instead.*

What some people don't understand about new clothes is it's not about the clothes. It's the promise of how happy you'll be when you wear them, the wonderful things you'll be doing in them, how people will look at you and say, yes, there's a woman who really likes herself. Usually, my clothes are well made and simple and attractive. I'm a well-dressed mother. Today, though, I buy clothes and jewelry and hair clips that say I'm an interesting woman. I'm unexpected and chic. I have style. I'm someone to be reckoned with.

Back in the suite, I unpack my new clothes and shoes, take a long shower, using the hotel products so I smell different and exotic. Wrap up in the luxurious hotel robe and check my email, ignore the messages from Adam and click on the restaurant links Jenny's sent. Ooh. Fancy. A little scary, too, but beautiful.

I call Jenny and talk to the girls, listening to them tell me about playing dress-up with Aunt Jenny, baking cookies with Aunt Jenny, sitting in Aunt Jenny's cupboards. I miss them so much it makes my chest ache.

But it's good for them to be away from me once in a while—I know that. It's just that I always pictured a getaway weekend under different circumstances. Like Adam and me, taking this trip together, because it's our tenth anniversary.

I picture dressing up again, putting on more makeup, the new clothes, and heading out to one of the beautiful spots Jenny recommended. Alone. With a book, maybe.

But I'm suddenly weary. I can't. Not tonight.

But I am starving.

Once again, I call room service, and when the bell-man arrives with my cart, I apologize, saying I've just got too much work to catch up on. Besides, I tell myself, I've always wanted to stay in this hotel. This is a dream come true. Once again, I eat on the rooftop deck, and I nurse my wine until the lights start to go on. The girls will be going to sleep by now.

I miss tucking them in. I haven't even been gone a day, and I'm homesick. I'll watch a movie, that's what

I'll do. In bed. In total comfort, without one single in-
terruption, an entire movie. I'll bring the wine with me
and wear my pretty pajamas and how great will that be?

Tomorrow, I'll go out to one of those restaurants, no
matter how beautiful this hotel is. Maybe someone will
come to the city to meet me. Kathleen, maybe? No, she
mentioned her parents were coming to visit this weekend. Not Elle, not Claudia. They'd sniff out something
like a shark smells a drop of blood in the water. It's been
hard enough, being around them at school.

Most of the contacts in my phone are child-related.
I scroll through the list. Dr. Cato, their pediatrician. Dr.
DeSoto, their dentist, just like in the book by William
Steig, which the girls adore. Donna, the lovely babysitter. Emily's Mom, whose first name I've never managed
to catch but whose daughter comes to play at our house
sometimes.

Gus Fletcher.

Not child-related.

Gus Fletcher of the smiley eyes. He emailed me his
number after the barfing incident, and I put it in my
phone. I did that for a reason, didn't I?

Without waiting another second, I hit his number.
He probably has a date. It's nine o'clock on a Saturday
night. If nothing else, he's out with friends. I pray it
goes to voice mail.

"Hello?"

I jump at the sound of his voice. "Gus?"

"Yes?"

"It's… It's Rachel. Rachel Carver. Rachel Tate
Carver?"

"The woman with the pukey kids?"

I smile. "Hopefully they're not puking right now, but yes."

"Just for the record, you're the only Rachel I know. The last names aren't necessary."

"Oh. Okay." My toes curl. It's safe to say I've never in my life called a guy for social purposes. I was always the callee, not the caller.

"What can I do for you, Rachel?" His voice is warm.

"Well, I'm staying in the city this weekend, and I was wondering if you might want to have a drink or dinner with me. Tomorrow. Sunday."

There's a long pause.

"I owe you, after all," I say. "You were a prince that day. And it was nice to see you again."

"In that case, yes. I accept."

"Really?"

"Yes."

I'm smiling. "Great! I'm staying at the Tribeca Grand."

"Nice."

"You have no idea. Want to come see my suite? It's pretty amazing."

"Sure. Seven o'clock?"

"Seven is perfect. See you then."

I'm having drinks with a nice man tomorrow who is not my husband.

A slight warning chimes in my brain. Things are messed up enough without me…without me doing… doing what? I would never cheat on Adam. Even now. I'm sure Gus knows that, too, but I'll be sure to reinforce that idea tomorrow.

Still, the idea of being with him, almost on a date— *almost* being the key word here—is deliciously dangerous and enticing, like a dark chocolate soufflé waiting at the end of a meal.

You know you shouldn't, but you also know you will.

Jenny

✦ ━━━●━━━ ✦

I NEVER REALIZED how much I loved solitude until my nieces came to visit.

Also, how great it was to eat an entire meal without something spilling, breaking, dropping or being flung somewhere. Also, the thrill of going to the bathroom by myself.

We got through Saturday just fine. Today, they seem possessed by demons. Starting at five forty-three in the morning, no less.

Because I'm Aunt Jenny, Purveyor of Fun, the girls seem to have morphed from their previously angelic selves—that is, the way they act when my sister is around—to little cyclones of chaos and destruction. Their reverence for my house and its newness is gone. They throw things, eat things, spit things, climb things. After a hectic lunch, I find Grace standing on the counter, hitting the light fixture with a wooden spoon.

"Grace! Honey, no! That's not safe." I scoop her off the counter, only to see a tiny butt sticking out of the cabinet where I keep the food processor and its razor-sharp attachments. "Rose, is that you?" I pull my niece out by the legs. "Get out, honey, there are sharp things in there."

"I love sharp!" she says, trying to wriggle back in. "I *want* sharp! Auntie, you so mean! I! Want! Sharp!"

Dear God.

Grace begins hitting the cabinets with her wooden spoon, which I have failed to take from her. She gets Rose in the head, making Rose scream like her fingernails are being pulled off.

"Oh, honey! Are you okay?" I ask, wrestling the spoon from Grace's hand. "Here. Let me get you some ice. Grace, say you're sorry, baby."

"I'm not," Grace states, pushing out her bottom lip. "It was a accident!"

"Well, tell her you didn't mean it, and you're sorry she got hurt."

Grace looks as though her insides are boiling. "No! It was a *accident*! Accident!"

Soon, I shall call the exorcist.

It dawns on me that Charlotte is missing. "Stay here," I order the wailing duo. "Charlotte? Lottie, where are you, angel?"

The front door is locked, thank God, so she couldn't have gone outside. Living room, no. Downstairs bathroom, no. Pantry, no. I race upstairs. The guest room, no. "Charlotte! Answer Aunt Jenny right now!"

If she does answer, I can't hear her over the banshees in my kitchen. "Charlotte!"

She's in my bathroom, sitting in the sink, idly kicking her feet and looking out the window. "Auntie!" she exclaims happily. "I'm peeing, Auntie!"

I mutter a curse. She's peed, all right. She failed to take off her overalls, however, and that means a whole new outfit.

There's a crash from downstairs. I don't have time to

change Charlotte, so I pick her up, grimacing, and dash downstairs, where I find three broken mixing bowls, apparently pulled from the cupboard.

"Is anyone bleeding?" I ask.

"I bleeding," Rose says. "Right here." She holds up her hand, which is unmarred by blood.

"You're not bleeding."

"Inside, Auntie. I bleed inside."

Shit. Could she be right? Is she hemorrhaging? Should I call Rachel?

"Here." Grace opens the baking supplies cupboard and pulls out a bag of chocolate chips. "This fixes bleeding."

"Fanks, Grace!" Rose says happily, tearing open the bag. Two pounds of chocolate chips scatter far and wide.

"Poop! It poop!" Charlotte shrieks, wriggling like a fish in my arms.

"It not poop!" Rose screams.

Grace begins stomping on the chips.

My God.

I look at the clock. It's 3:30 p.m. I have *four hours* to go till bedtime. Minimum! An hour and a half till wine is socially acceptable. But no, I can't have wine! I'm the only adult on the scene. This is *terrible* news!

The front door opens and in comes Loki. And Leo.

"Hey," he says, looking at my nieces. "Shut up, okay?"

They fall silent. "Who you?" Rose asks, folding her arms over her chest.

"I'm Leo."

"Why you here?"

"I own this building. Why *you* here?"

"Aunt Jenny, that why."

Wait. He owns this building? Since when?

Charlotte is lying on the floor, eating chips without the use of her hands. Talented child. "Leo," I say, "meet the triumvirate of terror better known as Grace, Charlotte and Rose Carver, my beautiful and angelic nieces."

"What you dog's name?" Rose asks, sidling up to Leo and looping an arm around his knee as she sticks her thumb in her mouth.

"Loki. He eats noisy little girls."

Rose smiles around her thumb at that.

"He's not very frien—" I start to say, then stop as Loki lies on the floor and rolls onto his back, offering his stomach. Leo kneels down and takes Rose's hand.

"He wants you to pet him," Leo says, and sure enough, Loki's stumpy little tail starts wagging. Grace and Charlotte join in, chattering at once. "Loki, that's a funny name," "Loki, don't bite me," "Loki likes me," "Loki no eat me!"

Leo looks up at me. "Want company?" he asks. "My lessons are done for the day."

"God, yes," I tell him.

Thirty minutes later, the kitchen is cleaned up, Charlotte is in a fresh outfit and Leo and the girls are sitting at the table, making things out of an organic version of Play-Doh from a kit nauseatingly called Little Minds Create, which I have on hand for their visits. Charlotte is not creating, opting to smash blobs of clay into the seams of the table.

"Sing us songs," Grace demands.

Leo glances at her. "There once was a girl called Aunt Jenny," he begins obligingly. "Her nieces were Pooh, Plum and Penny. They loved to make messes, and dress up in dresses, which was fine because Jenny had many."

"Not bad," I murmur. He has a nice singing voice. Of course.

"Juilliard. Limerick Songs 101."

"I not named Pooh," Rose says, putting a blob of Play-Doh in her mouth. "I Rose."

"Not for eating, sweetheart," I say, scooping out the blob. Child care is not for the squeamish.

"What are you making, Leo?" Grace asks.

He holds up his sculpture, which is made of pink clay and has bulbous green eyes and four legs. "It's Loki," he says.

The girls laugh, the sound so beautiful and pure my heart squeezes. "Loki's brown and white and gray and black," Grace says. "Not pink."

"He has hints of pink," Leo says. "Also, sparkles." He takes some of the sequins that come with the Little Minds Create kit and makes his clay dog a collar. "We can't forget his purple spots," he adds, reaching for the lavender clay.

"Loki not pupple!" Rose says.

"Or the yellow stripes," Leo says, winking at her. She smiles back, another female succumbing to his charms.

In the end, Clay Loki looks like a demon, but the girls adore him. "Can I have him?" Charlotte asks.

"Mine!" Rose yells.

"*I* want Loki the most!" Grace says.

"It's for your Aunt Jenny," he says, handing the sculpture to me.

"Girls," I say, "would you like to watch a movie?"

When they're lined up on the couch, mesmerized by *My Neighbor Totoro*, I get started on cleaning up the craft mess in the kitchen. Leo comes in, stepping over the real-life version of his dog.

"Thanks for coming up," I say.

"I owed you."

"Did you?"

He shrugs.

I get a toothpick to dig out the clay from where Charlotte squished it.

"Want me to start dinner?" he asks.

"Um...yeah. Sure."

"What do the little princesses eat?" He opens the fridge and surveys my stock.

"Everything not nailed to the floor."

"Spaghetti and meatballs?"

"They love that. I even have sauce. Homemade, no less. One of the few things I can make." I open the pantry and take out a quart of spaghetti sauce and a package of pasta. Leo gets some ground turkey, milk and eggs from the fridge and starts rummaging around in my cupboards.

It's dangerous, I think, to be playing house with a man who doesn't want a relationship. Who professes to be for recreation only. Who says he doesn't like babies but is fantastic with toddlers and children, who sends out mixed messages of jealousy and friendship and unreachability, if such a word exists.

But it's so, so nice, too.

"Did I hear you right? You own this building, huh?" I ask.

He glances at me. "Yeah."

"That explains your wretched skills as a super."

"It does, I guess."

"Why do my rent checks go to the real estate company and not you?"

"Because it's easier to have them handle it. And I

asked them not to tell my tenant I was the owner. Didn't want you to think I was a real estate magnate with piles of money."

"The next Donald Trump."

He smiles, then breaks an egg into the ground turkey. "I'll work on my comb-over."

"Don't you dare. You have the most beautiful hair on the face of the earth."

"True."

"My nieces adore you," I say, taking out some lettuce that's hopefully not too old.

"Of course they do. They're female, aren't they?"

I roll my eyes. "You and that ego."

"I'm sorry I was such a rotten date the other night," he says, not looking at me. My knees soften dangerously. "I'm jealous of your ex-husband, in case you haven't figured that out."

"Aren't we all. He has the perfect life."

"Not because of that, dummy."

I peek at the girls, who are blessedly engrossed in the movie. Loki has joined them, curled up next to Grace, his head in her lap. "Why would you be jealous of Owen?"

"Because you're still hung up on him."

Swooniness and irritation roll around in my heart, a sensation I'm thinking of calling The Leo. "Why would you care? You're not interested in me. You're gay where I'm concerned, remember?"

"I'm allowed to be contradictory. That's not just reserved for you women."

"So what's the contradiction? You want my complete and undivided attention so you can ignore me?"

"Yes. That's it exactly."

"You know, if you ever decided to be straightforward, we could maybe have something here."

"Recreation only, sweetheart."

"Right. You were born to be married. You should father a dozen kids."

He puts the meatballs in the sauce, then washes his hands. "I was married once."

The shock must show on my face, because he... Well, hell, he never told me. "What happened?" I ask.

He doesn't look at me, opting to keep lathering up his gifted hands. "She left me."

Ah. No wonder he knows so much about my feelings on Owen. "You want to talk about it?"

"I don't." He raises his eyes to me, and they're clear and neutral. "But I do want to watch that movie with the girls."

With that, he walks out of the kitchen. I hear him say something to the girls.

So his heart was broken, too. And I guess he's not over his wife; hence the "recreation only" bit.

It's oddly cheering, knowing that Leo's divorced. So I *was* right. He was born to be married; he just picked the wrong woman.

And maybe I could be the right woman.

I ignore the faint warning that chimes somewhere in my head. The old *Easy, there, let's not pick out the fabric for the gown just yet* chime. I'm heartily sick of that sound, let me tell you. And, please. Leo is watching a movie with three little girls. He loves his stinky old dog to the point of the ridiculous. He can make meatballs. He is the essence of family man.

Dinner is a sloppy, happy affair. The girls have fallen deeply in love with Leo and demonstrate this love by

chewing up their meatballs and showing him the contents of their mouths, draping spaghetti over their noses
and heads, and blowing bubbles into their drinks. Loki
lurks under the table, cleaning up the food that rains
down.

Leo sings them songs and pretends to play the piano
on the table. Even seeing him pretend to play is a weird
sort of thrill. His hands are huge, his fingers long and
fluid, almost. He sings along to that, too—*Bah bum, bababa bababa bababa BAH bum*. He doesn't eat much,
but he does have a glass of red wine. Just one.

The top floor of my house is locked. It contains the
owner's stored stuff, the Realtor said.

I wonder if I could pick that lock.

Hi, I'm Jenny, and I'm a stalker.

"Thank you for dinner, Aunt Jenny," Leo says, standing up and clearing a plate.

"Thank you for dinner, Aunt Jenny," the girls echo.

I take the girls upstairs and give them a much-needed
bath, then read them a story. "We want Leo to read to
us," Grace informs me.

"Yes, yes. Leo," Rose and Charlotte echo. Rose pronounces his name *Weo*, which is very damn cute.

"Leo," I call. "Your presence is requested."

There's no answer. "Maybe he's walking Loki," I say.

We finish the story, and I tuck them into bed. Then
we call Rachel, so they can tell her all about their exciting day—the chocolate chips, hide-and-seek, peeing in
the sink, Loki. "They've been great," I lie when it's my
turn. "How are you?"

"Oh, I'm good," she says, but I hear a note of uncer-
tainty in her voice. "I'm homesick, though."

"What are you doing tonight?"

"Meeting an old friend from Celery Stalk for drinks. Maybe dinner."

"Nice! Good girl, Rach."

There's a pause. "Has Adam called?"

He had. "Yeah. I just let Grace answer the phone. I didn't talk to him." Because I didn't want the girls to hear my death threats.

"I wonder if he's been with…her this weekend," my sister says.

I have no answer for that. "Listen. You just enjoy your dinner and the hotel. Send more pictures, okay? Love you."

"Love you, too."

"Why Mommy away?" Rose asks.

"She's having a little fun time away," I say.

"She has fun with us," Grace says, scowling.

"Yes. The most fun of all is with you girls. She loves you so much," I say. "But she also knows that Auntie loves you so much and so she shared you with me. You're my present!"

This assuages any pouty lips. I smooch the girls, breathe them in, get Charlotte to pee one more time, resettle her in the big bed. "I love you, my sweethearts," I say.

"We love *you*," they inform me.

Leo is not downstairs, though the kitchen is cleaned up. God loves a man who can clean up a kitchen.

Now I can have a glass of wine, and never in my life have I deserved one more.

I pour myself some cabernet and take it into the living room.

My sister sounded shaky. And that question—is

Adam taking advantage of her absence by being with his mistress… God.

I'd bet the farm that the answer is yes. I bet he's told Emmanuelle—such a porno name—that his wife doesn't understand him, and she's irrational and demanding, and God knows what else. That things haven't been good for a long, long time, but he owes it to her to at least try to work things out…but…you know how wives are. Not nearly as understanding as mistresses.

What did Dad tell Dorothy, I wonder? *My wife's obsessed with her job*? *She's not as young as she used to be*? *The sex feels very married.*

It may be time to find Dorothy and have a little talk. Or not. Jeesh, I have no idea.

Personally, I always thought married sex was the best sex. Owen and I knew each other's bodies, our favorite parts. There was the trust factor, the love, the like. It was always good.

I wonder how the sex is between Owen and Ana-Sofia. Life-changing, no doubt. Proof of God to my once-atheist husband.

My door opens, and in come Leo and Loki.

"Hey," he says. "Girls in bed?"

"Yep. Bet they'd love it if you went up and said goodnight."

"Nah. I'll just rile them up." He sits on the couch next to me. Loki lies down at his feet without snarling at me. A pleasant change.

Then Leo looks at me, and his eyes are soft and gray and have a hint of a smile in them, and my insides drop and tighten. He reaches out and touches my face.

Scratches my cheek. "You have some dried sauce here," he says.

"Ah. Thank you."

Then he slides his hand around to the back of my head and pulls me to him. One of my hands goes to his chest, and I can feel the solid thumping of his heart. "Recreation only," he murmurs, his voice scraping a part low in my stomach. "Got it?"

"Got it," I whisper back.

His eyes crinkle with a small smile, and then he's kissing me, and his mouth is... God, his mouth is good at what it's doing—a slow, gentle, thorough kiss that makes my insides leap and spark. He kisses the corners of my mouth, then my lips again, his tongue sliding against mine, shifting so that he's half lying on top of me, his long, rangy body covering me with its delicious weight. My hands slide up his arms, which are taut with muscle, across his shoulders and neck, all the while kissing him back.

"We can't... The girls are... So no..." I manage to say against his perfect mouth.

"I know," he whispers, kissing just under my ear. "This is just a make-out session." He kisses down my neck, making me clench and melt. "When do they go home, by the way?"

Then he pulls back and smiles at me, and it seems to me all I could ever want and all I ever hoped for is in that smile.

The warning chimes go silent under the sounds of us kissing and the happiness singing in my heart.

Rachel

—⋯—

When Sylvia, the Swiss concierge, calls to ask if I'm expecting a Mr. Gus Fletcher, I manage to say yes, send him right up.

If Adam knew I was having a man up to my suite, then going out for drinks and dinner, he'd be very, very uncomfortable.

Which is, I suppose, the point. Adam *slept* with another woman. I'm just having dinner with an old friend.

Doesn't make me feel less nervous. I blot my underarms with tissues and chug some water. Check my lipstick. Blot again.

And then there's a knock at the door, and I go to open it.

"Holy crap," Gus says.

"Yeah, I know. It's big. Kind of stupid, really. For one person. I mean, not that I mean anything by that. I just… I don't know. Hi. How are you?"

"I meant, holy crap, you look incredible."

I pause. "Oh. Thank you." I'm wearing one of the outfits from yesterday's spree—a red sheath dress that cost more than my first car. High, strappy metallic heels. The makeup. I also had my hair cut and highlighted and blown out.

He just looks at me for a second, then leans in and gives me a kiss on the cheek. "Nice to see you when you're not covered in vomit."

I smile, though I'm twisting my hands. "I get that a lot."

"Show me around. I'll probably never see a hotel suite like this again, so I want to drink it in." There's that smile that makes his eyes almost disappear into dark little crescents.

"Gus," I say, "I'm… Just to make sure we're clear, I'm not…you know. Coming on to you."

"I know. I'm not that lucky. Where does this stairway go to?"

"The rooftop deck. All mine. And yours."

We go up to admire it. "Gorgeous. So. I'm starving. Where are we eating?"

Because I chickened out last night and stayed in the hotel, I booked a reservation at one of the swanky places my sister recommended. We walk down the street, my heels occasionally catching on the cobblestones, until Gus takes my arm.

"Sorry," I say. "I'm trying a new vibe."

"You look beautiful," he says. "But you always did."

He's wearing a white dress shirt and jeans, black Converse high-tops. This makes him look much more famous and sophisticated than I do. I should just wear a sign that says Not From Here and Trying Too Hard.

"Oh, my God, I think that's Gwyneth Paltrow," someone says, and I turn to look.

"Where?" I whisper.

Gus laughs. "She was talking about you, Rachel."

"Really?"

"Really."

For some reason, this makes me feel a lot more confident. That, and Gus's hand on my arm. I've known him for longer than I've known Adam, and it dawns on me that I've really, really missed having him as a friend these past four years.

"Is this it?" He stops outside a restaurant.

"It is."

The maître d' looks us up and down, then crosses something off on his list. "This way, please," he says, and leads us to a huge booth in the back of the restaurant. It's a fantastic table. I know this because Robert Freakin' De Niro is in the booth next to us, talking animatedly to his companion. The actor looks up as we're being seated and gives a slight nod.

"Robert De Niro is sitting next to us, Gwyneth," Gus says in a low voice.

"I'm trying not to wet myself with excitement," I murmur back. "It's harder after having the triplets."

He laughs.

Gosh, I like him. I haven't been around a man I liked this much in what seems like a thousand years.

The art department at Celery Stalk was one big work space. I shared a massive desk with another woman, Liara, a tattooed and pierced lesbian who talked nonstop and educated me quite a bit about the wonders of her love life. My participation in the conversation wasn't really necessary. Liara was outgoing and fun and well liked… I was the workhorse, sort of.

Gus always asked me to work on his projects. He was—is—the concept guy. I wasn't flashy, and I wasn't full of bubbly personality like Liara, but I did good work, and Gus always appreciated it.

I never really got the impression he liked me until that ill-timed date request, and by then, it was too late.

We order a bottle of wine and talk, first about workmates, then about Gus, whose live-in girlfriend left him last year.

"Did you see it coming?" I ask.

He looks at me a long minute. "Yes. I couldn't tell if we should've tried harder or broken up earlier. Either way, it was tough."

"I'm sorry." And I am. I can't imagine someone leaving Gus, quite frankly.

He shrugs. "Well, I recovered. I always do. I thought about throwing myself in front of a train, but…"

"Anna Karenina did that. No one likes a copycat."

"I know," he says. "Besides, it's so nineteenth century. So I just listened to a lot of Beck and ate ice cream instead."

"Beck? Really? The train might've been less painful."

Another laugh, loud and unabashed.

Our dinners come, and we dig in. "Oh, my God," Gus says. "This may be the best thing I've ever eaten or seen anyone eat."

"It should be," I concur. "Bobby De Niro eats here."

"Oh, we're already on nicknames with him, are we?"

"Well, we're sitting next to him. I feel it's only right."

Gus's smile makes my stomach tingle. I drop my eyes.

The Old Rachel would never have had the guts to ask a cute guy to dinner, let alone engage in snappy dialogue. She never would've worn this dress. The New Rachel would only have done this out of spite.

I don't feel any spite right now. I just feel…happy. It's been a while.

"So tell me the truth," Gus says, putting down his

fork. His plate is clean, as is mine. "Am I here because you want to make your husband mad? Because I gather that this weekend is about him, sort of."

"My husband doesn't know you're here. And you're right, it is." I take a sip of wine. "We're having a rough time."

"You want to talk about it? I mean, I told you about my Anna Karenina moment. I owe you."

I look at Gus's nice face, the cropped hair, the omnipresent smile. "I'd rather not," I say. "Let's talk about anything but that, okay? I didn't ask you to have dinner because I wanted to talk about my husband, or make him jealous, or anything like that. I asked you because I couldn't think of a nicer person."

He looks at me for a long moment. "That might be the best compliment I've ever had," he says. Then he smiles and there's a warmth in my heart that has nothing to do with the wine.

WHEN WE LEAVE the restaurant, it's nearly midnight, and Tribeca now pulses with music from clubs and restaurants. "Feel like going anywhere else?" Gus asks.

I hesitate. "You can come back to the hotel. The roof deck is all mine." I feel foolish as I say it. A scorned wife spends lots of money to punish her husband. How original.

But the view from the deck is stellar. Liberty Tower is beautiful and poignant, the Woolworth Building stately and grand. I bring up a bottle of wine and Gus opens it, and we sit in our chairs and don't say anything, just look at the lights and listen to the sounds from the city below. I take off my shoes and wrap up in the soft throw the hotel has so thoughtfully provided.

"Rachel?"

He never shortens my name. Most people do. "Yeah?"

He gives me a long look. "I just want to say something. You know I always liked you. Had a crush on you."

"I actually didn't know that until you asked me out." A blush prickles my cheeks, and I'm glad for the dim lighting up here.

"Well, I did. I still do."

I look at him, but that's it, apparently. "I like you, too, Gus. But I can't do anything about that. I'm still married."

"I know. I wouldn't want you to. But I wanted to say it anyway." He sits up. "And with that awkward parting salvo, I should probably go."

I walk him to the door. "I'm really glad we did this."

He smiles. "Thank you for calling me. It was an honor."

Suddenly, there's a lump in my throat. "Good night, Gus."

"Take care."

He kisses my cheek, and for one second, I think about turning my head and kissing him on the mouth.

I don't. I close the door instead.

Whatever happens, this night is a little jewel for me to tuck away. A perfect night with a kind man who liked me and still does, more than ten years after he first asked me out. Who tried nothing, but was simply honest and charming and nice.

Then I go into the bathroom and wash up, hanging up my red dress with care. Floss. Brush.

There was a night before the affair, when I was brushing my teeth before bed, and Adam came into the bathroom and felt my ass and said, "Do you even know how beautiful you are?" and I laughed, because I had a mouthful of foam. I remember how lucky I felt, that my husband still wanted to feel my butt, still came on to me.

What happened to that guy? Was it because I fell asleep one time? Am I somehow responsible for this affair?

Lovely Gus aside, I'm married to Adam Carver. He took vows, but so did I. And in a flash, I realize that his affair hasn't killed my love for him. It muffled it. Embarrassed it. Shamed it. *I'm so stupid because I still love you.*

The woman at dinner, flirting so easily with a cute guy, sitting next to Robert De Niro... She's nice, sure, but she has a husband and three children and a foundering marriage.

Tomorrow is Monday, but I'll be going home. I belong home, in Cambry-on-Hudson, in my white house with the blue shutters, with my daughters.

I still might belong with Adam, too.

Jenny

WHEN I WAKE up in the morning, it's because there are three little warm bodies snuggled next to me. They rose at five, which is Satan's hour, as everyone knows, so I wooed them into cuddling with me so I could doze a little longer.

And think of Leo.

My whole body curls with happiness. We kissed for hours last night, the couch springs squeaking, a delicious state of horniness and warmth. We talked, too, murmuring sometimes, laughing. Ate ice cream around midnight. Kissed some more. And when he left, he pushed me against the front door and gave me a long, hot, lingering kiss. His hands slid down to my thighs, and he picked me up against him and I wrapped my legs around him, my back pressed against the door, and if it wasn't the horniest moment of my life, I don't know what was. Then he let me slide down against him, his hands going to my hair.

"Make sure your rent is on time," he murmured against my mouth, and then he smiled and was gone, and I staggered back to the couch and collapsed there, grinning like an idiot.

"Auntie? Auntie? I have to go baffroom," Rose says now, breaking me out of my reverie.

"Okay, baby," I answer.

It's raining outside, a steady, gentle rain. Monday, so the school bus rattles and sighs up the street, collecting the neighborhood kids. The girls don't have nursery school on Mondays, so it's just them and me for now. And maybe Leo, because his lessons won't start until 2:30 p.m.

Most Mondays, I go into the shop to work. Kimber Allegretti's dress needs another muslin mockup, for the ball gown this time. Poor kid. She's so not Cinderella... I'd much rather see her in something utterly sexy and Gatsby–era, lots of beading and a low back to show the tattoos she so obviously loves. The dress is supposed to be about the bride, after all...not about the disapproving mother-in-law. But Kimber wants to make Mrs. Brewster happy, so hopefully I can make a ball gown she doesn't hate.

I also have a bunch of sketches to whip up for some of the brides I booked at my open house. Some finishing touches on a beaded belt for a bride in Connecticut. But those can all wait. I'll work on Kimber's dress here, in the sewing room upstairs. This is the first time I've had the girls all to myself for more than a few hours, and I love it. It's a test-drive for motherhood.

I bet Leo would make a fantastic father. The way he is with Evander—and all his students, but especially Evander—the way he was with my nieces... You know, a lot of men say they don't want kids until they meet the right woman. Look at Owen. He didn't know, and now he adores being a father. And today, that thought doesn't even bother me.

I make the girls pancakes in shapes that allegedly look like animals, then wash them up and give them pots and pans and whisks and the ever-fascinating eggbeater so they'll be entertained while I clean up the sticky remains from the kitchen table. We draw; they love that I can sketch out dresses, and I let them color-in the pictures.

When the girls take their naps that afternoon—and God bless them for being good sleepers—I use the other upstairs bedroom to get started on the latest version of Kimber's dress. Mrs. Brewster would probably prefer a burka. There's modest—I've done plenty of dresses for people who don't want to show a lot of skin. And then there's this. I think the message is clear—Mrs. Brewster wants Kimber to know she's not right for her precious son.

Right on cue at 2:30 p.m., I hear someone talking in the courtyard down below. One of Leo's not-terrible students, a funny middle-aged woman who admitted to me a couple of weeks ago that she'd always wanted to learn to play piano and Leo's good looks gave her the impetus to start. I consider poking my head out the window, but I don't want it to seem like I'm stalking Leo.

I do, however, creep up to the fourth floor. It's quiet… obviously, it's quiet; I can't really see Leo pulling a *Flowers in the Attic* move.

I wonder what he keeps up here.

I find my hand is on the doorknob. It's locked, which is something of a relief, because while I like to think I wouldn't open it even if I could, I don't want to test myself. Probably, it's piles of music and some furniture. Nothing more than that.

But I'm hungry to know more about Leo Killian. I don't want to find out from snooping or Google. I want him to tell me. We started something last night. I could feel it.

When the girls wake up, I find a big box for them to play with. The three of them sit in it, giggling and pretending to be in a space ship, then turn it over and make it into a house for cats and baby rabbits.

I take a million pictures. Text Rachel a couple, because knowing her, she's getting homesick for them.

The phone rings, and I scramble to find it, hoping it's Leo. It's not. "Hi, Mom."

"Where's your sister?" she asks. "I got a text saying she was out of town with friends. Where would she go? And why?"

"She's just having a little girlfriend time," I lie. If Mom knew that Rachel was alone, she'd freak out. "The girls are staying with me."

"What? Why?"

"Because they're my nieces and I love them."

"Why didn't she ask me?" Mom demands.

Because you always let her know how difficult and exhausting they are. "Because I begged to have them."

"Auntie! I'm a cat! I'm a cat!" Grace makes a hideous hissing noise and curls her fingers into claws.

"And such a fierce one!" I say.

"I fierce, too!" Rose says. "I a fierce bunny!"

"Yes! So fierce!" I agree. "What can I do for you, Mom?"

"I'm a gentle cat," Charlotte chimes in, climbing onto my lap. "Purr. Purr, Auntie. Purr."

I love these girls so much. I kiss Charlotte's head, and she leans against me, a sweet, warm weight.

"I wish Rachel would take Rose to a speech pathologist," Mom says. "Grace and Charlotte speak so much better than she does."

"I think she's fine. And if there were a problem, I'm sure Rachel would be all over it, so please don't mention it to her."

"Well, between that and Grace's autism—"

"Mom! She shows no signs of that, okay? You should really stop telling Rachel she does." Charlotte crawls off my lap and scurries back under the box with her sisters. "And what about Charlotte?" I growl. "Got an armchair diagnosis for her?"

"I think she might be a lesbian."

I roll my eyes so hard I think I sprain one. "What did you need, Mom?"

"I just miss the girls, that's all. Rachel has been very hard to pin down lately, and I don't know why. I miss her. She's not telling me something, and I don't know why. You girls were always your own little club."

There it is, the eternal pang of sympathy for Mom. Always a little out of the loop. She puts herself there, but it doesn't mean I don't feel for her. "That's because you raised us to be close," I tell her.

She humphs. "Well, since you're the one in charge of my grandchildren, can I come see them? I love them, too, you know, and they're my *only* grandchildren, and God knows I had to wait long enough for them. And then you had to go and leave Owen just when he was ready to become a father."

My mouth falls open in shock. She knows that's not the case at all.

The fact that this waiting for grandchildren had to do with years of fertility issues for Rachel and Adam means nothing to Mom. The fact that she knows *I* wanted kids and the Fates are now laughing at me means nothing to her. The slow burn of anger evaporates the droplets of sympathy I felt a moment earlier. Someday, maybe, I'll get used to my mother's stealth attacks. Today is not that day.

"Guess who I saw the other day?" I ask, and yes, I'm being petty.

"Whom? Whom did you see, Jenny?"

"Dorothy."

For three seconds, there's silence. "Who's Dorothy?" she asks. Ha. She knows exactly who Dorothy is.

"She worked for Dad for a little while."

"Did she? Hmm. I don't remember." Her voice is haughty now.

"She was a single mom. We gave her some hand-me-downs, Rachel and I."

"If you say so. Can I come over or not?"

I hear a car door open on the street and look out the window. Uh-oh. It's Rachel, back a day early. "Mom, someone just pulled up. I'll talk to you later, okay?" Then, feeling guilty, I add, "Love you!" I hang up. "Girls! Mommy's here! Look out the window!"

"Mommy! Mommy's back! Mommy!" The girls run to the window and bang on it with their little fists. My sister looks up and her face breaks into a huge smile. She waves with both hands and blows kisses, then gets a few bags from her car.

"Come, Auntie!" Grace orders. "Mommy's here!"

When Rachel walks in, the girls launch themselves at her, and I can't help feeling a little ditched. For two days, they were mine to cuddle, soothe, read to and adore. Well, it's almost dinnertime. Maybe I'll convince Rachel to let them stay over one more night.

"Were you well behaved for Auntie?" Rachel asks, kissing them over and over.

"Yes!" Rose announces. "So behaved!"

"They were excellent," I say. "Such good company!"

The girls chorus to tell Rachel every exciting minute she missed. "Mommy, we ate canpakes!" "Mommy, we slept in Auntie's bed!" "Mommy, I peed by myself!" "We sang songs!" "Auntie's friend told us a song about us!" "He made a pink dog!"

"Leo came up to help when things got a little noisy," I explain. Saying his name makes my insides squeeze.

"Did he," Rachel murmurs, lifting an eyebrow. She turns her attention back to the girls. "I brought presents," she says, and the girls attack the shopping bags.

We make supper—Rachel is so much better at commandeering her daughters than I am—and then give them baths, read stories. They'll stay over one more night, Rachel says, and I'm so happy. We haven't had a sleepover for a long time, since Adam took a business trip two years ago.

I wonder if he cheated then, too.

Because I know Rachel has missed her daughters, I go downstairs while she tucks them in. I can hear her singing their favorite songs and a flutter of laughter as they say something adorable, no doubt.

If I ever get to be a mom, I hope I'm just like her. The yawning hole of want never fails to take me by surprise.

But maybe…just maybe…I can start thinking of little curly-haired children with musical ability and amazing smiles.

When Rachel comes, I pour us each a glass of wine. The rain has stopped for now, though the clouds are still thick. I turn on a kitchen light, flooding the room in amber light. "So. I didn't expect you back till tomorrow," I say.

Rachel sighs. "I got too lonely. I tried to stay. Went to the Cloisters today and had a nice lunch but the truth is, I just wanted to be back here."

"Did Adam call?"

She nods. "He emailed and texted. I didn't answer."

"And?"

"He keeps saying he knows it looked damning, but he's not back with her."

"Do you believe him?" I ask.

"I don't know. Would you?"

Are you even kidding? I don't answer.

She looks up. "Go ahead. Say what's on your mind."

I blow my bangs off my forehead. "Okay. Well, you gave him another chance. He was kissing that slut, which doesn't exactly fall under the purview of being a better man, does it? And if it walks like a duck and sounds like a duck…"

She plays with the stem of her wineglass. "I had dinner with a man last night."

My mouth drops open. "Did you?"

"Yep. Remember Gus Fletcher from my old job?"

I visited Rachel at work from time to time when she was at Celery Stalk. "Um…smiley eyes?"

"Yes. Him."

"I remember him as being very nice."

"Yes. He is. It was good to see him." The tears that have been making her eyes shiny slip out. "Except it was like I was pretending to be someone else. I don't know anything anymore, Jenny. I don't even know who I am. Last night was like a fake me, all dressed up, going out with a nice man, this haircut…and the truth is, I'd have rather been *home*. I'm not meant for hotels and restaurants, and we saw Robert De Niro, did I tell you that? We sat right next to him, and that's just not me!" She glances toward the living room and bites down on a sob.

"Rach, honey," I tell her. "You've been gone for two days. It's called escaping. Taking a break. That's allowed. That's even encouraged." I pause. "You just had dinner?"

She gives me a shaky smile. "Yes. And then we went back to my hotel room and had a drink. Up on the deck, not in the bedroom or anything. We talked, he left. He kissed me on the cheek, but nothing happened."

No. She's not the type. In all our life, I've never seen her so confused and sad as these past two months, and it makes my heart feel like it's in a vise. "Robert De Niro, huh?"

She smiles. "He nodded at me."

"Well, your hair does look amazing."

And now she laughs, and the vise loosens. "So you stayed in a gorgeous hotel, had a fabulous dinner with a nice man, and you saw a movie star… It sounds pretty great."

"It was."

"And, Rach, of course you're shaken up by this affair. You get to be mad. You trusted your husband a million percent, and he was fucking around—"

"Don't swear. The girls."

"They can't hear us. But he *was*, Rach. And maybe he still is! It's normal to feel like…like…" I remember how I felt when Owen told me we were getting divorced. "Like you're living in the wrong world."

Her face scrunches up. "Exactly. And, Jenny, God, I loved the old world, so, so much." She starts to cry in earnest, and damn it, so do I. "It's like when Daddy died," she says, wiping her eyes on the napkin. "Life was so perfect, and then it was over, and we never got that back. Do I divorce Adam? Do I try to stick it out? Sometimes I hate him so much, I think I might kill him, and then, yesterday, I *missed* him, Jenny. I missed him. And I feel like such an idiot because of it." The tears slide down her face, and there's such confusion there, such longing.

I press my lips together to stop my crying.

If Adam could see her now, would he still think Emmanuelle was worth it? That breaking the heart of this wonderful, lovely, generous, thoughtful human was somehow acceptable, because his orgasm was awesome?

The *bastard*. The cheating, lying scum bucket. There aren't words bad enough for him.

At that moment, someone knocks on my door. "It's probably Leo," I say, clearing my throat. "I'll shoo him away." The mirror in the foyer shows my eyes are shiny with tears, my nose is red, my face blotchy. Not my best look.

It's not Leo.

It's Adam.

"Is my wife here?" he asks.

I stare at him, hatred throbbing. So far as I'm concerned, he's lost the right to call Rachel *his* anything. "Go to hell, Adam."

"Jenny, please. Is my wife here?"

"My sister, you mean? My *sister* is here. I'm not sure if she's planning to be your wife much longer." My stomach twists in sympathy pain for Rachel. Once upon a time, I loved Adam Carver, his charm, his laugh, his sweetness with his girls. Now I want to kick him in the nuts. More than once.

He gives a martyred sigh. "Can you please stop trying to run her life and just tell her I'm here?"

"I'll ask *my sister* if she wants to see you. Until I know the answer, get off my steps. You're trespassing."

I'm shaking in rage. I close the door in his face, but gently, so as not to wake the girls, and go back into the kitchen.

My sister's face is white. "I don't want to see him. Not yet. I'll be going home tomorrow, but I can't see him tonight."

"Of course, of course," I say, kneeling down to give her a hug. "Stay right here. I'll be back in a flash."

I go out onto the stoop. Adam is obediently waiting on the sidewalk below. It feels good to look down at him like the dog shit he is. "She doesn't want to see you," I say. "For good reason. So. Bye."

He doesn't move a muscle.

"Adam, leave."

"Rachel!" he yells suddenly. "Rach! Honey, please! I miss you so much! You and the girls are my whole life!"

I'm down the steps in a flash, nose to nose with my brother-in-law. "Not here, ass-hat, and not now. She doesn't want to talk to you."

"Rach! Please, baby! It wasn't like that! You have to believe me! Emmanuelle is nothing to me!"

"Well, she was enough for you to fuck, wasn't she?" I hiss, jabbing my forefinger into his chest. "You have two seconds to get into your car, or I'm calling the police."

"Maybe *I'll* call the police, Jenny," he snarls. "You're the one assaulting me."

"With my finger?" I snap back. "God, I'm amazing. Or, you're a puny excuse for a man. I'm going with that one."

"Rach! Rachel, please!" he bellows past my head.

"Adam, be quiet," Rachel says from the doorway. "The girls are asleep."

Adam's face screws up. "Rachel, please."

I have never in my life hit a person, but, my God, I want to now. I glance back at my sister, who's biting her lip. "He's leaving. Don't worry."

"I'm not leaving," he says to her, his voice breaking. "I'll sleep on this sidewalk if I have to. But I'm not leaving till you talk to me."

"Adam, go home," she says, but her voice is hardly convincing.

"You heard her," I grind out.

"Fuck you, Jenny," he mutters in a very different tone than he's using with my sister.

"Go *home*, Adam!" I snap. "You made this mess, so grow a pair and deal with it! She doesn't want to see you!" I poke him again, hard.

And that's when the perfect storm hits. The sidewalks on this street are erratic, veined with tree roots thanks to poor arborist choices fifty years ago. Adam, driven by my forefinger's Thor-like strength—or rage, as the case may be—takes a step back, trips over a bump and lands on his ass against a metal garbage can, which clangs into a parked car.

Right as a police car happens to be driving down the street. There's the blip of a siren, lights start flashing.

I'm guessing it looks like I am indeed assaulting him.

"Jesus, Jenny, take it easy!" Adam says, loud enough for Rachel to hear. He flips me the bird, but subtly.

And sure enough, it works. "Jenny! What did you do? Calm down!" She runs down the steps.

"Nothing! Rach, he fell. Tell her you fell, you little worm." I take another step toward Adam, fully intending to give him a hand up, but someone puts his arms around me from behind. Leo. "What are you doing?" He lifts me up—easy for him, since he's a good six inches taller—and carries me back a few paces, as if I'm an actual threat. "Put me down!"

"Calm down, Jenny, and be quiet."

"I just poked him, okay? He fell because he's an uncoordinated cheating asswipe."

"Shush," he murmurs into my ear. "You don't want to get arrested."

That has quite the wallop. I freeze. Yeah, okay. I can see how this looks bad. Adam cowering, Rachel wringing her hands, me towering over the fallen.

Crap.

The cop gets out of his car. Rachel crouches by Adam's side. "Are you okay?" she asks, putting her hand on his shoulder. She never could tolerate someone being hurt.

Crap on a crutch.

"Sir," the officer says, "do you think you can get up?"

"I think so," Adam says. He never was stoic. The man once drove himself to the ER for a *cold*, convinced that his stuffy nose was pneumonia. It used to be a funny story. "My back hurts. I think I strained it when she pushed me."

"I did not push you, Adam! He fell on his ass! He tripped!" I sound like an abusive husband explaining why his wife has a black eye. Leo's right. I'm going to get arrested.

"Stay right where you are, lady, and quiet down. Ma'am," the cop says to Rachel, "please step over here." He lifts the radio on his shoulder and adds, "We've got a domestic here, 11 Magnolia. Possible injuries."

Within two minutes, there's an ambulance on the street. Legions of neighbors—who generally seem to like me but are now giving me strange looks—have come out to enjoy the drama, and I'm trying to look extremely unthreatening and gentle. Which I *am*.

Adam turns down the offer of an ambulance; I guess it's protocol to call one, even when the vic is faking.

Rachel is questioned by a police officer. Adam is questioned. I'm questioned. When I ask if this is really necessary, the officer coolly informs me that DV— domestic violence—calls can be the most dangerous. Leo is questioned as a witness—and sadly, tells the truth—he only saw me standing over my brother-in-law. Loki barks hysterically from Leo's courtyard, adding to the whole *Cops* feeling of the evening.

"Can I take my dog inside?" Leo asks. "He's old and confused."

"Sure," the cop says. "I need to ask Mr. Carver a few more questions."

Leo looks at me. "You know where I live," he says.

"Yeah. Thanks." He squeezes my hand, then goes to his true love.

It's awfully lonely without him. I catch Rachel's eye, give a half grimace, half smile.

She looks away, and my heart sinks so fast I feel sick.

"Okay," the cop says when he comes back to me. He cocks an eyebrow. "He's not going to press charges."

"Against the sidewalk? Because that's why he tripped. These are a hazard, you know."

"Ma'am, look," he says. "These situations can get very ugly. Okay? Just try to keep your temper."

"I don't have a temper," I say.

"Don't make me write you up."

"Thank you, Officer," I amend.

"That's better."

Adam signs a piece of paper, glancing at me.

I don't like the way Rachel only left his side to check on the girls. The bedroom windows are open, so we'd hear them if they needed anything.

I think my babysitting days have been curtailed for a little while.

I have to give Adam credit. He played that perfectly. No wonder he got away with an affair.

"Let's go inside to talk," Rachel says when the cops have left and the neighbors drift back to their homes. I'm still standing on the sidewalk, not sure what to do.

"No," Adam says. "Look, Jenny hates me, I get that. I deserve that. But, Rachel, we can't fix our marriage if you're staying with her. I love you. I love the girls." He pauses. "I miss the way things were."

And those are the magic words, apparently, because Rachel wavers.

"Please, baby," Adam whispers, and if he hadn't flipped me off and milked that fall, I might be pulling for him. But I know better.

Rachel does not know better. All of a sudden, they're hugging, and she's crying and he's murmuring, and I can't help it, I hear myself saying, "Rachel, you gotta be kidding! Don't fall for this again! You deserve better than this scumbag."

She pulls back and whirls on me. "That scumbag is the father of my children, Jenny," she hisses. "We have a family. It's easy for you to give advice because you don't know what's at stake!"

Her words slap me in the face. "Rachel, I just—"

"It's not your business," she says.

"You made it my business! I've been here for you since that first day! How can you say that?"

"Well, I don't need you right now, okay? I appreciate everything you've done for me, but Adam's right. This is for him and me to figure out. Not you." She looks at Adam. "Let me get the girls and we'll go home."

"I'll come in and help. If that's okay with you, Jenny. If you'll let me pollute your house long enough to get my daughters."

"Yes. I...I... Fine."

My hands are shaking. I'm furious with Rachel for being so naive—again! She didn't even know what a crotch shot was! And then, oh, hey, it was just an accident; Adam would never cheat on her, and of course he *was*. Even Leo, who was a complete stranger, knew that.

She wants me to look out for her, and I do, and then I get blamed for it. She needs a shoulder to cry on, and it's mine, and then I'm blamed for being angry.

It's so fucking unfair.

Five minutes later, I watch as the girls, who could sleep through being eaten by zombies, are packed into the minivan. Rachel pulls away, giving me a terse wave. Adam doesn't bother saying anything. Then, when he's just about to get into his car, he turns to me and says, "I'd appreciate it if you didn't fill her head with inflammatory images, Jenny. You're just making things worse."

"Me? Your *whore* is the one who filled her head with images when she sent that picture!"

Adam smiles at me. He *smiles* and gets into his car,

and I'm left alone on the street, the DelFuego kid across the way bouncing his basketball.

It starts to rain again, and my tears slash hot and fierce through the cold on my cheeks.

"Jenny. Come inside." Leo's voice is soft from the doorway.

I turn around and obey. I don't quite make it into his apartment before I'm bawling.

"How can she be mad at *me*? She just… How am I suddenly the bad guy here?" I sob. Leo looks around, then hands me a roll of paper towels. I take it, blowing my nose as he leads me into his ever-immaculate living room. "She gave him everything! Three beautiful children. Her heart, every hour of the day devoted to that family, to him. She thought he practically parted the Red Sea, and he goes and sleeps with some slut."

That stupid, squeaky sound is me, I realize. I hate this. I hate my Ugly Face of Crying, hate the sobs that rip out of my throat, hate that my sister is mad at me and back with Adam.

Loki, who finally sides with me for once, starts crooning. He comes over and puts his head in my lap.

"Why don't men appreciate what they have? Why do they screw everything up? Why, Leo? Why?"

"I don't know, honey," Leo says quietly.

"She *knows* he's still sleeping with her. She's not stupid. He and that woman were making out in his office on Friday, and now Rachel's hugging him in the street! Why would she give him another chance? Can you honestly forget that your husband lied to you, over and over and over…" My voice breaks off into a squeak.

"I've missed eighty percent of what you've just said,"

Leo says, putting his arm around me. "Only Loki can hear you now."

Loki lies down and puts his muzzle on my foot. I blow my nose and try to get myself under control.

"My father cheated on my mother, did you know that?" I say, my face spasming. "Everyone thought they had the perfect marriage, but he cheated, too. And then he died, and I couldn't even be mad at him."

Leo kisses my hair and doesn't say anything.

"I should've told."

"Why?"

"Because then maybe he wouldn't have gone to buy that Brain Freeze."

"So you control the world, then? Good to know."

"Don't laugh at me." But it's nice here, my head on his chest, the warm smell of him. We were kissing last night. It seems like a week ago. "Do you think I should tell Rachel about our dad?"

"I have no idea."

"Please, Leo."

"Sweetheart, I honestly have no idea. I'm not good at this stuff." But he's stroking my hair, and it feels so good.

"I'm afraid that if she knows about Dad, then she'll justify staying with Adam."

"Loki, what do you think?"

"I hate that she's mad at me. I'm the good guy here."

"You are. You're a very good sister from what I've seen."

That makes my eyes fill again. I pull another paper towel off the roll and blow my nose. "I don't understand men," I say brokenly. "They have everything, and then one piece of tail makes them throw away everything that's good in their lives just for…for what? For sex? Is sex really that important that you'd screw over your wife and children and make them feel like dirt? Like they're stupid and unimportant?"

Did the same kind of thing happen with him? Maybe he could pipe up and make me feel a little less freakish, all my emotional misery eviscerated, hanging there like intestines.

"Do you have any idea, Leo?" I ask, lifting my head to look at him.

"I don't."

I put my head back on his chest. "And even if they don't cheat," I say, my voice small, "they find some way to break your heart and make you wonder what you ever did wrong. But they don't have time to answer you because they've already found the next love of their life, and you're just left standing on the street corner, asking yourself how the hell you didn't even notice your husband stopped loving you." I'm crying again.

I guess we both know who I'm really talking about.

"Loki, what did she say?" Leo asks, but his face is kind. He frames my face with his hands. Kisses my forehead, then my cheek. "Not all men break hearts," he murmurs. "Now mop up so I can kiss you."

There's that smile again, but there's something else in his clear blue eyes. Kindness. Sympathy.

Sadness.

Did he break his wife's heart? It doesn't seem as if he'd be capable of that, funny, kind Leo. No. His heart was the one that took the hit.

I wipe my eyes and blow my nose. Not the sexiest sound in the world, I realize, but he just looks at me, the smile, the eyes, the unfairly beautiful hair.

I'm fairly sure I'm in love with Leo Killian.

"Are we finally going to sleep together?" I ask.

"Yes," he says, and he does kiss me then, kisses me for a long time, cups my face in his hands, threads his fingers through my hair and kisses me and kisses me until my heart throbs with wanting him, and my whole body is tight and coiled and helpless with this, with soft, hot want that blots out all the ugliness from earlier. Then he takes me into his bedroom and makes good on his promise.

Makes very good.

Rachel

❖

I DON'T KNOW if I believe Adam about when the affair ended. I almost feel like it doesn't matter, because I'm just so tired. I'm tired of myself, tired of him, tired of the confusion, the sadness, the panic. I just want to watch *Game of Thrones* and think about nothing except how much I like Tyrion.

But I believe what he said in the street—he wants me back. A weekend without the girls and me was exactly what he needed—a glimpse of the life he'd have with a fractured family, going days without seeing Charlotte, Grace and Rose.

Without me.

The house is not exactly a mess when we get home from that debacle at Jenny's, but my absence is graffitied throughout the downstairs. The unloaded dishwasher. The clutter of mail on the counters, the unfolded laundry in the basket. It's evidence that he was *here*. Not with her. The plate on the coffee table, the single empty wineglass, sticky red residue in the bottom, tell me that this weekend, he was too scared to be with her. The slut. The home-wrecking whore.

Relief wraps around me like a blanket.

We get the girls in bed and tuck them in, and as Adam

kisses each girl on the head, he whispers, "Daddy loves you."

And he does. I know he does.

We look at each other. I'm not sure what to do next.

"Let's talk," he says, reaching for my hand.

We sit in the living room, and he gets me a glass of wine. Touches my shoulder. "That was some scene at Jenny's," I murmur, because I'm not sure what else to say.

"It was surprising," Adam says drily.

I will die if this gets out—Jenny Tate and Rachel and Adam Carver, fighting in the street until the police were called. This entire spring, I've been grateful to my sister for a thousand reasons, but tonight is not one of those times. She's always so…*sure*, always taking charge. (I conveniently dismiss the fact that I asked her to do just that.) But honestly. What if the girls had woken up and looked out the window to see their aunt shoving their father?

I hate the way she sometimes treats me as if I'm slightly dim. Mom, too. We're not.

My anger toward her helps the other, more complicated feelings to slink to the back of my brain.

"How was your weekend?" Adam asks, and it's funny, I can barely remember. It was like a dream I had a long time ago. The suite, the view, the shopping… Gus.

Him, I remember.

"It was nice," I say. "I bought out SoHo and saw Robert De Niro and stayed in a ridiculous suite."

"You deserve it, babe," he says. "You deserve everything and more."

Whatever. I can't imagine Gus saying that. It's too trite.

"Adam, you have to be done with Emmanuelle." Her name is bitter in my mouth. "If I even suspect you're not, it's over between us. No more chances."

"I am done, Rach. I swear. I swear on our—" *girls*, he's about to say, but I cut him off.

"Don't. Don't ever swear on the girls."

"Okay. But I'm really done. You mean everything to me, Rachel. I've learned my lesson."

Why did you need to be taught, Adam? Why didn't you know that already? "I don't want you working with her. That's too much to ask. Find another job." I'm quite demanding, aren't I? This New Rachel has some qualities to recommend her, after all.

"Okay. I will, babe. You're right. I'll talk to Jared tomorrow."

"Good." I drain my wine. "I'm whipped. Let's go to bed."

We don't make love. But when I wake up in the dark, his arm is around me. I can't tell if I'm glad about that.

WE HAVE ONE more session with our marriage counselor. Donna babysits—she thinks we're going out to dinner. I don't ask Jenny, as I usually do. I'm still furious with her. I recognize that this isn't fair, but I need to be furious with someone. She can take it. She's the tough sister, after all, treating me as if I'm too fragile to have a real life.

Again, I'm not being fair.

Adam tells Laney the story of his encounter with Jenny as if he's in a bar, entertaining his workmates. She must have trained her face to be impassive, because her expression doesn't flicker.

"How did you feel about that, Rachel?" she asks.

"I was very angry," I say calmly. "I don't like having my marital problems broadcast."

"It sounds like Adam was the one broadcasting."

"I was desperate," Adam says. "I felt like if Rachel stayed one more hour with her sister, we'd never have a chance."

"Why?"

"Because Jenny… She never liked me."

I give him an incredulous look. "That's not true."

"Well. I think she was a little jealous of Rach and me. She had this protective thing going on with Rachel—not that you needed it, babe—and when I came along, I think she felt deposed."

"Why would she feel deposed, do you think, Adam?"

"Because Rachel loves me more," he says simply.

I don't respond.

"I'm sure Jenny has very strong feelings about your affair," Laney says.

"Look," I interject, not wanting to talk about my sister. "The point is, Adam and I are staying together. I'm tired of talking about it."

"Me, too!" Adam says with a relieved laugh.

"Okay," she says, her tone measured and calm. "A lot of couples want to do just that—put the event behind them. What can happen sometimes is that you think the issue has been dealt with, and then something flares back up."

I'm tired of flares. I never used to have flares.

She gives us the old therapist pause, waiting for one of us to speak.

Neither of us does.

She must read something in my expression. "If I can be of any further use, don't hesitate to call."

"Thank you. You've been very helpful." My tone is terse and unfamiliar even to my own ears. New Rachel in her sexy heels, bought in the city.

Like something Emmanuelle would wear.

LATER THAT WEEK, when the girls are at school and Adam's at work, I go to Bliss. As always, the beauty of my sister's work is a sensory shock—the gleam of fabric, the sweet beauty of a neckline, the glitter of a beaded bodice. Her talent is stunning, and this shop…it's warm and welcoming and breathtaking all at once.

As is my sister. I owe her an apology.

"Hello, Doris Day," Andreas says.

"Hello, Rock Hudson," I answer. "Is my sister here?"

"She's got an appointment in fifteen minutes. Kimber, as a matter of fact. But she's free right now."

Jenny appears on cue. "Hey!" she says, flushing. "Come on back."

I go into the dressing room with her, where a huge muslin dress hangs against the wall. I sit on the couch—apricot satin, something I helped pick out an eon ago, it seems. "Jenny, I'm sorry," I say.

"I didn't push him, Rachel. I poked him, and he tripped."

I nod.

"So you're back together?" she asks, focusing on something over my head.

"Yes. We're working through it. And we're getting there."

She can barely look at me, and a flash of Old Rachel, that stupid softhearted idiot, clamors to get out and beg her to hug me.

"Jenny," I say, "I need you to be okay with that. I

can't have you hating my husband and the father of my children."

"I get that," she says. "But don't punish me for knowing what I know. What you *told* me. I can't help hating him."

"That's exactly what I'm talking about!"

"Well, I *do* hate Adam! He hurt you! He broke your heart!"

"So what are you going to do?" I snap. "Make my life worse because the two people I love best can't stand each other?"

"No. No." She takes a sharp breath, her lips tightening. "I'll forgive him, but not because of him. Because of you. It's going to take some time. I can't just forgive and forget. I mean, have you forgiven Owen?"

My head jerks back. "Owen married someone else and popped out a baby. So no, I haven't forgiven him. He didn't see the error of his ways." God, that sounds so sanctimonious.

"And Adam has?"

"Yes! Is that so hard to believe? I wish I hadn't told you anything. I'm sorry I dragged you into it, but for the love of God, stop judging us. You know you'd have taken Owen back in a heartbeat. You still would."

She tips her head in acknowledgment. "That was true for a long time. But it's not anymore."

"Why? Because you have a crush on Leo? Be careful there, Jenny. He's going to break your heart next. You always see what you want to see. Don't be naive."

"Isn't that a tiny bit hypocritical? You thought a crotch shot was tree fungus."

We have never fought before. Bickered, yes, when we were teenagers, over using up all the hot water, or borrowing clothes without permission. But not like this. This is getting ugly. I can feel my heart tremble with the ugliness of it, but I don't know what else to say.

Mercifully, Andreas knocks. "The future Mrs. Brewster is here!" he coos, and in comes Kimber, Jared's mom and a lady I've never met.

"Oh, hey!" Kimber cries happily. "Rachel! Hi, Jenny! Mom, this is Rachel Carver, one of my bridesmaids! And this is the amazing Jenny!"

I stand up and give Kimber a hug, press my cheek against Mrs. Brewster's and shake Kimber's mom's hand. "I'm Rachel," I say. "Nice to meet you, Mrs. Allegretti."

"Oh, it's not Allegretti. It's Puchalski. Kimber's dad passed away when she was just a little thing, and after a while, I got remarried, but it didn't work out, so… Well. Too much information, right? Anyway, it's really nice to meet you. Call me Dorothy."

Mrs. Brewster, as usual, is staring at the rest of us as if we're toads.

I immediately like Dorothy. "Kimber's told me a lot about you."

"She's my darling. My best friend, right, honey?"

"That's right, Mom. So! Jenny, let's get going, shall we?" Kimber sees the dress hanging against the wall, and her smile falters.

I look at my sister. Her face is…weird. She says nothing.

"Kimber, your hair!" I say to cover. "You colored it."

"Yeah, well, I… It's more appropriate, I think. You know. Brown instead of pink. Right?"

"I loved the pink," her mom says, getting a glare from Mrs. Brewster. Dorothy raises an eyebrow in return. Good for her. About time someone didn't lick that woman's shoes.

"Would anyone like coffee?" Andreas asks.

"No, thank you," Mrs. Brewster says. "Let's get this done." My sister breaks out of her paralysis.

"I'm Jenny," she says to Dorothy. "Jenny Tate."

Dorothy flinches, then smiles, though it seems weirdly pained. "Hi!" Her voice is hearty. "Dorothy."

"We saw each other at the vet's office that night," Jenny says. "How's your bird?"

"Right, right! He's fine. Thank you. And your friend's dog?"

"Also fine." Jenny turns to the bride. "Come into the changing room, Kimber, and let's see what you think." She takes Kimber by the arm and steers her off.

"How have you been, Eleanor?" I use Mrs. Brewster's first name, just because it irritates her. New Rachel doesn't care. I've known the woman since I was five, for the love of God.

"I've been well," she answers. She doesn't ask how I am.

We wait, mostly in silence. Though Dorothy was initially friendly, she's tense now. Then again, Mrs. Brewster could make a baby sloth feel tense. Dorothy cracks her knuckles, earning a twitch from Mrs. Snotty.

Then Kimber comes out, and the first word that leaps to mind is *puritan*.

Kimber smiles uncertainly.

"Oh, baby," Dorothy says. "You look… Well, you're beautiful." Her eyes fill with tears.

"Is it okay?" Kimber asks, her eyes darting between the two mothers.

"It's fine," Mrs. Brewster says. "At least we can't see those hideous tattoos."

"How rude!" Dorothy snaps.

"And true," Mrs. Brewster responds, icicles dripping from her tone.

We can't see *any* skin, for that matter. The dress is not ugly, per se, but...well, it's not my sister's best work.

But Jenny is only looking at Dorothy. Which is weird.

"Jenny, will the actual dress have some detail work on it?" I ask.

"I think it should," she says, snapping out of her funk. "The satin is stunning, but it's a little plain, so I was thinking some crystal beading—"

"No. She's getting married in my husband's church, not Las Vegas," Mrs. Brewster interrupts. "She should look as decent as possible."

"What are you implying?" Dorothy asks, and again, I give her a point for going up against the bitchy old dragon. How Jared got to be so nice is thanks to his lovely dad, that's for sure. "My daughter *is* decent. She could wear a sack and look decent."

"If you say so," Mrs. Brewster says. "But she's marrying the son of a Congregational minister—"

"The son of a preacher man," I say, referencing the old Dusty Springfield song, and Kimber's face lights up.

"That's our favorite song!" she says. "That's how we met! I was singing at a bar, and—"

"As I was saying before you interrupted, *Rachel*, she should show some respect for the church and the family she's marrying into."

"And maybe you should show my *daughter* some respect, Eleanor," Dorothy says.

Kimber wrings her hands, which are laden with silver

rings and the one big honking diamond. "Mom, Mom, it's fine. I love this look. It's good. It's beautiful." She turns to Jenny. "It'll be great, right?"

Jenny's face softens. "Yes. You'll be stunning, Kimber. I bet you ten bucks Jared cries when he sees you. I've been to a lot of weddings, and I can tell which grooms are going to cry." She smiles, and I feel a rush of love for her.

God, I hate fighting.

She seems to read my mind and smiles at me, too.

We'll be okay.

And though I can't admit it—to Adam, because we're trying to rebuild things, or to Jenny, because it wouldn't help her forgive Adam—I wish *I* was the one who pushed Adam down in the street and called him names. Who stood there like a mother lion defending her young. Who was mad enough that the police thought she might do some harm.

My sister is fierce.

I hope my daughters would be like that if their husbands cheated. I hope they'd poke and swagger and tolerate absolutely no shit.

Not like their mother.

Not these days.

Jenny

———◆———

W<small>HEN</small> I <small>GET</small> home the day of Kimber's latest fitting, I need a glass of wine. And Leo. I could use Leo.

But Evander has Leo at the moment; the kid is playing something that's fluid and lyrical and the tiniest bit sad. I let myself in. Leo told me it was better than me lurking in the courtyard like a stalker, but I think he wanted me to have a key for girlfriendy reasons. He glances at me, winks and turns his attention back to his prodigy. Evander doesn't pause; I doubt he knows I'm here. The music grows, swelling into something more fiery and insistent, then gentles again, the notes so soft I feel them more than hear them. The boy's arms seem boneless, they're so graceful, and his face, even in profile, is intent, completely connected to the music.

I wait till the piece is over, and indeed, Evander startles a little when he sees me. "Hey, buddy," I say.

"Hi, Miss Jenny," he whispers.

"That was so beautiful," I say. "I felt it in my heart."

His face blossoms into a beautiful smile. He's missing an incisor, new since last week, which makes him even cuter, dang it. "Thanks, Miss Jenny. I'm glad."

"Are you flirting with my girlfriend?" Leo asks. "Because knock it off, mister. I don't stand a chance against you." Evander's smile grows. "Okay," Leo continues. "Next piece. Bach's Two-Part Inventions, Number Five, E-Flat Major, your favorite key. You can make googly eyes at Miss Jenny later. Miss Jenny, have I mentioned that Evander will be auditioning for Juilliard's pre-college program?"

"Really? Wow! Evander, that's great!" I have no idea what that is, but it sounds kick-ass.

"Yes, Miss Jenny," he says, sliding his eyes to meet mine for a second.

"It's for extremely gifted children," Leo says, cocking an eyebrow at his student. "Who practice a lot." He looks up at me. "Evander is staying for dinner, Miss Jenny. Would you like to join us?"

My heart nearly tumbles out of my chest. This is what I want, this easy of-course-we're-together relationship, none of the angst, the wondering, the will-he-call-me phase. "Miss Jenny would love to. Let me go upstairs and change." I pet Loki, who wags his stumpy little tail—progress—and tolerates me fondling his soft, triangular ears. Then he gives me a snarl, my lovey time used up. But I guess as stinky old dogs go, he's not so bad.

As I leave, Evander begins a bouncy, ridiculously complicated piece.

The fact that I saw my father's mistress today—and that she now knows who I am—is muted by having someone to come home to. Even so, my heart thumps sickly at the thought.

Kimber's mother is my father's mistress. Jesus.

I change into jeans and a soft gray cashmere sweater, take my hair out of its twist, slip in different earrings and pour a glass of wine.

My phone rings, and I glance at the screen before answering. "Hey, Owen."

"Hi, stranger! I've barely talked to you this week."

In fact, I haven't talked to Owen since just after his dinner party. "How's it going?"

"Oh, not so bad. Just wanted to hear your voice."

I've known Owen long enough to catch that note in his voice. *Not so bad* is his term for *everything's going to hell*.

And that last line borders on romantic. Maybe. His voice still gets to me, the deep, gentle timbre. I no longer remember the sound of my father's voice, but I think it was similar.

"What's going on?" I ask.

"Ah, nothing. You free for dinner one of these nights?"

I pause. But there's no reason for me not to see Owen and Ana-Sofia, just because I'm sleeping with Leo. "Sure. Let's see. Thursday?"

"I can't that day. Giving a lecture at Columbia. How about Friday?"

Friday is date night. Everyone knows that. "Um… maybe. Can I get back to you?"

"Of course." There's a pause. "I miss you."

"I miss you guys, too." I don't, I realize. Once, I counted days in between when I could call them again, so as not to appear too needy and lonely. Just a good, good friend.

"This would just be you and me. Is that okay?" Owen says. "Ana-Sofia has something that night."

"Oh, okay. I'll get to see Natalia, though, right?"

"Well, I was thinking a restaurant. We've found a great nanny."

Yeah. And being alone with my ex and his child, playing family, is probably not healthy. "Sounds good."

He doesn't answer.

"Owen, is everything okay?"

"Yes, yes, of course. I'm still at the hospital. I just… I don't know. I really miss you. I don't think I've ever gone so long without seeing you."

"Except for when you were with Doctors Without Borders," I remind him.

"Right. Remember that time when I called and you were at a wedding? I was so screwed up with time zones."

"I remember." That was back when we were in love. When he called from somewhere in Indonesia, and I smothered my cell phone and scurried out of the blue-and-ivory splendor of St. Thomas Church and onto Fifth Avenue so I could talk to him, hear his voice, tell him how much I loved and missed him. And he told me those things back.

Yeah.

That was years ago. Five, maybe? We were still newlyweds then.

"I have to go," I tell him. "I have a date."

"Oh! Uh, okay. Sorry, Jenny. Have fun. Let me know about Friday. Take care, honey. Bye."

Honey. Force of habit, or just affection. I call my brides *honey* all the time.

I hang up, bemused. While I wouldn't wish anything bad to befall my ex-husband, I can't deny that it feels kind of great to have him miss me. To be the one with plans.

Speaking of, two very attractive gentlemen are waiting for me downstairs, so downstairs I go.

AFTER DINNER, EVANDER's mother calls. Leo talks to her in a low voice for a few minutes, then looks over at me. "Can you drive Evander home?"

"Sure." I've only had the one glass of wine. "Is your car in the shop?"

"No. Let's go, Wonderboy."

It's a given that Loki comes. Leo doesn't seem to go anywhere without him. We drive through Cambry-on-Hudson to a scruffier section of town, closer to the gravel quarry. Evander gives me directions, not Leo, which surprises me. I thought he drove Evander home from time to time.

The James residence is a two-family house; down the sidewalk is a cluster of teenagers who yell and curse and roughhouse in the loud way of teenagers, then go silent as Leo and Evander get out of the car and go into the house.

The kids turn their attention to me, and the loud talking resumes. Their message is clear—*look at us, be afraid of us, we own this street.* I smile. It goes unreturned.

But Leo is only gone a minute.

"How is it for Evander, do you think, being a musical prodigy in a neighborhood like this?" I ask when he gets back in the car.

"Tough," he says. "His parents aren't sure they want him to keep on playing."

"You're kidding!"

"I wish I was. I'm trying to make it easy with the free lessons and taxis and keeping him for dinner, but it might be a matter of time."

"So he can, what? Sell drugs with these kids?" I point to the knot of children, the smell of pot thick in the air.

"That would be racial profiling, Jenny."

"Half those kids are white, and can you not smell that? That's marijuana, dear boy."

He runs a hand through his glorious hair and sighs.

"I thought you drove Evander home every week," I said.

"No. I don't drive students. Too much liability."

That makes sense. But he's tense, his fingers tapping on his knees, as if he's playing the piano. "So what's the pre-college program?" I ask.

"It's a weekend school for prodigies. Very intense, but if he gets in, he's almost guaranteed to be accepted at Juilliard for college."

"He's that good?"

"He's that good. He's quite possibly great."

Imagine that. It would be incredible to go see Evander playing at Carnegie Hall someday, to be able to say *I knew him when he was little. My husband was his teacher.*

Not that I'm getting ahead of myself.

"Why don't I ever hear you playing?" I ask.

His fingers stop moving, and he shrugs. "I play sometimes. You just might be at work when I do. I don't know."

I believe I've just been lied to. "Well, will you play for me when we get home? I'd love to hear you."

He gives me a look.

I'm not stupid. I've crossed a line. First of all, I just said words a man hates to hear—*when we get home.* Technically, we're not living together, despite being in the same building, despite sleeping together every night but two these past couple of weeks. And secondly, I asked to hear him play... Not the first time I have, and not the first time he's said no. You'd think a pianist would play the piano, wouldn't you? Especially, ladies and gentlemen of the jury, for his *girlfriend*, and he did call me his girlfriend. Evander is a witness.

The silence is getting to me.

"Jenny," he says at a stop sign. "Remember when I said I was recreation only?"

"Yes. I also remember when you said you were gay as far as I was concerned, which I believe I have disproved."

"I meant it about the recreation thing. We're friends with benefits, okay?" His voice is gentle.

Shit. Already, there's a lump in my throat. "So that rules out piano playing, does it?"

"Among other things, yes."

"Like the locked room upstairs? Listen. I've read *Jane Eyre*. That better be a red room of pain up there, and not your ex-wife."

"What's a red room of pain?"

"Never mind." Though I'm fairly sure I know the answer, I can't seem to help myself from asking the next question, either. "What about being my wedding date when Kimber and Jared get married in a few weeks?"

"I don't do weddings. You know how you women are. You read all sorts of things into it, then trample each other to catch the bouquet."

I nod, doing the old *it's fine, really, I don't mind a bit, hey, who needs a date to a wedding? We chicks love going stag.*

Most men don't relish weddings. It's fine. Leo and I have only been together a short time. He'll get there.

"So guess what?" I say brightly. "I saw my father's mistress today. File that under the heading of small world, because she's the mother of one of my brides. In fact, the bride herself once got hand-me-downs from Rachel and me."

Leo, always interested in my personal problems—though he never shares his own—glances at me sharply. "Wow."

We're home again. Loki rises stiffly and burps in my ear. I turn off the ignition and stay put, my hands still on the wheel. "So she recognized my name, and now I know she knows I know. You know?"

"Uh…sure." He smiles a little. "Were you okay, seeing her?"

"It was shocking. A little distressing." I swallow.

It made me miss my dad, oddly enough.

Leo tucks a strand of hair behind my ear, his eyes intent on the task. "Would you like me to come to your apartment and you can tell me about it and cry on my shoulder, and then we can fool around?"

"It's kind of our thing, isn't it?"

He smiles again, that heartbreaker smile, because, hand to God, that's the best smile I've ever seen, so wide and unexpected, his whole face transformed, and that slightly tragic shadow flies out the window when he smiles.

No doubt. I'm in love.

Rachel may be right. This is a disaster waiting to happen.

Rachel

❖

A FEW WEEKS after my weekend in the city, a package arrives. It's a gift-wrapped book from a little bookstore the next town over—*Darkly Dreaming Dexter* by Jeff Lindsay. There's a handwritten note card, too. How rare is that? "Thought you might like this. —Gus"

I know the premise of the book—the serial killer who only offs the bad guys—but I never had the guts to watch the show on TV. Neither did Adam, who has no tolerance for gore.

I think Gus is probably wrong. I've never read that type of book. But the fact that he thought of me—*is* thinking of me—is a little pearl in my day. A day which could use a whole string of pearls, because the girls have had springtime colds for six days now, and they view blowing their noses on the same level as having their hands held over an open flame. I've smeared Vicks VapoRub on their chests and the soles of their feet—it works, trust me. I ran the humidifier and cuddled and made chicken soup and got up in the night when Rose cried because "my tongue is hard!" Gave them long baths and ran the shower so the room would steam up. Slept in the guest room with Grace the night her cough was a little scary, took her to the pediatrician the next day with the other two to rule out pneumonia. Somehow, the cold made Charlotte revert back to pants-wetting, so I had to change her outfit four times one day, and she insisted on wearing the red turtleneck which is so hard to get off her extremely round head, and she screamed when it got stuck.

And still, I managed to keep them happy.

So today, when all three are finally mostly over their colds and back on their regular sleep schedules, I pour myself a glass of wine and sit down on the screened-in sunporch. It's that time of early June when the sun sets over the Hudson in a long, lingering fade of pink and yellow, and the birds serenade each other in long ripples of song.

I bring the book with me and start reading.

I was wrong. Gus was right.

I *love* the book.

I only go in when it's too dark to read, and then I curl up in my big chair and keep reading. Adam is doing something on the computer, surrounded by papers and files. He's grouchy, but I'll hand it to him. No more long days at the office. He's home by six every night. We've been doing couple things. Dinner with Jared and Kimber last week. Adam was devoted and affectionate and kind of a perfect date, but I found myself looking at Jared and wondering if I should warn him. Tell him never to cheat on Kimber, to take care of her heart, because it's clear that she loves him so, so much.

Obviously, I didn't say anything. I don't think Jared's the cheating type. I'd swear to it, really.

Very conveniently, Emmanuelle has left Triple B. Adam told me last week. He told her he couldn't work with her and he'd be looking for another job. Surpris-

ingly, she jumped ship and took another job in the city
before he needed to quit. It was a huge relief; I wouldn't
run into her at the grocery store or post office. And
Adam said he was glad, too; he did love working so close
to home. Translation: *I'm a devoted family man, see?*

I didn't quite believe him, so I drove into Ossining,
tracked down a pay phone and called Triple B and asked
for Emmanuelle in a bad British accent. "Ms. St. Pierre
no longer works at this office," Lydia said. "Can I trans-
fer you to—"

I hung up, relieved and disgusted with myself at the
same time.

But she's gone.

So I win.

Adam looks up from his work. I can feel his stare,
but I don't stop reading. This book is a little barrier. A
gift from a *male friend*, and since I never did tell Adam
about Gus, it feels delicious and secret.

Adam and I are sleeping together again. Having sex.
A couple of times, anyway. I can't say I'm really in the
mood, but we have to, almost. That's what husbands and
wives do. We are, however, using two condoms.

"Why are you reading that book?" he asks now,
scowling at the cover.

"It's giving me ideas on how to get rid of your body,"
I answer without looking up.

"That's not funny," he says. "Honey. Really."

Oh, it's pretty funny. But I grant him a little smile
over the pages, then keep reading.

A FEW DAYS later, I make plans with Jared to have lunch.
School is winding down for the girls; next week is their

last, so I want to do a few grown-up things while I still have the time. Donna is happy to pick them up.

I consider stopping by Bliss but decide against it. Jenny and I are not quite back to normal; I know she wishes I'd just divorce Adam. Life is so black-and-white for people without kids. Or something. I don't know. But I'm New Rachel now. I don't need my sister as much as I used to. Not in the same way, anyway. I don't know if that's good or bad. The thought does, however, make me feel like I can't breathe. Maybe that's why I'm reaching out to Jared a little more; I miss the old me.

Jenny came to the house last weekend for my birthday—my fortieth—and gave me a beautiful necklace and a card that said, "You're the best mother I know." Translation: *I understand you're doing staying with him because of the girls.*

But am I? Or am I staying for me, because I don't want to admit failure? Emmanuelle's gone. He chose me, but I still feel like a failure.

"Rachel!" Jared gives me a big hug as he comes through the restaurant door. "How are you?"

We talk about Kimber and the ongoing blood sport that is his upcoming wedding; his mother has caused three wedding planners to quit, and Kimber is trying very hard to make Mrs. Brewster happy.

"Make sure your mother doesn't run roughshod over her," I tell Jared.

"I'm trying. It's just that Kimber wants Mom to like her."

"*That* will never happen," I say before I can stop myself. This New Rachel. So rude. "I'm sorry. What I mean is, is anyone ever good enough for your baby?"

He smiles. "I keep telling Kimber she has to stand

up for herself. It's not a secret that my mom's a control freak. Imagine when we have babies. But Kimmy just says let's get through the wedding, because it doesn't really matter to her."

"Well, then, she's a saint," I say. "And her mom is very nice, too. She might give your mom a run for the money."

"I know!" Jared says happily. "Finally, someone will. Now, listen. You can say no if this will be too much, but do you think the girls would like to be flower girls?"

"Oh, my God, you will make their lives! Yes, of course! Thank you!"

"It was Kimber's idea. She loves kids."

Our meals are served. A salad for me, a giant steak for him. I tell him a few stories about the girls, because he's one of the few men who really seems to get a kick out of the antics of toddlers.

He's always been a true friend.

"Jared," I say as I eat my salad, "did you know Emmanuelle St. Pierre?"

"Sure," he says. I can tell immediately that he doesn't know about their affair. Jared is as transparent as a golden retriever.

"So whatever happened to her? I heard she left the firm."

"Oh, no, actually," he says, wiping his mouth. "I'm surprised Adam didn't tell you, since he recommended her for the position. She's with our Manhattan office now. She's the new head of litigation."

I don't move for a second. Then, realizing that a response is required, I nod. "Oh."

"Were you guys friendly?"

"No. Not at all."

"Well, she's got a kick-ass apartment in Trump Place," he says. "She had all of us partners down for a cocktail party last week. Very nice. Didn't Adam mention it? He was there, too."

My heart seems to have stopped.

"We drove in together. It was fun. Grabbed a beer afterward before we headed home. It was nice. He and I don't talk much, to tell you the truth. I mean, at work." He stops chewing. "Rach? You okay?"

"Yep."

"You sure?"

"Um…yeah. I just had a weird bit of lettuce or something." I smile and drink some water.

Adam recommended his mistress for a promotion and went to a party at her place.

Funny, how that hasn't come up in conversation.

I WAIT UNTIL the girls are in bed that night to fight with Adam. "So you lied to me again," I say calmly. "Emmanuelle didn't quit. She got a promotion with Triple B. Thanks to you, I hear."

He looks at me, a look of faux confusion/innocence on his face, same as the night he expressed his moral outrage that I thought him capable of an affair. At least I've learned how to tell he's lying. "I told you about that," he says.

"No, Adam," I grind out. "You didn't."

"I'm sure I did, actually."

"You didn't! You said she took a job in another city!"

"Well, she did, Rach. She's working in Manhattan. I don't understand the problem. You didn't want us working together, and we're not." He raises his eyebrows in the patented "women are so hysterical" look. I could cheerfully shank him right now.

"What you told me, Adam, was that she got a better offer from somewhere else."

His face tightens. "Look," he says, and his voice is hard. "She could've had a fucking field day with me. She could've made things public, complained to the partners, whatever. Instead, she and I made a deal."

"And all of this is news to me."

"I told her I'd recommend her for the promotion so long as she didn't say anything."

"So she blackmailed you, got a promotion and now lives in a swanky apartment in Manhattan, where you recently visited. Well done, Adam. You really drew a line in the sand, didn't you?"

"You're misinterpreting things again. You wanted a solution, I found one. I don't have to leave Triple B, and we get to keep my salary and my 401(k) and the health insurance, and no one knows a thing about the affair. Can you imagine those bitchy book club friends of yours if they knew about this? They'd eat you alive."

He comes over to me and takes my hands. "Seems to me like we all win here," he says in a gentler voice. "Honey. She's gone. I'm here. I'll probably never see her again. Can't we put this behind us? Please?"

"I want to, Adam, but it seems like every time I think we're moving ahead, I learn something new, find out some other little lie." My voice picks up speed. "I want to move on, but you're the one who brought this into our lives. You're the one who changed me, and I never wanted to be changed to begin with, and I hate myself these days!"

With that, I burst into tears. Sobs jerk out of me, taking me by surprise, and I cover my face with my hands, unable to stop the noises.

It's the first time I've really cried in front of him since I found that horrible picture. "Oh, sweetheart," he says, pulling me into his arms, and I hate that it feels so good to be held, and I hate that we fit together so perfectly, and I love that he knows just how to rub my back and stroke my hair. I love him. I hate him. And I'm so tired of feeling both ways.

"Baby, please don't cry," he murmurs. "Let's go away together. Let's have a second honeymoon. I love you, Rach. I love you so much."

I nod, simply because I'm too tired of being angry. I've got nothing left. Except for the girls, I'm empty.

"We'll have the girls stay with my mom, or Jenny," he continues. "We can go to Paris, how's that? Or Turks and Caicos, you always wanted to go there, right?"

And so it's decided, when I'm done crying, that we'll go the week after Jared and Kimber's wedding. Adam will call the travel agent. I won't have to do a thing. "And I get to see you in a bikini," Adam says with a wink.

So because of their affair, Emmanuelle gets a promotion and a raise, Adam gets a vacation, and I got an STD panel.

Through my bleary, weary eyes, I can see that the kitchen is sloppy and sticky with crumbs, as Adam offered to do cleanup tonight. It's still lovely, but up close, it's grimy. The stove pans need to be scoured, and there's spatter over the knobs. The flowers I picked last week are dying in the mason jar, and I can smell the hint of decay.

It feels like this house will never be clean again.

Jenny

✤ ━━━ ◆ ━━━ ✤

DESPITE LEO'S "RECREATION only" warnings—a phrase I'm becoming heartily sick of—this feels an awful lot like a relationship. He's been wonderful since the fight in the street. We drove upriver to the Vanderbilt estate and strolled around, held hands, even, then ate at a diner where the cheesecake was apparently made by God. Last night, we went to an utterly terrifying movie about demonic possession, which made Leo laugh and me cower (though that may have been because he put his arm around me when I did). When we came home, we ended up making out on the couch, then the floor, then my bedroom, where several home runs were scored.

So I'm pretty sure I was right about him. The recreation-only thing… That's temporary. That's what men always say. This particular man just needs to relax a little, to trust again. How special and meaningful those words sound! Once we've spent a little more time together, he'll see. I'm very trustworthy.

And he's getting there. Just the other night, I woke up in the middle of the night, and Leo was looking at me, his head propped on his hand. Just looking. I started to say something, but he put his finger over my lips and kissed me, soft and hot, and pulled me on top of him, and he smiled at me. You know who does that? Men who are in serious relationships, that's who.

This is driven home when I come home on Tuesday night. It's pouring, a lovely, soaking rain tap-dancing on my Monet–print umbrella as I walk down the street from where I parked to dear #11, my favorite house on the street.

There's a bizarre sight—Leo Killian on a ladder in front of my door, cleaning out a gutter. It's bizarre, because I can't imagine that Leo knew gutters needed to be cleaned. But there he is, soaking wet, his hair plastered to his forehead, his T-shirt—More Cowbell—clinging to his lean frame, jeans soaked.

My ovaries twitch as I walk up the steps.

"Hello, tenant," he says, scooping out a handful of leaves. "The gutter is clogged, and I didn't want you to get wet, fair maiden that you are with all those expensive clothes and cruel shoes."

"So you're actually taking care of this building," I say. "Let me document this historic moment with a photo." I pull out my phone and snap a shot, and there he is, smiling down at me, that wide, cheeky grin, his blue eyes crinkling. I'll be keeping this one, that's for sure.

Leo throws down another handful of wet leaves, then waits a second, assessing his work. "There. That wasn't so hard after all."

"You sound surprised. Scooping leaves out of gutters is hardly Rachmaninoff's Third Piano Concerto."

He jumps off the ladder and pulls off his work gloves. "My God. You know who Rachmaninoff is! I'm so turned on right now." He cups my face in his big hands and kisses me.

"Don't get too excited," I murmur against his mouth.

"I just looked up 'hardest piano pieces' so I could work it into the conversation and impress you."

"I'm impressed." He kisses me again, right there on the front steps, for everyone in the neighborhood to see, and I drop my umbrella and kiss him back, not caring one bit about the rain.

"Jenny?" comes a voice from the sidewalk. "Jenny? What— Is that— What's going on here? Do you even know this man?"

And there goes my happy.

"Hi, Mom," I say. "No. He's just some homeless guy who was sitting here, but I was lonely, so I asked him if we could make out."

"And I said yes," Leo adds. "She said she'd feed me afterward and give me ten bucks for booze, so why not?"

Mom looks at us both, frowning. Like a cat, she hates being wet, so she's wearing a huge black rain poncho, rain boots, a clear plastic rain hat and has a doorman-size umbrella. Her expression says Not Amused.

"Mom, this is Leo Killian," I say. "He's my…" Crap. He's my what? Landlord? Boyfriend? Fuck buddy?

"Her lover," Leo says, grinning. My heart melts a little more. Not just at the word, but because he's tweaking Mom. Solidarity, you see.

Mom flinches. "Oh, Jenny," she says in a voice leaden with disappointment. "I told you a rebound was a bad idea. You're still hung up on Owen."

"I'm only interested in her from a physical point of view," Leo says. "Still, maybe we can talk about it over dinner. I cooked."

He cooked.

"Lasagna," he murmurs. "Salad. Garlic bread. Red wine. Don't read into it."

"I'm totally reading into it." I turn to my mother. "Come on in, Mom. Want to stay for dinner?"

Fifteen minutes later, Leo has brought up the food, we've both changed into dry clothes, Mom has been convinced that he's not actually a homeless man, and we're sitting around my kitchen table, Loki snoring at our feet. Leo's charm offensive isn't working on my mother—he's not a pediatric plastic surgeon, after all—but it sure is working on me.

"You can make a living, teaching piano?" she asks dubiously.

"No. That's why I mooch off Jenny."

It had occurred to me that this town house is a fairly pricey piece of real estate. And that, while Leo has a steady stream of students, it's a little hard to imagine that he bought a town house in Westchester County with that income alone. Then again, he also composes a little, he said once. I guess that pays a lot.

"So what are your intentions toward my daughter?" Mom asks. "She's still in love with her ex-husband, you know. Owen. A doctor. He and his wife just had a baby."

"I'm really not, Mom. But thanks for sharing."

"I've met Owen. I wasn't impressed." Leo raises his eyebrows and leans back in his chair.

The gauntlet has been thrown.

"Not impressed with Owen?" Mom squeaks. "He's wonderful! He's a *doctor*. You should see his work. He changes lives."

"He dumped your daughter."

"Now, now," I say, pouring wine into Leo's glass. "You'll dump me, too, someday."

Mom huffs. "Then, honey, why are you wasting your time with this...piano teacher?"

"She has needs," Leo says. "Physical needs. You understand, right, Lenore?"

She glares. I bite down on a smile.

Dinner is something of a battle, as is usually the case when the angel of death is trying to kill joy. Mom is definitely off-kilter, punishing me for not telling her about Leo, even though she would've lectured me about how Owen really was the perfect man and I blew it and the world shall never see his like again, etc., etc.

But it's nice to have someone on my side, in a way that Rachel never is, because being on my side would mean she wasn't on Mom's side, and she wants there to be no sides at all.

"So guess what?" I say when we've all had two helpings of Leo's excellent lasagna. "I've been asked to make a wedding gown for the grandniece of the King of Liechtenstein. Or maybe it's his second-cousin. Anyway, she's a minor royal! Isn't that cool? And I think I'll be asked to come to the wedding. Just in case of a dress emergency, but still. Liechtenstein in the springtime. Should be nice."

"Too bad it wasn't Norway," Mom says. "Now *that's* a country I'd love to see."

"I think you missed the point," Leo says. "Jenny has been asked to make a gown for a princess."

"Oh, I know. She's very talented. It's just that I've always wanted to go to Norway."

"Then book a flight," he says pointedly. "Congratulations, Jenny. That's incredibly impressive. I'm sure your mother is very proud. Are you proud, Lenore?"

"I already said I was."

"No," Leo says in a silky voice. "You didn't."

"Fine. Jenny, I'm very proud of you. I just think Norway is a beautiful country. I didn't realize that was a crime."

Her face is folding in on itself, and there it is, the reluctant pity. I like that Leo is defending me, but...well, it's my mom. I'm used to her and her little pecks and veiled insults. She feels like the odd man out, it's clear.

"I'd love to go to Norway, too," I say, channeling my sister. Besides, this is just Mom's way of being part of the conversation. She's not deliberately malicious.

Time for a subject change. "Leo, how's Evander doing?" I ask. "Evander's one of Leo's students, Mom. He's a real sweetheart."

Leo gives me a dark look. I kick him under the table. "He's doing well. Very well. Should be more than ready for the Juilliard audition."

But Mom has been injured, and she won't let us forget it. "I'll let you two get to your night," she says, standing to clear the table. "I was planning to drop by Rachel's anyway."

"I'll clear, Mom. Thanks for coming." I hug and kiss her, and Leo says it was nice to meet her, but she gives him her kicked-dog look and slinks away.

I grab my phone for a quick text to Rachel. *Mom's on her way. You've been warned.* "Don't be too hard on my mother," I say to Leo. "She means well."

"Does she?" he asks. "I kind of hated her."

"Well, she's my mother, so get over that."

"No, I don't think I will."

"You have to."

"Actually, I don't." He folds his arms across his chest and looks at me, lifting an eyebrow.

Ah. Right. The "recreation only" phrase is sure to follow.

"True enough," I say. "It's not like you're going to end up her son-in-law."

"Correct."

The word makes my heart hurt. Something flickers through Leo's eyes. Sadness. Heartache. Something.

Then he smiles, and it's so unfair, because that smile promises all sorts of things—happy, sunshiny days and long nights filled with ice cream and laughter and sex.

His eyes stay sad.

God, I wish the man would talk to me.

"Give us a cuddle, what do you say?" he says, and pulls me against him.

I'm so stupid with men. Jeesh.

Then he kisses me, softly, and his fingers slide into my hair. "I don't like anyone picking on you," he murmurs.

"Except you," I say, not kissing him back.

"Exactly." He pulls me against him, and when I fail to hug him, he wraps my arms around his waist. "Come on, now. I made you dinner. I thought about you all afternoon. I defended your honor and fixed your gutter."

"It's really your gutter. I just rent it."

"I'll clean up the kitchen if you forgive me. And also rub your feet."

"Done. I can't believe your wife left you."

The words are out of my mouth before I think about them. Leo's expression freezes.

However, the words have been spoken, so...

"Why did she, anyway?" I ask as gently as I can. "You know all my dirty laundry. You can tell me yours."

He lowers his gaze to the floor. Rubs his hand over the top of his head. The clock on the mantel ticks.

Then he takes a deep breath and says, "You know

what, Jenny? We're not gonna talk about that, because we don't have that kind of relationship, and we're not going to. I'm sorry, but I have certain…limitations. And true intimacy is probably one of them."

My throat tightens. "Wow, Dr. Phil. That's very profound."

He doesn't smile.

If I were smart, I'd break up with him right now. *Listen, Leo, you're a great guy, but we want different things. I wish you only the best, but I want a family. I want true intimacy. I want someone to love me.*

The clock chimes the half hour.

"A clean kitchen and a foot rub, huh?" I hear myself say. "What woman could resist that?"

His smile is my reward. *After all*, a more chipper voice says in my head, *he's practically living with you. What he says and what he does are different things. He'll come around.*

I recognize this is not necessarily true, so I preach it all the harder.

As I said, I'm pretty stupid about men.

A FEW NIGHTS later, I get home a little late. One of my brides came up from the city to have dinner and show me her wedding album; she was basically the perfect client, letting me make her whatever I thought suited her, and the result was a glorious mermaid dress that's gotten me four new clients. This happens a lot; my brides and I become friends. There's something very intimate about making a dress for the big day; it's like a window into the personalities of the players involved. In Jo's case, the personality is lovely, and I hug her as we part.

"Hey, I didn't even ask," she says. "Are you seeing someone?"

I hesitate, then answer. "I am, actually."

She lifts an eyebrow. "I get invited to the wedding," is all she says, then blows me a kiss and gets into her car.

It's an awfully nice thought. And Leo, despite his words, is acting like the world's best boyfriend.

I believe I shall pop in on him and rock his world. The sun has just set, and the sky is a Maxfield Parrish–blue. What could be more romantic?

But when I pull up in front of our house, I see a note taped to the courtyard gate.

My heart is already sinking as I get out of the car.

Lessons are canceled for today due to an emergency.

Oh, God. I pull out my phone—there are no new messages or texts—and hit his number. It goes right to voice mail. "Leo, it's me. I'm at home, and I saw the sign. Call me right away, okay?"

Maybe he left me a note. I run up to my door, where there's nothing, and then dash inside and look around. No note anywhere a person might ordinarily leave a note, not by the phone, on the counter or table, on the fridge. Nothing.

I've got a bad feeling about this. Why didn't he call me? Did his mom take a turn for the worse? Or did he get hurt somehow, maybe trying to use power tools again, or a car accident, or—

But wait. There's his car, parked just a few spaces down from mine. I've only seen him drive it once or twice, but that's his car.

I go back down into the courtyard and knock. There's no answer. I try the door. It's locked, but I have a key.

My heart is shuddering with dread.

I open the door and flip the kitchen light on. We spend much more time at my place than his. As usual, the house is immaculate, soulless as an IKEA showroom.

I go into the living room and turn on a light there, then leap back with a shriek.

"Leo! Jesus, you scared me."

He squints at me.

Oh, dear. That's a good-size glass in his hand, and the liquid is clear. I'm betting it's not water. A bottle of Grey Goose on the coffee table confirms my Sherlockian suspicion.

"You okay, h—buddy?" I almost say *honey*, but I'm a little afraid to, for some reason.

"Jenny. I'd like to be alone," he says, enunciating carefully.

He's in the exact middle of the couch, and in this impersonal living room, he looks like a prop, sitting with his back straight, like he doesn't quite know how to sit anymore.

"What happened?" I ask.

"Loki died."

"Oh, no! I'm so sorry, Leo." I sit next to him and put my hand on his leg. He takes another sip of his drink.

"Well. He was old, as you so kindly pointed out."

I bite my lip. "I'm sorry. You… He had a good life."

"Did he, Jenny? Do you really know?"

That's a weird question. I take my hand off his leg. "I know you loved him and took really good care of him," I say.

"That is true. Yes."

"How old was he?" I ask.

"Fifteen."

"That's… Wow."

"Don't bother telling me it was his time and he's at the Rainbow Bridge and at least he's not having seizures and arthritis pain anymore." Another healthy sip. "I'd sell my worthless soul to have him back. That stupid dog was all I had left."

The words knife through my gut.

He has his students, after all. He has me.

But at the moment, he doesn't look as if he wants to be consoled.

"I know how much you loved him," I say quietly, "and I'm really sorry for your loss."

He laughs. "You have no idea what I've lost."

"I guess not."

He looks at me with those fathomless eyes, the entire ocean of everything and nothing. Everything he feels, and nothing he wants me to see.

Then, oddly, he leans forward and kisses me on the forehead. "Even though you're very nice, I'm going to say good-night," he says. "I believe I'm drunk enough to pass out now, so I'm going to bed."

He stands up, sways, and I jump up and take his arm. "I'll get you tucked in."

"Do what you gotta do."

I lead him into his bedroom. Like the rest of the apartment, it's blandly attractive. On the night table is *Pet Sematary* by the master of sleep deprivation, Stephen King. I slip it onto the floor so Leo won't get any ideas.

He can't seem to figure out how to get his T-shirt off. "Let me help, okay?" I pull it off, noting rather a lot of dog hair on it, and my throat tightens. I want to ask if it was a gentle death, if Loki went in his sleep, or drifted away courtesy of a kindly vet…or if Leo had to carry him out in a panic, the dog seizing or yelping in pain.

Based on Leo's state right now, I have a sinking feeling it was the last one.

Leo manages to get his jeans off. I pull down the covers, and he wastes no time getting in. His eyes close instantly, like Rose's do the second she hits the mattress.

"Do you want me to stay?" I whisper, stroking his hair.

"No." He opens his eyes a crack. "No, thanks, I mean."

"You sure?"

"Yes." His eyes close again.

I get him a glass of water for the night table, take *Pet Sematary* with me and go into the living room. Put the bottle of vodka in the freezer.

What I want is for Leo to come out of his room and ask me to stay. I'd make him scrambled eggs and toast, and we could watch a movie, and he'd put his head in my lap and tell me he loves me, and he's glad I'm here. That in the end, Loki liked me after all, even if it was just a little bit.

But he doesn't. I listen at his door for a few seconds, but I don't hear a sound.

I GO DOWN to check on Leo the next morning, extra cup of coffee in hand, but he doesn't answer, and I don't want to let myself in again. He might be getting some much-needed sleep. And I have two consultations. My sister's coming in after the girls' nap, because they're going to be flower girls in Jared's wedding, and I offered to make their dresses.

So I text Leo instead.

Thinking of you. Call me if you want & I'll see you later.

Despite my worry over him, the day goes by surprisingly fast; after my first consultation, I get a call from a reporter. *Hudson Bride* wants to do a feature on Bliss and custom-made wedding dresses, so I invite the woman to come over. She brings a photographer to take pictures of the dresses on the showroom floor, me with a sketch pad, me sewing, Andreas peering over my shoulder, and one of me with my second bride of the day, who's overjoyed that she gets to be in a magazine. Then I kick them out to focus on my client, who wants "Grace Kelly meets Gwen Stefani," whatever the hell that would look like, and pumps me for my feelings on the Kardashian weddings. I can tell we're not going to become friends.

Though I never check my phone during a consultation, I do now. Ah ha! Leo has texted back.

Thx.

Worry, irritation and disappointment twang through me. It's not that I'm unsympathetic. It's that I'm *dying* to be sympathetic. I want to hug him, to be there for him. I know he loved Loki, I know he's a little bit heartbroken, but come on. Give me more than three letters.

Finally, my bridezilla leaves, a half hour after her allotted time, and my sister comes in, the three girls in tow. "Auntie!" they cry, charging me.

"Sugarplums!" I answer, hugging them all close to me. I kiss them over and over until they wriggle out of my arms and charge around the room.

"Don't touch anything, little demons," Andreas says, and they erupt in giggles and attack his legs. "Jenny, save me," he says, making them laugh harder. He's serious, of course, but part of his healthy paycheck involves dealing with flower girls. Especially when they're related to me.

I take the girls into the consultation room with Rachel and mock-interview them. "Is this your first wedding? It is, I see. And your favorite color is sparkle? Mine, too. I'm thinking that you should all look like princesses. Do you agree?"

I take their measurements, and for once, all three of them are angelic at the same time, giggling as I wrap my green tape measure around their adorable little potbellies. Rachel and I talk easily about the dresses—we're going with the classic flower-girl look of white satin and tulle with pink sashes and crowns of pink silk flowers.

"Yes, yes, crowns, Mommy!" Grace says.

"Crowns! Crowns!" Charlotte chants.

"I want pupple," Rose demands.

Finally, I ask Andreas to entertain the girls for a few minutes. "No," he says.

"You have to. I'm your boss. I'll fire you if you don't."

"Ooh. I'm shaking. Besides, I have a novel to write."

"How about I give you an extra day off? You can spend all day writing."

He hesitates.

"Two days. Jeesh. They're just children, Andreas."

"Fine, you win. Come on, girls." He heaves a sigh. "I'll get you a cookie at the bakery if you promise not to bite me."

"Is that okay?" I ask my sister. She's really strict about snacks.

"Go for it," she tells Andreas, giving him a twenty, which he brushes off. Secretly, I think he loves children.

The girls chorus and jostle for his attention. "Andreas, I hold your hand!" "I want your hand!" "No, Rose, I called it!" "Stop it!" "I had it first!"

"Dear God, kill me now," Andreas mutters with a fabulous eye roll. "I'll be back as soon as humanly possible. What did I say about biting, blondie? Knock it off."

They leave. It seems very quiet.

"How's it going?" I ask.

"Good. Things are good," she answers.

"I'm glad." There's an awkward pause. "Rachel, I just want you to be happy and have everything you deserve." My words are stiff and tight…and sincere.

She smiles, a little sadly, and my throat tightens. "I know. Thanks. Same to you, of course." She pauses. "Adam and I are working on things. We're getting there. I have to believe that we'll get past this."

"Sure. And, um, some people do." Now would be the time to tell her about our father, I guess.

But I can't. She doesn't know, and she hasn't known, and why on earth would I poison her memories of him? Until I saw Dad kissing Dorothy, he was perfect in my eyes. Rachel still gets to have that.

"How's Leo?" she asks.

"He's… Well, his dog died, so he's pretty down."

"Tell him I'm really sorry."

"I will. Thanks."

"So you two are a couple?" she asks.

"Well…sort of. You were right, though. He's a little closed off. But wonderful, too."

She nods. "I miss you," she blurts, and then we're crying and hugging and thank God, because I've been so afraid that things would never get back to the way they were, that Rachel, my darling sister and best friend, would keep me at arm's length forever because of what I know about her shithead husband.

I lied to her. I will never forgive Adam.

"I've missed you, too," I say.

"Mom's been like a shark with blood in the water," Rachel says, grabbing a tissue and wiping her eyes. "She knows something's up."

"I know. She's been calling me daily to try to pry something out of me."

"You won't tell her anything, will you?"

"God, no!"

We laugh, and thus bonded over that eternal go-to for siblings—their parents' flaws.

"Maybe…well, maybe Leo and you and Adam and I can go out for dinner sometime," Rachel suggests. "It'd be nice to get to know Leo a little better."

I nod, my smile slipping a little. "I'll ask. Like I said, he's a little blue." I already know that, just as he refused to come to Kimber's wedding with me, he won't want to have dinner with my sister and her husband. Too familial.

But at least Rachel and I are back to normal. Thank God for that.

As I'm closing up the shop that night, I see Leo across the street, waiting for me, and my heart, that schizophrenic organ, leaps, cheerfully forgetting all my earlier worries. "Hey!" I call, waiting for a car to pass so I can run across the street—in heels, no less, an incredible life skill. "How are you?" I hug him, and he hugs me back, quickly but hard.

"I'm good," he says. "Sorry about last night." His eyes flicker away from mine, then back. "Can I walk you home?"

"Of course. Are you hungry? We could eat out."

"No, I'm fine. I can cook you something at home, if you want."

At home. That sounds nice.

And yet never have Leo and I eaten in public together, not in COH. We had that one lunch at the diner, an hour north of here.

"Sure," I say.

He doesn't take my hand as we walk.

Shit.

Somehow, I know he's about to break up with me.

"I got a call the other day," he begins, and already my eyes are filling with tears. "There's a music program in Spain. Two weeks. I wasn't going to go, because of Loki, but now I think I will."

"What about your students?"

"Piano teachers take vacations, too, Jenny."

"What about Evander and the Juilliard thing? Doesn't he have an audition?" That edge of panic in my voice—so attractive.

"He does, and I already gave him his practice pieces, and I'll be back before the big day."

"Well. Sounds like you have everything covered. What a fun trip. When do you leave?"

"Tomorrow."

Jesus. "You flying out of JFK? Want a ride? I can drive you." He stops walking. So do I.

Here it comes.

Leo, I love you. It's not a rebound. I genuinely love you. I want to fix you. I think about you constantly. I love the way you smile, laugh, touch me. I want you to tell me why your wife left you. I want you to love me back.

"Jenny," he says, looking back up at me, and his eyes are sad and beautiful and such a pure blue today, "maybe we should—"

"You know what?" I blurt. "Go to Spain. That's gonna be great! Just what you need. And when you get back, let's see where things are. Okay? You've just lost Loki, and this isn't a great time to…you know. Do anything. This is a fun thing we have going. Maybe when you get back, we can talk."

"I think we—"

"No, no! Nope. Let's… We'll see each other when you get back. You know what? I'm starving. I'm gonna run back to Luciano's and grab some eggplant parm. You want something?" I smile brightly—and falsely.

"I'm fine," he says. That horrible sadness ripples through his eyes.

"All right, then. Well, listen. Have a wonderful time in Spain. Forget your troubles and enjoy."

He nods, and I hug him, and he turns his face into my hair and holds me for a long, long moment.

And so our breakup is wordless, because I may be dumb, but I'm not stupid. I don't want to burden him with a sobbing female the day after his beloved dog died. Or ever. I don't want Leo Killian to be sad ever again.

I pull back and pat his cheek. "Have fun," I say, and my voice is normal now, and I manage a real smile.

Thank God I'm busy over the next two weeks—three weddings, four emergency alterations. I babysit my nieces, visit my mom, go into the city to have dinner with friends. Owen had to cancel our Friday night date, which was a relief. Then Andreas and his boyfriend decide to get married in a very spur-of-the-moment ceremony at City Hall, followed by one of the best parties I've ever been to in my entire life, to which Tim Gunn not only showed up, but once again remembered me by name, asked after my work and kissed me on both cheeks. See? Just because my own love life sucks doesn't mean I'm miserable.

Except I feel misery pulling at me like quicksand, like one of those crawling zombies on TV. But I just can't go there, can't be that woman who depends on a man to make her happy.

It's now July; the weather is hot, so I sit in the backyard with the sprinkler on, breathing in the smells of summer, the sharp scent of water on the grass and hardy hydrangeas, the thick, sweet smell of roses that grow along the fence. I drink a glass of wine, wondering why I fall for the wrong men. If I should move from this apartment—I should—if Leo and I did indeed break up—we did. If maybe I was wrong—I'm not—and two weeks in Spain will show Leo that I'm perfect for him—it won't.

We've been sleeping together for five weeks. We've only known each other since April, but—and I realize I don't have a lot of credibility here, given the Owen situation—

But I never felt so at home, so right, so happy with anyone as I did with Leo. I felt safe in myself, and looking back at my years with Owen, I realize that I was always a little shaky, like I had to try too hard to be worthy of him (I know, I know).

With Leo, I'm just me, and no matter what he says, or will say, I felt…loved.

Even if he was only in it a quarter as much as I was.

If I could meet his ex-wife, I'd take her aside and shake her and say, "What did you do to him, bitch?"

I bet it was cheating. I bet that's why he was so great with my sister that first day. It seems like an eternity ago. It seems like yesterday.

Just for the heck of it, I stop by Evander's house one evening; his parents are a little suspicious of me, but they let me in when Evander calls me by name. The little apartment is clean and filled with good smells. Evander's artwork hangs up in the kitchen.

The boy is loved.

I ask how the practicing is coming along, and his eyes slide to his parents, then back to me. "Fine," he says.

"You must be so proud," I tell them.

"We are, we are. We just want him to have a good job someday, and maybe piano…maybe that doesn't pay so well," his father says.

His mom nods. "Maybe he shouldn't spend so much time on something that's more of a hobby."

There's an awkward silence. They're his parents, after all. But Evander is looking at me with those huge brown eyes, silently begging me to defend him.

"Leo thinks your son is very special," I tell Mr. and Mrs. James. "And though I don't know anything about music, it does seem that God has given your son something very precious." They have a crucifix on the wall. Can't hurt to play the God angle. I silently apologize to God for being a callous user.

"It is, Mommy. It's precious," Evander says.

"I know, baby," she says, putting her arm around him. "Well. Thank you for coming."

I wander back home, the muggy air and mosquitoes taunting me.

Then, very late Saturday night, fifteen days after Leo left, I hear a car pull up to the house. A door closes; there are voices, and before I can stop myself, I'm lurking at the window behind the curtain, like Rochester's crazy-pants wife in *Jane Eyre*.

Leo is home. The taxi pulls away.

There's a knock on my door, and when I open it, there's Leo, smiling that incredibly happy smile, and he wraps me in his arms and says, "I couldn't wait to get back to you, Jenny Tate, I love you so much, you have to marry me or my head will explode" or something equally goofy and romantic and of course I'll say yes, and why wait, and we'll go to... We'll...

With the windows open, I can hear him opening his door. Not mine.

It takes me hours to fall back asleep.

I guess I have to move.

Tears slide out of my eyes into my hair. I'm such an idiot, falling—tumbling—in love with a guy who told me over and over he doesn't want a relationship. First of all, this apartment is perfect for me. For that reason alone, I shouldn't have mixed business with pleasure.

Except I couldn't help falling for him. My sad, happy landlord who loves children and dogs and women and is somehow the loneliest man on earth.

When I wake up, it's misting out, that irritating not-quite rain that still ruins the day. I get dressed and go downstairs. Guess I'll go to Rachel's today. Or into work. I can't stay here and wait for Leo to not come up.

Then I see him out my window, leaving his courtyard. He's wearing a suit.

Right. It's Sunday.

In a flash, I decide to follow him. I know, I know,
it's stupid, but I'm out the door before the voice of reason even puts down its coffee cup. Leo's already a block
ahead, his long legs making me almost trot to keep up
enough to see him. I stay back enough so as not to get
caught. At least I grabbed my cell phone before I left.
I can always pretend to be talking or texting. How did
people stalk without them?

Leo stops in Cambry-on-Hudson Florists, where I get
an arrangement every Tuesday morning for the shop.
He's a regular customer, too; he always brings his mom
a bouquet, which she sometimes sends back. I duck into
the café and get a latte. Hey. I work downtown. Perfect
excuse if he busts me. *Leo! Welcome home! Nope, just
on my way to work, not spying on you one bit.*

I get my drink and lurk a minute more until he comes
out, heading down the street once again. He shifts the
bouquet—wait, it's two bouquets, almost identical,
sunflowers and red roses. Okay, maybe he has more
than one relative in the nursing home. Or more likely,
maybe his mother's roomie has fallen in love with him.
In fact, I'm surprised Leo doesn't have a bouquet for
every woman there.

Three more blocks. Five. Seven. He crosses the park
that overlooks the mighty Hudson, then takes the west-
ern path. Dang, he's fast, across the street already, going
into the entrance of Silver Elms Assisted Living Facility, where my mother worked so long ago.

Okay, good. I need a few minutes to catch my breath,

anyway. Plus, it might be a teensy bit obvious if he caught me in the lobby of his mother's nursing home.

I wait until I figure it's safe, then go into the building.

This is monumentally stupid. I know his mom is here. This *Harriet the Spy* stuff isn't going to illuminate anything.

"Can I help you?" the receptionist asks.

"Oh! Um…well, no. It's raining out, did you know?"

She looks at me without expression.

What the hell.

"A friend's mom is here, I think? I thought I might visit her. Mrs. Killian."

"We don't have a Mrs. Killian," she says.

"Um…funny, I swore my friend just came in. Her son. Leo."

"Oh, Leo? He visits Mrs. Walker every week."

Different last names. Ah. "Right! That's right. She got remarried."

"Mrs. Walker's in room 227," she says, pointing to the hallway to the left of the desk.

"Okay."

She waits, so I swallow and head down the hallway.

I have no intention of visiting while Leo is here. Or ever, really. I'll just find a bathroom, wait a second and then leave. I don't even know what I'm looking for.

And then I hear Leo's voice, and what can I do except hide like an abject idiot? I duck into a closet and press myself against the wall, my heart thudding. Someone—a woman—is quite distraught. I think it must be Leo's mother, because though I can't make out the actual words, I recognize the rumble of his voice, soothing and calm.

Then there are footsteps, brisk and firm. I risk a peek out. There goes Leo, out toward the lobby.

He's still holding a bouquet of flowers.

Well, I'm invested now. I'm already damp, have already hidden in a closet. May as well go for the home run.

Leo is damn fast. But I see him, crossing the park once more, not headed toward downtown, or home.

No, he's heading to the far side, which adjoins a place I haven't been in a very long time.

The cemetery.

I stopped going to see my father's grave in college. Before that, we'd make the annual pilgrimages, Mom and Rachel and me. Dad's birthday, Christmas, Easter, Father's Day, the anniversary of his death. I hated it every time. It never felt as if Dad was there, and it made Mom even more maudlin than usual. Rachel would just get quiet and teary-eyed. Me, I'd be in an agony of fidgeting and impatience, itching to get out of there.

I wonder if Dorothy's been here. If she's seen Dad's grave. Watered his flowers. Talked to him, the way I haven't let myself since the day Dr. Dan confirmed what I'd seen all those years ago.

Leo's already through the gates.

I'll be spotted if I follow him in there, so I lurk under a giant pine tree in the park, the misty rain dripping from the needles, the smell of the tree rich and deep. Leo disappears from view. I wait.

It doesn't take long. A few minutes later, he comes out, hands in his pockets, head bent against the rain, which has turned heavier. The shoulders of his suit are darkened with moisture. He doesn't look my way, just heads back toward downtown, toward home.

Except his home isn't really a home. It's a place to live, but it's not a home, and my heart feels thick and leaden, because it's dawning on me just why that is.

I run into the cemetery and walk along the lane. It's easy to spot the bouquet; the yellow sunflowers glow against the dark gray granite.

I walk over to the grave.

Amanda Walker Killian
Beloved wife, mother and daughter

Leo's wife would've been thirty-five.

Rachel

———※———

IT RAINS ALL day Sunday, which means the girls are climbing the walls. Adam preempts me by letting them watch a movie at 10 a.m., which means I won't be able to plop them down at the witching hour, which is four until dinnertime, when they seem possessed by demons. Limited screen time is a hard-and-fast rule; I don't want kids who can't sit still without a device in their hands, so I mete it out carefully.

Now Adam's used it up, which I didn't realize until I was done cleaning up the breakfast mess. Adam put them in front of the TV because he's working in the den. Or playing *Soldier of Fortune*. Or watching porn. Or who knows what? He's been on his superbest behavior these past few weeks. I know he's trying.

The weather also means there will be more of a play mess to clean up later on...a deeper mess, because if the girls can't go outside and run off some energy, they're more creatively destructive than usual. One time, when I thought they were napping and I was folding laundry— Me Time—they tore up eight rolls of toilet paper to make snow. Another time, Grace flooded the bathroom so she could "be a goldfish, Mommy."

Already, they're bickering over who gets to sit on

which part of the couch. Charlotte keeps taking Rose's sippy cup for no reason. Rose is angry that I didn't let her drink wine with breakfast—"or ever, Mommy! You so mean!" Grace is scowling at the movie, because she wanted to watch *Dexter* instead, which I recently bought on DVD. Shockingly, I said no.

On impulse, I stick my head into Adam's office. He whirls around in his chair and closes his laptop. "Hey!"

Not a good sign.

"What are you working on?" I ask.

"Oh, some briefs. Boring stuff." He smiles. I can't tell if it's genuine.

"Which client?"

"Bloomfields. You know. The strip mall owners?"

"Right. Listen, I'm gonna take off for the day, okay? See you later."

"Wait! Where are you going?"

"I'm just a little itchy. I don't really know yet."

"Maybe we can all go somewhere," he suggests.

"No. I want some Me Time." I smile. I can't tell if that's genuine, either.

"When will you be back?"

"I don't know. I'll call you."

Ten minutes later, I'm in the BMW. I don't ask. I don't even tell. I pull out my phone and call Kathleen from book club. "Hey, it's Rachel. I know this is spur-of-the-moment, but do you want to go on a little day trip with me? Right now?"

"God, yes. This weather is killing me."

"Pick you up in five minutes, then."

She runs to the car when I pull up at her house, laughing. "I feel like I'm playing hooky," she says. "We're supposed to go to see Brett's parents today. And you know how it is. We go in, the kids start tearing the place to shreds, and Brett decides that now is a good time to fix his parents' furnace. Anything other than talk to them. So, yeah, I'm thrilled that you called." She laughs merrily and closes the car door. "Where are we going?"

"To spy on my husband's mistress," I say.

Her mouth falls open. "Well, holy shit, Rachel." She gives her head a little shake. "Let's get going, then."

DEAR OLD GOOGLE gives us Emmanuelle's address, courtesy of a search for *Emmanuelle St. Pierre, Trump, recent real estate transactions, Manhattan*.

We find on-street parking—a sign, Kathleen says, that God has blessed our mission—and go in the lobby. The thing is, it's a big building. I have no idea what to do now.

"Can I help you?" says the doorman.

"Um…uh…" Shoot. I have no game.

"We're interested in moving here," Kathleen says. "Is there an empty apartment we can see?"

"You'll have to make an appointment with the manager," he says.

"Oh, I get it. You discriminate against lesbians."

Wow. She *definitely* has game.

"Uh, no!" the doorman says. "No, we don't. We have several same-sex couples here."

"Sure, you do. But you can't even let us *look* at an apartment," Kathleen says. "Good thing I'm a civil liberties attorney."

"Look, lady, don't bust my balls, okay?"

"You immediately assume that because I'm a lesbian, I'm also a ball-buster. Interesting." Kathleen puts her arm around me. "I can't wait to file suit, babe. They wouldn't even let us see an apartment."

The doorman throws up his hands. "Fine, fine. Sign in here. I need to see your licenses."

"I'm French," I say, not bothering with a fake accent. There's no way I'm putting my name on any list in Emmanuelle's building. "I don't have a license."

Kathleen signs in, shows her license, grinning at me.

The doorman makes a call, and within a minute, a tiny little man comes into the lobby. The doorman speaks to him in Spanish, glares at Kathleen and off we go.

Our tiny guide leads us to the elevators, swipes his card and pushes the button for the eighteenth floor. My ears pop. Kathleen gives me a gleeful look, which I return. My heart is leaping with an almost-unfamiliar sensation—fun.

I told her everything on the way here. Somehow, I know she won't gossip.

The maintenance person lets us into Apartment 1819. He holds the door for us but doesn't come in.

The apartment is very nice. Unfurnished, of course. An amazing view of the skyline. Parquet floors, a small but elegant—and boring—kitchen with granite countertops and stainless-steel appliances. The walls are white. It's sleek and impressive and sterile. Oh, sure, someone could make it cozy. But call me a reverse snob; I doubt anyone who lives in this building is going for cozy.

"Any idea which floor she lives on?" Kathleen asks.

"No. This was all very spontaneous. But how cool that we get to see this, right?"

"Absolutely."

"You ever wonder what it would be like to be the person who called this home? Like, what if we didn't have kids and we were single and got to look out over this skyline every night?"

Kathleen smiles. "I lived in an apartment like this," she says. "When I was a news producer. Had the great view and the white couch and all that. And I tell you, I didn't do a lot of looking out over the skyline. It was more come home, work and collapse into bed at one o'clock in the morning. All my friends were self-important assholes, more or less—I was, too, mind you." She sits on a stool at the breakfast counter. "All I really wanted was to pop out a couple of kids and live in the suburbs."

I nod. "Well, somewhere in this building is Emmanuelle."

"I bet she has a white couch."

"Yeah. And really expensive vodka." My Chardonnay seems so provincial.

"Oh, yeah. Drinks it straight up, no doubt."

"Wears a thong every day."

"And Christian Louboutins."

"She actually does have those," I say.

"And a *giant* vibrator," Kathleen says, and suddenly we're laughing and snorting till tears run down our faces. Then our little friend comes in, and says, "All done, *si*?"

"Yes," Kathleen says. "Thank you. *Gracias.*"

"I'll buy you dinner," I say. "There's a great little Italian place in the Village that's been around forever. I haven't been there in ages."

"Sounds perfect."

And then, as we're walking back to the car, I see Emmanuelle, half a block away and coming straight for us.

"Shit," I hiss, grabbing Kathleen's arm and dragging her across the street. "It's *her*. Get down, get down!"

We crouch behind a Mercedes, then peek.

There she is. My husband's lover.

She's wearing yoga pants and sneakers and a T-shirt. Her red hair is in a ponytail. A canvas Whole Foods bag dangles from one hand, a plastic Duane Reade bag from the other. A brown leather purse is slung over one shoulder.

She looks…ordinary. Without the clothes and red lipstick and postmodern shoes, she's not quite the Angelina Jolie femme fatale I picture every time I think of her.

"Duane Reade," Kathleen murmurs. "Bet she's on drugs for syphilis."

I start giggling again. God, I haven't laughed like this in ages.

Then Emmanuelle stops, and Kathleen says, "Shit!" and pulls me down lower so we're sitting on the sidewalk, both of us wheezing with laughter.

I peek out again.

Emmanuelle has stepped in gum. Or dog shit. At any rate, she's scraping off her shoe on the curb.

"Karma, bitch," I whisper, and that sends us off into more paroxysms of laughter.

Emmanuelle lifts her shoe so she can inspect the sole. Then she hops awkwardly, and her Whole Foods bag upends.

One giant red apple rolls into the gutter. A green glass bottle—Perrier—breaks. Green leaves rain down from a salad container.

"Damn it!" Emmanuelle says. She picks up the detritus of her groceries, then stomps off into her building.

I'm not laughing anymore.

Imagine taking the trouble to schlep to the grocery store for one sad, low-calorie meal. A wet Sunday afternoon spent with nothing but work and a sleek apartment. No little voices, no husband, no burgeoning grocery bags filled with all the things required for a family of five. No good smells or happy music. Just quiet and self-imposed distractions and one apple for dessert.

I wonder if she really needed to go out, or if she was just climbing the walls.

"She must be lonely," I say, based on nothing but that grocery bag.

"She's earned it," Kathleen says. She stands up and looks at me. "Don't you dare feel sorry for her."

"I kind of do," I murmur.

She rolls her eyes. "Let's go get dinner," she says. "I'll drive this bad-boy home so you can drink. You need it."

It's funny. As we drive down the West Side Highway toward the Village, I feel more like myself than I have in ages.

Jenny

—◆—

WHEN I GET home from the cemetery, I go straight to Leo's door. "Hey, Jenny," he says as he answers. His eyes rest on my face a second, and something comes over his expression. "Okay," he says, as if he already knows what I've seen. He probably does. He's always been a mind reader where I'm concerned. "Come in, then. Get into some dry clothes first."

Though I could just run upstairs and change into my own clothes, I don't. Instead, I accept the bathrobe he hands me and go into the bathroom, strip off my wet clothes and towel off my hair. My reflection in the mirror shows a white face, made even paler by the contrast of my wet hair.

Leo's bathrobe smells like him. I wrap it tight around me—it's warm and flannel and his, and I'm cold, no matter that it's summer.

He's waiting for me in the living room, in the chair across from the couch. There's already a box of tissues there, as if he knows I'll cry. My eyes are already full.

"So you went to the cemetery," he guesses.

I nod.

"And you saw my wife's grave."

"Yes," I whisper.

He sits forward, his long-fingered hands clasped loosely, and looks at the coffee table. "Right. Well. I was married for three years. We were in a car accident. Amanda was seven months pregnant with our son. They...they tried to deliver him, but he was already gone." His voice breaks a little, but that's all.

I take a tissue and blot my eyes, then another and another, and try to speak. "Oh, Leo, I'm so sorry." The words have to be forced from my locked throat.

Leo's words seem to press him downward with their horrible weight. His elbows rest on his knees, and he stares at nothing.

As the rain murmurs in the gutters and hisses on the flagstones, Leo tells me the story he wanted to keep from me, a story I don't want to hear—a woman, an ambulance, the shocked sobs of onlookers, the panicked shouts of the paramedics during their heroic—and futile—efforts to save a mother and her unborn baby.

As he tells the story, Leo isn't exactly calm. He's simply...gone.

Finally, he clears his throat. "Loki was her dog," he says. "She had him long before she had me." He gives a half smile, but it doesn't quite make it.

"Leo...why didn't you tell me?"

He sighs, sounding so tired that I wish I could wrap myself around his heart and protect him.

"I liked being something other than the tragic widower," he says. "After they died, all our friends... You remember that woman in the Hungarian restaurant? She was Amanda's best friend." He runs a hand through his hair. "All anyone could see or think about was that day. I was a walking reminder of a horror story. I *was* the horror story."

God, what a burden to carry—not just the grief of his unspeakable loss, but the...the brutality of that ending.

"That's why I moved here," he says quietly. "I was kind of...absent that first year. I don't remember a lot of it. And then her mom got diagnosed with Alzheimer's and started going downhill fast, so I moved here to be closer. I didn't have to run into people who knew me." He looks at his hands. "Amanda didn't grow up here, but her mom lived here for years. She wanted Amanda buried close to her."

I nod.

"The, uh...the worst part," he says, looking out the window, "is that we were late. We were going to her baby shower, ironically. I was driving. She said the highway would be faster. But I knew better. Half a mile from the restaurant, we got T-boned in an intersection. Not a scratch on me, but she died." He hesitates, then adds, "Almost right away."

Almost. The image is too horrible.

How do people live through so much? I have to fight to keep from sobbing, but a little squeak escapes my throat just the same. "Leo," I whisper, but that's all I can get out.

"I know," he says. "It's a fucking nightmare. Just one that you don't wake up from. So once her mom moved into Silver Elms, I bought this place, gave a concert at the elementary school, started getting students so I could do something other than drink, though the truth is, I'm hugely fucking wealthy, thanks to the lawsuit against the driver."

"And Amanda's mom? Mrs. Walker? How is... Is she aware?"

"No. Losing Amanda and the baby...it pretty much

felled her. She's lucky, though. She's forgotten all this. She doesn't even remember Amanda anymore." His voice breaks a little, but he clears his throat. "She thinks I'm her son, and I don't have the heart to tell her I'm not. Amanda was her only child."

"That's very kind of you."

He gives a short, bitter laugh. "Yeah, well, since I killed her daughter and grandson, it's the least I can do."

"Leo, you can't—"

"Am I forgetting anything?" He cuts me off. "Oh, the fourth floor. Some of her stuff. Some of our stuff. All our pictures. Is there anything else you want to know?"

I bite my lip. "Is there anything at all I can do for you?"

"No. But thank you. You've been…very…distracting." He tries again for a smile and again fails.

"Did you have a name picked out for the baby?" The question comes out of left field.

He blinks, and currents of sorrow traverse his face. "*Sean*. I liked *Sean*. She was leaning toward *Daniel*. But I just think of him as…baby." He swallows hard. "I got to hold him for a minute, but he was already… He's buried with her."

This time I can't suppress the sob.

Leo rubs his eyes with one hand. "Okay. Well. I'm sorry I had to tell you all this. It was three years ago."

"No, no. I wish I'd known before."

"I'm so glad you didn't. I never wanted to get to this point, the point where you'd know. I mean, I guess I would have, eventually. I just… I liked the way you saw me, Jenny. I shouldn't have rented to you, because the second I saw you, I knew you'd be trouble."

He does smile now, the most heartbreaking smile I've

ever seen. "But when I said I was for recreation only, I meant it. I don't ever want to be in that position again. It's not that I can't love you. You're very lovable." He looks at me with terrible kindness. "It's just that I don't want to. Not because of you. Because of me." He's quiet for a long time, the rain pattering on the flagstones outside. "When she died, she took everything. I can't get over it. I can't play anymore, I can't—I can't be involved with someone else more than I was with you. The truth is, I'm just killing time."

The pain in my chest swells hard and sharp. "Leo, don't say that. I know I can't imagine how—"

He reaches across the coffee table and takes my hand. "Whatever you're about to say, please don't. I've heard it all before. Please just stay the Jenny who thinks I'm a lazy womanizer with bad handyman skills."

I swallow loudly, and two more fat tears spill out of my eyes. "Okay," I whisper.

Because I've got nothing. There are no platitudes I can dole out, no wisdom I can share, and my love isn't going to save him, because some things—and some people—are beyond repair.

But I stand up and go over to him and wrap my arms around him, and he hugs me back, his head against my chest, my tears leaking into his hair. "I do love you, you know," I whisper.

"Thank you." He looks up at me for a long moment. "I'm sorry if I broke your heart."

"It's fine." We both give a little laugh at my stupid answer, though mine is choked with tears.

And then I go upstairs, still in his bathrobe, because there's nothing more I can do.

THE NEXT MORNING, my eyes are nearly swollen shut from crying. Good thing the shop is closed. A sobbing wedding-dress designer isn't that great for business.

Leo has sent me an email.

Thank you for the sympathy. I do appreciate it. You have seven months left on the lease, but it might be best if you moved. If you don't want to, I'll be happy to find another place. Even if I do own this building. —Leo

It seems telling that he can make me smile even as I'm crying yet again.

I call the Realtor and tell her I'll be looking for a new rental.

But I can't quite bring myself to pack just yet. And I don't want Leo to have to hear me packing. I answer his email and tell him I'll be looking for a place of my own, so no need for him to leave. I also tell him I'm going to stay with my sister for a while and help with the girls.

And then I go upstairs to the fourth floor and sit on the stairs in front of the locked door and cry for Leo's lost wife, pray that she didn't know what was happening. I cry for the baby, who went from one otherworld to the next, sliding right past ours, past his father.

But mostly, I cry for Leo, for the horror and terror he must've endured in the time between *almost* and *right away*, and after, as the paramedics tried to save his child, and the heart-crushing loss he's endured all these months since.

My sister welcomes me with all the love and gentleness that defines her. She tells Adam to give me some space, and I have to hand it to him; he's very nice over the next few days. The girls are a balm; it's hard to stay in bed, weeping, when a thirty-pound child launches herself onto your stomach, never mind three of them at once. When I walk into work on Tuesday, Andreas takes one look at me and says, "Jesus. Do you want to talk about it?"

"I do not," I answer.

"I'm getting you a coffee and three doughnuts," he says. "Back in a flash." His kindness makes me feel almost worse, and he senses it, so after an awkward pat on the shoulder, he goes back to his laptop, reading me lurid scenes from his novel, which is no longer a gay erotica but now a gritty crime story set during the time of Richard the Lionheart.

The week drags by. In order to get out of town, I opt to spend a couple nights with my mother. Yes. It's come to that.

"It's so nice to have you here," she says, and it's odd, not having a guilt trip attached to those words. We're sitting on the porch on Saturday night, watching the highly gifted children of Hedgefield zip by on their bikes and scooters, all of them appropriately helmeted and chaperoned.

"Will you make me tuna casserole tomorrow?" I ask.

"Oh, sure, honey," she says. "It's so bad for you, though."

"But good for the soul."

Mom smiles. "So is it Owen? Are you jealous? Has him becoming a father finally hit you?"

"No, Mom. I fell for someone else. And it didn't work out."

"You never did choose that well," she concurs.

"Oh, come on. You think of Owen in the same league as Jesus and George Clooney."

She laughs. "I don't know about that. He was always a little sanctimonious, don't you think? Owen, that is. George Clooney is perfect."

I stare. "Um…yes, actually, that's a fantastic word for him."

"I was going through some of your father's things the other day," she begins.

"Oh, yeah? Why is that?"

"No reason. Just to see them." She looks at her hands, seeming embarrassed at her devotion.

But now that I know about Leo, I understand better, and shame pricks my conscience. I never did cut Mom a lot of slack when it came to Dad. I always thought she should move on.

"You must miss him so much," I say.

"I do."

"A friend of mine lost his wife and child." Predictably, my eyes fill. "I don't think he'll ever get over it."

"Of course not," Mom says. "You don't get over it, ever."

"So how do you keep going?"

She sighs. "Some days, you don't. Some days, you're just stalled." She takes a sip of her iced tea. "You know what I miss? I miss complaining about him. There was such a guilty luxury in calling up a friend and telling her just how aggravating my husband was."

I wipe my eyes surreptitiously. "I thought Dad was perfect."

"No husband is perfect. Not even Adam."

My glance flickers her way. "What makes you say that?"

"Oh, sometimes I think he looks at other women a little too long," Mom says.

Well, well. Mom is more observant than I gave her credit for.

Since I seem to be staring at her, she shrugs. "All men do, I suppose."

My decades-old secret stirs. I wait a beat, then ask—finally. "Did Dad?"

She doesn't answer for a minute, just swings her foot, clad in its ever-present sneaker. "Well, no. But there was a time when… I don't know."

"What, Mom?"

She shrugs. "When I thought he might've had a little…thing for someone. A crush. A midlife crisis." She's carefully not looking at me.

"What if he did?" I ask.

She takes a long sip of her iced tea. "He probably didn't," she amends. "And even if he did, he loved me."

I look at her, my mother the widow, who has let that one loss define her as nothing else. She's sixty-five years old. If I tell her Dad *did* have a thing for someone, what would it do to her? Would it free her? Crush her?

"He sure did love you," I say. "But you know he would've been remarried two weeks after your funeral."

She laughs. "Yep. You're right about that. He was helpless outside of that dentist office."

A hummingbird hovers at her hanging basket of lobelia, the buzz of its wings low and sweet. "Mom, did you ever think how that day might've been different? How, if you could've changed one little thing, Dad might not have died?"

She looks at me sharply. "All the time. You know, I almost called him at the office to ask him to pick up the dry cleaning. But I forgot. If I hadn't, he'd be alive today."

Well, holy crap. Seems I'm not the only one with a little guilt. "I…I thought something similar. If I'd said something, then he wouldn't have gone to that store."

"Don't feel guilty, honey. The only people who were responsible were those idiots who shot him."

Suddenly, I'm crying before I even knew I wanted to cry. Mom scootches over on the glider, and I sit with her arms around me and bawl like a little baby. "I miss him," I say, and she kisses my head.

"I know, honey. I know," she says, and for once, she just let me have my grief without trying to up the ante, and I cry and cry and cry, and honestly, I can't remember when I've loved her more.

A hundred memories are unchained all at once— Mom taking care of me when I had the pukes, Mom coming to get me at school when my period came for the first time and I almost passed out from cramps and the evil gym teacher wouldn't let me out of class. How I hated when my teeth were loose, and she—not Dad the dentist—would be the one to gently tug the baby tooth from its bed.

"Mom, I hate thinking of you living the rest of your life on your own," I say, wiping my eyes and nose on my sleeve like the classy person I am. "You've never wanted to date?"

"No!" She says it as if I've just asked her if she's ever wanted to eat a baby hedgehog. "Your father was enough for me. Some of us are better at being alone than others. Rachel and I, for example, are fine with our own company."

"What? Who? Is that a joke?"

"You're the one who was born to be married." She

takes my hand. "I'll find you a nice man to date, honey. Don't worry. You won't be an old maid for much longer."

"Gosh. That's so sweet, Mom." But I put my head back on her shoulder, and we watch the kids go by, and the wind dries my tears and flutters my hair.

WHEN I GET back home the next afternoon, music—if you can call "The Wheels on the Bus" music—seeps out of Leo's place. I creep up to my place to grab a few things. The Realtor has some apartments she wants to show me, but for now, I'll go back to Rachel's.

I check my voice mail—two missed calls, both from Owen. Right. I was supposed to have dinner with him, but we never rescheduled. The thought of going into the city makes me tired. If he wants to see me, he can come up here.

As I'm getting some clean underwear, I see the little pink clay dog Leo made when the girls stayed with me. It's been on my bureau since that night.

Without further thought, I go down to Leo's.

I glance through the window and see Austin, son of a Hungry Mom, banging out "Lightly Row"—I know all the beginner songs, horribly. The mom is staring at the back of Leo's head.

I knock on the door, loudly. "Leo? Can I see you for a second?"

"Lightly Row" stops—praise Jesus—and some pounding begins from Austin's destructive little fists. His mother doesn't tell him to stop.

Leo is at the door surprisingly fast. "Hi."

"Hi." Suddenly, I feel stupid. I didn't really plan this out. But there he is, and I haven't seen him for six days, and my heart lurches and wobbles.

He looks tired.

I clear my throat. "Um...how are you?"

"Good. And you?"

"Fine! Great. Good. Um...I wanted you to have this."

He looks down at the pink Loki. A faint smile comes to his face, and my whole soul seems to expand. "Thank you, Jenny."

"Leo!" Austin bellows. "I'm *bored*!"

"Don't yell, Austin," his mother says in a singsong voice.

"Hang in there, buddy," Leo calls over his shoulder. He looks back at me. "How's apartment hunting going?"

"Good. Listen. Leo. I just want to tell you this one thing."

"Okay." His eyes are such a pure blue today.

"You didn't break my heart," I say. "You filled it up. And I do love you, but I also understand what you can and can't do. I just hope that I'm a happy memory for you. That's what you are for me. I'll always think of you and smile and be glad that I was with you and got to know you."

His mouth opens slightly.

"I'm! So! Bored!" Austin roars, punctuating each word with a fist-bang.

"He's bored," I say. Leo's smile is fast and then gone. "You get back to it," I say. "I just wanted to tell you. And to give you Loki."

"Thank you, Jenny." His voice is achingly deep and gentle.

"You bet. I know how you love pink." I give a shaky smile and get while the getting's good.

Evander's mom pulls up as I'm heading up the stairs. "Miss Jenny," the little guy calls as he gets out of the car.

"Hey, buddy." If he sees the tears in my eyes, he doesn't comment. "How's practice coming along?"

"Fine, thank you." He has such nice manners. "Leo says I'm ready for my audition."

"Then I bet you are."

"Would you come?" he asks. "To Juilliard?"

I'm momentarily shocked out of my sorrow. "Um... wow! Thank you, honey!" He beams. "Just make sure it's okay with Leo and your parents."

"My parents can't go. They have to work."

My sore heart tugs. "Well, you ask Leo, and if he says yes, I'd love to. But either way, I know you'll be great. Because you already are."

He has the smile of an angel, this kid. My throat tightens even more as he goes into Leo's. I'm going to miss Evander. A lot.

I go inside my own apartment.

It seems so long ago that I moved in. All my furniture loves it here. I love it here. The brick walls, the bang of the radiators, the arched doorways, the claw-foot tub, the tin ceiling in the kitchen, the black-and-white tile floors in the bathroom... I wish in one sharp, abrupt swell, that I could stay.

What a beautiful word that is. *Stay with me. Stay home. Stay alive.*

In another impulsive move, I pick up my phone and call the Realtor. "Hey, Jill," I say. "I think I'm ready to buy something. Let's forget about renting, okay?"

She's thrilled, of course. She promises to email me some listings and schedule some visits.

After I hang up, I take one long look around, trying to etch the feeling of living here on to my heart so I won't forget.

There's a picture of my nieces as newborns on my mantel, the three of them in soft pink sleepers. Rachel kept them in the same crib for three or four months. They're touching in this picture; Grace in the middle, one hand on Rose's, her arm looped through Charlotte's.

I want kids. I want a daughter or a son. I want to be a mother. I also want to be a wife, but it doesn't seem fair to try to find a husband when I'm pretty sure I'll be in love with Leo for a long, long time.

I Google a few terms, find a phone number and dial it. When a woman picks up the phone and says, "Department of Children and Families," I say, "Hi. I'm interested in becoming a foster parent. Can you tell me how to get more information?"

Rachel

———— ✽ ————

Jenny stayed with us for ten days. She seems different in her heartbreak over Leo than she was with Owen. With Owen, she was stunned, like an animal clipped by a car.

Now, she seems…gentled. Her edge is gone when she talks to our mom, and though she's so, so sad, there's something else, there, too. Kindness. Grace. I'm not sure, exactly.

When she told me about Leo's wife and baby, I slept in the girls' room that night, cuddling with each girl in turn, crying into my pillow. It certainly puts my issues with Adam in perspective. If I lost the girls…well. There are some thoughts that are intolerable, to which suicide truly seems like a happy alternative.

Poor Jenny. She wants so much to fix things for everyone—me, Mom, now Leo. But some things are unfixable.

On the marriage front, things are…fine. I'm feeling oddly neutral these days. Adam was furious that I went to see Emmanuelle. I found that rather uninteresting. When he asked why on earth I'd *stalk* her, I just shrugged and said I wanted to see where she lived, free country and all that. He seemed very concerned that I had "reopened a can of worms."

"Whatever, Adam," I said. "I don't care what you think. It was fun, spying on her."

"That's so unlike you," he said. "It's sneaky, Rach." His face was flushed with anger.

"Right. You're more the sneaky one, aren't you?" I smiled sweetly at him and left the room.

The girls will take swim classes this summer, and Donna will watch them one day a week so I can have Me Time for exciting things like grocery shopping, a nearly impossible job with three kids grabbing every sugary thing they can find. I can also get the car serviced. Repaint the porch. Clean out the cellar.

I've been talking with Kathleen a lot, bonded by our spy mission. She asked if I knew anyone who might house-sit for them while they're in Nantucket. Jenny volunteered, saying she didn't want to impose on Adam and me any longer. She still hates Adam, I know. Oddly, I appreciate it, since that luxury is denied to me, now that we're together again.

I got what I wanted, I guess. I'm here, in this home that I worked so hard to insulate from the problems of the world, our happy little bubble. The girls have their father every night. Adam has a newfound respect for me, the New Rachel, for the glittering, sharp edge that's emerged like a razor in the grass. When I think about my old self, I feel pity and yearning at the same time. Poor Old Rachel, the sweet, naive idiot. And lucky Old Rachel, so completely happy.

There's one niggling thought I can't shake, one that keeps me awake at night.

What would I tell my daughters if they came to me with the news that their husband had a mistress? That he told her, my precious daughter, that sex with the other woman was amazing? *Stay and work things out. Oh, and get that STD panel ASAP, darlings! But do stay. Take all that hurt and betrayal and just ball it up and swallow it. Want to bake cookies?*

When Owen told my sister he didn't want to stay married anymore, she was out of the apartment the next day. The next day! At the time, I thought she was being a drama queen, to be honest.

Now I have a very different view. He told her he wasn't in love with her anymore, and she left. Bing, bang, boom.

The first morning without Jenny, before I can think about it too much, I decide to update my résumé. Then, on a whim, I check Craigslist.

There are three jobs for graphic designers in the COH area. Two are part-time.

I reply to all three. If they want to interview me, we'll take it from there. It might be nice to be something in addition to Mommy. After all, my own mom always worked, less when we were really small, more when we were older. I always loved picturing her at work at the nursing home, giving her clients a way to pass the hours that was filled with the good smells of paint, the rustle of paper and bright colors.

I loved working at Celery Stalk. I loved having co-workers despite my social anxiety, loved hearing their stories, going out for the occasional lunch.

Maybe I should call Gus and see if they could use me.

On second thought, no. If I'm going to have a job, I want to do it on my own. I want it to be new, where I can make a fresh start.

Later that day, when I'm doing errands, I run into Mrs. Brewster at the post office.

"Rachel, I've been meaning to talk to you," she says without preamble. "Do you have time for a coffee?"

This is certainly a first. "Sure."

We go to Starbucks, a place I'm sure Mrs. Brewster has never graced with her presence. I order a silly drink with lots of whipped cream and caramel sauce; she orders a cup of tea. No sugar, no cream, no milk, just lemon. It sums up her personality perfectly.

"What can I do for you?" I ask when we're sitting.

She wipes off the table with a napkin. "Well. I'll get right to the point. You and my son have been friends for many years."

"Yes." I take a sip of my mocha-whatever.

"I'm wondering if you're interested in him. Romantically. I always thought you'd make a lovely couple."

I choke. She hands me a napkin. "Excuse me?" I manage.

"You and Jared. You obviously have feelings for him."

"I— What?"

"Women and men don't stay friends because they *like* each other, dear. You and Jared. It would be a vast improvement over that white trash he's smitten with."

"His fiancée, you mean? Your future daughter-in-law?"

"Yes."

I open my mouth, close it, then open it again. "Mrs. Brewster, first of all, Jared and I are only friends. Second, his wedding is in ten days! He loves Kimber. And third, I'm married!"

"I've heard things are not quite…happy…for you, Rachel."

Heat flares like sunspots on my chest and cheeks.

"Did you. How nice of you to call and see how I was doing, in that case."

"I would never pry."

"But you're…what? Pimping me your son? Or are you telling me to make a pass at him? I'm unclear."

She lifts an eyebrow. "I'm saying that I think he's making a terrible mistake, and if he were aware that you had romantic feelings for him—"

"Which I don't."

"—then he might be open to calling off the wedding to that ridiculous Kimber person." She pauses. "We're quite well off, you know."

"Oh. Okay. So if I do this, will you pay me? A lot? A million dollars?"

Her eyes harden. "Fine. Make light of the problem."

I put the lid on my coffee. "You're the only problem here, Eleanor. Have some faith in your son, for heaven's sake." With that, I stand up to leave. "I won't tell Jared about this little meeting—for now—but if I hear you bad-mouthing Kimber again, I will in a New York minute. I can only imagine how disappointed he'd be in you." I pick up my bag and my coffee and stride out of there.

My first thought in the car is to call Gus. To say, "So guess what? Someone just offered to pay me to seduce her son," and hear his wry answer, something like, "Welcome to my world."

But I don't. I like Gus, and it wouldn't be fair to lead him on in any way, not with Adam and me back together. So I call my mom instead. "Oh, good for you, Rachel!" she says when I'm done. "I always thought she was a condescending pain in the ass. Who'd have thought you had it in you?"

This New Rachel brings something to the party, after all.

And even though I didn't call him, the thought of Gus and his smiley eyes keeps me company for the rest of the day.

Jenny

$\div\!\!\!-\!\!\!\bullet\!\!\!-\!\!\!\div$

I FINALLY MEET Owen for brunch.

I had suggested dinner up near me, but Owen, like so many New Yorkers, hemmed and hawed at the thought of driving "all the way" to Cambry-on-Hudson. He and Ana-Sofia have only come out the one time, for the opening of Bliss. So I caved. Later today is Evander's audition, and since I had to be in the city for that anyway, here I am.

We meet at a place we used to go to with friends in our old life. I haven't seen Owen in weeks and weeks now, and for a flash of a second, my eyes pass right over him as I scan the restaurant—*woman in yellow Stella McCartney, check; Asian man with baby in stroller, check; hipster with wool hat on, check, it's July, buddy, isn't the hat a little ridiculous?—hang on, back to man with baby...*

It's Owen. I smile and make my way to the table.

"It's so good to see you," he says, taking both my hands in his and kissing me on the cheek. "You look wonderful!"

"Thanks. You, too. Hi, Natalia! I didn't know you were coming today, pumpkin!"

She smiles up at me. She really is a beautiful baby.

"Ana-Sofia was supposed to have her today. I'm sorry."

"Are you kidding? Natalia's my favorite of all three of you. Aren't you, sweetie?"

"Would you like to hold her?"

"Yes, please. I even brought my own hand sanitizer." I slather up, then reach out for the baby.

Her head has that hypnotically wonderful baby smell, and her hair is silky. As she did when she was first born, she reminds me of a seal with her huge dark eyes and shock of black hair.

"Can I get you a drink?" the waitress asks. "Oh, your baby is so cute. She looks just like you."

She's talking to me.

"Oh, she's not mine. But she is cute," I say.

Owen is looking at me with a smile.

Kind of a dopey smile.

"I'll have a mimosa," I say.

"Same for me," my ex echoes.

"Coming up!" The waitress bustles away.

"So. How are you?" Owen asks.

"Good. Fine. I'm looking for a house," I say, kissing the baby's head. Really, I kind of wish Owen would go away and leave me to inhale his daughter's good smells.

"Excellent! A house! How wonderful!" he says, his abundant enthusiasm immediately irritating me.

"How's Ana-Sofia?" I ask.

"Oh, she's fine. The usual."

"Kind, hardworking, utterly beautiful?"

Owen looks uncertain. "Yes, I guess so." He sighs. "I don't know. All this happened so fast…getting married, the baby. My head is still spinning."

"Oh, well. That's life, right?"

"I don't know. Sometimes I miss us."

"Us? You mean, you and her before Natalia?"

He gives me that slightly bemused smile. "I mean you and me."

"Is that right," I say, and my voice may be a little loud.

"Well, I've always missed us. We were never the problem."

What? Men are so… Natalia is starting to fuss a little, so I turn her toward me, and with a sigh, she settles against my neck.

"What do you mean, *we* were never the problem?" I say, my voice low because of the baby, and hard—because really! "You didn't want to be married to me anymore, Owen. That was actually a very big problem."

He has on his Dr. Wonderful face. Compassionate yet concerned yet reassuring. "I just wonder if Ana and I rushed things."

"Well, of course you did. That's hardly news."

He smiles. "I know. It just… It seemed fated at the time."

"And now?"

"Not so fated." I blink. "Things were so perfect at first. It really did seem like it was meant to be. But now… I don't know. We barely talk anymore. She's always tired and acting like a martyr because she's nursing, and I say just bottle-feed—it won't kill her—and she acts like I suggested throwing the baby in the Hudson. And Natalia doesn't sleep for more than a couple of hours at a stretch. I actually fell asleep in my office the other day. Me. Can you imagine?"

I'd respond, but I'm too stunned. Owen is *whining*. Owen. Whining. He of the Perfect Life.

His hair is starting to thin.

"Sometimes I just wish I could go back in time and be with you, that's all." He gives me a sad smile.

I put the baby back in her stroller/car seat/cappuccino maker, since I think my glaring would have more effect if it wasn't over the head of a beautiful sleeping child.

"You don't get to say shit like that, Owen," I say.

His eyebrows jump in surprise.

The waitress brings our drinks, and while I'd like to toss mine in his face, I might get the baby wet, and also I'm quite thirsty. I chug it down. "Would you like to order now?" the waitress asks.

Owen smiles at her. "I'll have the—"

I hold my hand up. "I'm sorry," I say to the waitress. "We're in the middle of something. Sorry. Can you come back in ten minutes?"

"I'm really hungry," he says, and you know, I've forgotten that. Owen has to be fed every four hours or he gets a little bitchy. That's the only word for it.

"Ten minutes," I tell the waitress.

"I'll have the salmon Benedi—"

"Owen!"

"I'll give you ten minutes," she says and backs away from the table.

"You're upset," he says.

"Yes, Owen. I am." I take a deep breath. "Look. You divorced me. You found me lacking somehow."

"No, I didn't."

"Yes. You did." The words come out from behind clenched teeth. "And then you found your soul mate and you have this perfect baby, but you whine to me? Me? How dare you?"

"Jenny, all I meant was—"

"I don't think we can be friends anymore."

The words surprise us both.

But in the nicest way. For me, anyway.

Suddenly, I feel a lot lighter than I have in a long time.

"Look," I say more gently. "I'm sure that being a new dad is hard. And now that you and Ana-Sofia have been married a little while, reality is setting in. But you don't get to complain about that to me. You *left* me. I wanted kids, and you didn't, and now I don't have any and you do. So you're a little tired. So Ana's boobs are used for something other than your recreation. Grow up."

He starts to speak, but I don't let him. I'm kind of on a roll, actually.

"And furthermore, I don't think it's healthy for me to stay close with you. I'm tired of pretending it's all happy and great and the three of us are friends. We're not. You're my ex-husband. She's the woman who took my place. I don't *care* if you're both nice people. I'm tired of soothing your guilty conscience by appearing at dinner parties twice a year and getting a phone call every other day. Okay? You dumped me. It's fine. I'm fine. But enough already."

I stand up. So does he. "Jenny," he says, rubbing his hand over his mouth. "I—I'm so sorry."

"I accept your apology." I look down at the baby, this beautiful child I helped into the world. "Keep me on your Christmas card list, okay?"

Then I give him a quick hug and leave, snagging a cheese danish from the pastry counter on the way out. "Put this on his tab," I tell our waitress.

"You bet, sister." She winks.

I wander down toward Lincoln Center, where Evander will be auditioning, eating my danish and eavesdropping, dodging the people who are engrossed in their phones, half hoping that Darwinism will take place and they'll fall down an open manhole. But it's a beautiful summer day, I'm walking along Central Park West and the pastry is excellent.

I'm happy, I realize.

It's good that Owen and I broke up, because the truth is, I never fit in that life. I loved it—and I loved him—but I didn't fit. It was a life meant for someone else—Ana-Sofia, I hope, because I truly do like her and don't want Owen to end up one of those sad, lonely clichés of a man, with three ex-wives and children he never sees.

And while Leo and I didn't work out…

I don't know how to finish that sentence. I'm better off for loving him? So corny. So true.

Life is good, even without all the elements in place. I love my small family, my sister and nieces, my mom. Even Adam, because if Rachel loves him, I will, too. I love Andreas and my work. And soon, hopefully, I'll be on the road to becoming a mother. A foster mom at first. After talking to the social worker the other day, I said I'd be open to an older kid. I have my first interview in two weeks, after my background check clears.

I get to Alice Tully Hall, that strange and wonderful building of sharp angles and light, and already my stomach is cramping. Evander is eleven. Eleven! How these kids endure the pressure, I have no idea.

I'm directed down a hallway. There's Leo, wearing a dark brown suit and purple shirt and tie. The perfect curling hair. The mercurial face I love.

My heart, already rabbiting along in my chest, kicks into tachycardia. He jerks his chin at me, a sign that things aren't going that well. Evander is sitting on the floor, knees drawn up to his chest. "Hey," I say. "Here's our boy."

"Nice to see you, Miss Jenny," Leo says, but he's cracking his knuckles and the lines around his mouth are tense.

"You ready for this, killer?" I ask Evander, who hasn't looked up.

He doesn't answer.

That doesn't bode well.

"He's a little nervous. As is everyone who tries out for this," Leo says, trying to sound firm and reassuring. But I can sense the panic under his words.

"Sure. But you'll ace this, honey." Not that I know a damned thing.

A girl of about fourteen comes out of the door. Her face is red, and she's crying. She doesn't pause, just runs down the hall. Her mother follows, calling after her, "Sweetie, don't be upset! You did your best. It's okay!"

Shit. Are they eating children in there?

"Jenny, can I ask you a question? Evander, be right back." Leo takes my hand and practically drags me down the hall a few paces. "He's freaking out."

"What can I do?" I whisper.

"I have no idea. And even if he gets in, I'm not sure his parents are going to let him do this. But right now, all I want for him is not to puke." Then his eyes meet mine, and his expression gentles. "Hi."

The simple word reverberates in my stomach. "Hi."

"It was good of you to come."

"Well. I love that kid."

Leo smiles a little.

"So what exactly does he have to do?" I ask.

"He has to play three pieces, all of which he's been

working on for months. He's got them down cold. But he's saying he doesn't think he can play piano at all today."

"Why?"

"I don't know, Jenny!"

Then the door opens. "Evander James?" A smiling young woman comes into the hall. "Are you ready?"

Evander doesn't answer.

"This is us, buddy," Leo says, going back and extending his hand.

Evander takes it wordlessly and stands up. We're ushered into a dark room.

Holy crap. It's the actual Alice Tully Hall. I remember, because I think I dozed off here on more than one occasion, when Owen dragged me to hear an orchestra from Slovakia or Transylvania or somewhere.

The stage is huge, furnished only with a gleaming black grand piano. Lights glare into our eyes. There are rows and rows and rows of seats.

Four people sit in the front. Three men: two clean-shaven with frizzy hair, one bald with a white beard; and one woman who looks like Diane Sawyer and is wearing a really nice red St. John suit. All the same, they all look as if they're about to sentence us to death.

"Evander James?" asks a man with a white beard.

Evander nods, his eyes on the floor.

Some paper is shuffled. "Ready when you are," the woman says.

Evander doesn't move.

Oh, no.

"He's a little nervous," Leo says. He kneels down next to his student and whispers, "Listen, pal. You're ready for this. You're more than good enough."

"I can't," Evander whispers back. I put my hand on his head.

"Why not?" Leo asks.

"Because."

This is the kid who plays "only" five or six hours a day. Who said music was his best friend. Who touches the piano as if it's a shy animal and he wants nothing more than to take it home.

"What's the matter, sweetheart?" I ask, crouching down next to him.

His lip is trembling. "Because...because when I play, it's to let the music out, because there's music inside me and I *have* to let it out, and right now, there's no music in me and all I can hear is...afraid."

Tears spill out of his eyes, and he looks at Leo helplessly.

Leo looks just as helpless.

I turn to the judges. "Can we have five minutes?" I ask firmly. "I'm sorry. Is that possible?"

"Sure," says White Beard. "I have to make a phone call anyway."

I take Evander by the hand and lead him back into the hall, because standing on one of the most prestigious concert stages in the world isn't going to calm anyone down. I feel sick myself, and I'm just a bystander.

"Is there a practice room here?" I ask Leo.

"Good idea," he says, loping down the hall. "Come on, this way."

I lead Evander after him. His hand is sweaty, and tears are dripping down his cheeks. "You look really handsome," I tell him.

"Leo bought me a suit," he whispers.

Of course he did. He'd probably buy this kid a house.

Leo tries a door. It's locked. He tries the next one; that one's open, and he holds the door for us. Praise be, there's a piano inside.

"Okay, bud," Leo says, "just sit down and let it flow, and then we'll go back into the concert hall—"

"I can't," Evander says. "There's nothing inside me. The music is gone."

Leo bites a fingernail. "Well, I understand, but this isn't the time to—"

"Leo, play something," I order.

"What?"

"Play us something."

His eyes flicker to mine. "I—"

"Evander needs to be filled up with music. Fill him up."

The boy's face looks suddenly hopeful.

"Right," Leo says. "Um…right."

He hesitates a second. "We have five minutes," I say, fixing him with the look I reserve for nasty bridesmaids. The "shut up and smile" look.

It works. Leo takes a deep breath. "Got it."

Five minutes to calm this kid down, who, if he's as good as Leo thinks, could have a future the likes of which one in a million people gets to dream about. One in ten million, even. I sit down on the floor—there are no chairs—and pull Evander down with me.

Leo goes to the piano, takes off his jacket and sits down. "Any requests?" he says, and his voice is shaking a little.

"'Piano Man,'" I suggest.

"Liszt's Hungarian Rhapsody Number Two," Evander says.

"You're both evil," Leo mutters.

He puts his hands over the keyboard—they're shaking, too—and then, with a glance back at Evander and me, the famous notes thunder out. Even a troglodyte like me recognizes the Hungarian Rhapsody. Thank you, Tom and Jerry cartoons.

Leo's posture is stiff and proper. But then he leans in a little...then a little more. He's being hypnotized, almost, his entire being becoming involved with the piano.

After the first few bars of music, his hands don't just play the notes...they ripple and flow, sometimes almost bouncing off the keys. His focus becomes so singular, as if the music has reached out and grabbed him, and he's just channeling it now. It looks like he's seducing the music out of the piano, and though I know nothing about piano performance, I can see that to be great, a pianist has to do just that...seduce the instrument, win it over, become part of the great, beautiful piano and the music itself.

And Leo *is* great.

His hands move so fast that his fingers blur, and his expression changes with the music. His lips move, as if he's talking to the piano. The melody goes from grandiose and somber, climbing faster and faster to something different, and just as Leo himself can go from dark to light, from tragic to gleeful.

Evander chose well.

Leo's hands move up the keyboard, and the notes become lighter and faster and faster, and then Leo smiles.

And when he smiles, I swear the earth stops rotating.

Finally, finally, I see him in his true self, melded to the piano, to the golden, dancing notes that leap and swirl and fill the room with their bright light.

I don't realize I'm crying till Evander puts his arm

around me. The boy gazes at Leo, a faraway look on his face.

The door behind us opens. I glance back and see the judges. All four of them. "Is that Leo Killian?" the woman asks.

"It is," says the man with the white beard.

Great, golden chords crash from the piano. Leo hasn't noticed his audience has grown. I'm fairly sure we could all spontaneously combust, and he wouldn't notice. His hands are crossed over the keyboard—really, why on earth is he not playing at Carnegie Hall and La Scala? Surely this isn't average, even at Juilliard. Surely this is godlike playing.

Finally, in a clatter of utterly joyous noise and rippling hands, Leo finishes. His hands fly up, and he almost leaps back from the piano as if he's been electrocuted, and stands there, a little stunned, sweat darkening his shirt. He's breathing hard.

"Imagine what you could do if you practiced," one of the judges says drily.

"I heard four mistakes," another says, and honest to God, really? I suppose it's their business to know, but really?

Leo doesn't answer. He goes to Evander and kneels in front of him—in front of both of us, really, but he only has eyes for the boy. "Ready?" he says.

Evander nods. He's smiling.

Leo looks at the judges. "This is my student, Evander James," he says.

"Nice to meet you, young man," the man with the beard says. "And nice to hear you play again, Leo."

"Maestro." He gives the man a faint smile. "Good to see you."

The man gives him a long look, then glances down at Evander. "Shall we, Mr. James?"

They gesture for Evander to come with them, and Leo stands, then offers his hand to me and helps me up.

"That was…" My voice chokes off.

Leo gives a courtly nod. He's sweaty, and his hands are still shaking. He seems almost shy now.

Then he takes a breath and grabs his jacket, and we go down the hall to the great concert hall.

Mrs. James is there, wearing scrubs and clutching her big purse against her. "Is it okay that I came?" she asks.

"Are you kidding? You're just in time," Leo tells her, guiding her in.

When Evander sees his mother there, his beautiful face lights up. A lump hardens my throat, and I wipe my eyes on my sleeve.

We take our seats and Evander bows to the judges and begins.

He aces it. I can tell because Leo smiles the whole way through.

When he's done, and the judges are asking him questions and telling his mother what a special gift he has, when the maestro guy shakes Leo's hand and claps him on the back, I catch Evander's eye and blow him a kiss, then put my hands over my heart. He smiles, my gift.

Then I slip out the back, the music from Liszt's Hungarian Rhapsody Number Two—now the most perfect and beautiful piece of music I've ever heard—echoing and ringing in my soul.

Rachel

---❖---

ON THE MORNING of Jared and Kimber's wedding, the plan is for me to shower and get ready while Adam watches the girls. We'll put them in their flower girl dresses at the last possible second to avoid any accidents.

I take my time. For the past three and a half years, showers have been a necessity, not a luxury. Today, I shave my legs, condition my hair for the entire three minutes. I use a different shower gel, the really nice stuff Jenny gave me for Mother's Day.

I can't wait to see the final version of the wedding gown she made for Kimber. Somehow or another, I know she'll pull it off. It looked a little drab at its last incarnation, but Jenny's never made a dull dress in her life. All those changes Mrs. Brewster wanted didn't make her job easy, but I know the dress will be stunning.

Oddly enough—given my advanced age of forty— I'm really looking forward to today. I haven't been to a wedding in a long time, and even after these past few months and my schizophrenic views on marriage, I think Jared and Kimber will last. There's a part of some wedding ceremonies where the minister asks the guests if they'll support the couple. My answer will be a wholehearted yes.

It still galls me that Mrs. Brewster thought she could buy me off somehow. Or separate Kimber and Jared. That same night, Adam and I had dinner with the happy couple, and I watched them, their long looks at each other, the flush in her cheeks, the way Jared reached out to touch her ear, as if he couldn't go another minute without a little caress.

I remember feeling that way about Adam when things were new.

I also remember my own smugness…that somehow, because I was so careful and well behaved—the attentive listening, the regular sex, my self-appointed role as #1 Fan of Adam Carver—our marriage was insulated. That what happened to those other foolish couples would never happen to us because I was so on guard against it.

I lost myself in becoming Adam's wife, and later, the girls' mother. I forgot to be a person, too, a person who was well within her rights to say, "I'm too tired, tonight, honey. How about a back rub instead? I would really appreciate it."

And while Adam cheated, and I don't excuse that, maybe I had a little more of a role in that than I wanted to admit.

Well. Time to get on with this.

I put on my bridesmaid dress, which is an ice-blue sleeveless chiffon. Pretty, if a little boring. Luckily, the Mrs. Brewster-approved hairstyle for bridesmaids is a French twist, which I can do myself.

I sit at my dressing table and start doing my makeup. Foundation. A little powder. Blush. Eye shadow. Mascara. Lip gloss.

I like my face. I have a few crow's-feet, sure. My skin's not as elastic as it used to be… I gained a lot of weight when I was pregnant, as one tends to do with three babies inside, and it shows.

But this is the face of a woman who's been through a lot, a woman who has lost a lot and held on to a lot, too.

This is the face my daughters love, the face they look to for comfort and unconditional love, for patience.

For wisdom.

For guidance.

Adam comes in. He's already dressed in a dark blue suit, the same type he wears to work every day. Men have it so easy. "The girls are watching a movie," he says. His eyes look me up and down, a slow, appreciative sweep. "Wow. You look amazing, Mrs. Carver."

"Thanks. You're not so bad yourself."

He smiles, and I feel that old stir of attraction for him.

Then his phone buzzes. He takes it out, looks at it, puts it back without answering. Smiles at me once more.

"I want a divorce," I say.

I don't know who's more surprised. His mouth opens, and I glance at my reflection, almost as if I'm checking to see who's speaking. It's New Rachel...but it's Old Rachel, too. There's no anger in my face. There's just...me.

I will not stay married to a man I can't trust. Forget the sex, forget Emmanuelle. My husband lied to me, more than once, and he will lie to me again. My heart knows the truth. It always has.

I deserve better.

"I can't believe you're bringing this up again," he says. There's a hardness to his voice, and I'm oddly unaffected by it.

"I'm sorry, Adam. I can't stay married to you."

"Look, I've told you a thousand times. I'm *sorry*."

"I'm sorry, too."

And I am. I'm sorry it won't work between us, but something is cracking open in my chest, and instead of heartache, it feels more like…certainty. These past few months of not knowing how to be, of trying to see this situation from every angle…they're over.

I know what to do.

His face flushes with anger, something I've seen more in the past three months than in the past ten years. "So you're going to be an independent woman? You're gonna work full-time?"

"I don't know yet. But yes, I'll get a job. And move, if we have to." I'm oddly at peace with the image, abruptly aware of how much I've been carrying—shame, secrets, anger, loss, hurt. And now, those seem to be floating away and dissolving into the air.

"We?"

"The girls and me. I love this house, but if we have to downsize, that's fine, too."

That rattles him. The house, and me staying home, have always been his ace in the hole. His expression changes to worry. "Rachel," he says. "Please, honey." He comes over and kneels at my side. Takes my hand. "You don't really want this. Just forgive me already. Get over it." He flinches. "I mean, put it in the past."

But *get over it* is really what he means.

"Adam," I whisper, "if one of our daughters came to you and told you her husband had cheated, that he couldn't help himself because the other woman was just too hot…what would you tell her? What would you tell Grace or Charlotte or Rose?"

His gaze drops to the floor at the mention of their names. "I'd tell them to work on it. To stay." He looks back up at me.

"Really? Even after he lied to her, after he'd had sex—amazing sex—with another woman while she was home teaching our grandchildren their ABCs?"

Suddenly, his eyes fill with tears. He yanks his hand from mine. "No. I'd punch the asshole in the fucking face and tell him to stay the hell away from my little girl."

"Of course you would," I say. "Because they deserve better. And so do I, Adam."

He wipes his eyes. "I can do better."

"Show me your phone," I say.

"What?"

"You just got a text. Show it to me."

He's been beaten. "Give me another chance," he says.

"No. I don't think Emmanuelle was a fluke, and even if this was the first time you cheated, I don't think it'll be the last. I can't be that sad little wife who stays home at night, hoping her husband really is working late and not screwing another woman. I have to be more than that."

He huffs in indignation. "Well, I'm not going to be an absentee father," he says. "I'll want joint custody. I love them, too, you know." Again, his eyes fill.

A wave of mourning for our old life rolls over me, taking my breath away. So, so sad that it's gone, that lovely fantasy. "It doesn't have to be ugly," I say. "You're a good father. I want the girls to see the best in you. We'll always be their parents, and I have no intention of hating you."

"Gee, thanks."

He's bitter. His actions have come home to roost, and he's not getting his way, and he'll be angry.

I can handle it.

"Do you want me to come to the wedding?" he asks.

"Or do you want to make a big announcement and make sure everyone hates me?"

"Let's be a happy family today," I say. "Because we have been that, and we can be again. We just can't be married." I pause. "But you don't have to come if you don't want to."

He swallows and wipes his eyes again. "I do. I want to see the girls do their thing."

"Okay."

One last time to appear as a happy family. I bite down on a sob.

Then something crashes in the girls' room, and he stands up. "I'll get them ready." He gets up and heads out of our room, but pauses in the doorway. "I'm sorry," he says, and this time, the words mean more than all the other times he's said them.

"Me, too, Adam."

And so my marriage ends, just an hour before Jared's begins.

I hope Adam and I can be that couple who stays friends. That he'll come here for Thanksgivings and Christmas mornings. That we'll always care about each other. That we'll be kind to each other. I'll try for that. I hope Adam will, too.

But a huge weight has been lifted from my shoulders, as if a rock has rolled off my soul.

No. As if I pushed it off, and stand blinking in the sun.

Jenny

⋅◆⋅

WHEN MY PHONE rings, I fall out of bed reaching for it, because my night table seems to have been stolen. Wait. Where am I?

Oh, right. I'm house-sitting. There is no night table. And it's six thirty-two in the morning, people! I'm single and childless! I don't have to get up at six thirty-two! That is the one perk of my single, childless life!

The phone is still ringing. There it is, on the chair. "Hello?"

"Jenny?"

"That's me."

"It's Kimber."

Uh-oh. I recognize that whisper…the Whisper of Cold Feet. "Hey!" I say heartily. "Today's the big day! Are you excited?"

"I think I need to…call this off. I just… I tried on my dress, and I realized… And Jared… I don't…" There's a lot of squeaking going on.

"Okay, sweetie, okay. Take a breath. Is it a problem with the dress?"

"Yes," she manages. "And everything else."

This is not the first time a bride has fallen apart at the sight of herself in her wedding dress on the big day.

Kimber may have gained weight in the ten days since her last fitting—the most common reason for wedding-day meltdowns. But I have a feeling it's not that. "Do you want to meet me at the shop?"

"I...I guess so."

"Great. I'll be there in twenty minutes. This is going to be fine, Kimber. Trust me."

I shower faster than a cat and put on the pale yellow dress I planned to wear to their wedding. Err on the side of hope, I always think. That philosophy hasn't always worked out—Leo, anyone?—but I can't seem to help it.

I haven't seen Leo since Evander's recital. I sent Andreas over to my apartment to pick up a few things, but Leo didn't seem to be home. Mrs. James did call me to thank me for befriending her son. Yes, Evander got into the Juilliard program. Not that I had any doubts.

I wonder how Leo is doing.

For a second, I can't seem to straighten up.

Yearning snatches at me, startling in its hunger.

I miss him so much.

But I promised him he didn't break my heart, and so I summon a memory of his breathtaking, transformative smile and swallow hard. I loved our short time together. It made me very happy. I laughed a lot when I was with Leo, and so did he.

So I wipe my eyes and pull my hair up into a ponytail. I may have to be at my sewing machine, after all. I have a bride to comfort and a job to do.

Kimber is waiting at Bliss when I arrive, the huge dress bag draped over her arm. Her eyes are red.

Her mother is with her. Dorothy doesn't quite meet my eyes, and her face is tight with anxiety. She twists the hem of her shirt—the same nervous gesture she used that day in the supply closet.

For a flash, I can picture them, Dorothy and my beloved dad. The memory is so acute that I can almost smell his aftershave and hear the rain that poured from the sky that day.

"Come on in," I say.

"I can't go through with this," Kimber begins.

"Well, let's talk about it inside. Come on. I'll put on some coffee."

It's too early for customers; we open at ten on Saturdays. Andreas isn't here yet—have I mentioned how early it is?—so the shop is ours.

Kimber and Dorothy follow me into the dressing room, and I busy myself making coffee. "Gorgeous weather," I comment mildly, and Kimber bursts into tears.

Ah, brides. I hand her a box of tissues and a cup of coffee and sit down next to her. "So what's going on?"

Kimber doesn't answer, she's crying so hard. I rub her back and look at her mother.

"Last night was horrible," Dorothy says. "That dried-up old hag kept sticking it to poor Kimber every chance she got. But she's like a stealth bomber or something. Subtle and mean and polite at the same time."

"Yeah, I've known her my whole life. She's good at that."

Dorothy looks grateful for the camaraderie. "So anyways, Kimber tried on the dress this morning and just lost it."

Kimber blows her nose. "I want her to like me," she says wetly.

"She won't," I say. "She doesn't like anyone."

"I tried so hard," Kimber says with a hitching breath. "I mean, Jared's her only son, and I know I'm not good enough for him—"

"Oh, please. He's so happy with you."

Kimber's mouth wobbles. "I saw myself in that dress, and I just knew… I'll never fit into his world."

I look at her, this pretty, lively girl who grew up without a dad, who once wore my hand-me-downs. Who lights up a room by walking in, and who won over a confirmed bachelor by singing a song. "Oh, Kimber," I say with a smile. "You *are* his world."

Dorothy's face softens.

"And really," I continue, "are you going to leave him to deal with that dragon all by himself? I thought you loved him!"

"I do!" Kimber says. "I love him so much I can't believe it's real. I never knew I could feel so happy. All I want is to be with him, but his mother is going to make our life miserable, and nothing I do will be enough."

"You're absolutely right. It won't be enough for her. It'll be more than enough for Jared. And she's not going to like you, Kimber. But she might respect you."

"That's exactly what I was telling her," Dorothy says.

I look at Dorothy. "Kids. They never believe their own moms."

Dorothy smiles at me, a little uncertainly.

"Come on," I say, standing up. "Try on the dress for me, and let's see what we can do to sex it up a bit. Because, Kimber…you're going to the chapel. And you're gonna get married."

Kimber smiles for real this time, though tears still course down her face. "Okay," she says. "Okay, and thanks."

Five minutes later, she puts on the dress.

It's not ugly. Please. I don't do ugly. The fabric is gorgeous, if heavy, and it fits Kimber perfectly. The seaming is flawless.

But it is horribly plain, completely without ornamentation. No lace, no crystals, no draping. And it covers her up from neck to fingertips to toes.

I tilt my head and consider my bride, feeling a pang of guilt. My job was to make *her* happy. Not Mrs. Brewster, and so what if she wields her country-club influence and bad-mouths me? I don't need her approval.

I do need Kimber's.

"Do you trust me?" I ask.

"Absolutely," she says.

I make a few marks, but this is easy, really. I have the tingle of inspiration. I'm in my element.

I'm back, in other words.

I help Kimber out of the dress. "This will take an hour, hour and a half," I say. "You're welcome to stay, or I can drop the dress off at your house. Whatever's easier."

"We'll come back here," Dorothy says. "Kimber, baby, let's go to the drugstore and get some hair color. I miss the pink."

Seems as if I kind of like my father's mistress. Go figure.

"Okay. Let me just wash up a little. I have raccoon eyes, I bet." Kimber goes into the bathroom.

Which leaves Dorothy and me alone with the elephant in the room.

"Thank you for this," she says.

"Of course. I should've made her a better dress to start with."

"Well, she really did think it would win her points with that old battle-ax." She twists the hem of her shirt again and looks at the floor.

"Dorothy, I think you knew my dad," I say lightly. "Didn't you work for him for a little while?"

Her face flushes, but she meets my eyes. "Yes. He was... He was a very nice man. I was so sorry to hear about his death."

And in that moment, I see that Dorothy truly loved my father. My father who didn't choose her, didn't become Kimber's stepdad, who stayed with his wife instead.

I forgive her. But mostly, I forgive him.

"He was a great dad," I say, and my voice is husky. "Rachel and I were really lucky."

Kimber pops out of the bathroom, looking much improved. "Okay, Mom. Let's go."

There's sewing to be done, and my scissors are scalpel-sharp, hissing through the satin. I cut and pin, iron and sew, the satin fabric sliding effortlessly through the machine, the whirr and hum of the machine one of the happiest sounds I know. Yards of discarded fabric lay in heaps around me.

I find that I'm singing "Son of a Preacher Man." Always loved that song. I grab some springy, faintly pink tulle, that joyful fabric, and add that onto the skirt, a drape here, a twist there.

In the fabric sample room is an entire wall devoted to bling. Belts and beads, hairpieces and tiaras, lace and netting. I choose a thick rope of Swarovski crystal beading and a blingy 1920s-style hairpiece and run back to the workroom.

When I'm done, I'm a little sweaty, but man, oh, man, this dress is perfect. Perfect for Kimber.

"Holy crap," says a voice, and it's Dorothy's. They're back, and Kimber's hair is once again bright pink. She's beaming.

"Better?" I ask.

"I love it," Kimber breathes. "Oh, Jenny, I love it."

WHEN I GET to the church at quarter to ten, my sister is already standing outside with the girls. Adam and Mom are there, too. I dole out kisses—even Adam, as I am the world's best sister—then exclaim over my nieces, who look like they belong on the cover of *Martha Stewart Weddings*. "Auntie, Auntie! Aren't we so pretty?" the girls ask, twirling so their skirts billow.

"So beautiful! Oh, I love your shoes, too!"

Mrs. Brewster, too, is here, wearing a floor-length bile-green dress.

"Where's Kimber?" my mother asks.

"She's running a little late," I answer as Grace tugs my hand and Charlotte petitions to try on my heels. "Mrs. Brewster!" I say. "Such a happy day, isn't it? And that color matches your personality perfectly."

Her nostrils turn white. She looks like she swallowed a live eel and is trying not to let it out, her mouth is clamped shut so hard. Guess her dreams of her son being left at the altar have been snuffed out.

Rachel seems awfully Zen today. She nods at me to come over; the other bridesmaids are arriving, one enormously pregnant with many piercings. Good, I think. Good for Kimber.

"You look gorgeous," I tell my sister. "And happy."

She glances at the girls; Grace is going through my

mother's purse, and Charlotte and Rose are running around Adam. "We're getting a divorce," she whispers. "I told him this morning."

"Oh, Rach!"

"No, it's good. He was really... It's good."

I seem to be crying. Rachel fishes a tissue out of her clutch for me—always prepared, that's her motto. I blot my eyes. Here I wanted nothing more than for Adam to crawl away to a cold and slimy hole, but all of a sudden, I feel so *bad* for him. He glances over and meets my eyes, then gives a sad smile. "I'm sorry, Rachel," I whisper.

"Yeah. Me, too. But I feel...lighter."

"I'm glad, too. Sorry and glad."

"I know exactly what you mean." She smiles, and she looks so peaceful and so sad at the same time. "I'll need you a lot the next few months."

"You've got me."

Rachel gives me a quick hug, then obeys the photographer, who's trying to herd the bridesmaids together.

"Jenny!" Mom calls. "Let's go in, honey. I want a good seat."

Light floods in through the tall, clear windows of the Congregational church. Mom and I sit near the front. I wonder if this is a preview of how things will be—me as Mom's escort for the various funerals and weddings and fund-raisers, the years passing by.

But before too much longer, there will be another one of us... My foster child. It won't be happening too fast, since I don't have a permanent residence just yet, but the social worker said she didn't foresee a problem. My background check cleared, and I've already been looking at cases and pictures online of kids who need a home, imagining each one as mine.

"You look very pretty," Mom says. "Yellow usually makes you look like you need a liver transplant, but not today." That's my mama. Unable to give a compliment without somehow insulting me, too. She herself is in her "don't look at me" uniform—black pants, white men's dress shirt.

"I love you, Mom," I tell her with a smooch on the cheek.

Jared goes up to the altar with his best man. His father stands there in his minister's robes, smiling. The music starts and my nieces earn a universal sigh of rapture as they walk down the aisle, Grace solemnly and methodically scattering her rose petals, Charlotte following too closely behind her, Rose hamming it up by tossing handfuls of petals into the air. They join Adam at the front, and he kisses them, smiles and wipes his eyes.

He's a good dad. Since forgiveness seems to be the order of the day, I find myself forgiving him, too. He'll suffer enough without me adding to it. The best thing I can do for Rachel and my nieces is be friendly. And so I shall. I'm incredibly mature, it seems.

The bridesmaids file in, smiling. My sister is the prettiest, of course.

And then the doors open, and in comes Kimber, holding her mother's hand.

Mrs. Brewster's mouth falls open. Not in shock and joy, either.

But everyone else, it seems, heartily approves.

Kimber's dress is a sleeveless minidress now. Bateau neckline, the crystal-beaded belt accentuating her voluptuous curves, the skirt of the dress poofing out with the same light ebullience that radiates from the bride. Her tattoos are on full display, and as she walks down the aisle, the scoop back of the dress shows off her angel wings. From the front, she looks almost demure; from the back, like a sex kitten. The dress is bright and fun and fresh, just like the bride herself, and sure enough, I glance at Jared and, yep, he's a weeper, God bless him. He looks absolutely gobsmacked by love.

Kimber is beaming. Almost floating.

Rachel turns to look at me and gives me the thumbs-up.

"Now *that's* a dress," my mother says.

WHEN THE CEREMONY is over and I've gone through the reception line and been thanked by Jared and Kimber and complimented by dozens and glared at by Mrs. Brewster, I slip off to my car. "Where are you going?" Mom asks.

"I'll catch up later. I have an errand to do," I say. "Save me a seat."

I have to pay a visit to someone.

My father is buried not too far from a stand of pines, on a little knoll in the cemetery. My heels sink into the rain-softened grass, and the sharp, rich smell of pine fills the air.

I forgot how beautiful it is here. Rachel has planted purple-and-pink petunias on Dad's grave, their colors bold and cheerful.

I put my hand on the warm granite of his gravestone. "Hi, Daddy," I say.

The wind brings the smell of smoke and meat; someone not too far away is having a cookout. Dad, too, loved to grill.

I'm glad my father didn't suffer. But oh, how I wish I could've said goodbye.

"Thank you for everything," I whisper now.

Then I stand up, my knees creaking a little. I look over toward the grave of Leo's wife and unborn baby, but I won't go there. It's not my place.

But I will go see her mother. Leo said he was the only one left, and that's just too damn sad. It won't matter if she knows me; I'll at least be there. I'll tell her I'm her son's friend, and that will be enough.

The nursing home is just on the other side of the cemetery, a two-minute walk. The sky is so blue today.

Inside the air is heavy and stale, despite the flower arrangement on the coffee table. The receptionist, a different one from the day I trailed Leo, is on the phone. She waves me in. Room 227 was Mrs. Walker's room, as I recall.

I go down the hallway. The patients' names are written outside their doors in childish handwriting with drawings of flowers and animals. There's probably some kind of adopt-a-grandparent program going on here. I bet Rachel would know.

I stop outside Room 227. Elizabeth Walker, the sign reads, and there's a picture of a cat and a tree with two branches and a giant crow. I peek in, then jerk back.

Leo's in there.

"Jenny?"

Shit, I'm busted. Feeling my face burn with heat, I show myself. "Hey. I'm sorry. I didn't know you were here. It's Saturday, and you usually come on… Well. I just thought I'd stop by."

He stands up. I forgot how tall he is. Two weeks without seeing him, and I forgot that.

"Who is this?" Mrs. Walker asks. "I don't know this person! What do you want? Don't steal from me! The last people took everything!"

I guess coming to visit her wasn't a great idea.

"It's okay, Mom," Leo says, and his voice is so gentle and kind I can feel it in my chest. "She's my friend. Her name is Jenny."

"Hi, Mrs. Walker." Leo's mother-in-law seems far too young to be here. Her skin is beautiful, her hair thick and blond-gray, but she's very thin, and her eyes have a lost, frightened look.

"I don't know you," she says, her eyes flicking toward Leo.

"She's nice," Leo says. "Sit down, Jenny."

"Don't steal my things," Mrs. Walker says.

"I won't," I tell her, trying to look responsible and caring, though fearing I look guilty as hell.

"How are you?" Leo asks me.

"Fine. Good." I glance at Mrs. Walker and lower my voice. "I'm sorry. I was visiting my father's grave and I thought of... I thought maybe Mrs. Walker could use some company."

He stares at me for a second, his eyes achingly sad. "That was very nice of you." He sits back down. "You look very pretty, by the way."

"Oh. Right. It was Kimber's wedding. One of my brides, remember?"

"Bride?" Mrs. Walker asks, looking at Leo. "Is this your wife?"

Oh, God. The words scrape my heart. I can't imagine how Leo must feel. This poor woman, who can't remember her daughter, her only child, the baby she raised and loved.

And yet, this lucky woman, who can't remember that her daughter is gone.

"No," Leo says, clearing his throat. "I'm afraid my wife died."

Something flickers across Mrs. Walker's face, like an autumn leaf blowing across a field. Then it's gone.

"Well," she says. "I'm sure she loved you very much."

The words fill the room, and I have to bow my head under the leaden weight of sadness.

"Yes," Leo says.

I stand up. I can't cry in front of Leo, will not add my tears to all the grief he carries every day. That would not be the act of a friend. That would not be a gift. "I should go. It was very nice to meet you, Mrs. Walker," I say. I stick out my hand, but she just looks at it as if she's not sure what it's for. I end up putting my hand on her shoulder, very briefly.

Then I look at Leo. "Take care of yourself," I say. "It was good to see you."

"You, too."

I go out the door, walking briskly but not running, down the hallway, into the lobby, out onto the sidewalk, tears dripping off my cheeks. Why did I walk here? Why didn't I drive over?

I'll walk back to the church, then drive to the country club. Mom and I will have a good time, and I'll dance with my nieces, and who knows? Maybe I'll even meet a nice guy.

But I really don't want to. There's only one guy I want.

"Jenny."

I lurch to a stop and wipe my eyes hastily.

"You're faster than you look," Leo says.

"Hey."

"Thank you for visiting her."

"I'm sorry. I didn't mean to upset her."

"No. She's always like that."

I nod. The breeze whispers past, drying the tear streaks on my cheeks. "How are you?"

"Fine. Good." He smiles, and I realize he's echoing me from earlier. Then his smile falls away. "Actually, I'm kind of a mess." He takes a deep breath. "Ever since Evander's audition, I've been playing. Badly. It…brings a lot up, you know?"

I nod. After seeing him play with his entire heart, yes, I would guess it does.

"The thing is, Jenny… I guess I wasn't really for recreation only. And I don't really want to keep on being… tormented. So I'm working on forgiving myself. They asked me to teach at Juilliard in the fall. I've been playing a lot, because something shook loose that day, and it's pretty much like hitting the keys with wooden mallets, but at least I'm doing something, and I can see that I'm rambling now, because I'm kind of terrified."

"Why?"

"Just living can be pretty terrifying. I don't know how you do it. You're always so damn optimistic."

"Sorry." I feel the start of a smile. "I'll work on that."

"Also, I'm worried that you'll realize you can do a lot better than me."

My heart stops. "Good point," I breathe.

"I'm hoping you haven't figured that out yet, but I feel morally obliged to mention it." He looks at me, some of his nervous energy dissipating, leaving him with just that still intensity. "I miss you."

My eyes fill. "I miss you, too."

"I'm irritating and damaged and pretty manic sometimes, not to mention—"

"I just took you back, didn't I? Quit while you're ahead."

His arms go around me, and he hugs me so close and hard that my ribs creak, and I hug him back just as hard, and then he kisses me, a long, perfect kiss, and my heart feels so full that it hurts in a wonderful, warm ache.

Everything I want is right here. Right now.

"I knew you were trouble," Leo says.

"I love you, too," I answer, and he laughs and hugs me again, and I breathe in his good, clean Leo smell, my heart splitting open with happiness, overflowing with love.

I used to think that somewhere along the line, I'd find the key to that perfect life, the way Rachel seemed to, and that once I had it, every day would be golden and easy, and everything would fit. But life isn't like that. There are only perfect, glowing moments, like this one, and then there are the everyday moments that weave them together into a shimmering path that can always be seen, even in the dark.

"You still need a date for that wedding?" Leo asks.

"Only if you want to go."

"I do." He smiles down at me, then takes my hand, and we walk down the street together, past the park, past the cemetery, into the beautiful summer day.

* * * * *

Acknowledgments

There are so many people who contribute to an author's work, and I am exceptionally fortunate to work with some of the best and kindest in the business. As always, a thousand thanks to my brilliant agent, Maria Carvainis, and her able staff—Elizabeth Copps, Martha Guzman and Samantha Brody. At Harlequin, thanks to my wonderful editor, Susan Swinwood, and to Dianne Moggy, Craig Swinwood and Loriana Sacilotto for their unwavering faith and encouragement. Sarah Burningham at Little Bird Publicity is smart, funny and fabulous, and Kim Castillo at Author's Best Friend is steadfast, generous and utterly lovely.

Wedding dress designer Dianne Keesee gave me a generous gift of time, information and several beautiful sketches while educating me on wedding gown design. Ronald Giannattasio was kind enough to answer questions about the world of a classical pianist, and Linda Cork was incredibly helpful describing the life of a Juilliard student. Any mistakes are all mine.

Thanks to Paul Stigliano for unwittingly giving me

material for this book (I believe that's called "theft," but my phrasing is nicer). Thanks especially to Huntley Fitzpatrick for the hand-holding and her rock-solid conviction that the hardest parts to write would be the best parts to read. And for simply being wonderful, thanks to Robyn Carr, my dear, darling friend.

To the three great loves of my life—husband, daughter, son—thank you for making me happier and prouder than I ever knew I could be. The laugh-till-we-spit-out-our-food stuff is pretty great, too.

And thank you, readers, for spending a few hours with this book. It is truly an honor.

USA TODAY bestselling author

SARAH MORGAN

**introduces *From Manhattan with Love*,
a sparkling new trilogy about three best friends
embracing life—and love—in New York.**

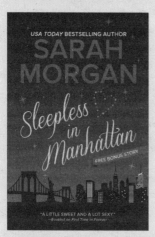

Cool, calm and competent, events planner Paige Walker loves a challenge. After a childhood spent in and out of hospitals, she's now determined to prove herself—and where better to take the world by storm than Manhattan? But when Paige loses the job she loves, she must face her biggest challenge of all—going it alone.

Except launching her own events company is nothing compared to hiding her outrageous crush on Jake Romano—her brother's best friend, New York's most in-demand date and the only man to break her heart. When Jake offers Paige's fledgling company a big chance, their still-sizzling chemistry starts giving her sleepless nights. But can she convince the man who trusts no one to take a chance on forever?

Pick up your copy today!

Be sure to connect with us at:

Harlequin.com/Newsletters
Facebook.com/HarlequinBooks
Twitter.com/HQNBooks

HQN™

www.HQNBooks.com

PHSAM915

REQUEST YOUR FREE BOOKS!

2 FREE NOVELS
FROM THE ROMANCE COLLECTION
PLUS 2 FREE GIFTS!

YES! Please send me 2 FREE novels from the Romance Collection and my 2 FREE gifts (gifts are worth about $10). After receiving them, if I don't wish to receive any more books, I can return the shipping statement marked "cancel." If I don't cancel, I will receive 4 brand-new novels every month and be billed just $6.49 per book in the U.S. or $6.99 per book in Canada. That's a savings of at least 19% off the cover price. It's quite a bargain! Shipping and handling is just 50¢ per book in the U.S. and 75¢ per book in Canada.* I understand that accepting the 2 free books and gifts places me under no obligation to buy anything. I can always return a shipment and cancel at any time. Even if I never buy another book, the two free books and gifts are mine to keep forever.

194/394 MDN GH4D

Name	(PLEASE PRINT)	

Address		Apt. #

City	State/Prov.	Zip/Postal Code

Signature (if under 18, a parent or guardian must sign)

Mail to the **Reader Service:**
IN U.S.A.: P.O. Box 1867, Buffalo, NY 14240-1867
IN CANADA: P.O. Box 609, Fort Erie, Ontario L2A 5X3

Want to try two free books from another line?
Call 1-800-873-8635 or visit www.ReaderService.com.

* Terms and prices subject to change without notice. Prices do not include applicable taxes. Sales tax applicable in N.Y. Canadian residents will be charged applicable taxes. Offer not valid in Quebec. This offer is limited to one order per household. Not valid for current subscribers to the Romance Collection or the Romance/Suspense Collection. All orders subject to credit approval. Credit or debit balances in a customer's account(s) may be offset by any other outstanding balance owed by or to the customer. Please allow 4 to 6 weeks for delivery. Offer available while quantities last.

Your Privacy—The Reader Service is committed to protecting your privacy. Our Privacy Policy is available online at www.ReaderService.com or upon request from the Reader Service.

We make a portion of our mailing list available to reputable third parties that offer products we believe may interest you. If you prefer that we not exchange your name with third parties, or if you wish to clarify or modify your communication preferences, please visit us at www.ReaderService.com/consumerschoice or write to us at Reader Service Preference Service, P.O. Box 9062, Buffalo, NY 14240-9062. Include your complete name and address.